P9-ECM-129

ZANE GREY

Shadow on the Trail

WALTER J. BLACK, INC.

ROSLYN, NEW YORK

BY ARRANGEMENT WITH HARPER & BROTHERS

FOREWORD

IN MY reading of historical books on our American frontiers, and in my many trips to wild places in the West, and my early contacts with great westerners like Buffalo Jones, Buffalo Bill, Joe Sitter and Vaughn, Texas Rangers, Wyatt Earp and Dick Moore, gunmen, and my old guides Al Doyle and John Wetherill, one of the remarkable things in western life was the way desperate characters and hunted outlaws disappeared without leaving a trace, never to be heard of again.

Henderson, one of the Billy the Kid gang, was a case in point. Henderson was a bad man, a desperado, a killer, marked by sheriffs from Abilene to Santa Fe. But he left Billy the Kid just before that deadly young man helped to instigate the Lincoln County War in New Mexico, and was eventually with his gang and many others wiped out. Henderson was never heard of again. What became of him?

Another case in point, and one which particularly inspired this novel, was that of a young lieutenant of Sam Bass, the notorious Texas bandit and bank-robber. Very little was ever known of this young outlaw, Jackson by name, during Sam Bass's life, and nothing at all after Bass's death.

When Sam Bass and his gang attempted to rob the bank at Mercer, Texas, they were surprised and attacked by Texas Rangers and citizens, and in a terrific fight all the robbers were killed except young Jackson.

He rode out of town supporting the mortally shot Bass in his saddle. The pursuing rangers came upon the dying Bass sitting up under a tree along the roadside. He died there. But nothing could be seen of Jackson except his tracks, and though the rangers rode this outlaw down for years, acting upon a hundred clues, he was never found.

What became of Jackson, as well as of so many desperate outlaws of those early days? Of those who were never heard of again!

For a novelist of western historical life that query was one of intriguing interest. Some of them, surely, turned their backs upon the uncertainty and inevitability of the evil life. Some of them, surely, were not as black as the wild frontier painted them. It is conceivable that some of them reformed, and lived useful hidden perhaps remorseful lives in out of the way corners of the vast West.

It is within the province of the creative writer to take upon himself the task of imagining and portraying what might have happened to one of these vanishing outlaws. And that is what I have tried to do in *Shadow on the Trail.*

ZANE GREY

Altadena
December 1, 1936

Shadow on the Trail

CHAPTER ONE

THE whistle of the Texas Pacific express train nerved Wade Holden to dare one more argument against the unplanned holdup and robbery his chief had undertaken. Standing there in the dark night under the trees with the misty rain blowing in his face and the horses restlessly creaking leather, Wade thought swiftly, realizing the peril in speaking ill of men Simm Bell chose as comrades for a job of banditry.

"Listen, Simm," whispered Wade close to the ear of the lean dark outlaw beside him. "It's too sudden, this holdup. We've got the big bank job all ready."

"I've a hunch," replied Bell, with the force of one who never brooked opposition. "We're ridin' through this country. Bad weather. Passed the towns at night. No one has seen us. Wade, I'll get you a bunch of money like pickin' it off bushes."

"But these two strangers. We don't know them."

"Blue says he knows them. That's enough for me."

"Chief, I don't trust Randall Blue," returned Wade, with effort.

"Son, what're you sayin'?" asked Bell, in gruff amaze. His big eyes glowed in the gloom.

"I know what I'm saying. I don't trust Blue. Ever since I saw him talking to that ranger, Pell. He's—"

"What? You saw him?"

"I did. They had a serious talk. I believe Blue has agreed to double-cross you."

"Hellsfire! Would you face him with that?"

"I'd be only too glad."

"And you'll kill him. I see. . . . Son, you're a bad hombre when you go against a man. But I'll not have you splittin' my band."

"Simm, you read that last notice of reward offered for you, alive or dead. Ten thousand dollars!"

"Cap Mahaffey has raised the ante. I'm somebody worth gettin' now. But those damned rangers will never get me alive."

"They'll get you dead, though. That Texas bunch has been after you for two years. They'd had you but for your many friends. Let's not risk this holdup with Blue. And ride on our way to meet the gang. Blue will not know of our bank job at Mercer."

"I told him, Wade."

"God, you've ruined us!"

The train rumbled into the dimly lighted station and rattled to a halt with the engine down at the end of the platform.

"Come on, Wade, I'll get you some easy money," rasped Bell, dragging his young companion with a powerful hand. They ran across the road. In the yellow flare of light Wade saw Blue accost the conductor with a sharp. "Hands up!" The other two men, who called themselves Smith and Hazlitt, would by this time be climbing aboard the engine to take care of the engineer and brakeman. In a moment more Wade heard harsh voices in the engine cab.

"Here's the express car," whispered Bell. "That express messenger is openin' the door. Well, of all the luck! Leave it to me, Wade, but look sharp."

They stole along the car to the door that slid to a halt. Behind a leveled gun Bell stuck his head and shoulders into the car. "Hands up!" called the robber, low and menacingly. "If you squeak, I'll bore you!"

The messenger slowly straightened with hands up, his face turning white. Bell leaped up into the car. Holden followed with drawn gun.

"Cover him while I look round," said the chief.

The express car was well lighted. Wade saw a few boxes ready for delivery. A large iron safe stood back against the far wall. Bell gave it a heave.

"Too heavy!—Force him to open it."

"I can't. That's the Wells Fargo safe. They don't give me the combination."

"Open up or we'll kill you!"

"Kill and be damned. I can't—I tell you."

"Looks like he's telling the truth," interposed Wade.

"What's in these?" demanded Bell, kicking some oblong packages lying beside the safe.

"I don't know," replied the express messenger.

The robber glanced around for some kind of implement and espied an ax. Seizing it he struck the top package a hard blow. There was a musical jingle of coins.

"Money," Bell cried out and struck open the end of the package. Gold twenty-dollar coins rolled out.

"Double eagles! Look at 'em, pard. Pick them loose ones up." With a bound at the messenger, Bell felled him with a blow of the gun. "How about my hunch, boy? Easiest job we ever had! . . . Slide those packages to the door."

Bell leaped down upon the platform to peer with eager hawk eyes back toward the station. "Blue's comin'. Hurry . . . Blue, run forward and get your pards."

Wade filled his coat pockets with the loose coins, leaving some on the floor. Then he closed the end of the package Bell had broken and carried it to the door. The next one he slid across. By the time he had moved the five bundles, Blue had returned with his two partners.

"Each grab one and run for your hoss," ordered Bell, fierce with gleeful excitement.

Wade leaped down and grasped the last package. It was heavy and he needed his gun hand to help. Thus burdened he ran after the dark form ahead of him. In another moment he was out of the flare of light and in the gloom. Shrill cries pealed from the station. Wade reached his companions more by sound than sight. Two were already mounted.

"Hand it—up," panted the chief. "Did I—have—a hunch?—

Ha! Not a shot! . . . Where's the boy? . . . Here you air. . . . Lift 'er up. . . . How about that for—some easy money? No ranger can—connect Simm Bell—with this job."

Wade removed his cloth mask and mounted to take the extra package that his chief held on his saddle.

"There! We're all set. . . . Ride close to me. . . . Look sharp—for that road across the track—to the south. . . . And here comes the rain—to wash out our tracks."

Wade Holden rode behind Smith and Hazlitt. It seemed significant to him that the robber chief placed himself in front beside Blue. They all rode so close together that they could have touched each other. Rain began to fall heavily. Wade had a waterproof coat tied on his saddle and in removing this he had to shift the package that Bell had handed him. Somehow it did not seem so heavy and hard as the others. He squeezed it. Through the thick wrapping paper and cardboard he felt the contents was currency. He was about to apprise Bell of this discovery, when it occurred to him that such intelligence could wait to be divulged later.

The trotting horses soon left the station behind in the black night. Shouts and calls died away. The discharge of a shotgun back there elicited much glee from the chief. He was the only one of the five who broke the silence and he jested, bragged, crowed as was his wont after a successful raid. But that did not deceive Holden. He knew his chief.

The rain became a steady downpour. Wade rested his package endwise on his saddle and buckled it under his coat to keep it dry.

"Hold on," called out Bell, presently. "We're passin' that turn-off. . . . Blue, I thought you knew the road."

"I do. But it's so damn dark," explained the other.

"Well, I've been along here myself if you want to know," replied Bell, gruffly, and rode to the left across the track.

Wade sank comfortably in his saddle for another of Simm Bell's long night rides. The sandy road gave forth little sound from hoofs, except an occasional splash of water. The road ahead appeared to be a pale obscure lane dividing two walls of gloom. After a while Bell grew tired of his volubility. Then the quintet rode on somber and silent, each occupied with his own thoughts.

Holden's were not what might have been expected of a young desperado who had been in a train holdup netting thousands of dollars without a fight. He had an unaccountable, unshakable feeling of impending calamity for his chief. And he loved this free-handed robber. He had stood by Bell of late against his better judgment. The robber had gravitated from little inconsequential stealings to bloody crimes. His name had become notorious from the Kansas border to the Rio Grande. He had incurred the wrath of the Texas Rangers, and that, together with the price on his head, spelled doom for Simm Bell. He was cunning, brave, a hard fighter, but he was not particularly keen-minded.

Nevertheless, Holden did not see how he could sever his connection with his chief. He did not care very much what happened to himself, but he would have liked to steer his friend away from obvious disaster. He and his family owed Bell a good deal. Wade's father had been a Missouri guerrilla during the Civil War. After the war he came home a crippled and ruined man. Bell had been one of his lieutenants and for some years he had practically taken care of the Holdens. But Simm too had been ruined by the free life of a guerrilla. He did not take kindly to farming. In the succeeding years he drifted to more vicious ways and took Wade with him.

That explained Wade Holden's presence there on this lonely Texas road, a robber, red-handed, already at twenty-two notorious for his quick and deadly gunplay, and marked by the Texas Rangers along with Simm Bell. Wade had grown bitter and hard. He suffered few moments of remorse. Hope had almost died in his breast. He could look back and see how inevitably he had been forced out of honest ways. He had never had a chance. And all there seemed left for him now was to die fighting by and for his chief. Through the long hours of night that sense of loyalty grew to a passion.

They rode on through the long dark hours at a steady trot. They passed isolated ranch houses at intervals and one village where all but watchdogs were wrapped in slumber.

It rained hardest during the dark hour before dawn. Then with the gray break of day the rain let up and there was a prospect of clearing weather. Sunrise found Bell leading his men off the road into a wood where, some distance in, they halted in a grassy glade.

"We'll rest the hosses and dry off," said Bell, cheerily, as he dismounted. "That farmer back aways is a friend of mine. We can get grub."

"Wal, Bell, if it's all the same to you, we'll be ridin' on," said Smith, a freckled, evil-eyed man.

Bell straightened up but he did not bat an eyelash. He had been prepared.

"Smith, it's not all the same to me. And who do you mean by *we*?" he returned, coolly.

"Me an' Hazlitt hyar. We're ridin' on with our share."

"Who'n hell said anythin' about your share?" queried Bell, sharply, and deliberately he lifted the heavy package of coin off Smith's saddle, and then, even more forcefully, repeated the action with Hazlitt. When he turned to Blue, however, that worthy was in the act of dismounting with his treasure. Bell relieved him of it and laid it beside the others on a log. Holden got off his horse and placed his package on the log, too, but apart from the others.

"I kept mine dry," he observed, and covered it with his coat. This precaution was only a blind. Wade did not want to be hampered if trouble ensued. Manifestly Bell had struck a false note. Smith and Hazlitt looked ugly but uncertain, as they got down on cramped legs. Wade had a covert look at Randall Blue. He was under thirty, a tall man, fair and not bad looking. Wade distrusted his shifty gaze, his ready tongue and smile. Bell watched the three men while he uncinched and threw his saddle. His big black eyes held a sardonic gleam.

"Wal, Bell," began Smith, presently, "nobody said anythin' aboot a divvy, but shore thet was understood."

"I always pay men who work with me," replied the leader.

"Pay! . . . Wal, what do you aim to pay us?"

"Reckon one of them packages more than squares your work in that little job."

"Wal, we don't reckon thet way," said Smith. "What's more we ain't bein' paid. We want an equal divvy. There're five of us, an' five bundles of gold. One for each of us."

"Blue, what's your angle on that?" inquired Bell of his confederate, and both look and tone were curious.

"Strikes me fair," rejoined Blue, nervously.

"Wade, what you think?"

"Chief, you had the idea and planned the job," said Holden, quickly. "If this was your regular gang you'd divide as always—share and share alike. But I wouldn't do that here."

"My sentiments exactly," declared the chief, with satisfaction. "Smith, you and Hazlitt take one pack of this gold and go on your way."

"Nope. I won't agree to thet. You'll give Blue one pack. An' he didn't take as big a part in the job as Jim an' me."

"Blue used to trail with me."

"Wal, I hev my doubts about his trailin' with you now. . . . Ask him who he was sendin' telegrams to yestiddy, when we hit the railroad at Belton."

"Telegrams!" ejaculated Bell, and slowly turned to Blue with a singular vibration through his wiry frame. "Rand, did you send telegrams yesterday?"

"Yes. I wired my folks not to expect me home soon," replied Blue, suavely enough.

"But you told me you *told* them before you came to meet me."

"I know. But my telegram made it definite," added Blue, his lips just shading gray.

"Ahuh," grunted Bell, subtly changing.

"Chief, he's a —— liar!" interposed Holden, sharply. The

moment had convinced him of the correctness of his suspicion. Blue was a traitor.

"Mebbe he is, at that. But let's settle with these hombres first," said the robber, caustically. "Smith, do you and Hazlitt accept what I offered?"

"I should smile we don't," snapped Smith viciously, his weasel eyes glinting. They betrayed nerve, purpose, and an estimate of Bell which put Holden on instant cold guard. For some reason Smith did not take Bell's young comrade seriously.

"All right then. You get nothin'," retorted the robber chief.

Smith's reply was to draw his gun. "Bell, you'll divvy or—" he rasped.

Holden deliberated a moment, divining the instant for his interference. Simm Bell laughed. He had been in such situations before.

"So you throw your gun on me?" he jeered.

"I shore do."

"What's your idee?"

"You agree to a square divvy."

"Simm Bell never goes back on his word."

"You'll go back on it now—or I'll kill you an' take all this gold!" rang out Smith, beginning to quiver.

Holden flashed into action. His shot clubbed Smith down bloody-faced and limp. His second, delivered while Hazlitt was drawing, took that worthy in the middle and cut short a curse of rage. Hazlitt's weapon exploded and went spinning while he fell over the log and began to flop all over the grass. Bell drew his gun and deliberately put a stop to both ghastly sounds and struggles.

"Once more, boy," he said, grimly. "I reckon I'll be owin' you considerable one of these days."

Blue had reacted surprisingly to this scene. He was white of face, clammy of skin, wholly unnerved; and it was at the younger man that he stared. Holden stepped over the dead Smith to shove his gun into Blue's abdomen.

"Blue, you've double-crossed the chief," he declared hard as ice.

"I saw you talking to Pell. I guessed that deal. You planned with the rangers to trap Bell—betray him into their hands."

"Yes—yes, I did," cried Blue, hoarsely. "They had me. They put the job up to me. . . . I listened—I consented. But I—I didn't mean to do it."

"Liar!"

Bell pushed Wade back and faced his friend. "My Gawd, Rand, you didn't plot with rangers to trap me?"

"What could I do? Pell had me dead to rights on that unco raid," cried the man, huskily, realizing how near death he was. "I was recognized. None of the rangers have ever seen you. Pell asked what you looked like. And I lied. . . . They made me choose between arrest and agreeing to—to a plan to trap you. I had to do it, Simm—but I swear to God I meant to double-cross them, not you."

"Blue, you're lying again," thundered Holden. "You wired Pell we'd planned to rob the Mercer bank."

"No, I didn't," shouted Blue, livid of face, plausible, perhaps convincing to Bell, but not to Holden.

"If you deny it again, I'll bore you."

"Simm, he hates me. He's jealous of your friendship for me," protested Blue gaining strength. "I do deny it. I swear—"

Bell knocked Holden's gun up in the nick of time. It boomed and the powder blackened Blue's face.

"Hold, you blood-spillin' young devil," yelled Bell, evidently wrought up between the opposing forces. But his dark visage was ashen and his brow clammy. His trust died hard. "This man has befriended me. I can't let you kill him on suspicion." Then he pushed Holden back and confronted Blue. "Rand, it looks bad. Fork your hoss and slope. I'm givin' you the benefit of a doubt. But if you have double-crossed me you'd better ride to the end of the earth. Because I'll track you down and kill you!"

Randall Blue leaped astride his horse and spurred it into the brush with a crashing disregard of his person, to disappear at once in the spring foliage. Bell kept listening to the swish of branch and crack of twig until these sounds ceased.

In a cold sweat Wade sat on the log, reloading his gun, his damp hair falling over his furrowed brow. Bell placed a hand on his shoulder.

"Thanks, son. I reckon you saved my life again," he said, with feeling. "But I couldn't let you shoot Blue."

"Man alive! Didn't you see his face?" expostulated Holden.

"Yes. It worries me. But I don't see through things quick. . . . Let me think. What to do now?" He sank on the log to lean his head on his hands. After a moment of concentration he looked up, his old forceful self again.

"I'll walk over to this farmer friend—forget his name—and fetch some grub. I'll make a deal with him to hide our hosses and let us have a buggy or spring wagon. We can make as good time with that. And be less likely to excite suspicion. That little raid will fly over Texas. Won't Mahaffey and Pell roar? Ha! Ha! . . . Boy, I told you I'd get you some easy money."

"Simm, I reckon my package holds bills instead of double eagles," said Holden.

"You don't say. Good! I'll give you some of the gold, too."

"What'll we do with these?" queried Wade, indicating the two dead men without looking at them.

"Search the greedy hombres and cut some green brush to throw over them. . . . I'll be back pronto."

Two days later Bell and Holden were approaching the hamlet of Belknap, Denton County, Texas, in an old spring wagon drawn by a scrawny team of horses.

They looked like two uncouth farmers. The wagon appeared to contain camp utensils, bedding, food supplies and hay. No observer would have suspected that under the seat hidden by tools and old canvas reposed a fortune in gold and currency.

At a crossroad the travelers were overtaken by a party of horsemen.

"Ahuh. Rangers. I'll do the talkin'," whispered Bell.

There were ten men in the group that halted Bell, lean, hawk-eyed riders, heavily armed and superbly mounted. The foremost, evidently the leader, leaned from his saddle to scrutinize Bell and Holden. He was not young. Robust of build, thin-lipped and square-jawed, bronzed so darkly that the hair of his temples looked white, he was a man to remember.

"I'm Captain Mahaffey of Company Eight, Texas Rangers," he announced in a sonorous authoritative voice that matched his frame. "Have you seen anything of a bunch of horsemen, five in number, riding south on this road?"

"No sir, we haven't," drawled Bell. "We seed a niggah on a mule about—"

"How long have you been on this road?" interrupted the bronzed ranger, impatiently.

"Wal, lemme see. We dropped in on this heah road sometime this mawnin', comin' from Yorkville, where we stayed all night. I reckon about midmawnin'."

"Where are you going?"

"Me an' my brother air bound for Denton County to homestead some land over there. We ain't shore jest where."

"I see you've got a Winchester behind you on the seat. What's that for?"

"Nothin' pertickler. We jest fetched it along with what we owned."

The officer seemed baffled. "Boys, it looks like that gang of train robbers rode through last night or yesterday. They're in the breaks by this time. We're stuck. Pell's tip came too late."

"Mister Ranger, has there been a train holdup?" asked Bell, wonderingly.

"Yes. Three nights ago. A Texas Central express car was robbed at Hailey. The robbers made off with thirty thousand dollars. Looks like a Simm Bell job. Did you ever hear of him?"

"Simm Bell?" mused the robber chief, reflectively. "I reckon I've heerd thet name somewhere."

"Ha! Ha!" laughed the captain. "If you're a Texan you must have lived on the Staked Plain. Thanks, homesteaders, and good luck."

"Same to you, Cap. Hope you ketch thet Simm Bell," replied Bell, jocularly, and whipping the reins he clucked to the team and started on. Holden's keen ears were attuned to catch any more from the rangers.

"Beaten again!" rolled out the captain, his deep voice ringing. "That robber Bell has too many friends in Central Texas. But if it's the last ranger job I ever do, I'll ride the man down!"

"Simm, did you hear that?" whispered Wade, glancing over his shoulder to see the rangers turn east on the crossroad.

"Hear it? Hell yes! . . . And that was old hawk-eyed Cap Mahaffey himself!" ejaculated the robber. Then he grew gleeful. He chuckled. He laughed outright. "Fooled him good! By gum, that was worth somethin'. What'd ole Cap have said if he'd found out we got that thirty thousand under this here seat?"

"He'd have said a lot and done more," replied Wade, seriously. "It was a ticklish place for us. And for them! If they'd started to search this wagon, I'd have killed Mahaffey. They'd have filled us full of lead. . . . I'm darn glad you fooled Mahaffey. Kind of like his face. I'll never forget it."

"Huh! I'll never forget what he said," growled Bell. "Ride the man down! . . . Sounds like he meant that. Aw hell! Talk takes no skin off my back. Talk is cheap. And I've sure got friends in this country."

"Enemies too, Simm. Don't overlook that."

"He said Pell's tip was too late. What'd he mean, Wade?"

"I don't know. Maybe Blue wired Pell."

"Aw no . . . no! Rand wouldn't do a dirty trick like that."

"We'll see. But at least we've got a hunch to lay off on that Mercer bank job."

"Lay off nothin'," returned Bell, with an impatient snarl.

"Simm, we've got plenty of money for a while. We can hide up in Smoky till all this blows over."

"After we bust that Mercer bank. Them rangers took some other hosses' tracks for ours. Makin' for the breaks east. They're off our tracks. It'll be just the right time. Lawd, won't ole Cap roar!"

"I'm leery of it," replied Wade, gravely.

"Well, you can keep camp in the Hollow and wait," said Bell, sarcastically.

"Chief, did I ever fail you?" queried Wade, poignantly.

"No. And that's what surprises me--your turnin' yellow now."

"I'm not yellow. . . . It's for your sake. I tell you I feel sort of queer lately. You're gettin' too reckless. It's not for myself, Simm. What do I care for myself? My folks are dead, except my sister, Lil, as you remember. She's married now. She knows I went to the bad."

"You been with me since you were sixteen. And now you're grown up. What'll become of you when I get bored? . . . Makes me think I've given you a tough deal, Wade. But I never thought about it that way."

"Don't mind me. I'll be all right if you only use some sense. . . . Simm, you've been more to me than my own Dad. I—I'd hate to see you killed."

"Well, son, then you'd better ride away from Texas 'cause I'll probably stop lead sooner or later. I'll never hang, that's sure."

"Don't talk to me about riding away," rejoined Wade, bitterly. "Where'd I go? What'd I do? . . . Here's the village. Are you going to stop?"

"Yes, long enough to buy some more grub and likker for the gang. Look sharp to see if the rangers doubled back."

CHAPTER TWO

SMOKY HOLLOW was the favorite hiding place of Simm Bell after one of his raids.

It lay in western Denton County which was sparsely settled over that rough country, and was a deep wide gorge at the headwaters of Clear Creek and so densely wooded that it made an almost impenetrable jungle.

No posse of Texans or company of rangers had ever trailed Bell within many miles of that covert. The reason was that the few inhabitants of the region had a great deal to lose and nothing to gain by informing on the robber's whereabouts. Bell was kindly and generous. His friends profited by steering inquisitive strangers or officers of the law away from the wilderness of western Denton County.

By driving unremittingly all next day Bell and Holden had arrived at the wooded rim of the gorge late in the afternoon. They unhitched the wagon and hid it in a clump of tamaracks.

"It might come in handy," remarked Bell. "But the hosses we'll give away. Not a bad idee. The rest of the outfit we'll pack down the trail."

"Like hob we will. Not in one trip or two."

"That's so. I'm not very smart. How much can you pack?"

Holden was buckling on his heavy gun belt. "Reckon my saddle, my rifle—and my package of bills, if it *is* bills."

"By gum, we haven't opened that yet. Make sure now, boy."

Wade drew his knife and slit the heavy wrapper, tore open a corner to expose the neatly tied end of a packet of greenbacks.

"Fifties! . . . And I gave you that bundle! Well, son, I'll not go back on it. . . . Now I'll go down after the gang. Reckon two of them packs of coin are all I can carry. You stay here. Better hide your share. I'll give you a handful of gold pieces so you can jingle them in your pocket."

With grunts of satisfaction and effort Bell started down the trail burdened with all he could carry. Wade took his saddlebags, his coat and his share of the loot back into the woods a little way, and sat down to examine his prize and decide what to do with it. The operation of opening the package, which he performed with rude hands, was naturally exciting, but Wade did not gloat over the many neat bundles of greenbacks. Singularly enough, money did not mean much to Wade Holden. Here lay more cash than he had ever seen at one time in his life. Its first effect on him was to revive a once cherished boyhood dream of a cattle ranch, but a dream that had gradually faded as he drifted into outlawry with Simm Bell. He smiled bitterly at the ghost of that dream. Too late! But what to do with all this money? He hated drink and he was a poor gambler.

Wade mechanically began to count the money. There were two packs of fifty-dollar bills aggregating five thousand dollars. Then he found two bundles of one-hundred-dollar bills, the sum of which made ten thousand. Here he began to sweat, and his fingers trembled. Besides these, there were packages of twenties, tens and fives, which he did not take the time to count and add. The twenties he hid in the lining of his coat, where money had secretly reposed before. The smaller bills he stowed away in his saddlebags. The packets of large bills fitted in the inside pockets of his loose leather vest and there he determined to sew them securely. This done, Wade repaired to the trail and sat down to wait.

The sun was sinking in the west and a cool breeze stirred the treetops. Spring had come to the breaks and the foliage was almost full-leafed. A dreamy murmur of running water arose from the green depths. Wade heard wild turkeys clucking. He was glad to get back to Smoky Hollow. He could rest and fish and hunt once more, and wander by himself without eternal vigilance. It struck him suddenly how good—how wonderful to be free forever of that need to listen, to watch, to be ready to ride, ride, ride. But what a foolish thought!

At length voices disrupted this strange mood that had of late obsessed him. Soon a low whistle wafted up. Holden replied with the same birdcall. It was not long then until he saw Arkansas' lanky figure and red bewhiskered visage ascending the trail. After him plodded the thickset swarthy Bill Morgan and last came Pony Heston, the blond giant of the gang. They climbed with unusual eagerness though saving their breath. Arkansas' grin made a wide gap in his red face.

"Howdy, son," he panted. "Where's all—thet yaller coin—the boss raved about?"

"Ark, did Simm tell you about that fool holdup?" asked Wade.

"He did. An' I—shore cussed him. But all the rest—of the gang —took it like pie."

"Here. You rustle these two packs. . . . Pony, you take this one and what else you can carry. . . . Bill, you lug the rest."

They all talked at once, husky-voiced, gleeful, like boys who had broken into a watermelon patch. Wade got them started down, then followed, so burdened with his load that he fell behind.

Bell, like a fox, had more than one hole to his burrow. There were several trails leading down into Smoky Hollow. But all of them were dim, and no ironshod hoof had ever cut into them. Hunted men learned to be careful how and where to step. Wade had never been on this particular trail, or any of the others that zigzagged into it.

From the surrounding hills above, this deep hollow appeared to be full of blue haze, which gave it the name Smoky. It was miles long, and its branches were endless in number.

Gradually the eager robbers ahead of Wade descended out of hearing. He deposited his burden in a likely place and sat down to rest. The dreamy sweetness of this wilderness stole over Wade anew. He could see the tunnels in the green foliage—deer and bear trails—leading down. A glimpse of sunset gold through an aperture in the canopy overhead reminded him that the day was closing. He started down again. A flock of wild turkeys had been scratching under the oaks. A whirr of wings and a crash of brush attested to heavy birds in flight. The murmur of the stream increased in volume. And as he descended, the slope grew less precipitous and the timber larger. Nevertheless the underbrush was so dense that he had to crawl in places, an ardous task with his burden. He rested in another pleasant spot and became conscious of a boding labored discontent with his lot. It was only when he returned to the tranquillity and security of this hiding place that such a mood assailed him. This time it seemed stronger. He could not understand it, unless his keen intuition foretold a tragic end to Simm Bell, and that dread haunted him.

Golden twilight fell before him, augmenting the beauty and mystery of the gorge. He saw the level floor before he descended to it. Great oaks, walnuts, elms stood in stately confusion, marking the center of the hollow where the creek wound its alternately swift and eddying way.

At the brink, where the clear stream flowed shallowly over flat stone, Holden deposited his burden again to kneel and drink. How cold, how sweet this water!

He went across, and before twilight had yielded to darkness he espied the light of a campfire through the trees.

When Wade arrived at camp to drop his burden it was none too soon for him. "Howdy, men," he replied in answer to greetings, and he threw off his coat and wiped the sweat from his hot brow.

If Wade had expected to find a hilarious company he missed his guess. Gilchrist, the red-shirted cook, was busy at his campfire, upon which pots and kettles steamed. Oberney, a weazened little Texan with a visage like a rat was laboriously and greedily counting gold coins. Tex Corning stood tall and slim in the firelight, his sallow face and drooping sandy mustache giving him an appearance of solemnity. Morgan, Pony Heston, and Muddy Ackers stood expectantly before Bell, who had a bottle of whisky in his hand. Nick Allen, the cowman of the gang, was lifting a cup to his bearded lips.

"Wal, heah's to you, Simm," Arkansas was saying, and drained his cup.

Wade soon ascertained that the fact of rangers being on Bell's trail accounted for the comparative seriousness of the robbers. Gilchrist soon called them to supper. They ate mostly in silence, hungry men of the open. After the meal Bell produced some cigars which he divided equally, as was his wont with everything.

"Boys, I'm dog-tired, but I reckon I'll smoke and talk a bit before turnin' in," he said. He lighted a cigar with a burning stick and settled back against a log, his powerful dark face somber in the firelight. Then without his usual braggadocio and levity, especially ridicule at the expense of the railroad people and the rangers, he briefly told the story of the holding up of the express train.

"I've divided that gold among you all, takin' the smallest share myself," he went on. "Maybe it was a fool job, in view of the big bank deal on hand. I reckon it was. But it's done. There's no more to say, onless we figure on whether Rand Blue double-crossed me or not. I'd like your angle on that."

"What's yours, chief?" queried Heston.

"I just can't believe Rand would be so low-down. But Wade made him admit he'd agreed with Pell to trap me. Rand swore to God he had to do it or go to jail. I reckon I still have faith in him."

Three of the gang who had been with Bell and Blue in several recent robberies backed up the chief. Three others who knew Blue better were noncommittal.

"Wal, I never liked his eye," was Nick Allen's contribution to the hearing.

Plainly the chief suffered under the lack of unanimous faith in his friend Blue. "Boys, I forgot to tell you that Wade tried to shoot Rand. I knocked up the gun. So you don't need to hear Wade's angle. . . . Arkansas, you're glum as an owl. Are you agin Blue?"

"Boss, I shore don't like the look of it one damn bit," said

Arkansas. "But if Blue did go over to the rangers to save himself we'll know pronto. My advice is not to take thet chance. Blue has been heah with us. I'd say it'd be wise to rustle for the breaks of the Rio Grande an' hole up for six months."

"After we raid that Mercer bank?" queried the chief, gruffly.

"No. Thet job can wait. Let's go pronto."

"When we put off jobs we never do them."

"Which so far has turned out lucky for us."

"I'll do what I've never done before. Put a deal to a vote."

One by one he questioned his men, first as to the advisability of deserting Smoky Hollow, and secondly whether or not to rob the Mercer bank. Wade and Arkansas were the only two members who voted to leave the camp at once and give up the Mercer job.

"That settles the deal," said the chief, without his usual animation. "My vote wouldn't count one way or another. . . . We'll rest up tomorrow, get in the hosses, hide this camp outfit, and when night comes hit the road for Mercer. Next day we'll raid that bank as planned and then light out for the Rio Grande."

Holden left his comrades in high spirits and unrolled his bed some distance from the campfire. He had just stretched out comfortably when he heard Bell tramping around calling him.

"Over here, chief," he replied.

Bell came stalking black against the fire flare and sat down beside Holden. He puffed at a cigar which he did not know had gone out.

"What's on your mind, Simm?"

"Kinda hard to get out, boy," replied Bell, haltingly for him. "But it's been botherin' me the last day or so, since we run into Cap Mahaffey. That old geezer sort of galled me. '*Ride the man down*!' . . . Damn his Texas soul!"

"Simm, he meant it. Mahaffey is on his mettle. He'll have to catch you or get out of the ranger service. You've caused it a lot of grief."

"Ahuh, I reckon. It's not ticklin' me much just now. . . . Boy,

I've got the queerest feelin' of my life. Not one of my hunches! It must be that cold creepy thing I've heard people say comes over you when somebody walks over your grave. . . . Anyway, here's the idee that's been growin' on me. Suppose tomorrow night you give us the slip an' light out of Texas forever!"

"*Simm!*" whispered Wade, aghast.

"You're still only a boy," went on Bell, hurriedly. "I kinda feel responsible for you. The idee of gettin' jailed never bothered me, 'cause I never will be. I'll go with my boots on. But somehow it oughta be different for you. Your mother was a good woman. And Lil is a fine girl. You've had schoolin', and you're a darned handsome boy. . . . It occurred to me—for you to leave the gang—ride away—far away as Arizona that I've heard is so wonderful. . . . Turn honest, Wade! That's been done before by outlaws far worse than you. Curb that gun-throwin' instinct of yours. And go straight. I wish you would, Wade. It'd be a load off my mind."

"Thanks, chief," replied Wade with emotion, as he pressed the outlaw's hand resting on his bed. "But no. I won't do it. . . . Not while you're alive!"

"Aw, I'm sorry. I was afraid you wouldn't," replied the chief, gloomily. "But Wade—if I should be—"

He broke off huskily. His dark face looked haggard in the dim firelight and his big eyes burned.

"Simm, is there any hope that you might do—what you ask me—after this big job?"

"Gawd no! That's too late, even if I wanted to. But for you, boy. . . ."

"All right, Simm. If they get you—and not me—I promise."

Mercer was a good-sized town in central Texas, having one long main street, the middle block of which consisted of the important stores and saloons. Opposite the hotel on the corner stood the Mercer bank building, a new structure more imposing than the modest edifices that neighbored it.

The noon hour of this particular spring day appeared to be less affected than usual by the lazy siesta-loving habit of Texans, for there were pedestrians on the sidewalks and vehicles moving along between.

Four horsemen, riding close together, turned out of a side street a block down from the hotel almost precisely at the same moment that seven other riders appeared from an opposite direction. They trotted their horses toward each other.

"Boss, I shore don't like the way them people air fadin' off the street," observed Arkansas.

"'Pears like Tex is leadin' his gang a little fast," added Pony Heston.

The four horsemen had reached a point almost opposite the hotel, diagonally across from which frowned the stone-faced bank, when Wade Holden seized Bell's arm and hissed:

"Hold, chief! I saw sunshine glint on a rifle barrel in that open window above the bank!"

"I seen it, boss," corroborated Arkansas, coolly. "We're ambushed."

"*Blue!* . . . Damn his treacherous soul!" growled Bell.

Wade's keen gaze roved swiftly everywhere.

"Boss, make a break—quick!" advised Arkansas, sharply.

"But which way?" rasped Bell, wise too late.

Wade saw a man in his shirt sleeves appear at an open door. He was not a ranger, but probably a citizen too excited to wait for orders. He raised a rifle and fired. Wade heard the sickening thud of the bullet striking flesh. Bell was knocked clean out of his saddle. Arkansas snatched at the bridle of the rearing horse.

Swift as a flash Holden dropped out of his saddle. He leveled his gun at the fellow who was again aiming the rifle, froze with deadly precision and fired. That man pitched up an exploding rifle and fell out in the street. Other shots rang out with the pounding of hoofs. Bell was getting to his feet.

"Rustle, Wade," shouted Arkansas. "Help him up!"

Wade boosted his chief into the saddle, then leaped into his own and whipped out two guns. Heston was galloping away swaying to and fro. A volley of shots burst from the upper story of the bank. Wild yells, thunder of hoofs, boom of guns accompanied the flight of Tex Corning's horsemen, as they tore down the street in the opposite direction. Wade saw one saddle emptied. He wheeled his frightened mount after Arkansas who was supporting Bell in the saddle with one hand and firing his gun with the other. Wade took snap shots at the puffs of smoke from the open windows above the bank. The street was deserted. Rifles cracked from the hotel. Bullets whistled all around Wade, to strike up the dust on the street. Suddenly Arkansas plunged headlong out of his saddle, to slide into the gutter. His horse broke its gait. Wade sheathed the gun in his left hand and reached to support the reeling Bell. Then their horses turned the corner and stretched out for the open country.

"Simm, are you bad hurt?" called Wade, poignantly.

The robber shook his shaggy head in doubt. He had lost his sombrero; his hair hung damp over a pallid brow. With one hand he held to the pommel of the saddle; he had the other inside his coat clutched in his shirt.

Wade overcame his fears. What was a bullet wound to Simm Bell? Wade remembered when his chief had carried away three pellets of lead from a fight, one of which was still in him. Wade no longer heard shots. Only the rhythmic beat of swift hoofs! The country road stretched straight ahead, a lonely yellow lane between unfenced rangelands. If Simm could hang on they were safe. The ranger service had no horses that could run down these two racers, chosen and trained for the very work they were now doing so effectively.

Holden looked back. No pursuers in sight yet! But he knew there would be soon. He looked ahead. Miles—to the broken country of timber and brush.

Bell swayed heavily in the saddle. Wade held his arm to keep him from falling. The fleet horses were now running even, and at that gait would soon reach the cover ahead. If Simm could only hold out! Once in the woody hills Wade could evade pursuers and look to his chief's wound. But his heart sank. Bell acted strange for a great robber who at laughed at posses and rangers for years. He was hard hit.

"Wade—I can't—stick on," he panted, hoarsely.

"Simm!—You must," cried Holden, suddenly sick with dread. "Only to the woods! . . . It's not far. Simm, remember what Mahaffey said."

"No hope, boy. I'm done. . . . Go on—alone. Save yourself."

Bell pulled at his bridle, slowing his horse. Wade had to follow suit, just managing by dint of effort to keep his chief from falling.

"We mustn't stop!" cried Wade, tensely, looking back fearfully. "No riders in sight!"

"Got to. . . . It's the end—boy. . . . Run for your life!"

"No," flashed Wade, in frantic passion. He turned the horses off the road under a wide-spreading elm, and leaped off just in time to catch the lurching Bell. The chief sank under the tree to lean against it. His face was ashen white. There was dew on his brow and a terrible light in his eyes, a bloody froth on his lips.

"My God! . . . Simm!" burst out Wade, in terror.

"Shot clean through, boy . . . and I'll go—with my boots on. . . . Who did it?—A ranger?"

"No. Some man in his shirt sleeves. I killed him, Simm!"

"That's good. . . . I saw Arkansas fall—shot plumb center. . . . What happened to Heston?"

"He rode off hard hit."

"And the rest—of the gang?"

"They turned back. I saw one saddle empty. They must have run into a hail of lead."

"Ahuh. . . . Look, boy. Any riders in sight?"

Wade leaped up to peer down the road. A group of eight or ten horsemen had turned the bend.

"Yes! Rangers!" exclaimed Wade, stridently. "Coming slow. Tracking us. Two miles or more back."

Bell opened his coat with his free hand. The other still clutched his shirt. Blood oozed out between his fingers. At the sight Wade uttered a loud cry and sank to his knees beside his friend. That bloody shirt, that clenched hand, meant only death. Wade could have shrieked in his misery. Prepared as he had been for this very thing, its presence was heart-rending and insupportable.

"Oh Simm! Simm!" he moaned. "If you'd only listened to me!"

"Too late, boy. . . . I'm sorry. . . . Here, take this." And he handed a heavy leather wallet to Wade. "Never mind the gold . . . too heavy." He thrust the wallet in Wade's coat pocket. "Fork your hoss—and ride. Remember your promise."

"No. I won't leave you," blazed Wade, leaping up to snatch his Winchester from the saddle-sheath. The rangers were coming on, in plain sight. Soon they would see the two horses under the elm.

"Go, you wild boy! Do you want me to see—you killed? You can get away."

"Simm, I can kill the whole bunch."

"Suppose you did? You'd have—the ranger service after you. . . . You'd never--be safe."

"I'm going to bore that —— Mahaffey. I see him now."

Bell cursed Wade to leave him.

"I'll stick, Simm," replied Wade, coolly, as the numb misery left his breast. His fighting heart leaped.

"Wade!—You'll force me—to tell you—somethin'. . . . And you'll hate me."

"Never!—But I reckon I'll go before you, Simm, so keep your secret."

The ranger posse was now less than half a mile away. In a moment surely they would see the horses and guess the situation. All Wade asked of fate was for them to keep on in a body. He had ten shots in his rifle. There would not be many rangers that would escape unscathed. But if they scattered to ride and surround the elm, then his hope would be futile. Then he saw that a stand of bushes down the road must hide the two horses from the rangers. And he calculated this cover would persist until the posse got within a hundred yards.

"Boy, you're not—listenin'," said Bell, huskily.

"Chief, there's no more to say—except good-by," replied Wade, darkly.

"Run, boy . . . for my sake!"

Wade shook his head, grimly gazing down the road. He was calculating distance. The rangers were coming at a jogtrot. Captain Mahaffey, square-shouldered and stalwart, his bronze face gleaming, rode beside a ranger who was bending from his saddle, his eyes glued to the horse tracks they were following. Ambush on an open road and level plain never occurred to them. They were going to ride right into death.

"Wade—won't you obey—my last order?"

"No, chief, I won't."

"My wish—my prayer?"

Wade kept silent. He was afraid to look at Bell lest he weaken. There was something in the robber's voice he had never heard before. Besides he wanted to be ready to shoot the instant the rangers came on from behind that line of brush.

"Simm, in less than a minute now Cap Mahaffey will be biting the dust," said Wade piercingly.

"Boy, don't kill him . . . don't kill *any* ranger . . . that's why I—lasted so long."

"I'll kill them all. . . . There's eight of them, Simm. . . . Only another hundred steps!—Less. Not one has a rifle out. What a chance!—They got us, Simm, but at dear cost."

"Lower that rifle!"

Wade heard but paid no attention to this, although a strange stifled cry from his dying chief tore at his heartstrings. Wade raised the rifle higher, his mind active and deadly. He gloated in his one gift, an instinctive and unerring skill with firearms. At that distance he could kill three or four of these rangers in less than half that many seconds—before they could swerve their horses. And a fiendish joy possessed him. Luck was on his side. If at his first shots they did not scatter like quail that would be the end of Mahaffey's squad.

"*Wade!*"

It was not the inflection of command in Bell's voice that struck through Wade. The rifle wavered half leveled. Mahaffey's rangers rode out from behind the line of bushes.

"Wade, I'm—your real father. . . . Your mother loved me. . . . Jim Holden never knew."

"Oh, God!" cried Wade, stricken to the soul. That had been the bond between him and this robber chief. A bolt shot back within his breast. He wheeled. He leaped back to kneel.

"My father! . . . Oh, why didn't you tell me long ago?"

"I couldn't, son. I'm glad—now. . . . Go!—Run for your life! Let me die—knowing—you got away—your promise—"

Bell's words failed, but the look in his eyes was one Wade could not disobey. It wrung the words, "I'll keep my promise" from him. He passed a swift shaking hand over Bell's pallid face, and it appeared that with that first and last caress a beautiful light began to fade in the big wide eyes.

Shrill yells brought Wade erect. He shoved the rifle home in its sheath and in a single spring made the saddle. The spirited horse leaped as from a catapult. Above the yells and shots, Mahaffey's stentorian voice pealed out:

"Ride the man down!"

CHAPTER THREE

HEAVY gunshots close behind Wade as he spurred his horse into flight caused him to turn in the saddle. Bell was sitting up, his hands extended with red-flashing guns. His shots upset the charging band of rangers. They spread on each side of the road to give the elm a wide berth. One ranger toppled from his saddle and another had to be supported. Wade saw Bell fall forward on his face.

Wade let out a terrible cry and turned his dimmed gaze ahead. Simm Bell had expended his last ounce of strength to halt the rangers for a few moments, in which time he knew Wade's fleet horse would get far in the lead. That was the Texas outlaw's last gesture. Wade knew he had seen his father die.

The abrupt transition from hate and blood lust, from iron nerve that scorned death for himself, to the anguish of finding his father only to lose him the same moment, and the realization of the terrible need of escape to keep his promise,—this rending change bowed Wade in his saddle, exceeding the sum of all the bitter moments of his life. It worked through him like a convulsion, his physical being at the mercy of the violence of his mental strife. To flee for his life—to resist halting and fighting those rangers with his last gasp—this took strength and will born of the exceeding love and grief that transformed him.

It seemed that his mind received a strange flashing illumination in which the blackness disappeared. He would escape. He would live to fulfill the pledge he had made his father. It gave him such unquestioning faith that no pursuit, no hardship, no future menace could ever eradicate it.

When Wade raised his head again to look back he saw six rangers in pursuit some three hundred rods behind. Two of the original posse had been eliminated. The sextet, riding two abreast, were holding their own with Wade. He recognized the broad-shouldered Mahaffey, that implacable ranger captain who could ride and fight with the most noted in that intrepid service. Mahaffey would ride him down if that were possible, and failing that, Wade knew they would resort to rifles to stop him alive or dead.

Wade forced himself to desperate calculation of chances. He must not make a mistake. The rangers, long used to the pursuit of criminals, seldom blundered. Wade's horse had exceptional speed and strength. The rangers used wiry little Mexican mustangs that could run all day without giving out. But in a short race of from five to ten miles they had no chance with Wade's big black. Wade knew that they would soon ascertain that. Probably old horsemen among them could see that the black had not yet extended himself.

Leaning back, Wade untied his slicker which contained a blanket rolled around a pack of provisions and some bags of Bell's gold. It weighed fifty pounds or more. Wade let it slide off to roll in the road. His ideas was to lessen the burden of his horse and possibly check the rangers. When pursuing train or bank robbers they never passed by discarded packs. In this instance Mahaffey evidently ordered one of his men to halt and see what the fugitive had abandoned. The others kept on without slackening their pace.

Wooded rolling country lay no farther ahead than between two and three miles. The road appeared to turn into a defile between green hills. The grass growing in the middle of the road attested to its being but seldom traveled. There was a hamlet ten miles west of Mercer, but not this far south. Somewhere across country ran one of the thoroughfares that wagon trains used when working north and west. When Wade reached this he decided he would cross it and strike more to the south.

No doubt Mahaffey felt sure of his quarry, else his men would have resorted to rifles long ago. Wade dreaded that contingency.

The intervening distance was not great enough; a good rifle shot could hit him or his horse before they could get out of range. Yet Wade felt his best game was to hold the black in, let the pursuers keep about the same distance or else gain a little, until he reached the wooded country. Once there, he would decide on his course.

The next time Wade looked back he saw the sixth rider coming up from the rear and gaining on his fellows. He rode a fast horse, undoubtedly the fastest of that posse. It appeared to be a lean mustang, rather rangier than the others and a horse to fear.

"Save yourself, Blackie," called Wade to his running mount. "Steady now! Hold in."

The horse lessened perceptibly that tendency to stretch lower and faster. His hoofbeat a light regular rhythmic tattoo on the hard road. Blackie was just getting warm. He had been a young race horse before Bell stole him to train him to show his heels to rangers.

The wide plains of the rangeland began to fall behind in timber-bordered wings. Wade was fast approaching the wooded country. Soon he saw it from the height of a ridge which sloped down into a valley. Then he ascertained that this was just one of the timbered creek bottoms so prevalent in Texas. But it was cover and in the thick of it he would be hard to head.

Wade resorted to a ruse that might throw his pursuers off the track. He did not wait until the road reached the woods, but left it and cut across in plain sight of the rangers to ride into the brush.

They would have to track him, which rangers were trained to do. They seldom lost a trail but they would have to go slowly, while he could accommodate his gait to the lay of the ground. A thicket of brambles and scrub oak offered poor travel on horseback. Wade turned to the right and rode as fast as he could under the trees, over logs and through brush to the shallow creek into which he spurred Blackie despite a possibility of quicksand. The horse had difficulty but made the crossing without getting mired. Twice Wade came within an ace of riding out upon the road again. Creek bottom and timbered belts narrowed between hills. Wade feared he might get boxed in, and halted his horse at a point where he could peep over the brush to see back along a quarter mile of the road.

This would give Blackie a rest, while the ranger horses would still be going. It struck Wade that Mahaffey might be too keen to send all his men into the brush to work out his tracks. Some of them might keep to the road. Wade bent far over, away from his creaking saddle, to listen, and his reward was a sound of hoof-beats on the road beyond the bend. Without a moment's hesitation he urged Blackie out of the brush into a run. His shrewd guess was that the rangers could not hear the running of his horse as he had heard theirs.

The advantage was Wade's. Down in the Hollow the shadows proclaimed that the afternoon was far advanced. If he could keep the rangers behind him until nightfall his escape was assured. As he did not know the country, it was imperative that he stay on the road until forced off.

Blackie ran easily along the winding creek-bottom road. It grew rocky and rough, necessitating a lessening speed. It followed and crossed the creek, wound through dells of elm and sycamore where slants of golden sunlight lightened the green gloom. Flocks of wild turkeys and troops of deer were disturbed at their drinking. The lessening volume of the creek and the little ledges of rock over which it poured convinced Wade that he was approaching its source. When the road began to climb away from the creek then Wade knew he would soon be out from cover.

So it turned out. Wade found himself once more in the open rangeland. It was, however, more undulating than the country surrounding Mercer. To his surprise and concern he found that the creek bottom had doubled back with the road, making a wide bend. What if the rangers were aware of that?

The black ears of his horse shot up. Wade turned his gaze from left to right. Three riders were sweeping across the plateau to head him off. One was Mahaffey and another was the ranger on the lean buckskin mustang.

"Out, Blackie! Run!" yelled Wade to his horse, and goaded him with the spurs. The black leaped as if he had been standing still, and in a few moments of dead run the danger that the rangers might head off Wade was over. They dashed into the road a full hundred rods behind. But not so far that Wade failed to hear Mahaffey's far-carrying yell of baffled rage!

A peculiar familiar hot hiss in the air close to Wade's head was followed by the crack of a rifle shot. Wade glanced back over his shoulder. The lean ranger was out in front of Mahaffey and the others. His mustang had free rein and was running, stretched low, on the instant a puff of white smoke rose. If Wade had not instinctively ducked he would have gotten a bullet through his middle. As it was, it cut him across the top of his head, tugging away his sombrero. The hot sting was like the gush of blood out of Wade's heart, burning along his veins. These rangers would drive him to fight. They would force him into a corner. But no! They could never catch him.

Bending low and forward Wade called to the horse. "Run Blackie! . . . Oh, run away from them! . . . So I can keep my word to him!"

Bullets were striking up the dust in front of Wade. His pursuers were all shooting. They had the range. But for the difficulty of aiming true from a running horse they would swiftly have put a stop to Wade's flight. He looked back. The lean ranger on the buckskin mustang had the lead on his comrades. Mahaffey was second and he was shooting a carbine. The third rode to one side behind him and he had a rifle to his shoulder. Far back on the road the other three rangers hove in sight.

Blackie drew away from his pursuers in a manner that must have caused Mahaffey deep chagrin. But the rangers favored endurance in horses above racing speed. Their trails were long and the record of the service was that it never failed. The lean rider was reloading his Winchester. Mahaffey shot with more haste than judgment. His bullets skipped along the dusty road. The third man was more dangerous. His lead whipped up the dust behind Wade. He was shooting to cripple Blackie.

The horse bore a charmed life. In less than two miles he doubled the hundred rods between him and the rangers. He grew hot and settled into his swiftest, a pace that blurred the sides of the road in Wade's sight. In a desperate flight Blackie could hold that gait a long while without killing himself. He knew what depended on him and the fighting heart of his racing sire throbbed in him. Farther and farther he drew away. Mahaffey ceased to waste more ammunition. The time came when a third ranger gave up shooting, but still came tearing on at the top speed of his mustang. It was the lean rider on the buckskin that Blackie had to beat. This ranger gradually fell back. He was already beaten, except for that rifle.

Wade felt something wet and hot trickling down his left arm. Blood! He experienced no pain. Could that blood come from the wound in his head? Changing the bridle over to his left hand he felt his arm. He had been shot through that arm without knowing it. The bone was still intact. A gloom descended upon him. Were they to kill him after all? How implacable these rangers! Something—perhaps justice and right, gave them that unswerving ruthlessness.

Blackie, with his magnificent stride, ran almost out of range of the relentless pursuer. Only a few more rods! The lean rider was aiming high. His bullets, almost spent, no longer whipped up the spiteful swirls of dust. Then almost at the moment of victory one of those missiles caught Blackie somewhere in the flank. He broke and plunged, then recovered to go on.

"Oh hell!" cursed Wade, frantically, feeling the change of muscular rhythm in the horse. Once more Wade's deadly wrath flamed up, not for himself but for his faithful horse. If Blackie fell, Wade would be right back where he had been under the elm, when his father's poignant revelation had saved Mahaffey's life. Wade reached down to jerk the Winchester from its sheath.

Yet somehow he did not give up. A nameless feeling, more than hope, would not die.

But Blackie did not go down. He recovered his stride enough to increase the advantage he had gained until he was out of range. That appeared to be his limit. That he held. Wade had no way to ascertain where Blackie had been hit or how serious it was. No blood showed on his flanks. Certainly no bone had been touched for the horse was running hard, still fast enough to keep the lead.

"Oh, Blackie—you grand horse!" cried Wade, huskily, as the fever of rage passed. He had loved many horses, but all that he had felt was little to what Blackie inspired. Once more Wade attended to the road ahead, and the hour, and his pursuers.

The road was now wide, bare of grass, thickly packed with tracks of hoofs and wheels. He had come into the main artery of travel west. A wagon train had left those fresh marks. It could not be far ahead. The last rays of the setting sun flushed rough heights of land to the fore.

Behind Wade, a half mile or less on the road, came Mahaffey and his two rangers, and about a like distance behind them galloped the other three.

For miles then the race held that way, with the edge wearing off the speed of the ranger's mustangs and Blackie slackening perceptibly.

The afterglow of sunset failed. Twilight crept out of the breaks of rough land ahead. Wade's hope revived. Blackie must have sustained only a superficial flesh wound. Night was near at hand. Wade resisted a feeling that he should swerve off the road, find cover in one of the many rugged ravines yawning black from the level of prairie, and after nightfall work southward. But before he yielded to it the road entered a pass with steep gravelly banks. It would be time enough when he got through here.

He kept on, trying not to believe that Blackie had broken his gait again. But soon Wade had to credit his senses. The horse was laboring. Gathering darkness favored Wade as well as the widening of the pass into a steep-walled gorge with clumps of trees and thickets on each side of the road. Water gleamed in the gloom under the left wall. If overtaken, Wade saw that he might hide, but he could no longer climb out. It might develop that he should have climbed out before. The rangers would be gaining now. Another straight stretch of road would betray his plight to them.

It came, traversing a wide amphitheatre with unscalable walls and scanty timber, through which the road ran straight toward what might be a gateway into open country or a still narrower pocket.

Wade had no choice. As Blackie thundered on with weakening stride, Wade kept looking back. When he saw the rangers emerge from the pass, much closer to him, and heard their yells, a coolness of despair settled down upon him. At the worst, he could only die and he would not die submissively. Only he would exhaust every possible chance before turning at bay.

The thoroughbred under Wade would go on till his heart cracked. But Wade began to pull him, intending to leave the saddle before being shot out of it. A last time he looked back. He could make out the group of dark riders against a pale skyline. They were within easy rifle shot of him, but he calculated that the black shadows in front of him made him invisible to them. Through the trees ahead he imagined he saw a pin-point of light. The road turned, a dim lane between trees close to the looming walls. He could elude his pursuers on foot.

Wade hauled Blackie off the road, and leaping down he gave the noble heaving horse a last pat, and broke into a run. He soon got out of the trees into another open space. Fleeing across this, Wade gained a thin line of brush. Pausing to pick his way he heard the pound of hoofs behind and excited shouts of men. The rangers had found Blackie.

"Spread out! Ride him down!" roared the inexorable Mahaffey.

Wade crouched there like a beast cornered. His chest heaved and his tongue clove to the roof of his mouth. The rangers would soon be upon him. Spread across that narrow canyon they could drive a rabbit out of its covert. The instinctive drawing of his gun was a sign that Wade had all but abandoned hope. Against a rage of despair he ran on.

The canyon boxed. A bulging wall drove him into the road. It made another bend. When Wade got around it he heard the crashings of brush not far behind.

Suddenly the walls appeared to fall away on each side. That box had been a gateway into another oval. Rounding a thicket into a glade he came upon horses that startled him so he nearly dropped. They were riderless. Snorting, they thumped away. Hobbled! Then he saw lights beyond a fringe of trees. Camp fires! His distraught mind received the sensations and groped for their meaning. He had run squarely into the wagon train that had been ahead of him on this road and which he had forgotten. It had halted for the night, surely blocked his escape. Still he went on, swerving to the left, hoping to get by under cover of the wall. He passed horses, oxen, canvas-covered wagons, always keeping himself behind the fringe of trees. Beyond this appeared an open space bright with fires.

Wade bent low and glided from tree to tree, making for the darkest place. At last he crawled to the edge of some bushes and lay still, burning hot, his heart bursting, dripping wet with sweat, his strength and endurance not equal to his spirit. He strove to control his whistling breath. In a moment more he moved on and peeped out.

A little tent had been pitched in the open not twenty feet from where Wade crouched. Beside it a girl knelt, placing sticks upon a camp fire that had begun to blaze. She was humming a tune. Her tent sat somewhat apart from a great prairie schooner, beyond which blazed the fires of a big caravan. Out there sounded a merry hum of voices. He saw men and women busy around camp fires; he smelled smoke and the fragrance of frying ham. All the way across this space bright fires blocked Wade's escape. He could not hope to pass unobserved, but he would have to take the risk.

Wade stood up, swallowing hard. It was the end. He felt terrible bitterness of regret that he had not stayed back to die fighting with his father. Then an insupportable memory crushed back his weakness. While he lived there was a chance. Suddenly his glance came back to the girl.

She stood up in the light of her fire, a grown girl, slender and dark. The instinct that had actuated Wade when he gripped his gun swayed him now.

He strode out to confront her.

"Girl—for God's sake—hide me!" he panted.

She recoiled, her big dark eyes flaring with fright. They took in Wade's white, blood-streaked face, and the dripping hand he held out beseechingly. But she did not scream.

"Who are you?" she whispered, in sudden excitement.

"I'm a—fugitive," he panted. "Rangers after me. . . . They've shot me—twice. . . . They're close—on my trail. . . . They'll kill me! . . . For mercy's sake—hide me!"

She stared at him as if fascinated. Her wide dark eyes quickened to dispel the fright.

At that instant a commotion broke out in the camp, caused by pound of hoofs and shout of men.

"Who comes there?" yelled a man, no doubt the leader of the caravan.

"Mahaffey's Rangers," came the booming reply from beyond the trees.

"What you want?"

"We're runnin' down an outlaw. He's heah. Just fell off his hawse—shot bad. Saddle all bloody. Look sharp, you—campers! . . . Ride men—he cain't get away. Ride him down!"

The girl darted to her tent. "Quick! Hide in here," she whispered opening the flaps.

Wade leaped to fall inside. She slipped in after him and drawing the flaps close she peeped out.

CHAPTER FOUR

WADE sank down on a soft bed of blankets. The awful clamp around his heart eased its icy grip. Against the light of the fire outside he saw the profile of the girl as she peered out. Pounding of hoofs, babel of voices, shrill whistles resounded.

"They've ridden on," whispered the girl, turning to Wade. "That ranger, Captain Mahaffey, is my uncle!"

"They'll come—back," he panted. "Your—uncle?"

She watched and listened again at the aperture, during which few moments Wade recovered his breath. The stitch in his side pierced like a blade. Shadows of flames flickered on the tent. The fire outside crackled. The clip-clop of trotting horses lessened in volume, and also the shouts. Only the steady hum of talking men continued.

"What are—they doing?" asked Wade, huskily.

"Riding to and fro—everywhere," she replied, the dark velvet brightness of her eyes strained to perceive objects at a distance.

"How far does this canyon go?"

"It opens right heah into the prairie."

"Could I climb the bank?"

"No. Too high and steep."

Silence ensued while the girl continued to peer out. Wade watched her expressive profile and listened, trying to decide what his next move should be.

"I'd better go back . . . climb out below somewhere," he muttered, despondently. But hope resurged. He would elude these bloodhound rangers.

"You stay heah. Dad's men are watching. . . . Besides you're wounded. You were staggering."

"Yes, I'm shot. My head burns. But I can't feel the other. . . . Only I'm bleeding so."

She gave a slight start and whispered fearfully: "There! They are riding back. . . . Up to Dad and the men by the fire."

"Let me look."

"Oh, be careful. They're so close."

Wade bent forward to peep between the flaps of the tent. Less than a hundred paces away sat the closest of the rangers—the lean rider on the buckskin. Mahaffey, his big face red in the firelight, was in the center of the line. They had halted not far beyond the first canvas-covered wagon where the men of the caravan stood waiting.

"Well, Cap, no luck, eh? We could have spared you the trouble. No man has come through our camp."

"Hell! I saw him get off his horse," replied Mahaffey, in ringing impatience. "My ranger, Jim Thorne, saw him, too."

"Yes, an' I got warm blood on my hand from his saddle," vouchsafed the lean rider.

"We're wasting time. He's hidden right in this camp," declared Mahaffey. "Pen, you're trail boss of this caravan?"

"I am. Bound for New Mexico," rejoined the leader.

"All right, sorry I'll have to search your camp."

"Go ahaid. But I reckon yo're exceeding yore authority."

"A captain of Texas Rangers can search any place or arrest any one."

"I know all about you rangers," replied Pencarrow, dryly. "I said go ahaid. But be careful. My wife and kids air in this outfit. And so air other families."

"Do you think we're greasers?" demanded Mahaffey hotly.

"No. I'm only giving you a hunch."

"Off, men!" ordered Mahaffey, peremptorily. "Search the camp. He's crawled in somewhere. Search the tents—the wagons, in and out. Everywhere a jack rabbit could hide."

Wade sank back on his knees. The girl, still holding the tent flap aside, turned to see his tortured face.

"Oh, they're hounds!" she exclaimed. "I had another uncle once who wasn't a ranger. . . . They shot him!"

"Must make a break," said Wade, desperately to himself, and he drew his gun and started to rise.

She pushed him back. "Stay here. I'll save you. . . . Get under the blanket. . . . Far over." As Wade stretched out she covered him from foot to head. He lay still, his heart throbbing painfully, slowly awakening to the reality of the girl. She was good; she had nerve. He pushed down the edge of the blanket so he could see. She was watching again, breathless and intent. The curve of her full lips appeared contemptuous.

With strained attention Wade listened for sounds outside. Only the continuous flow of talk came to him, not distinguishable. How slowly the seconds dragged! Mahaffey would make a thorough search. Wade shook under the blanket. Tremendous exertion and emotion had verged on panic. But he began to recover, to find himself. This girl herself was a Texan. She would outwit the rangers.

"They're coming," she whispered, peering out. "Left our wagon to the last. Dad's with them. . . . And if he's not hopping mad I don't know him."

Wade began to distinguish voices. "Pen, I do my duty as I see it," Captain Mahaffey was saying, testily.

"Mahaffey, there are other things in the world besides your damned ranger service," returned Pencarrow, coldly. "For instance the feelings of honest people and their regard for personal property."

"Men, heah's the last wagon. Look out now." Mahaffey pounded on the iron-bound wheel with the butt of a gun. "Hey, young fellar, I'm gettin' tired callin' you to come oot. If you have any sense you'll surrender."

A moment's silence ensued fraught with suspense.

"Not thet hombre, boss," drawled one of the rangers. "He'll die like Simm Bell died—with his guns bellerin'."

"He's out of shells. Never shot once at us," said another.

"Thet shore stumped me," declared Mahaffey, as if mystified. "Men, we cain't overlook that. I saw him kill Wess Jenkins, the bartender who shot Bell off his hawse. We just found that rifle with only one shell exploded. Strange."

"Cap'n, I seen Holden standin' by his hoss under the elm where Bell dropped. An' he had thet rifle at his shoulder. He could have cleaned us."

"Holden, if you're in there come out," called Mahaffey, ringingly. "I'll remember thet so far as we know you've never shot at a Texas Ranger."

Wade listened to all this with bated breath. The girl knelt at the aperture, strung and intent, singularly cool.

"Go in, men, an' dig about," ordered Mahaffey in chagrin.

There were forthcoming sundry sounds and voices that attested to a thorough search of the wagon.

"No good, boss," declared a ranger.

"All right. Come out. . . . Heah's another tent. Have a look in thet."

The girl slipped the flaps together and with deft hands tied the strings. That left the tent opaque and dim from the firelight outside. She crawled upon the bed, and getting to her knees she began to take off her blouse.

"Mahaffey, thet's my daughter's tent," said Pencarrow. "If she's there no one opens it."

Thuds of boots and jingles of spurs told Wade of the approaching group of men. He covered his face with the blanket so that he could peep out with one eye.

"I don't care a damn whose tent it is," declared the crabbed captain.

"Wal, you will care if my lass is in it," returned Pencarrow, coolly. "Jacqueline, air you heah?"

"Yes, Dad. Is supper ready? What's all the fuss about?" she replied, calmly.

"Rangers heah, lass. Yore uncle Cap Mahaffey. They're searchin' our camp for an escaped outlaw. Can they see in yore tent?"

"Texas Rangers! . . . My uncle? Indeed they cain't. I'm undressed."

She had only removed her blouse which she was in the act of laying on the bed. Her white rounded arms and breast gleamed palely. Wade could see her on her knees, with her little dark head erect like that of a listening deer, her big eyes black as gulfs in the gloom of the tent.

"Excuse me, Jackie," spoke up Mahaffey, deferentially. "How long have you been in your tent?"

"Only a little while. I built my fire—then came in to change for supper."

"Did you see a man slippin' along?"

"No."

"Did you heah any one runnin'?"

"No."

"Thank you. Sorry to have disturbed you. . . . Well, men, we're stuck for the thousandth time."

"Boss, he's given us the slip," said the ranger whose voice Wade now knew.

"By gad, he has."

"Cap, who is this outlaw an' why air you so set on catchin' him?" asked Pencarrow, curiously.

"I reckon it's young Wade Holden, right-hand pard of the robber, Simm Bell. But some of my men don't agree about thet. Holden is a gunman, a desperado, an' the most dangerous of thet gang. One of them, Rand Blue, turned state's evidence to save himself. He was in the robbin' of the express car on the Central less than a week ago. An' he wired Sergeant Pell thet the gang was due to rob the Mercer bank. We frustrated thet raid. In the fight we about cleaned up this gang. Only three got away, not countin' this man we're after. He was with Bell an' two other robbers, when Wess Jenkins took to shootin' too soon. At thet he bored Bell. An' got killed himself by young Holden. We tracked Bell an' this fellar out of town—to a tree where evidently Bell fell off his hoss or had to give up. Holden—if it was him—rode off. An' as we gave chase Bell opened up with two guns, killing Sergeant Pell an' cripplin' another ranger before he fell daid over his guns."

"Ah! So thet was Simm Bell's finish!" ejaculated Pencarrow. "Reminds me of Wess Hardin an' Buck Duane."

"Simm Bell was not in the class of those Texans," rejoined Mahaffey. "He was an ordinary robber. He had a faculty of makin' friends. Thet's what kept us from gettin' him long ago. But he died great, I'm bound to confess."

"I reckon this news will go good in Houston?" queried Pencarrow, with dry shrewdness.

"It shore will," declared the captain, emphatically. "Politics! One party has been advocatin' a discontinuance of the ranger service. An' they shore been raggin' us."

"Ah, I see. Thet accounts."

"No, it doesn't altogether," retorted Mahaffey with temper. "A ranger is trained to ride down his man. But for thet, Pencarrow, Texas would still be unsafe to live in. Young Holden was the most dangerous of Bell's gang. A marvelous shot with either a six or long gun. Cold nerve. Absolutely fearless. A mere boy in years. . . . I just cain't understand why he didn't use thet rifle on us. Probably this robber with Bell was not Holden at all. That's my explanation. But I'll ride him down if it takes all summer!"

"Wal, you better have supper with us an' take his trail again in the mawnin'," drawled Pencarrow. "For my part I hope he gets away."

"So it appears," returned Mahaffey, tersely. "But thanks for your invitation. We're all in. Thet hombre shore gave us a run."

As their voices trailed away a clanking ring of iron against iron proclaimed suppertime for the caravan.

"They've gone. He's given up—the old devil," said the girl, fervently, in a low voice. "That's our supper gong. I must hurry."

"Don't forget you were changing your dress," returned Wade, with the shrewdness of the fugitive.

"So I said. But I won't. Dad will not notice. And the rangers haven't seen me." She was slipping on her blouse when suddenly she ceased. In the pale light he could see her bend over her hand. Then she started violently.

"It's all bloody!"

"No wonder. I've bled all over your blankets. Be careful to wipe it off before going to supper."

"Will you stay right heah until I come back? It's safest. Then I'll bind up your wounds and—and we'll see. . . ."

"I'll stay," he replied, soberly.

She rubbed her hands on something soft and completed the task of getting her blouse on; then she seemed struck by a thought.

"Air you—Wade Holden?" she asked, with her quaint Texas accent.

"I wish to God I could deny it," returned Wade, bitterly.

She made no further comment and opened the tent to go out, tying the flaps behind her.

Wade was left alone, victim of contending tides of emotion and thought. Simm Bell—his father—had yielded to the fierce desire to check the ranger's pursuit and he had chosen to kill Pell rather than Mahaffey. Indeed, at last the robber had died as he had always sworn he would die—with his boots on and guns in hands. Wade reveled in that. The loquacious robber chief had risen to the heights of battle in the end and his last act, his last thought had been for his boy. What a bloodhound Mahaffey was—a Texan with one set purpose! Wade felt that even if he escaped now he would never be safe. He must get away that night and leave no track and go far. This girl—what was her name?—Jacqueline Pencarrow—had saved his life. An unutterable gratitude—something that waxed against his somber bitterness—welled up in Wade's heart. Girls had played no part in his life since he had taken to evil ways. Seven years! He could not remember with interest any girl except his sister Lil. And he recalled his mother. That she had loved Simm Bell instead of the wandering guerrilla rebel, Jim Holden, sank deep into Wade's mind, there to be accepted.

Presently Wade realized that despite a whirling of thought and feeling he was gradually sinking to faintness or slumber. Loss of blood had weakened him. He still felt the hot trickle down his sleeve. Sitting up he carefully put aside the blankets and removed his coat. There was a hole in the top of his shirt at the left shoulder. The wound was just a furrow in the flesh. He must bind it to stop the bleeding. Taking his scarf from his pocket he looked about for something to make a pad to place over the wound. He found a soft garment lying on top of the girl's open box and, folding that inside his shirt, he bound it securely with the scarf.

Then he waited for her, resisting the temptation to peer out. Apparently there was only one mess, for all the laughter and talk sounded from one direction. Members of the caravan with their ranger guests were making merry over the meal. Somehow they seemed heartless. Here he crouched, burning with wounds, starved and thirsty, a hunted man no better than a mad dog. Then he thought of the girl. She had a heart. She had saved him without a thought as to who or what he was. She represented the saving grace of woman, of which he had heard but with which he had had little contact until now. And she stood between Wade and utter hatred of the world.

Light footsteps sounded outside. She had come back. Wade heard the crackle of fresh wood thrown upon the fire. A blaze lightened the interior of the tent. Then the flaps were untied and she slipped inside with a momentary flash of firelight. She carried a parcel which she deposited on the bed.

"I thought I'd never get away," she whispered. "The men are excited and the women fussing over the rangers. I fetched some pieces of meat, salt, matches, all the biscuits I could steal and an apple. You must be hungry."

"I haven't had a bite since night before last. But I'll wait. . . . I must tell you that I took some garment or other off your box and used it to bind this gunshot on my arm."

"Garment?—I—I wonder what," she returned, and dropped on her knees to feel around the box. "Oh!"—

"It was white and soft," he said, seeing her confusion. I'm sorry. But I had to have something."

"You took my—my chemise."

"I didn't look at the—the thing. It's too late now."

"No matter. You can throw it away."

Wade did not make any reply. All at once the singular situation struck him, aside from the stark tragedy of what had crowded his mind—death, pitiless rangers and wild flight—imminent peril. A young girl, probably sixteen years of age, had taken him into the privacy and protection of her tent. He was only a hunted creature to her. But to him she loomed great as the influence he had lost since he left his mother—that spirit called woman—in this case kind and cool and clever to save.

"Where's your other hurt?" she asked, practically. "There's blood on your face."

"On the top of my head," he replied, bending it for her survey. Gently she parted his matted hair.

"Ugh!—A long groove—clotted with blood."

"Run your finger along. See if it's deep. Never mind if it hurts. I want to know."

After several attempts she succeeded in complying.

"Pretty deep. But the bullet didn't go in. It just cut," she whispered, hopefully.

"That's good. I thought maybe the little brains I had were oozing out."

"You haven't any to spare," she said, with a hint of her father's Texas drollery. That seemed a subtle imputation of how brainless it was for a young man of his evident attainments to be a robber—to put himself at the mercy of rangers. Wade had shame enough left to feel the shaft sink deep.

"Your hair is all matted. And the blood has dried on your face," she went on. "I'll get some water. I can reach the pan."

Wade sat there with head bowed. Presently she began to bathe his face and then the wound. The cold water stung but it refreshed him. The combing out of his matted locks was an ordeal.

"That's all I can do. I haven't anything to put on the cut. . . . Where's your hat?"

"Lost. The bullet that tagged me took it flying."

"I have a sombrero," she whispered, and leaning back she reached over her pillow. "It's too large for me. Let's try it on."

"Just made for me!—Well . . . I won't try to thank you, Miss Jacqueline Pencarrow. . . . And now I must go."

"Not yet. The fires are still bright. Wait!—Let's make it a good job. You lie down and rest if you cain't sleep. I'll sit up and watch for the best time."

There was no denying her sagacity any more than her incredible generosity. Besides, Wade felt the need of rest and sleep. Since this girl wanted him to owe her more, he lay back without another word and closed his eyes. The marvel then was to feel himself go fading into oblivion despite the pangs of wounds and the aches and the whirl of his mind.

Sometime in the night Wade felt sleep being shaken out of him. He was conscious of it without being able to awaken.

"Wake! Wake!" came a whisper in his ear, from lips he felt. He stirred. He groaned and opened his eyes. Black shadows of foliage quivered on the moonlit tent. A pale light showed the girl kneeling beside him.

"Oh, you were so hard to awaken!" she whispered. "I feared you were daid. . . . It's mawning. They're all asleep. You must go."

Wade sat up with difficulty. "Morning! You stayed awake all night?"

"Yes. It was nothing. The hours flew. . . . This is the safe time. Go!"

While she knelt to open the tent flaps Wade got into his coat to button it up. Then he found the sombrero and put that on.

"Heah. Don't forget your food and this canteen."

He received them from her, aware that her little hands were

shaking. Then she moved to draw the tent flap in. A waning moon shone low over the ragged wall. All appeared gray and wan, and silent as the grave.

"Go to the left," she whispered. "Keep close to the wall. There are no wagons or tents. . . . Good luck, Wade Holden."

As Wade reached the tent door he could see her face clearly in the moonlight. It was small, oval, earnest and youthful, with the daring that went with youth. But the big deep eyes were unfathomable. All his life he would remember them.

"Bless you—girl!" he whispered, huskily, and slipped out to glide into the shadow of the trees.

Then he straightened up to peer around. The huge wagons gleamed weirdly in the moonlight. Fires were long dead. Nothing stirred. By straining his ears Wade caught a tinkle of running water. Beyond the camp he could slake his thirst. Stealthily he glided for the left wall close by, and as he moved, the tip of the moon sank below the rim of the opposite wall. Before he stepped he made certain where to place his foot; there would be no snapped twig, no imprint in dust, no disturbed tuft of grass. He had progressed a few rods when a perceptible shade darkened the canyon. The moon had gone down. Dawn was not far away. One by one Wade passed the gray prairie schooners. The canyon opened wide, the left wall sheering south, black with timber and thicket. The creek turned away from the road in the direction Wade had chosen.

He halted to breathe deep of the cold air. He felt a wondrous exaltation. Free! And that dark life lay behind. He gazed back toward the camp, trying to pierce the gloom and see once more that little tent and his dark-eyed savior. The rangers who rode men down sank into insignificance beside a slip of a girl. If his fate had been for them to catch him, his steps would never have led to her.

Wade glided on and left no tracks. He accepted Jacqueline Pencarrow as someone more spiritual than real, as a barrier against hatred, as a reward for his promise to his father and the strength to withhold his gun from rangers.

CHAPTER FIVE

WADE'S great task was to travel on yet leave no trace. This proved to be a job for an Indian, not a white man used to boots and horses. Fortune favored him in that the grass was thick and short, and devoid of dew.

At a spring which poured from a crevice in the bank, Wade refilled the canteen, and then drank all he could hold. He went on refreshed.

The morning broke, sunny and bright. Mocking birds and wild turkeys, deer and rabbits gave music and movement to the cool spring morning. Wade noticed these things but took no pleasure in them. He was a somber, vigilant man, bent on saving his life.

Mahaffey would scour the immediate vicinity of the caravan camp in an endeavor to strike Wade's tracks. The chances were that he would not find them. If he did Wade would know before the sun stood overhead. Failing that, the rangers would have recourse to their old habit of circling ahead through the country, touching at all settlements, ranches, camps, everywhere a fugitive might go for food. They would never guess that Wade had food enough for a week, salt for a month, and need never approach a house or town. But Texas Rangers were not to be gainsaid. If he did not get out of the state they would capture or kill him eventually. And the vast stretch and heave of western Texas had to be traversed.

Wade followed the creek to its headwaters. There in a shady spot he drank again and ate sparingly of his food. By this hour he would have traveled fifteen or eighteen miles from his starting point. He did not know the immediate country, but he had a general idea of the direction he should take to work south of the arid slopes of the Staked Plain, a region few men ever crossed on foot. He must keep off roads and avoid the habitations of men. No railroad crossed the country south of the Texas Central. Every step he took would lead him into more unsettled country. By keeping high up along the plains he would be able to ford the rivers where they emerged from the plateau. Eventually he could strike west for the Pecos River, west of which there were no laws, no rangers, nothing but wild cattle and wild men, rock, cactus and sagebrush.

He camped that night on a stream many miles farther on, and if he left any tracks they would be obliterated by a remnant of the last great herd of buffalo. Wade recalled then the fact of the rapid extermination of the buffalo by hide hunters. If he remained on this broad track he soon would be among the camps of these butchers. That year, 1878, would see the end of the great shaggy beasts of the plain.

Wade slept that night like a man whom neither pursuit nor worry could keep awake. Next day the wound on his arm burned and throbbed. He untied it and removed the bloody pad, remembering it to be the folded garment he had appropriated in the girl's tent. It was not then a thing of beauty but he kept it. Then he washed the wound which had healed over but was swollen and painful. Binding it loosely, he went on his way.

Three days later he entered a grassy zone despoiled by the ghastly carcasses of skinned buffalo. Hundreds lay in plain sight. Wolves and coyotes, vultures and buzzards swarmed everywhere. The stench was sickening. Soon Wade heard a distant boom, boom, boom of buffalo guns. Below him, along a river bottom, black moving patches and clouds of dust from which came the continuous boom was a scene of carnage that he wanted to avoid. At sunset he fell upon a camp of hunters. There were a dozen or more burly, bearded men, some dust-begrimed and bloody-handed from the day's work, others emerging wet and hairy-breasted from the creek. Wagons loaded with hides stood ready to be hauled away; horses and oxen grazed along the creek; buffalo hides pegged to the ground half surrounded the camp.

These hunters asked Wade no questions, but they invited him to eat with them. A wayfarer on foot meant little to them. There were thousands of hide-hunters on the Texas plains.

Wade was glad to rest and eat with them. They appeared to be merry fellows, from all over the country north and east, among whom Wade recognized no Texans. They were making money which no doubt accounted for their jovial hospitality.

"Want a job skinnin' buffs or peggin' hides?" asked the leader. "Two bits a hide."

"Thanks. I don't believe I do," replied Wade, resisting a desire to accept.

"Did ye ever skin a buff?" asked another.

"No."

"Wal, if you haven't, you'd make about two bits a day for a month."

They all laughed at the joke.

"Got a horse you'd sell?" asked Wade casually.

"Lots of 'em."

"And a saddle?"

"Yes. I can oblige you. How much'll you pay?"

"I couldn't afford more than twenty-five dollars."

"Sold."

Next morning Wade found himself mounted on a staunch horse with a pack of buffalo rump, biscuits, salt, sugar, coffee and a few utensils tied on the back of his saddle.

"Where bound, young fellar?" asked the buffalo hunter with a shrewd and kindly look of interest.

"Fact is, I don't know where I am," admitted Wade.

"Two hundred miles west an' a little south of Waco. Where do you want to go?"

"West of the Pecos."

"Long ride, stranger. Cross the next river an' strike west along it. Avoid direct south. Thet country is overrun with hide-hunters and Injuns. Leave the river where it comes out of the bluffs an' travel southwest. It's rough goin' an' water scarce. Somewhere you'll cross the cattle trail for the Pecos."

"Thanks, hunter," replied Wade, gratefully.

"You're welcome." And as Wade rode off he added, "I never seen you atall!"

Day after day Wade rode west, always alert and keen-eyed, ever looking backward on his trail. But as the days multiplied and he never saw a settler's cabin or a horse, or crossed a road, something began to ease off him like a gradual lessening of a burden. He had always wanted to be alone but now he knew loneliness as he had never before experienced it.

The river forked at the foot of the hills. Such a beautiful spot Wade had never seen. Wonderful trees spread green canopy over glades where deer and turkey did not run from him. Bear and panther followed him curiously. The deep pool where the streams joined was full of fish. Wade spent a day there, cooking venison for his jaunt into harsher wilderness. Early summer had come to this part of Texas.

Next morning Wade arose to make an early start. Some days he had had to spend time finding his hobbled horse. But that did not occur in this camp. The sides of the horse were full and round. He would need that in the days to come. Wade left the lonely sylvan spot with regret. How wonderful to have had a ranch there! But sure delight was not to be his in Texas.

He headed away from the river, just enough south to keep to the foot of the slope. When he emerged from the river valley he saw the real Texas spread away to infinitude, gray and vast, a rolling barren of sagebrush.

His chief concern now was water. But at this season, along the bulge of the western plateau, there could hardly be a day when he would fail to find a stream or water hole. His horse was a walker, covering three miles and more an hour. Soon he left the game trails and the birds and rabbits behind. The solemn noon hour found Wade a moving dot in a wasteland of green. The hours passed insensibly. His habit of looking back had become fixed, but it never yielded sight of living things. Before sunset he crossed several little willow-lined threads of water, and before dark he selected a grassy swale for a camp. That time Wade did not hobble the horse. He had long since established friendly relations with this meek and stout steed. They were dependent upon each other. His camp tasks were simple. He built a fire to make coffee and heat a piece of meat. He had allowed himself one biscuit a day. His freedom was so glorious, the strange companion he had found in himself so intriguing, that the sameness of his simple fare never palled upon him.

He ate and afterward waited the passing of the hours to twilight and night. For years he had camped in secluded places. But this was different. No drinking, quarreling, gambling, garrulous companions! No sense of incomprehensible loyalty to his chief or fear for him! All that seemed long ago, gone into the past of which only the one memory crystallized.

That night Wade was free of the mourning of the wolves, the yelping of coyotes. He had grown to love these sounds and felt lonesome in their absence. He lived in the present. His desire to escape from Texas was so strong that it absorbed what time he gave to calculations. The past was fading. The future did not intrude. That would take care of itself. The moment, the hour, the night occupied him. He slept on his saddle blanket with his saddle for a pillow.

In the rosy morning, when Wade took stock of supplies, he found that he had ten biscuits left and enough coffee to last with them. He headed into the gray beckoning distance.

When those ten biscuits were gone Wade knew he had traveled ten days.

By imperceptible degrees the character of the plant life changed. From sagebrush he passed to dwarf mesquite and other thorny growths, excepting cactus which he saw rarely. The ground grew scaly with scant grass and a little mixture of sand. Wade entered this zone with misgivings. It was not the treacherous *braseda* of southern Texas, yet it might well check his progress and eventually take toll of his horse and himself. By standing in his saddle Wade could see how the vast thicket gradually sloped away from him toward a darker line of green. That would be a stream. And from there the brush-darkened land appeared to rise slowly toward dim ghosts of gray bluffs in the west.

This was a crucial moment for Wade. He could not turn back. Southward the dense growth thickened. To go north was forbidden by the barren plateau in that direction. To travel westward was his only course. Grim and fully aware of his danger Wade rode into the brush, taking the sun for a guide.

And at once he appeared plunged into a labyrinth of lanes, aisles and glades surrounded by impenetrable thickets. He could not ride in a straight line. He had to zigzag, double upon his trail, break through thin barriers of brush, and go around. The soil was too barren to support a complete covering of brush, which fact was fortunate for Wade, as otherwise he would not have been able to make any headway.

He kept on and the sun mounted hot. From time to time he wet his dry mouth and throat, but he was sparing of his water. The horse sweat copiously and by and by the perspiration began to pour down Wade's face. He tied his coat on the cantle. Relently he pressed westward, indomitable and resourceful. He rode until darkness forced him to stop. His horse went without grass and water at that camp.

Wade slept a few hours, then lay awake, a prey to worry. When it was light enough to see the opening in the thicket he saddled and addressed himself to a critical day.

The morning was cool and sweet. Wade's horse nipped at dewey tufts of scant grass and at occasional tips of bushes. Hope resurged in the fugitive. He would get through. Jack rabbits, few and far between, were the only living creatures that crossed Wade's sight. He husbanded his horse's endurance and was more sparing of his water. The sun grew hot and by the time it was directly overhead. Wade felt it almost unendurable.

Then the brush seemed to close in on him, so that the avenues grew scarcer. This fact had one good side—the denser it grew, the closer it came to water. But he had to break through wherever that was possible. The thorns tore at his legs and the heat and dust told mercilessly upon him. As he toiled on, his thirst grew almost maddening. Half his water was gone. He took a good swallow and determined he would save the remainder for the next day. He could last two more days without being in an extremity. But could the horse hold out? Wade was finding this beast enduring and game. And once again he was learning what it was to be dependant upon a horse.

All obstacles increased. By midafternoon he was a ragged and begrimed man, lost in this wilderness of thorn, beginning to feel near the end of his mental and physical resources. His horse labored in distress.

By sunset a horror of his predicament beset Wade. His passion to live mounted to a frenzy. And this infernal wall of tangled branch and thorn, the suffocating dust, presented such brutal terrible barriers to life that Wade sometimes doubted the sanity of his unabated spirit. His intelligence told him that he was still a long way from physical collapse. The thing to fear was the effect of the heat on his mind. And it seemed that the sun was burning a hole through the top of his sombrero. He filled the crown full of leaves. He rested in a shady place, pondering the situation. Soon night would intervene again. He decided to give the horse free rein and keep on.

As Wade pondered thus, the horse gave a snort, scattering caked frother from his nostrils, and started on of its own accord. Wade took that as an instinct of self-preservation. He let the animal make its way through the brush. Then followed hideously long and racking hours till the sun set. Relief did not come, so great had been the effort and the strain. Wade was fighting terrible discouragement when the horse plunged out into a wide road.

Wade stared incredulously. It was not a delusion or a mirage. A wide yellow road bisected this appalling maze of thorn. Wade looked down in thanksgiving, as if he had not before had solid ground under his feet. Cattle tracks! He studied them, here, there, across the road. He bent down in the saddle. Horse tracks! Fresh upon the cattle tracks! He deduced that a big herd of cattle had passed there a day or so before, and not later than an hour ago horsemen had ridden in the same direction. Wade was an expert on horse tracks. His profession had taught him that hard lesson.

This was the road the buffalo hunters had spoken of—a cattle trail leading to the Pecos. Wade rode on, profoundly struggling with a change of mood. Something unknown, big and vital, lay ahead in the future.

Sunset had not long yielded to the gloaming hour when Wade heard the ring of an ax. It made his heart leap. Then he became aware that his horse scented water. Turning a bend he came almost abruptly upon a camp set in an opening where a creek gleamed, running over rock. A camp fire blazed. Men rose at his advance.

"Hullo, thar," called out a rough voice that was a challenge as well as greeting. A burly man, gun in hand, would have blocked Wade's progress.

"Niggah or white man?" he queried.

"Wait . . . water," replied Wade in husky choked voice, and fell out of his saddle to bend to the stream. He drank, his horse with him, and the thought came to him that if he had ever appreciated water before, it had been nothing to this. Then he got up like one cramped from long riding. The big man who had accosted Wade stood by, reinforced by two companions. Wade had seen enough hard characters in his day to recognize these.

"Come to the fire. Let's hev a look at you," said the leader.

"Reckon I'm in luck," replied Wade.

There were six in the group, all matured men, significantly different from the robust hearty hide-hunters. These men were mostly lean, dark-garbed, clean-shaven, with hungry glittering eyes. The leader stood hatless, a man of lofty stature, wide-shouldered and heavy, his visage like a crag with slits of fire for eyes and a thin hard line for lips.

"What's yore handle?" he asked.

"No matter. It changes as I rustle west," said Wade with a laugh. He had the ease which intimacy with such men gave him.

"Lost in the brush, hey?"

"Yes. Two days. I came from the head of the Blanco."

"Ahuh. Been with the hide-hunters?"

"Yes."

"Air you a buff hunter?"

"No."

"Trail-driver, mebbe?" queried the leader, with an appreciative survey of Wade's lithe build.

"No. I'm on the dodge, if you must know," retorted Wade, crisply, with an edge to his voice that did not invite undue curiosity. "I'm worn out and starved. Will you feed me? Or must I go on?"

"Stay, stranger. We got plenty of grub. An' if you're on the dodge our hand is not agin you, thet's shore."

"Thanks a lot," replied Wade, gratefully, and hastened to relieve his horse of saddle and bridle. He carried these to an open spot not obtrusively far from the campfire, and untied his coat and pack from the cantle. Then with soap and towel he repaired to the creek for a much needed wash. He removed his shirt, which was wet and torn and as black as if it had never been light. When he had washed it, and himself, there came a call to supper. Wade made tracks for the fire, to hang his shirt on a stick to dry and present himself with alacrity at the spread tarpaulin.

"Fall to, stranger, an' help yorself," said the leader. "This ain't no Santone dinner but there's plenty of what we got."

Wade heartily availed himself of the invitation. It was camp fare but wholesome, with a plentiful abundance of fresh beef. Wade ate until he could hold no more. Then, rising he thanked his host and complimented the cook. The men appeared disposed to be friendly, except a blank-faced Texan who watched Wade with suspicion. Wade got back in the shadow away from those searching eyes and removed his heavily-loaded vest to put on his shirt, not yet wholly dry. If these men sensed he had money, even a small sum, they would not scruple to shoot him for it. Wade felt glad to button up that leather vest.

"What about my horse, boss?" he asked of the leader.

"You're welcome to a nose bag of grain. An' there's some open patches around where yore hoss can pick a little grass."

That solved the problem for his animal. Wade whistled at his task while covertly he watched these men. At once he figured them to be a band of rustlers, sinisterly bent upon those cattle tracks in the road. Wade found a little open place up the creek where some grass grew, and here he led his horse and tethered him upon it. Darkness had set in now. And he contrived to carry his saddle and pack to the same place.

Upon his return to the campfire, his footsteps made no sound on the soft road, so he heard conversation not meant for his ears.

"Wal, even if he had anythin' on him, I shore wouldn't try to snitch it—not off a man who packs a gun like him. This fellar's a gunman, Nippert, take thet from me. One of thet wild Texas breed."

Nippert's reply was growled too low for the delaying Wade to distinguish.

"Another thing, Nip. If he's on the dodge he might fall in with our plans. An' believe me, with thet outfit of tough riders Aulsbrook won't be easy to relieve of cattle."

"Catlin, I know this cattle trail," replied Nippert. "At Horsehaid Crossin' we can waylay thet bunch an' never get a scratch."

"You told me thet before. But the Pecos is a hell of a long way off. An' if we do get the herd there we'll hev to sell in New Mexico. An' I don't know thet country."

"Jesse Chisum will buy every haid of stock an' ask no questions."

"Humph! Is thet jingle-bob cattle king open to trade?"

"He shore is. I happen to know."

A low hist from another member of the gang warned the two

rustlers of Wade's approach. When he arrived at the campfire Catlin offered his tobacco pouch.

"Roll one an' hev a seat, stranger," he invited in rough cordiality.

"Gosh, when have I had a smoke!" ejaculated Wade.

"Keep the bag. I got plenty more. . . . An' what'd you say yore name was?"

"I didn't say," replied Wade, genially, as he rolled the cigarette.

"Thet's so. You wasn't turrible sociable."

"Well, the fact is, my true name makes Texans—especially rangers—a little too interested in me, so I usually go by Jim Crow, or Sam Smith or some handle like that."

"Ahuh. I see. Much obliged. I ain't one damn bit curious about thet. . . . But whar you goin'?"

"I haven't any idea, except out of Texas," replied Wade, frankly.

"Friend, you got a hell of a ways to go yet, by road."

"How far to the Pecos?"

"Nip, how far to Horsehaid Crossin'?"

"For cattle thet depends on the grazin'. This spring it's good, once out of this thicket. I'd say twenty days, barrin' any holdup by Comanches or sich. Haw! Haw!"

"Twenty days for cattle," mused Wade, as if impressed.

"Wal, friend, thet means twenty days or thereabouts for us," drawled Catlin, blandly. "How about trailin' along with us? Plenty of grub an' good company."

"Thanks. Does that entail any obligation?" rejoined Wade.

"Not a damn thing. Take it or leave it. I like yore looks, if you're on the dodge."

"Straight talk. I appreciate it. But your men might not be so—so kind."

"I shore got an oncivil outfit," declared Catlin with a guffaw. "But I'm not apologizin' for them. Onct they know a fellar, they open up."

"I'll sleep on your offer," replied Wade, thoughtfully. "Twenty days to get west of the Pecos! That sticks in my craw."

"Stranger," interposed Nippert with animation, "you can make the Pecos in two days, across country, follerin' this creek."

"Through that thorn thicket?"

"Shore. It's tough. But you could get through without bein' lost. You could swim your hoss acrost the river an' find a trail up to Eagle's Nest. Thar's no law there. Only greasers an' hard nuts! Haw! Haw!"

"Excuse me. I'll take my chance on the road," replied Wade and turned again to the leader. "Say, would I seem to give offense if I voice a thought—that your twenty days to Horsehead Crossing must have some bearing on the cattle herd which passed along here recently?"

"No offense, stranger, an' it do hev a bearin'."

"Much obliged. I feel in more congenial company. It might be good for me to change my lone-wolf ways. But listen, man. I feel bound to tell you that if I threw in with you it'd increase the probability of your dying with your boots on."

"Haw! Haw! Haw! Well spoke, my young fellar!" ejaculated the rustler, won by the subtle remark. "Let me tell you—neither you nor Wess Hardin, nor even Simm Bell hisself could increase thet probability for Bill Catlin."

"All right. I'll think it over," ended Wade, abruptly stung and alienated by the allusion to his father. He bade them good night and strode away in the darkness. No doubt Simm Bell's ill fame had penetrated to the remote camps of Texas. All the more reason for Wade to leave Texas forever! Once he glanced back to see the dark faces of the rustlers lighted by the ruddy firelight. What a real western scene! Wade read it as clearly as if it had been a printed page.

He made his way carefully and searchingly to where he had left his horse and saddle. The glade was starlit and out of sight of the rustlers. Wade searched for another outlet to the road, and the moment when he discovered it made up his mind to leave there in the night.

With that in view, and his mind set on awakening early, he made his bed and went to sleep. When he woke up he knew he had slept long. Still the hour had not reached dawn. He had rested and so had his horse. Noiselessly saddling and bridling the animal, Wade led him out to the road and along it for a goodly distance before mounting. Once in the saddle, he walked the horse until there was no longer any danger of the rustlers hearing hoof beats, then he urged him to a lope.

Daybreak accorded Wade the welcome fact that he was out of the brush. He recognized that this dense growth had been a league-wide belt running down a draw which he had traversed endwise. There was grass again, and rolling sage country, growing to rocky breaks in the west, and climbing to the gray plateau in the east. The road headed almost due north. Wade rejoiced that he was on it, not many miles from the famous river beyond which he would be safe.

It would be sunrise before the rustlers discovered his departure. And they would be at some pains to try to figure it out. Catlin would lay it to the lone-wolf proclivities he had chosen to give Wade. Nippert would rage at the loss of a chance to rob someone upon whom he had smelled money. And he would suspect the very thing Wade meant to do, which was to acquaint the cattleman Aulsbrook with his peril. Still, Wade reflected, those rustlers did not know he had heard of their plan to ambush the cattleman at Horsehead Crossing.

Wade rode on, loping and trotting by turns. Daylight came with a redness in the east. It tinged the rolling land of rock and sage and grassy plain. Again Wade saw the outlines of pale bluffs, not so vague and ghostlike this morning. Down that endless range ran the Pecos, a stone-walled river, he had heard, fordable only at long distances, a rendezvous for outlaws, like the Rim Rock of the Rio Grande.

From a ridge top Wade sighted cattle grazing on a plain close to the road. Blue smoke marked the location of the camp of the cattle-men not five miles ahead. Wade urged his horse into a lope. Presently he made out riders coming in from the herd. When at length Wade reined in his horse at the camp he saw five men at their morning meal. A stalwart Texan of middle age, bronze-faced and sandy-haired, like so many Texans, rose to take in Wade with gray eagle eyes.

"Mawnin'," he said.

"Howdy," returned Wade, as he glanced from the cattleman to the others. They were lean rangy riders, young in years, like most of the cattle trail-drivers.

"What's yore hurry?" queried the tall Texan.

"Reckon I wanted to catch up with you."

"Air you alone?" And the eagle gaze shifted from Wade down the yellow road to where it disappeared over a ridge.

"Yes."

"An' what was your hurry to ketch up with me?"

"You're being trailed by an outfit of rustlers. Nippert and Catlin with four others whose names I didn't get."

"Wal, you needn't. Catlin is enough. . . . Suppose you get down an' come in. We're just havin' breakfast."

Wade sat down with them, aware of covert scrutiny.

"I'm taking you to be Aulsbrook," said Wade, presently.

"Thet's me. An' your name?"

"I'm not telling my right name. So you can call me what you like."

"Wal, eat yore breakfast."

Wade consumed more food and drink than minutes at this task. Then he made haste to explain: "I'm from over Blanco way. Got lost in that brush thicket. Last night I had the luck to break out in the road an' run plumb into a camp of six men. I knew their kind and I lost no time telling them I was on the dodge. That eased things. They made me welcome. After supper I overheard Nippert and Catlin talking. Nippert wanted to rob me—I reckon, kill me first. But Catlin didn't like the idea. He took me for a gunman and said I might help in the job at hand. Nippert knew the country. His plan is to let you drive in to Horsehead Crossing, ambush you there and make way with your herd. . . . I never let on I'd heard. But when Catlin felt me out I said I'd think it over. This morning before daylight I saddled and hit your trail."

The Texan scratched his stubby chin a moment, his gray eyes narrowing.

"Stranger, when I seen you comin' I reckoned you belonged to Catlin's outfit," he drawled. "So I'm askin' yore pardon an' thankin' you for the hunch."

"Boss, how do you know this heah hombre aint lyin'?" queried the foremost of the tall riders.

"Wal, Bert, there's times when you have to take a man for what he says he is," rejoined the cattleman, thoughtfully. "But I'm willin' to listen to you."

"I ain't got much to say. I was only thinkin'. This stranger has an eye an' he talks straight. Besides, if he *was* in thet outfit, he'd hardly be likely to give way Nippert's plan of waylayin' us at Hawsehaid."

"Exactly. An' see heah, Bert. Mebbee some of this herd raidin' at Hawsehaid thet's been laid on the Comanches is the work of rustlers."

"Thet occurred to me, boss."

"Wal, Blanco—not knowin' your name I'll call you Blanco—air you ridin' on or trail-drivin' with me?"

"Is that an invite to clear out or join you?"

"You can take it either way. It's what you want to do."

"I reckon I'd like to help you if I could. God knows it's time I was turning my hand to something," said Wade with a suggestion of bitterness. "Besides I'd like to throw a gun on Nippert."

"Gun throwin' yore line?"

"I'm afraid it's all I'm good at."

"Wal, on this trail it's a damn good thing, an' don't you forget thet. How about a rifle?"

"Still better. I can hit anything with a rifle," replied Wade, with a smile at his modesty.

"Sam, get thet saddle sheath an' forty-four in the wagon," ordered Aulsbrook. "I'm a pore shot with a long gun. An' none of my boys air extra good."

"Then you take my word?" asked Wade feelingly. He was finding that his distrust of men might have been occasioned by his profession.

"I do, shore. How about you, Bert?"

"Boss, if I had to decide it myself I reckon I'd take him."

"Boys, any kick comin'?" queried Aulsbrook to the others.

"Nary a kick. We're daid lucky," replied one, heartily.

Sam returned with the saddle sheath, Winchester and shells which he turned over to Wade.

"Boys, I reckon Blanco lightin' out on them rustlers last night will change their plans," remarked Aulsbrook after some pondering. "They may not expect to find Blanco with us. But they shore know we know they're trailin' us. An' thet might make the suspense too much for them. What would be the sense of their waitin' to waylay us at Hawsehaid when they know they cain't surprise us?"

"No sense atall, boss," replied the cowboy Bert. "They'll foller along an' try raidin' us some night."

"Thet'd be Catlin. But Nippert is whole hawg or none. He's the brains of thet outfit, if not the boss. . . . What do you think, Blanco?"

"I'm not a cattleman. And these are the first rustlers I ever had to deal with. I'd say they're stuck."

"Fine—to say thet!" exclaimed Aulsbrook. "But what gives you the hunch?"

"It's not a hunch. I know."

Aulsbrook did not press the question. But his clearing brow was expressive.

"Sam, an' you Jim, clean up an' pack," he ordered. "Bert, you an' Blanco wrangle the hawses. Nick, you fetch in the team an' help me harness. Pronto now."

In less than an hour the herd was on the move. Wade sat on the wagon seat with Aulsbrook who drove in the rear. Wade's horse, minus his saddle, had an easy time with the rest of the *remuda*, grazing along with the cattle. The four cowboys rode, one on each side of the herd and two behind. They lolled in their saddles and smoked. Trail-driving was leisurely work.

"I like this," said Wade. "Poking along as if there wasn't such a thing as time. How many miles a day?"

"Wal, about ten, I reckon. Depends on the grass. We'll beat thet this trip. Never seen it so green."

"Where are you bound for?"

"Colorado. I can sell for twenty dollars a haid there."

"Whew! And how many head in this herd?"

"About two thousand. All longhorns. I might sell to Chisum, if he offers a good price."

"Chisum. . . . Jesse Chisum, the jingle-bob cattle king?"

"Thet's the man."

"What does jingle-bob mean?"

"Haw! Haw! You air a tenderfoot. Chisum slits the ears of his yearlin's so a piece hangs down, bobs up an' down. It's a brand no other cattleman ever copied."

"Nippert told Catlin that Chisum would buy this herd without asking questions."

"I daresay he would, the old reprobate. Chisum runs a dozen outfits an' when I was at Seven Rivers last he had a hundred thousand haid on the range. He moves cattle fast."

"Would you call that honest?"

"Wal, on the face of it, thet's the way cattlemen do if they air big an' rich enough to risk it. Chisum may not ask questions, but he knows cattle thet have been rustled. He knows somebody else will, particularly the beef buyers for the forts an' Indian reservations, an' he thinks he might as well underbid them. Nine times out of ten the cattle he buys air gone before the right owner turns up, which west of the Pecos he seldom does. I might never have turned up but for you, young fellar."

"But doesn't that encourage cattle stealing?"

"It shore does. An' the rustlin' of cattle these days is about as big as the honest cattle business. This is the heydey of the rustler. Why, the Lincoln County War is on right now."

"Excuse my ignorance of the West," said Wade, laughing. "What is the Lincoln County War?"

"War between cattlemen over heah in New Mexico. Both sides air wrong. An' there'll be a heap of blood-spillin' before it's over."

"Looks like I've headed for interesting times," mused Wade.

"Take my advice an' keep right on ridin'! New Mexico is wuss than Texas ever was. All the bad men thet the rangers have run out of the Big Bend an' the Panhandle have turned up in New Mexico."

That last bit of information cured Wade of any further desire for more at the moment. He watched the herd and the drivers and ever and anon looked back along the road. Aulsbrook did that also, perhaps not so often as Wade with whom the act had become habitual. The leisurely mode of travel, however, did not keep the hours from passing. When the riders bunched the herd on a grassy plain, Wade guessed that it was time for the midday rest. Aulsbrook drove on to meet his riders where some trees offered a bit of shade.

"Wal, boss, I reckon it might as wal be heah as anywhere," drawled Bert, with a glint in his eye.

"What might?" retorted Aulsbrook.

"Our little set-to with Catlin. He's comin'."

Aulsbrook strode out from behind the wagon to crane his neck and gaze back along the road they had traversed.

"Wal, I don't see any hawses."

"Boss, you're not lookin' right. . . . Over there, off the road."

Across the grassy plain Wade sighted a dark group of horsemen and as many pack animals; and he was not only startled but chagrined to find how vain had been his vigilance.

"By Gawd, there they air!" declared Aulsbrook. "Wal, what do you make of thet?"

"They cut across where the road bends."

"Haidin' fer us now."

The cattleman cursed under his breath.

"Bold move for rustlers. I don't like it. Catlin knows we're short of hands. Lay out the rifles convenient an' look to yore guns. They shore cain't bluff us."

CHAPTER SIX

WADE pondered an unfamiliar reaction for him—that of resentment and animosity which had nothing whatever to do with Simm Bell and the aftermath of one of his raids. This not unexpected move of the rustlers had resulted from a contact of his own. Left to make his own decisions, his very first fight after his escape from the rangers had to do with right and justice. It struck him deeply and when he realized that significance he felt an elation which mounted with his anger.

His first action was to saddle his horse. He did not miss the suggestive glance Bert shot over to Aulsbrook. Wade stopped short.

"Bert, I reckon you'll be damn sorry for that," he said, bluntly.

"For what?" queried the rider.

"I saw the look you gave your boss. And it said as plain as print that the distrust you had at first has come back stronger than ever."

"Wal, I ain't denyin' thet. All the same, I ask you if yore saddlin' up doesn't look queer?"

"Not queer enough to make me a dirty liar," snapped Wade. "After we get through with this Catlin gang I'm going to call you out for it." Then he turned to Aulsbrook. "I'm on the square with you. But if you don't have faith in me I'll return your rifle and make tracks north."

"Blanco, don't take offense at Bert. He's young an' hothaided—"

"Bert better take it back while he's got a chance."

"Take what back?" demanded the rider.

"You not only think I'm a low-down liar, but you believe I'm in with this rustler bunch."

"Wal, you'll have to prove to me you're not."

A hot retort trembled on Wade's lips but he choked it back and turned to the other man. "Aulsbrook, do I need to tell you this Catlin bunch is a hard outfit?"

"No, you needn't. They're comin' right up to us, thet's shore. I don't know what to make of it. Sort of a new trick on me. They're a shootin' outfit, but hardly right out in the open."

"My hunch is they want to see if I fell in with you, and in that case to get rid of me. Suppose you let me call their hand?"

"No. I'll do the talkin' ontil I see what it's all about. I'm gettin' riled at the gall of them," said Aulsbrook testily.

Aulsbrook stood out with Bert. The other riders began to open a pack, build a fire, spread a tarpaulin in preparation for a noonday lunch. Four Winchesters leaned rather conspicuously against the wagon wheels. Wade sat down in the background.

The rustlers left their pack horses nibbling at the grass on the other side of the road while they crossed to halt before Aulsbrook. Hard but indistinguishable words were exchanged between Catlin and Nippert up to the last moment. The latter's sallow visage did not invite civility.

"What you men want?" demanded Aulsbrook before either of the rustlers spoke.

"Wal, Aulsbrook," drawled Catlin not unamiably, "as my wants are second hand in this deal they can wait."

"We don't care a damn about yore wants or yore waitin'. What we want to know is why air you bracin' this outfit?"

"My pard, hyar, is het up about somethin'," replied Catlin, and with a sneer he turned to his lieutenant. "Now—you talk!"

Nippert did not immediately avail himself of that permission. His eyes gleamed like holes under his broad sombrero. He was slow to move his gaze from Aulsbrook to Bert and from Bert to the other riders. He could hardly see Wade yet. But Wade had a keen eye on him.

"Wal, what do *you* want?" queried the cattleman transferring his attention to Nippert.

"If I wanted a civil howdy I don't 'pear to be gettin' it," snarled the rustler.

"You won't get thet from us. So you might as wal ride on."

"Western custom not observed, heh?"

"I don't savvy just what custom you refer to."

"When Texans meet on the range they usually share a bite an' a drink."

"Texans, yes," rejoined Aulsbrook, caustically. "But not with rustlers."

"Rustlers?"

"Thet's what I said."

"Wal now, who'n hell told you thet?"

"Bah. We didn't need to be told. We've known for three days thet Catlin's outfit was trailin' us."

"Ahuh. So you deny bein' told?"

"Deny nothin'. I don't have to deny or affirm anythin' to you."

"Wal, then maybe you wont deny thet a young fellar rode in on you this mawnin'."

"I don't say yes or no. Thet's none of yore business."

"Aulsbrook, I see his hoss. An' thet's him hidin' back there."

Wade leaped erect and in two bounds cleared the others to face Nippert in the road. He let his sudden action suffice for words. But all his faculty of intuition focused on the possibilities of the rustler. Nippert was not in the least intimidated. His face wore a surly crafty look and his eyes hid little from Wade. This rustler would draw if given the slightest chance and that intention was forming in the back of his mind. Wade saw instantly that Nippert, drawing from the saddle, could never beat him to the gun. Wade grasped that probably Nippert wanted to learn how much Wade had known, what he had told, and then refute it. Which was to say that the wily outlaw thought he could carry a point and then do away with Wade. Catlin's attitude seemed one of intense curiosity and comical doubt of the issue. Only one of his men remained alongside Nippert, a small fellow with a crooked nose and pale blue circles under fishlike blue eyes. His front was nothing if not menacing.

After a full moment of scrutiny, Nippert rasped out:

"Sneaked away on us, after breakin' bread, huh?"

"I didn't sneak, Mr. Nippert," retorted Wade.

"Wal, you cleared out damn queer. An' I'm thinkin' thet you got a hunch from Catlin an' aimed to worm in with these cattle-men."

"What are you aiming at?" queried Wade, tartly, now fully satisfied that he had read the rustler aright.

"I'm aimin' to make you swaller what you told Aulsbrook."

"Why you dirty-mugged rustler—you couldn't make me take back anything!" ejaculated Wade, insolently.

Nippert was not equal to a control of passion, which weakness relegated him to a lower order of gun fighters. A leap of muscular contraction ran along his frame.

"Wal, you lied, whatever you told Aulsbrook. Bet you didn't tell what you admitted to Catlin—thet you was on the dodge."

"Ask him."

"I'm talkin' to *you*, young fellar, an' pretty pronto I'm liable to get tired of shootin' off my chin instead—"

"Bah! That's your game, windjamming. You can't bluff me, Nippert. I can see through you. It's not what I told Ausbrook that you're keen about, but how much I know."

"Ahuh. You ain't so pore at talk yourself."

"Take it straight, then," cried Wade in cold finality. "I heard you and Catlin talking. Your plan was to rob me—kill me in my sleep, I reckon—then trail along after this outfit, ambush them at Horsehead Crossing—where by God I'll gamble you have done the same trick before!—make off with the cattle and sell to Chisum without being asked any questions. . . . That's what I heard and that's why I rode on ahead to tell Aulsbrook. . . . Now, what do—you say?—"

Wade slowed at the last, realizing that the moment was imminent. Nippert's harsh curse preceded his spasmodic jerk. Wade was drawing from the instant Nippert's thin lips opened. The flash of his gun caught Nippert's hand on the jerk and the terrific impact of the heavy bullet knocked him out of the saddle, sending the gun spinning. His horse plunged among the others. Nippert's ally had drawn. But his horse reared as he pulled the trigger, spoiling his aim. Hard on that followed Wade's second shot. His adversary appeared hit, for his action broke and he could not hold the frightened horse. It galloped down the road with the rustler reeling in the saddle.

Wade menaced Catlin and the others. They had made no attempt to draw. Catlin hauled down his mettlesome horse.

"Hold, young fellar, hold!" he shouted, lustily.

"Catlin, I've a mind to bore you," rang out Wade in the grip of a fierce cold reaction.

"Wal, it'll be murder if you do," replied the rustler. "I'm not backin' Nippert. I was agin his deal. An' I couldn't change him."

Catlin gazed down at the man lying on his back, arms spread, his spurs deep in the dust, his sombrero beside his working face which all at once set icily.

"I told him. I told him!" he rolled out, as if called upon to judge.

"Throw him on his horse and move on with your outfit," ordered Wade. "Catlin, you fed me when I was starved. I'm remembering that now. But look out if we ever meet again."

"You bloody gun slinger! I had you figgered. . . . Hyar, men, one of you fetch Nip's hoss. An' the rest of you drive the pack train after Bill."

"Boss, Bill is down. Slid off in the road," replied one of them.

"Haw! Haw! He was a damn fool, too. . . . I *told* them not to draw on this hombre."

They loaded the dead Nippert on his saddle, remounted and took the road toward the north. Watching them, Wade slipped shells from his belt to reload.

"One of you pick up thet gun," said Aulsbrook, breaking the

silence. "Blanco, whatever their game was, you spoiled it. I'm in your debt."

"Hey you, Bert," yelled Wade. "Come out here."

"I was—wrong," replied the young rider, growing white.

"Too late. You called me a liar and you classed me with that outfit. Now you've got to go for your gun."

"But I'm—sorry. I apologize."

"Blanco, thet's no way to do," interposed Aulsbrook, hastily. "Bert never threw a gun on a man in his life."

"Well, it's high time he was beginning. Any man with a tongue as sharp as his has got to back it with a gun."

"Boss, what can—I do?" choked out the rider.

"Hell, you'll have to meet him if he insists. . . . But, Blanco, you struck me fine. Won't you let my cottonin' to you make up for his suspicion?"

"All right, if you put it that way," returned Wade, sheathing his gun. "Bert, you rubbed me wrong at a bad time. But forget it. . . . Aulsbrook, I'll ride out by the herd and wait for you."

Wade patrolled the herd during the noon hour. Aulsbrook did not appear to be in a rush. No doubt he and his riders had a good deal to discuss. Wade felt a grim satisfaction that none of them could doubt his status any longer, so far as his sincerity toward them was concerned.

Far up the road the rustlers halted and went out toward the grass, evidently to bury their dead. Wade knew where he had hit the second rustler and that he had ridden off mortally wounded.

The killing of these two men, though really in self-defense, worked powerfully and differently upon Wade. The cold mood of iron remained with him. His gloomy pondering centered around his own self-preservation and little on the fact of having again snuffed out life. If Nippert's ally had been a little quicker, a little better, he would have shot Wade. Beyond question Wade would meet quicker and better men out beyond the border. He would offend evil men and perhaps good ones; and it behooved him to realize that and to be prepared. Aulsbrook called him Blanco, a gunman. One name seemed as good as another, since he could not use his own. But he did not regard himself as a gunman. Nor had Bell's gang so considered him. Nevertheless he had not yet met his superior with guns. But this would inevitably come. Wade realized that he had to enhance his speed, his accuracy, and to do so he must practice, practice, practice. And that had to be done in privacy. It was one of the things he had not calculated on. His dream had been to go far away from Texas, to some place where men did not need guns. He began to suspect now that the farther he traveled west the more he would have to depend upon them. The ranger captain had sworn, ride the man down! That meant Wade must ride and hide for years before he could feel safe. Yet this stern enforcement was entirely aside from the hard facts of everyday meetings on the trails of the West.

In due time Aulsbrook came along in the wagon, and his riders pointed the herd once more up the road. Wade avoided close contact with any of them. Once he rode out to where he had observed the rustlers congregate; and as he had surmised, they had been engaged in burying two of their comrades. The remaining four had long since trotted north out of sight. Wade's deduction was that unless Catlin fell in with more of his ilk, Aulsbrook had nothing to fear from him.

The afternoon passed at the slow pace of grazing cattle. The riders drove until after dark before they came to water. Camp had to be pitched where firewood was scarce. Neither Aulsbrook nor his riders spoke unnecessarily that night, and Wade was not communicative at all. After supper he said: "Boss, I'd like to stand the night watch."

"All right. You an' Nick," replied the cattleman.

Wade rode out with Nick, who asked: "Shore you've stood guard before?"

"No. This is my first crack at cattle herding. What do I do?"

"Wal, it's easy along heah. Plenty of grass. No storms or buffalo to stampede the herd. But drivin' is shore tough on the Old Trail from Santone to Dodge. Onct was enough for me. . . . All you got to do here is fork yore hawse an' smoke an' watch. Keep the stragglers in. Thet's about all."

"Gosh! Gives a fellow lots of time to think. But I reckon I'll like it."

"Fine if you like loneliness an' night an' stars. Or if you have a gurl to think about. Haw! Haw!"

"A girl! . . . Oh, I see. . . . That would be a help," rejoined Wade, thoughtfully, and spoke no more. It seemed here was something he lacked. He had never had a girl; he never could have one. And he remembered Jacqueline Pencarrow with a strange melancholy. He never would forget her big dark wide eyes, fixed upon him with an expression beyond his understanding.

He rode to the far end of the herd, and drove in the few scattered longhorns. Most of them were lying down. The night was starry and cool. An intense solitude lay over the prairie like a blanket. A hum of insects enhanced the stillness. Wade listened and watched. These senses of sight and hearing had been marvelously developed in him. How good to exercise them as a cowboy instead of a fugitive train robber. In those first hours of standing guard, with the great herd indistinct in the starlit gloom and the enveloping lonely night all around him, Wade had born in him a love for such work.

He was sorry when relieved of duty. And he slept as if something that magnified the hours had stretched between noon and midnight of that eventful day.

By morning the strain had eased off Aulsbrook's riders and they were merry. They accepted Wade as one of them, a little in awe, perhaps, but certainly with friendliness and appreciation. Wade met them halfway and the hard crux of the situation passed. After that they easily adapted themselves to one another.

Days passed, long lazy solemn days, and short starry lovely nights, until Wade forgot how many lay back along the road.

He grew ever more fascinated by the country through which they were passing. In the distance it appeared a broken waste of rock and sage, but near at hand there were always flats and meadows and plains of grass. The herd did not lose weight, which fact pleased Aulsbrook.

At last the riders faced the long day's journey to Horsehead Crossing on the Pecos. Toward noon the grass failed and the country became more rough and barren. The scaly bleached ridges, the deep stony draws merged in the distance into a universal gray-green wasteland. Wade experienced a strong excitement at his first sight of the yawning canyon of the Pecos—the famous river with few fords.

Along the road, skulls of cattle adorned points of rocks, and skeletons and dried hides littered the wayside. The hot sun glared in the faces of the riders, the dust rose in clouds, the weary longhorns quickened their step at the scent of water. The ghastliness of that approach to the river increased in all the features so appallingly suggestive of barrenness and gray-stoned barriers, and thirst and death and decay. At sunset the herd topped the rise above Horsehead Crossing and ran pell-mell for the river. It was a stampede, checked only by the cool and shallow water.

Wade sat his horse a moment to absorb the character of that famous crossing in all its somber beauty and terrific solitude. Not even Comanches tarried there long. Wade caught the rude shape of the head of a horse in the bend of the river. All seemed so much greater than he had imagined—the desert, the strange river, the austere atmosphere hanging over it, and the magnificent spread of rangeland toward the west. Across here lay the country famed as "West of the Pecos" and to the north the far-heralded grassy land of New Mexico.

Aulsbrook crossed his herd before dark and camped beyond the western bank. After supper he, and Fred particularly, appeared to be in a jovial, not to say hilarious mood. Aulsbrook produced a black can-covered bottle from the depths of the wagon.

They drank, and pressed liquor upon Wade.

"I've sworn off," objected Wade.

"But just this once, Blanco," insisted the cattleman.

"Aulsbrook, I'll need a steady hand and eye in this west-of-the-Pecos land."

"Shore you will, Blanco, an' by Gawd!—you've got 'em. . . . I didn't tell you thet I was goin' west for good. An' I reckon yo're doin' the same. Let's drink to our good luck."

"That hits me deep," responded Wade, heartily. "One more, Aulsbrook, and then I'm through with the bottle."

Aulsbrook sold out to Jesse Chisum.

It was a difficult matter for a trail-driving cattleman to get past the great Seven Rivers Ranch. Wade recognized the cattle king's strategic location. Not one herd driver in a hundred could refuse a good offer after that grilling trip across the badlands of western Texas.

"Blanco, I'm takin' Fred with me to Arizona. The other boys have got on with Chisum. Has he offered you a job yet?"

"No. I've a mind to tackle him for one. Never saw such a wonderful country."

"I'd like you to go with me. I'd shore feel safer. This wad of money makes me sweat."

"Thanks, Aulsbrook. But I reckon I'd rather not."

"Why, Blanco? We've gotten along fine since—"

"That's it, Aulsbrook. Since! I'd rather be among strangers."

"Ahuh. I savvy. An' good luck to you. But let me give you a hunch. Chisum is runnin' ten outfits of cowboys. He always hires only the toughest nuts that ever forked a hawse. You won't have a bed of roses heah. The Lincoln County Cattle War is on. An' Chisum is part responsible for thet. He once had Billy the Kid an' his outfit heah. If you don't know, I'll tell you thet Billy the Kid is the chain lightnin' an' poison of this frontier. Chisum is daid sore at Billy now an' he had a lot to do with makin' Billy what he is today."

"What's that?" queried Wade curiously.

"Billy the Kid is all thet's bad on the frontier rolled into one boy of eighteen years."

"Gunman?"

"Wal, I guess. Deadlier even than Wild Bill Hickok. . . . Blanco, this range will be bad for you because you air a gunman."

"I'll take a shot at it," declared Wade, recklessly.

"Will you let me pay you wages for the month you rode with us?"

"I'd rather not take anything, Aulsbrook. The experience—my first as a cowboy—and the friendliness of you and your riders—that seems pay enough."

"As you like. I'll remember you, Blanco. An' listen, boy. Whoever you air an' whatever you've done thet made you—wal, stick to the man you air *now*. Adios."

Wade watched Aulsbrook and the cowboy ride away with regret. Later he sought Chisum.

The cattle king appeared to be in the prime of a wonderful physical life, though rumor said he had some incurable disease. He was a short, square, extremely powerful man, with the cold blue eye of the Texan, a broad strong face, thin of lip and prominent of jaw.

"Mr. Chisum, could you give me a job?" asked Wade.

"What can you do?" The curt query was accompanied by a swift stock-taking survey which told Wade one of the reasons why this cattleman wielded such power.

"Not much. I can ride and shoot."

"You're the rider Aulsbrook fetched in. Blanco, he called you, wasn't it?"

"Yes sir. But that's not my name."

"Names don't count out heah. . . . Aulsbrook told me you broke up Catlin's plan to steal his herd."

"I had a hand in that."

"Humph. What would you call a full house? . . . Those riders said you were a gunman. Any truth in thet?"

"I was never known as one."

"You're on. Forty dollars. Go to the store an' get a new outfit. You're pretty ragged. Then see Hicks, my foreman."

"Thanks, Mr. Chisum—"

"Hell! Call me Jesse."

"Yes, sir. . . . I think I'd like hard work—"

"Let me see yore hands," interrupted the cattleman, and when Wade spread them out, palms up, he grunted. "Ha! A lot of bronco breakin', hawse shoein' an' wood-choppin' you've done, Blanco, I don't think. But I like your looks an' I like what Aulsbrook said about you. Why didn't you go with him?"

"I'd rather be with men I—who don't know me."

"Ahuh. How about one of my outfits up in the foothills? They stay out for months an' never see a white man."

"That'd suit me fine."

"All right. We'll try you out. Mebbe later I'll need you to throw against thet Lincoln crowd. It's gettin' hot—thet mess. Tell Hicks. An' see me in the mawnin'. I'll be sendin' a message to Jesse Evans."

CHAPTER SEVEN

IT WAS midsummer.

The camp of Chisum's foothill riders stood in the edge of the pine belt and looked out and down over a hundred miles of silver and green New Mexico range.

Wade thought it the wildest and loveliest spot in the world. The pines were scattered as if they had been planted to adorn a park and the cool wind at that high altitude moaned or made music incessantly. Brown mats of pine needles, tufts of nodding grama grass, purple asters and golden daisies carpeted the ground. From back on the slope a stream tumbled with white cascade here and green pool there, to brawl right through the camp site.

A belt of luxuriant grass sloped for a few miles down to the bleached range of sage and yucca; and this belt held ten thousand head of steers, cows, yearlings, calves, all jingle-bobbed and as fat as butter. The herd required little guarding because they would not leave that zone of pure water and rich grass.

Whenever Wade looked down this slope his gaze encountered the grazing cattle, and the scene filled his heart with delight. He had found his place. A cowboy of the range until he could own a herd! Beyond the red-dotted slope the land fell away so gradually that it looked level, so deceitfully illusive as to distance. It was a bleached-grass and yucca-tufted plateau of New Mexico, vast in three directions, reaching to the dim bluffs and hazy mountains two hundred miles north, fading into the purple plain of the Panhandle to the east, and westward walled by a curving spur of the black foothills. Seven Rivers hid down in there, a hundred miles to the southeast. Winding ribbons marked the rivers. Far beyond them the Cimarron wound like a waving thread. Dots and patches might have been ranches or rocks. It was a magnificent scene, totally unlike Texas, a high country; walled in, irresistible to the lover of freedom and the wild. It was the mountain west—that marvelous region above the Great Plains.

Jesse Evans' riders of Chisum's Number Ten outfit were sprawled in the shade under the pines. Their job had many drawbacks, but hard work was not among them. They had little actual labor to perform except to brand a new calf when they rode across one. They had to keep watch for Indians and rustlers. Fighting the lions, wolves and coyotes that lived off the herd was fun for them. Besides these routine tasks, all they had to do was to live off the fat of the land, chop wood and do camp chores, which for nine husky cowboys who had graduated to this ideal job was not work at all.

Jesse Evans was foreman of this outfit. He was twenty years old, a towheaded cowboy with steel-blue eyes, lithe and bowlegged. He was famous for many things on that New Mexican frontier, but most notorious for his past friendship with Billy the Kid.

"Doggone it, Jesse!" Wade was complaining ruefully. "What have you got against me?"

"My Gawd! listen to thet, you fellars!" piped Jesse, lying back under a puff of cigarette smoke. "What have I *not* got agin you? Fust off you won't fight."

"Now Jesse, wouldn't I be a bright boy to provoke you to draw? If I have to get bored some day, as I'm liable to, I want half a chance for my life, which I wouldn't get with you."

"Huh. You're a slick talker, Blanco. I've thet agin you, too. How'n hell do I know I can beat you to a gun?"

"*I* know you can, Jesse."

"They always swore I could beat Billy the Kid to a gun," he went on, more seriously. "An' I reckon I could. Billy didn't think so. I hope to Gawd we never meet now he's on the outs with Chisum."

"From all I hear of Billy I'd like to see you meet."

"Don't say nothin' agin my old pard. I had to split with him 'cause he turned crooked. But I won't hear nothin' agin him."

One of the other riders, a tanned, sleepy-eyed boy, long as a fence rail, interposed with a laugh: "Jesse, you don't get enough work. You're spoiled. Stop raggin' pore Blanco. You know damn wal he's the best hombre Chisum has hired since we been with him."

"Wal, spose he is," drawled Jesse, trying to be nettled when he could not be. "He come here with all kinds of a rep as a gun-man, didn't he? Shoots the haids off all the jack rabbits, doesn't he? An' you cain't find a tin can without a hole in it. He's been the kind of tenderfoot I never seen before. You cain't make him mad. He'll lend you anythin' but his guns. Give you his last smoke. Stand your watch an' do your chores. He'll play two-bit poker but nothin' higher, an' did he ever win a dollar? Hell no! . . . Never says a word about hisself. Gets up an' leaves the campfire when somebody tells a dirty story or talks about his girl. . . . I ask you, fellars, what're you gonna do with a hombre like Blanco?"

The laugh that ensued attested to the foreman's encomium.

"Jesse, I'll tell you what," spoke up Wade. "I reckon we both have reasons not to bung up our good right hands. Let's have the boys tie our right arms fast to our sides and fight each other left-handed."

"With guns?"

"No. Just fists."

The proposal was hailed all around with loud acclaim. Apparently it intrigued the foreman.

"Thet's shore an idee. . . . Naw, I'll be damned if I'll risk it. No use, Blanco. I jest gotta give up an' like you powerful. If you wasn't so mysterious you'd make a real pard."

"I wish you were all my pards," said Wade, thoughtfully. "It's not my fault if you're not."

"Blanco, to stop teasin' an' honest to Gawd, you're a man after my heart," returned Evans, all at once different, showing a depth and intelligence his levity had hidden. "Now don't *you* take offense. 'Cause we all like you plumb much. But you don't savvy us cowboys like we savvy you. They say you hail from Texas. But you're no Texan. You came from somewhere north, which is nothin' agin you. But you never loosen up. You always have somethin' on your mind. You're *always* lookin' for somebody. You packed most a wagonload of shells out heah. An' you're always shootin'. You got the eye, the hand, the draw of a gunman. You've killed men, an' you bet, more than them two hombres thet Aulsbrook told us about last spring. . . . All to the good, Blanco. We don't like you less for thet. But 'cept in my case the boys air leery of you. Thet'd pass in time, if you stayed with us. But you won't stay, Blanco. Mark my hunch. You'll be gone before the snow flies."

Wade dropped his head a little and said nothing. He was both amazed and touched to be read so truthfully by this keen cowboy. He could not deny a word of that kindly estimate, though he had never until that moment thought of riding away. But now he knew that he would, sooner or later, and the realization filled him with regret.

"Hope I didn't hurt yore feelin's, Blanco," said Evans, presently.

"Hardly that, Jesse. You made me think about myself, which I hate to do. I reckon you called the turn on me."

"Wal, I like you the better for admittin' it. . . . Blanco, we all got a deep side, a bad side. Lord knows I've one. An' thet's what makes me so cantankerous. This job up heah is close to cowboy heaven. But, do you know I want to get back to the drinkin' an' gamblin' hells. I want a whirl at the painted girls. Thet's somethin' I'll bet you don't want. So cheer up, Blanco. . . . An' now you lazy hombres, what can we do in the way of earnin' our wages?"

"I'm workin' right now," replied a lean cowboy, with falcon eyes on the slope.

"Aw, Jesse, what'd you git serious fer, all of a sudden?" asked another.

"Come now, boss. Let's have a little game of draw. I got five bucks of yore's yet."

"By golly, I forgot," replied the agreeable Evans. "I'm gonna get thet back. Blanco, will you set in?"

"Not this game, Jesse. I see some dust clouds down the slope," returned Wade, gazing down.

"Boss, somethin' movin' down there," spoke up the sharp-eyed cowboy.

"Wal, Jack, for heavens sake you an' Blanco fork yore hosses an' see what it is. You're both always lookin'."

That little observation of vigilant eyes resulted in Jack and Wade discovering a band of Indians running off a score or more of cattle. The redmen were too far away to be classed as Utes, Kiowas or Commanches. They rode naked on wild ragged mustangs.

"They're making to go round the foothills," said Wade. "We might get a long shot, if we rustle."

"An' hev Jesse raise hell with us? Not much."

Half an hour later they broke in upon the quiet game of the cowboys in the shade. Jack did the talking. Evans began to swear like a pirate.

"Jesse, they didn't get more than twenty haid," explained Jack.

"Hell! What do I care about the cattle? These heah robbers trimmed me out of five bucks more," yelled the foreman. "An' now we gotta ride! Dogdone it, a cowboy's life is a ha—ard. . . . Saddle up!"

Wade had his first ride with Chisum's cowboys on the trail of raiders. He had often ridden for his very life. But that was nothing compared to what Evans put the posse through before they forced the Indians to abandon the stolen stock.

"Kiowas! Thet's the—second raid—this summer," panted Evans as his riders halted around him. "The boss—will be wild. Reckon we haven't been watchin' good. . . . No sense in—trailin' them slippery redskins! They're gone like quail in the sage. We'll let the cattle rest till dark, then drive them back."

It was far in the night when the cowboys reached their range with the weary cattle.

That raid appeared to inaugurate a busy period for Evans' riders. The Kiowas came back to be caught in the act. They escaped in a running fight with one of their number crippled, an example of Wade's long-range shooting with a rifle.

Not long after that incident they had a brush with rustlers, when Wade smelled powder again. Evans' riders turned back from a long chase.

"Cowboy rustlers, an' don't you forget thet," avowed Jesse, with fire in his eye. "We're gonna be dragged in thet Lincoln County War."

"Could them hombres hev been Billy the Kid's outfit?" asked Jack.

"They could hev, but they wasn't," declared Jesse, loyally. "Billy wouldn't steal from me—not in a million years."

"Wonder how thet cattle war is goin'?"

"Damn tough fer McSween's side. They'll get killed, the whole caboodle of them, even if they have Billy's outfit fightin' fer them. Thet war is gonna take in the range."

By September the need of constant vigil relaxed. A pack train with supplies brought Evans a message to stay out through the middle of October, then drive his herd down to the winter range near Seven Rivers. These riders also brought the late gossip of the cattle war.

October ushered in the wonderful autumn season for the foothills. Early frosts colored the oaks and maples. Higher up the aspens turned gold and the vines on the rocks showed red. For the first time in his life Wade had his fill of hunting. Deer and elk abounded, coming down from the heights. The lions followed the deer. Many a ringing chase Wade enjoyed behind the hounds. But all too soon that glamorous period passed; and Wade found himself trail-driving the enormous herd down to the lower ground.

It took the squad ten days to reach the Sycamore River Range, where this particular herd of jingle-bobs were to be quartered for the winter. That was within easy riding distance of Chisum's ranch. It was also on the edge of the disputed rangeland, the million acres of which Chisum declared verged upon his domain. There were other cattlemen, running far less stock, who aspired to that fertile range. And these were contending against one another, in dire risk of stepping on the toes of the cattle king.

The cowboys threw their bedrolls and packs under the cottonwoods on the riverbank. Stoke, the cook, drove his chuck wagon to a convenient shady spot. Evans sent out three riders with the herd.

"Wal, we've had a lazy time," he said. "An' now we're gonna get back to the cowboys' hell. . . . I'm kinda tired of meat an' beans an' sour-dough biscuits."

The foreman strove manfully against an obvious temptation. "Jack, you an' Sleepy ride in for fresh supplies. Make some excuse to hang around so you can heah all the news. Tell Chisum we're about eleven hundred haid stronger than last spring. Thet'll please the old devil, if anythin' can."

Wade tramped around in search of the kind of sleeping nook that he desired. This place could not compare with the wonderful camp up in the pines, but it was pleasant. The Old Trail of the caravans crossed the river close by, and that was something to stimulate thought. The Spanish padres had blazed that trail three hundred years before. Then followed the Spanish adventurers, later the French fur traders, then the American traders, down to the caravan freighters, the gold seekers, the pioneers, and the trail-drivers with their herds. What a trail of years and blood and dust!

He found a sandy spot enclosed by a thicket of sunflowers and marked by a fallen cottonwood. Here he fetched his few belongings. Never for a moment did Wade forget that he had a fortune hidden inside his leather vest, and thousands more in the lining of his heavy coat. He had never counted the money given him by his father that last dreadful day. Money was the least of his requirements. But the day would come when he would need it. He always kept a small pack of belongings ready to be tied on his saddle at a moment's notice.

Upon emerging from his covert, Wade espied a bunch of dark clad riders on dark horses grouped on the river bank apart from the camp. His pulse took a quick impetus. Jesse Evans' outfit was hard-looking enough, but beside these ragged wild horsemen they looked tame. Wade always had a keen eye for horses and these appeared to fit their riders.

Sauntering forward watchfully, Wade next saw Jesse talking to a youth of slight stature who had dismounted and stood holding the bridle of his horse. There was something impressive about that youth, but it had nothing to do with his battered slouch hat, his worn garments and boots. It was the way he stood, the way he packed his gun. He wore it on the left side, in a reversed position to that almost universally adopted by westerners. Wade was quick to grasp that this young man had a different draw.

"Come heah, cowboy," called Jesse Evans.

As Wade approached them he saw that Evans was pale and somehow visibly agitated.

"Shake hands with an old pard of mine—Billy the Kid."

Wade held himself under control despite the excitement that name aroused in him.

"Howdy," said the youth in a level cool voice, extending his hand.

"Howdy—Billy the Kid," replied Wade, warmly. "I'm sure glad to meet you. Jesse has talked about you a lot."

"Bet it wasn't good," returned Bill with a laugh.

Wade met and felt the clearest coldest eyes that it had ever been his fortune to gaze into. They seemed to search his very soul. Billy the Kid was not unprepossessing. But for a prominent tooth which he exposed when he laughed, he would have been almost handsome. It was a smooth, reckless, youthful face, singularly cold, as if carved out of stone. Wade's divination here recognized the spirit of the wildness of the West at its height. Billy the Kid was what the West had made him. He looked a boy, he had the freshness of a boy, but he was a man, and one in whom fear had never been born.

"Well, I can't remember Jesse ever speaking bad of you," replied Wade, choosing his words.

"Blanco, Billy has just come over from Lincoln," said Jesse, hurriedly. "His outfit killed Sheriff Baker an' some deputies. Thet cattle war will be fought to the bitter end. Billy says he's heahed of you an' he wants to talk to you. He didn't confide in me about what he heahed. But I'm worried. All I'll say is this. If Billy the Kid is yore pard you can bet yore life on him."

"Hold on, Jesse," rejoined the desperado as Evans turned to leave. "It's all right with me for you to hear what I've got to say if it's all right with him."

"Stay, Jesse," said Wade, soberly. He sensed incredible events. Like the fox long out of hearing of the hounds he vibrated to a distant bay.

"You call yourself Blanco?" queried Billy the Kid.

"No. That name was given me because I happened to say I'd come from the head of the Blanco River," explained Wade.

"Jesse, he's the man, sure as shootin'," declared the outlaw, turning to his friend.

"I reckon. Go ahaid an' get it off yore chest."

"But your right name is Holden—Wade Holden—an' you're the last of a gang of bank robbers?"

"I don't admit that," flashed Wade, shocked to the core of his being. He felt the blood recede from his face, leaving it cold.

"You needn't. But if you're really Holden, I'm your friend an' so is Jesse."

"All right . . . I'm—Holden," admitted Wade, hoarsely, his voice breaking.

"There's a bunch of Texas Rangers at Chisum's. They're huntin' you. They'll be ridin' out to meet Jesse soon as word arrives at Seven Rivers thet he's down from the hills."

"Yes, an' thet word will get there pronto," interposed Jesse, grimly.

"Holden, here's how I found this out," went on Billy the Kid, as evenly and matter-of-factly as if it did not send shuddering death to Wade's hopes. "Lately I got acquainted with a Texan named Blue. Footloose, an' wantin' to get in with us. He trailed with some hombres I have no use for. Well, this Blue is the man who connected Chisum's new gunman, Blanco, with Wade Holden. I reckon range talk drifted to his ears an' some rider who'd seen you at Chisum's described you to him. I don't know thet he tipped you off to the rangers. But Chisum would do thet. He'll stand for rustlers, an' even hoss thieves, so long as they ain't known to ride for him. Chisum an' I split long ago. He was against an Englishman named Tunstan who was my friend. Thet Lincoln County outfit murdered Tunstan. I've killed some of them. An' I'll kill Chisum before they kill me."

"But the rangers?—How'd you hear about them?" queried Wade.

"Just by accident. Run into Bud Slatten on the trail. He stayed at Chisum's last night. Bud's a good friend of Jesse's. We used to ride together. He told me all the news."

"Did he say what company of Texas Rangers?"

"No."

"Or who was the captain?"

"Bud didn't name him. Called him a red-faced, loudmouthed old geezer."

"Mahaffey? . . . My God!" muttered Wade.

"What's it mean if they get you?" asked Billy the Kid.

"Bullets or the pen—for life."

"I savvy it'd be bullets," put in Jesse Evans, darkly. His regard for Wade spoke there in bitter certainty.

"Blanco," went on Billy the Kid, as if to bury that other name. "Throw in with me. Come out in the open. I've got as sweet a bunch of men as ever pulled a gun. We'll drag the rangers into this Lincoln County War. They're an ornery houndin' outfit—these Texas rangers. An' by Gawd, this bunch won't go home with their man! . . . Shake with Billy the Kid on thet deal."

"Thank you—Billy," gasped Wade, sick and distraught. "It's good of you—to take me in with you—to offer to fight for me. . . . Let me think. . . . God knows—they'll get me. Ride the man down! That's their motto. . . . Oh, I always knew. . . . I never forgot. . . . Why not go out in the open? Fight it out!"

"Thet's the talk, Blanco. Come on. Put her thar," sang out Billy the Kid, his voice terrible in its ruthlessness; and once more he held out that slim deadly little hand.

Wade faced an appalling temptation. He seemed to be falling from a precipice. The suddenness of this peril to his freedom and life left him devoid of power to reason.

"Hold on, Billy, damn yore pictures," spoke out Jesse, just as ringingly. "This boy has got a chance yet. It's just hard luck he was found out. He must have been driven to whatever he did thet put them vultures on his scent. Let's help him, instead of makin' it shore death."

"Blanco, do you want to fight or run?" asked the young ruffian who had killed more than one man for each year of his life.

"I want to fight. . . . But—but—" cried Wade, fiercely.

Jesse Evans must have read Wade's soul.

"There's yore hoss, Blanco," he shouted, as if inspired, his eyes bright, his clutch like steel. "Fork him an' ride till hell freezes over."

A shrill whistle came from the dark group of horsemen on the river bank.

"Hey, Billy. Bunch of riders comin' up the trail."

"How far?"

"Three—mebbe four miles."

"Who are they?"

"Don't know. They're not cowboys or Injuns."

"Blanco, it's your rangers. Ride! . . . If I ever meet Blue again I'll bore him. Good-by," said the outlaw.

Jesse ran with Wade to where his horse was tethered near the thicket. Wade darted in to fetch his pack and coat. These Jesse helped tie on the saddle, and all the time he talked as swiftly as his fingers flew.

"Keep to the river bottom till you get over thet rise of ground. Then take the direction of the trail, but keep off it, on the grass. Ride—but save yore hoss. Keep on, but dodge Lincoln. . . . There! . . . I'll lie like a trooper to them rangers. I'll hold them—throw them off. . . . Ride, pard, ride!"

CHAPTER EIGHT

WADE raced his horse through the cottonwoods, but he looked back. With the old instinctive action his excitement increased to terror. There was hot wild blood in him that yearned to halt him, his back to a tree, to deal these hounds of the law death for death; but always a stronger power, neither physical nor primitive made him a coward.

He raced on through the sunflowers, under the trees, and he looked back. Jesse Evans and Billy the Kid stood watching. They waved to him. Billy's gang of dark riders gazed the other way, then rode down the bank into the river. When Wade looked again they were all out of sight.

His powerful horse ran easily, over the sand patches and through the grass. Once Wade saw dust far down the Old Trail and he thought he would hate the sight of yellow dust clouds all his days. At length he came to the end of the cottonwood growth where the land began a gentle rise except along the river. Wade rode up high enough to peep over the treetops and halted to look.

Presently over a distant ridge swept a band of horsemen, three abreast, riding in an orderly column. If they had been twice as far away he would have recognized them as Texas Rangers. They rode as if backed by law and justice.

Wade urged his steed, plunging down the slope to the river-bank, and here he turned to the left and kept to the grass. Eleven thousand cattle had worked down the river that day. His tracks would be lost like needles in a haystack. Gradually the terror left him. And he thought that he should never have waxed forgetful and secure. He would never grow so soft again. The sudden shock, when Billy the Kid told him that the rangers were there, had been a dreadful and devastating thing. For the moment it had robbed him of manhood and left him sick, nerveless, frantic. Even now he had to fight to win back cold grim defiance.

He came to where the river spread out in shallow sheets over wide sandy bars, and that place he remembered was where Jesse's herd had first come down to water. A rise of ground hid the long cottonwood grove and the range beyond. Wade rode off the trail, and keeping it in sight he set his horse to a steady lope.

After a few more miles he looked back to find that the ridge was out of sight. He breathed freely again. Jesse Evans had detained the rangers. They would probably camp there that night or ride back to Seven Rivers. What a narrow shave! And he owed his life to Billy the Kid—the most notorious and ruthless outlaw of the time. Wade would always remember that youth, the something inimical about him, the way he packed his gun, the cool quiet quality of his voice, the marvelous eyes.

The old trapper gave Wade a shrewd understanding look, not unkindly.

"Wal, I'm goin' up in the mountains to my cabin an' put in a winter trappin'."

"How do you make out? Any money in it?"

"Not any more. Used to be like diggin' gold. I've seen them days. An' tradin' with the Injuns. Thet was good business till the caravans drove the redskins to war."

"Do you get snowed up?" asked Wade, curiously.

"Wal, I should say. Thet's when I like it, after the crust freezes. Then I travel on snowshoes. Ever try thet, cowboy?"

"No. I'd sure like to."

"You're a clear-eyed chap. Come along an' spend the winter with me."

"What!"

"Come along with me. There'll be fine elk an' bear huntin' for a month."

"By heaven! . . . Does any one ever come to your cabin?"

"Never hev yet. It's high up an' hard to reach."

"But say, you don't know me," protested Wade, white-faced and tense at the idea. "I might be—be Billy the Kid—or some train-robber—or desperado."

"You might be, but you ain't. . . . I had a son once—way back across the big river. If he'd lived he'd been about your age now. . . . What say, young fellar?"

"I'll go. I'll work without wages. . . . But what'll I do with my horse?"

"Turn him loose up hyar a ways. There's a valley where deer an' elk winter. I can cache your saddle."

"Trapper, you're a Godsend! I'll take you up. . . . I swear you'll never be sorry."

Once again some unlooked-for dispensation had come between Wade Holden and hate, fear, desperation, perhaps evil. High above the foothills, in a sheltered mountain valley, the old trapper led him to a little log cabin with a huge yellow stone fireplace.

It took two days to climb up on foot. Wade worried about his tracks. As if in answer to his unconscious prayer the snow fell and they were as if they had never been. All his suddenly returning horror vanished over night.

With the wild eagerness of a boy who had yearned for such adventure, Wade entered into this life in heartfelt gratitude and joy. He chopped down trees and sawed and split wood; he hunted the game that was working down from the heights; he hung up a winter's supply of bear and elk meat and venison and wild turkeys. This meat froze into a perfect state of preservation. After weeks of toil, Wade worked himself into lean hard condition, capable of exertion and endurance he had not before possessed.

Then the snow fell in earnest and the mountain fastness was

locked in until spring. A crust that would bear the weight of a man soon formed. The trapper began to ply his trade. He taught Wade to travel on snowshoes, to bait traps and skin out the valuable furs.

The solemn white days, cold and nipping, with frost like diamonds crackling in the air, passed as if by magic. Time might as well have stood still. At night, when the day's toil was past and the good supper enjoyed, Wade would sit before the blazing logs and listen to the trapper's tales of the early days. Then, snug in his bed of furs, he would lie awake and listen to the roar of the winter wind or the piercing silence of the wilderness, or the mournful wail of wolves.

Spring came. Wade followed the old trapper down out of the mountains. His horse was gone. Wade walked like the mountaineer he had become, and at Santa Fe bade his friend good-by. Wade felt himself a changed man, if not in heart, surely in appearance. He had let his beard grow and when he first looked into a mirror he did not recognize himself. The beard concealed the lean hardness of his face. His intention had been to shave it off. But it was a mask. He had a barber trim it and then he thought he resembled an Englishman he had seen once. The beard had a tinge of gold that went well with his steel-blue eyes. Then he was struck by a look in his eyes that recalled Billy the Kid. Well, indeed, would it be to hide those eyes under a broad-brimmed sombrero.

Wade took the stage for Taos where he stayed a day, interested in the quaint Mexican village. Then he proceeded to Lamy, which was on the railroad. Albuquerque, with its colorful Mexican and Indian life, its idle tranquil days, held him for a while. He became acquainted with a trader who had a post at Shiprock. Wade accompanied him and took a job in the post. It was far out in the desert. He learned to like the soft-voiced Navajos. He did so well for the trader that he was sent out to buy blankets, wool, sheepskins from the Indians. And then it seemed to Wade that he had found his niche. He grew to love the desert with its dust storms, its vast levels of sage and greasewood, its purple and red-walled horizons.

But the winter changed his mind. The icy wind blew everlastingly.

In the spring Wade drifted west. Always he traveled toward the setting sun. He became a sheepherder for a rancher at Mariposa and held that job all summer, sharing the work with a Mexican. They drove their flock up on the cool plateaus. Wade had his old gun practice on jack rabbits and coyotes, sometimes on wolves and lions. In the fall they drove the increased flock back to Mariposa.

Wade spent the winter working in a lumber camp in the White Mountains, close to the Arizona line. The job was hard, the fare poor, the lumberjacks not to his liking. Another spring found him across the line in the territory that for years had lured him on. It was not disappointing, but different from the picture in his mind's eye. Timbered mountains alternated with sage ranges, clear cold rushing streams criss-crossed the country. Wade traveled from one cattle ranch to another, sometimes getting a job for a while, sometimes only a meal. When he rode into White River Ranch he thought surely this beautiful place must be the one of his dreams come true. He got work as a cowboy. But it developed at length that the owner of the Triple Bar was a Mormon and all Wade's riding comrades were Mormons. He liked them despite their proselyting, and they liked him or they would never have tried to make him a Mormon.

All went well until the rancher's buxom daughter began to make eyes at Wade. It was so obvious that he could not fail to see. Then the shyer he grew, the more he avoided the spoiled girl, the stranger became her infatuation. That precipitated the jealousy of a former favored suitor. Soon the day came when Wade once more rode away.

And as Wade penetrated this amazing Arizona land he knew that somewhere in its vast area he would find his place. He was not in a hurry. That old fear had lulled—he never looked back any more—and the erring past had faded as the months passed by. He drifted ever westward and as another winter drew near, sheered to the south where the sun shone warm. Cow camps, sheep camps, lonesome hamlets all the way to Tucson held him for a day or a week, according to their interest for him. He tried odd jobs in Tucson and passed the winter there.

Tombstone was in its heyday. Wade journeyed there. The gold fever was thick as dust over this mining-town center. It was full of gamblers, thieves, lewd women, adventurers, cowboys, travelers, besides the horde of miners. The humming town fascinated Wade. He tried his hand at mining. He was unusually lucky. Every place he touched yielded gold. He struck a small rich vein from which he gleaned several thousand dollars' worth of gold dust. This incurred the envy of a neighboring miner who advanced a prior right to the claim. Wade went to work in the Bird Cage, a notorious place where the populace of Tombstone flocked for entertainment, for drink and faro. Here Wade's good looks and kindness won the interest of a pretty dancer. Gossip had it that she was the property of a gambler called Monte. Wade felt sorry for her, but took no advantage of her interest in him. The gambler beat the girl. That unleashed the devil in Wade. Before a crowd in the gambling hall, he called the card sharp every vile name common to the West, threw the cards and chips in his face, drove him to draw his gun and killed him in the act.

Once again Wade was a marked man, but in a different way. He was patted on the back for killing Monte, and as that individual had been reputed to be swift on the draw, the duel brought Wade the old sobriquet of gunman. Wyatt Earp, Tombstone's most noted exponent of gunplay, witnessed the encounter between Wade and Monte.

"Texas gunman," he pronounced. "I don't care for any of his game."

So in the wildest town on the Arizona frontier, Wade, who had traveled under his middle name of Brandon, his mother's name, became known as Tex Brandon. And would-be killers, long-haired seekers for notoriety, drunken cowboys, and thin-lipped hangers-on of the gambling hells, placed Wade in the unenviable position of defending himself openly as well as from being waylaid in the dark. He crippled three men before he was forced to kill another. Friends Wade had made in Tombstone enjoyed his distinction and the gambler's girl made the most of his championship. But Wade grew distrustful of his position there and its trend. One spring day when the bloom was on the sage he rode away.

Southern Arizona proved too hot for Wade in summer. He headed north and day by day the heat tempered, the desert bloomed, the dim hazy walls beyond the horizon took shape and color. He spent summer and fall in the Tonto Basin and loved that wild valley of black timber and crystal brooks most of all regions of Arizona. But the Pleasant Valley War between sheepmen who were rustlers and cattlemen who were backwoodsmen was about to break out, and that conflict invited any stranger to depart.

Wade rode up over the Mogollon Rim and lost himself in the wonderful woodlands of silver spruce and scarlet maple and golden aspen, gloomed over by the great yellow pines. These woods were ranged by cattle herds, and riders Wade took care not to encounter.

November found him tired of a meat and salt diet, though he was loath to leave that magnificent forest. He found a winter's berth at Concha where he chopped wood and milked cows for an old widow woman who was glad to give him lodging.

Spring came again. It had a trick of surprising Wade. He counted the seasons on his fingers. Five. Five years that seemed ages since he had taken flight with Simm Bell out of Mercer!

"You're one of them sad-eyed, trail-ridin', guntotin' cowboys," averred the old woman, as he looked down upon her from his horse. "An' it's a pity. Such a nice sober quiet man! You should find yourself a woman an' settle down. If you don't, Tex Brandon, you'll come to a bad end."

Wade rode into a country that fascinated so greatly that he often checked his horse and sat at gaze. One vista succeeded another, with all of Arizona's multiple charms. Valleys of purple sage, watered by streams, bordered by pine forests yielded to a range of low foothills, grassy under the trees. Vast prairies of gray cedar flats stretched to the south, across which painted buttes and bluffs wavered in the air. Deep rock-walled, green-ledged canyons opened under his feet, from which the mellow song of waterfall floated upward. A wandering wall of purple rock held his gaze for long; spurs of red crags, like huge beasts, stood up out of the level. Dominating all was a group of white-spiked, black-belted mountains. And most illusive and calling of all was the vague mirage above the painted mesas, higher farther steppes of the desert, mystic and beckoning with their ghostly tracery.

"Howdy, rider. Get down an' come in," was the cowman's greeting, gray eyes scanning Wade from spur to sombrero.

It was the open sesame of the range. There was no place to go in. But the invitation was obvious. The cowboys stood or squatted or sat about with steaming tin plates and cups. The cook, a jovial fellow of uncertain age, thrust upon Wade more food and drink than he had had in days. This outfit appeared to be a friendly one of half a dozen riders and the two older men. They looked prosperous. Boots and garb, pack saddles and saddles, chuck wagon and utensils,—all bore testimony to a rancher not out-at-elbows.

"Have a smoke?" asked the boss, after Wade had finished a hearty meal.

"Thanks. Don't care if I do."

"Ridin' a grub-line?" asked the other, with interest. Wade always made a good impression.

"I reckon. But I can pay for what I eat."

"Never heard of that on an Arizona range. . . . Where you headin'?"

"I don't know. Just riding."

"Know this country?"

"I should say not. If I had ever seen this country, I'd not have left it."

"Good!" laughed the cowman. "Yes, it's God's country. Just now rich in beef an' long in rustlers. . . . What's your handle, stranger?"

"Tex Brandon."

"Heard of you, somewhere. From the Lone Star State, eh?"

"Yes. But I'm not a born Texan."

"I reckoned that. Are you lookin' for a job?"

"Yes, if I could get on with a clean-looking outfit like yours."

"Sorry, we're full up. Besides my boss is leery of these lone riders. He hires only boys he knows. Takes them young an' raises them. . . . Let me see. You could get on with Driscoll. But his outfit razzes the devil out of any new rider. Mason's foreman, Stewart, is hell to work for. Drill is always open, but pays poor wages. That leaves only Pencarrow an' he can't pay anythin'."

"Pencarrow?" repeated Wade, blankly. Then suddenly a bolt seemed to shoot back within his mind and memory trooped out with long forgotten names and places.

"Yes, Pencarrow. He's a Texan," went on the cowman. "Salt of the earth. He dropped in on this range four or five years ago. He had plenty of money. Bought Band Drake's place—a wonderful range. Finest view in Arizona. An' he built a ranch house that hasn't a beat anywhere. . . . Wal, before Pencarrow learned the ropes on this Cedar Range he throwed in twenty thousand head of cattle an' a couple hundred fine hosses. He had the grass, the water, an' he started big. Arizona shore gave Pencarrow a dirty deal. We're all ashamed of it. But he never asked our advice or help. . . . They cleaned him. So now he can't—"

"Who cleaned him?" interrupted Wade.

"Wal, the rustlers an' robbers an' hoss thieves. The Hash Knife got theirs. So did Bullon's Diamond B. An' every outfit of low-down riders in the country."

"You think Pencarrow would give me a job?"

"He would, if you trust him for wages."

"I can ride and shoot," said Wade, as if to himself.

"Wal, you look it, Brandon," returned the cowman, dryly.

"But at that you haven't the cut of a cowboy. You wasn't born on a hoss."

"I'm no good with a rope or following tracks, and I can't cook worth a damn. But I reckon I'll ask him anyhow."

One of the cowboys spoke up quizzically. "Stranger, how air you on milkin' cows an' diggin' post holes an' cleanin' out the barn?"

Wade's affirmative elicited a merry laugh from the group. They liked Wade's look and the simplicity that contrasted so markedly with it.

"Brandon, you can tell Pencarrow I reckoned he might take you on," added the cowman more seriously.

"Thanks. And who're you?"

"I'm Lawsford, foreman of Aulsbrook's three outfits."

"Aulsbrook!"

"Yes. An' he's another Texan, by the way."

Wade dropped his eyes to hide the flash that must have been there. What had his wandering ride led him to?

"Has this cattleman—Pen—Pen—carrow, I think you said—has he any family?"

"That's the hell of it. He's got a big family—the finest folk who ever came to Arizona. Good southern blood. Educated. Mother, grown daughter, boy and girl of fourteen. They're twins. An' two more born since Pencarrow came out here. An' from every luxury they're reduced almost to want."

"Tough!" ejaculated Wade, thoughtfully, as he tightened his belt, an action singular with him in that it preceded action. "Is the grown daughter married?"

"No. But that's not the fault of the range. She could marry any man jack of us. Fact is Jacqueline Pencarrow has upset this range. There's been more fights over her than over stock. But she can't see any cowboy or rancher. She's devoted to her father an' mother, an' the kids."

"Lawsford, how can I find this Pencarrow ranch?"

"Wal, let's see. Squat down here an' I'll draw you a map. . . . Take a beeline across this sage flat. Go through that belt of timber, keepin' straight for the bald-faced mesa yonder. Keep round that to the left. You'll strike a canyon, runnin' south. Follow along till you come to a trail. Go down, then turn an' go up this canyon until it opens out. You'll sure know when you get there."

"How far?"

"Reckon close to thirty mile. You'd better lay out with us here tonight an' then you could start early in the mornin'."

"That would be better. Much obliged," said Wade, preoccupied with thoughts too swift and changing to be grasped.

"Better let him go tonight, boss," drawled one of the cowboys with a look of deviltry. "Because Ben here might tell him how turrible pretty Jacque Pencarrow is an' thet there's no show on Gawd's green earth for a cowboy with her."

Wade said nothing. The blood beat in his ears. All at once he saw a ghost. A slim form under a shadowed tent—a light shining between the flaps—a sweet earnest face—and great dark midnight eyes!

"Say, Ben, you tell *us* jest how purty thet girl is," spoke up another rider. "I ain't never seen her. An' I'm powerful curious."

"Hell, there ain't no way to tell you thet. You gotta see Jacque Pencarrow," declared Ben, evidently an unsuccessful lover still loyal. "But she's tall, only not too tall. An' what a shape! You never seen such laigs. I seen Jacque once in a ball dress. Shoulders, arms, neck all bare! Lovely, boys, jest lovely, an' no sight for fancy-free cowpunchers, believe me. Her face is like no flower I ever seen, but it makes a fellar think of one. Red lips any man would die to kiss! An' eyes—Aw! like starlit deep wells!"

"Ben, you didn't like Jacque much atall, did you?" observed the prompter of this eloquent tribute.

Wade led his horse out upon the grass and removed saddle and bridle. He spread his saddle blanket and sat down to think. He lighted a cigarette that he did not smoke. It burned until it scorched his fingers, when he cast it away. Sunset, twilight, dusk passed while he sat there. The cowboys sang songs and told merry jests; the hobbled horses thumped over the grass; coyotes yelped from the cedar ridges; and night came with its trains of stars.

Pencarrow, Aulsbrook, the dark-eyed girl, never forgotten,

had given rise to whirling thoughts out of which Wade at length achieved coherence and sanity. The latter thundered at him the cardinal necessity to ride on, never to risk being recognized by Pencarrow and Aulsbrook, never to let that dark-eyed girl see him. The instant realization did not result in instant decision. Something obstructed his reaction to intelligence. Pencarrow had never seen him and Aulsbrook would not recognize him. It did not matter if the girl did, though Wade preferred she would not. She had befriended him; she had been his good angel. And she was in trouble. Her father, a bighearted Texan, openhanded and trusting had been imposed upon by the riffraff of Arizona. His family was suffering because of that. Jacqueline—the grown daughter, Lawsford had called her—she was helping her father in his extremity.

Suddenly there came a flashing light into Wade's clouded mind. It shot clear across the perplexed field of his consciousness. Like a bursting thunderbolt clarifying the murky atmosphere it burned away the little thoughts and fears. He had found his place. This wild corner of Arizona had called through the years. The opportunity to pay his incalculable debt to Jacqueline Pencarrow had come. What her father needed was a man, keen, ruthless, incorruptible. Only such a man as Wade knew himself to be could cope with that lawless element. Wade had the answer to the old futile queries—why had he been born the son of a man not his mother's husband? Why had he loved and cleaved to Simm Bell, robber and outlaw? Why had his life since boyhood been one of violence, flight, vigilance, hate and fear? Why had the footsteps of his horse led him to this Cedar Range? Why had he made that irrevocable promise to his father who had implored it with his dying breath?

All blessings in disguise, he thought in exaltation. "All to fit me for this big job. All to make me a man. . . . All for that dark-eyed girl!"

CHAPTER NINE

WADE sat his horse on the canyon rim and tried to see clearly, reasonably, when he knew his emotions were at a higher and different pitch than he had ever experienced. He wanted to make sure that the color, the glamour, the glory of this wild Arizona was not illusion.

The wonderful bright light came from a morning sun and a rarified atmosphere. But though they deceived him as to distance they were true to form and hue.

All the way across the desert—for despite its warmth and luxuriance it was desert—Wade had been led by revealing steps from one beauty to another, each varying and increasing its charm, until he halted awed and rapt on the edge of this blue abyss that Lawsford had called Doubtful Canyon.

Wade wondered at the name, which at first seemed rather ridiculous. How impossible to doubt its immense depth, its sheer red-gold walls, its hundreds of green-foliaged ledges where only eagles could light, its white cascades and shining pools, its murmuring melody of water and wind, its black dense thicketed floor, so far down, its many rugged-mouthed branching canyons, apparently as deep and large as the main one! Wade remembered Smoky Hollow back in Texas, which once had seemed such a safe retreat for robbers, and he smiled at the comparison. Smoky Hollow could have been lost and never found in Doubtful Canyon. But for its beauty, this gorge should have been called Centipede Canyon because of its many arms. This led him to the observation that all the branding canyons he could see were on the west side.

Wade's first calculation appraised the depth at over a thousand feet and the width more than a mile. But he did not trust his judgment. The Redwalled, blue-smoked rent in the earth grew on him the more he gazed. Then he began to understand why it was called Doubtful Canyon.

But where was Pencarrow's ranch? The Tonto basin supported ranches, but interspersed among its gorges and ridges were many valleys and bare flats and meadows where grass grew abundantly. Wade could not see an opening in the timbered bottom of Doubtful Canyon, except where the winding stream shone.

North toward the grand mountains, towering black and white above the desert, he discerned a broad belt of sage, of cedar, apparently level for many leagues, then gradually sloping to the irregular black line. He judged distance to the range, then multiplied it by three. Those calling mountains were over a hundred miles away.

In that direction the canyon widened and at the same time climbed toward the open country. The stream and the walls and the timber had their source somewhere in that distance, perhaps in that wide jumble of purple rocks which bordered the broad belt of desert.

Wade rode along the rim toward the south. When he could see the canyon, deepening, narrowing, thickening its rough features in that direction, he gazed spellbound. When the rough nature of the rim entailed detours he grew impatient to get back again, where he could look into the blue depths.

At length he came to a trail leading down. It was well defined and evidently much traveled. But like most Arizona trails it was steep and rough, full of loose rock, and zig-zagged down weathered slopes that groaned and slid under his horse. It followed along the shady base of cliffs, dipped over descents where Wade had to dismount and sheered down and down to the thick forest of pines and maples.

What had appeared level from the rim proved to be red hills and green swales, all supporting a dense growth of various kinds of timber. It was a dark cool fragrant jungle. The trail led into a large thicket that followed the stream in both directions. Wade turned to the north. The stream was really a river, clear, amber, eddying in pools, rushing among rocks, falling over ledges. Deer crashed into the brush; bear tracks crossed the trail; squirrels and jays scolded at this intrusion on their haunts. Every turn held a new surprise for Wade and when he came to a fan-shaped waterfall, from which the deeper note of falling water had arisen, he saw big dark trout lying along the pebbled bottom of the pool and all his pleasure seemed enhanced. The great sycamore trees gleamed white among the dark green; in sunny patches ferns and lilies and columbine nodded with the lazy floating of the air.

Three times trails left the main one he was following to cross the stream. But he met with none that turned off on his right. The red rims which he caught sight of infrequently, towered far toward the blue sky. Long before Wade reached a gradual ascent, a climbing of the trail among huge mossy sections of cliff, he had succumbed to the beauty and fascination of Doubtful Canyon.

At length a different kind of roaring stream arrested Wade's attention. It did not appear to come from falling and rushing water. It had a strange boiling, bubbling sound. He climbed presently to a lighter part of the canyon, marked by fewer and larger pines and spruces, and a low fern-greened bluff. In another moment the trail led out upon a gigantic pool from which came that strange gurgling sound. The stream ended there. This gigantic pool was a spring, fifty feet wide, clear as crystal, mirroring the trees and the rocks and boiling, bubbling in glorious abundance from under the bluff. This fountain, with its margin of ferns and flowers and mossy rocks, its leaping amber-glancing outlet, its green canopy of foliage pierced by rays of sun and gleam of blue, took precedence in Wade's memory over all other beautiful places he had seen.

He rode on and up. The trail divided, the right leading higher toward a no-longer-visible rim, the left winding gradually into open parklike country where straggling pines and gray rocks vied with purple sage flats, and timbered knolls led Wade's gaze out across the rolling grassy range toward the magnificent peaks. He had emerged from Doubtful Canyon and this must be Pencarrow's range. It satisfied even Wade's avid anticipations. And presently when he crossed a brook and rode around a clump of trees, horses appeared in the fields and he espied a long, yellow log cabin set among straggling pines on a low knoll, with the compelling panorama beyond.

The sun hung overhead; white ships of clouds sailed the blue; the desert brooded; a sage-sweet tang pervaded the air. But these did not overwhelm Wade. He sensed out of the elements a claim that no other place had ever made on him.

All that the past had taught Wade would be called upon here at the scene of Pencarrow's folly and ruin. There must be no half measures, no reluctance to employ a ruthless hand. Nothing but submission to his few gifts—an intuitive recognition of evil thought and nature in men, a clairvoyant and magnifying eye, a terrible skill with guns!

Wade settled that while he gazed upon this run-down ranch, still showing signs of past munificence. All the multiple and unknown angles of the Pencarrow tragedy must come with time. Wade's incentive was great. It equalled the vow to his father. In those moments of slow riding toward the ranch house Wade felt the last bolt of culminating change with which the years had rent him.

He reached the knoll. A gravel road circled it and climbed it at both front and back. To the rear, out among the scattered pines, had been erected a bewildering array of sheds, cribs, corrals dominated by a huge barn opening with wide doors through the middle. Wade followed the road toward the front.

It developed that this side of the knoll sloped but slightly and boasted open grassy lawn to the very sage. A wide porch ran the length of the front of the ranch house. Saddled horses stood bridles down. Harsh angry voices greeted Wade's eager ears. A white-haired man with gestures in which Wade read passion and despair, faced booted and belted riders, several of whose lean, taut forms and bent hawklike heads brought instant corroboration of Lawsford's story.

Wade's approach disrupted the altercation. He sensed an opportune arrival. The riders wheeled and stared with a sullen resentment and surprise. Fifty feet from them Wade slid off, left his horse, and began a very slow walk forward. He put in it and in his piercing survey of the group all the intense curiosity, suspicion and menace which obsessed him. He halted the instant he could see them distinctly.

"Dad, who is that man?" called a woman's voice, rich and vibrant.

"Another one, I reckon."

Wade did not let this answer nor a faint hint of remembrance of that feminine voice swerve him from intent scrutiny of the riders. They stood close together, silent no doubt, on account of Wade's singular approach. Two of them were young louts, marked by no distinguishing feature except viciousness. If they carried guns Wade could not detect them, which was almost equivalent to a surety that they were unarmed. The third had a leaden visage, seamed with innumerably wavy lines of age, and a sneaking eye of negative hue. The fourth possessed bold features, ugly and wolfish, emphasized by glinting eyes. These last two riders wore guns in their belts.

"Wal, Urba," snapped the third rider. "Mebbe when this stranger gets tired sizin' us up, he'll explain his gall."

"What'd ye want?" queried the one addressed as Urba.

"Ask yourself," retorted Wade.

"Wal, I'm askin' myself to tell you to get goin'."

The man threatened. But he did not possess the quality in bad men that Wade respected. Not one of the four gave Wade a sense of compunction. They did not even have the self-preserving power by which western men of quality gauged one another. Furthermore if the two armed ones felt provoked to draw on Wade, it would be too late.

A young woman emerged from the open door. Wade saw her over the heads of the riders. Wade could not tell whether it was her beauty or her magnificent dark eyes that struck at his heart. He recognized the girl who had saved him, grown into a woman.

"Dad, he's not one of them," she asserted, poignantly.

"They're all alike, only wuss as they come along," replied the man, bitterly. He stood erect, his white locks bristling, his fine dark face drawn with haggard lines, a Texan at the end of his rope.

"You're Pencarrow," asserted Wade.

"Yes, I'm Pencarrow," snarled the rancher, wearily. "What do you want heah?"

"Lawsford, foreman for Aulsbrook, sent me over. I want a job."

"Lawsford is no friend of mine."

"Oh, Dad, that's not true," interposed his daughter. "Mr. Lawsford has been friendly, in spite of Aulsbrook's enmity."

"Humph! To you, lass, because he's lost his haid over you. . . . Stranger, Lawsford's name is no bid to my notice."

Wade turned to the daughter and removed his sombrero. It required all his cold nerve—that gesture. But he would make the test at once. The four riders gaped from him to the Pencarrows, interested despite their resentment.

"You are his daughter?" asked Wade, courteous yet sharp.

"Yes. I am Jacque Pencarrow," she reurned, shortly, her wide eyes upon Wade distrustfully. But his presence, his force must have had its effect.

"My name is Brandon," went on Wade. "My errand here is to help your father—and you."

"Help Dad and me?" she queried, wonderingly.

Pencarrow waved aside the idea as he would have this intruder. "Jackie, don't listen to him. Haven't I taken in a score of riders to be fooled an' robbed? If he's not thet kind, he's only another lovesick cowhand come heah moonin' after you."

"Dad, this—this rider does not look or talk like that kind," replied the girl, with a vivid blush. "Thank you, sir, for your offer. But we have no place for you heah."

"Lady, you can't expect me to believe that," rejoined Wade, seriously. "Even if I haven't been told, I can see what this ranch needs."

"No doubt. I should have said that we can't afford to employ anyone," she replied with pathos.

"Nevertheless, I will stay," returned Wade with the force of a man who could not be denied. "Naturally your father has lost faith in men. But you are young and keen, Miss Pencarrow. Trust me. At least enough to tell me if these four riders are not enemies of your father."

"Indeed they are!" she flashed, passionately. "They belong to Band Drake's outfit. He cheated Father—and has never ceased to make demands since. They came heah this time—"

"Shet up, gurl, or it'll be the wuss fer yore old man," interrupted Urba, with a vicious scowl.

"Thank you, Miss Pencarrow," said Wade, swiftly. "That's quite enough. I'll step aside now and let these men take up their argument with your father."

"You will, huh?" demanded Urba. "Wal, what'n hell is to prevent me from bootin' you out of hyar?"

Wade laughed in the man's face and deliberately backed away to one side.

"Say, Urb, don't bother with him," spoke up his nearest comrade. "We're wastin' time. This hyar smart aleck is tryin' some Romeo guff on the gurl. Shore can't blame him, but he's a sucker for tryin' it."

"Pencarrow, my boss is out of patience with you an' I'm losin' mine," said Urba, insolently, to the rancher. "We came after thet thousand you owe Drake an' we're gonna get it."

"I don't owe Band Drake a dollar," replied Pencarrow, wearily. "I paid him for twice the haid of cattle thet he left heah."

"Thet's yore story, Pencarrow. Drake's word is as good as

yore's in this country. An' as there ain't any court or law to pass judgment it comes down to man to man. Yore cowboys hev quit you an' thet looks bad on this range. It'll go agin you."

"Quit me? Most of them were thieves in cahoots with these rustlers. The others hadn't the guts to stick to a cattleman who was good to them."

"Say, Pencarrow, you made a crack before thet riled me," declared Urba. "Are you castin' a slur at me?"

Pencarrow appeared too disgusted to reply to that. He was a sorely beset man, losing his grip on himself. There seemed to be some strong obstacle to his meeting these riders like a Texan. And Wade divined that it had to do with Pencarrow's family. All disputes in that wild section of Arizona were settled with guns, and Pencarrow feared he might leave his loved ones unprotected. These riders, and no doubt other gangs, had grown brazen because the Texan's hands were thus tied.

"Pencarrow, are you gonna pony up?" queried Urba, impatiently.

"If I had thet much money I'd never give it to Drake."

"Wal, yore hosses, then. We looked them over. An' I reckon them an' the bunch of cattle we cut out will square this little debt."

"No!" thundered Pencarrow, growing livid.

"Dad! Control yourself," implored his daughter.

"Jackie, please go in an' let me cuss these men."

"I shall not. You can curse them before me—or *I* will!"

"Aw, Urb, ain't she a pippin'?" drawled Urba's lieutenant. "Look at them eyes. An' them heavin' breasts!"

Wade gazed at the speaker, yet had the will power to stay his hand. But the speech, the burning glance of that lewd-eyed ruffian had sealed his death warrant.

"Wal, I guess," retorted Urba with a guffaw, and he walked halfway up the steps to leer into the girl's pale face. She shrank but did not flinch. "Jacque, I reckon you might save yore dad—"

Her supple body moved swiftly as her arm swept out. The

resounding smack was more of a blow. It staggered Urba and almost upset him. His hand at his bloody lips, he glared up malignantly. But the white fury of her checked his utterance.

"Get out of heah—before I shoot you," she cried. "I'm not afraid of you. And don't think I can't shoot you. . . . My father knows all about Band Drake. He's a cheat and a thief. He's worse —as *I* could tell. And you and your crew are his low-down tools!"

"Ahuh! You hell-spittin' cat! . . . So you come clean with all the old man hadn't nerve to say?" rasped Urba, brutally, and then he shot a baleful gaze up at the rancher. "Pencarrow, we're takin' yore hosses an' thet bunch of cattle. . . . An' by Gawd! you better hev a care of thet white-faced slut!"

He strode out with clinking spurs, his head still turned to the rancher, until he collided with Wade who thumped a hard left hand on his chest, shoving him backwards.

"Greaser, you've had your say. Now hear mine!" commanded Wade.

Urba appeared so completely astonished that he stood there, strangled with rage.

"Jackie, get in the house!" yelled Pencarrow, shrilly. His Texan keenness saw the imminence of catastrophe.

The girl backed away from the steps and inside the door. But she did not close it. Her dark eyes appeared all the wider for the shadow.

Wade fronted the two men who stood almost abreast with Urba a step ahead. At last the menace of the situation penetrated Urba's thick head.

"Bill!—" he yelped, "This hyar hombre—"

His comrade interrupted that trenchant call by dropping his hand toward his weapon. The move appeared more intimidation than draw. But it failed of both, for Wade's gun leaped and belched in the same instant. Bill fell against one of the other men who supported him a moment, then at a sucking terrible intake of breath dropped him like a sodden sack.

"Urb!" he screeched in warning where now no warning was

needed. He and his comrade slunk aside, ready to run but afraid.

When Urba took a backward step he almost tripped over the prostrate Bill, who appeared to be shuddering in the last throes of sudden death. Urba had turned a ghastly white. Only an idiot then could have been blind to impending fate. Wade held his gun low. It still smoked. The issue with the Ruffian was whether he would try to draw or cravenly accept the inevitable doom.

"Urba, I'd shot you along with your pard," said Wade in cold scorn, "but boring daylight through you isn't enough to pay for your insult to Pencarrow's daughter."

Wade swung the heavy Colt across Urba's mouth, knocking him flat.

"Man, don't—shoot!" bawled Urba, spitting blood from his mangled mouth. "I'll crawl! . . . I take it back! . . . 'pologize!"

"Pull your gun or I'll murder you."

"No! I ain't no gun-slinger. . . . Wait, Brandon. . . . *Wait!* . . . Aghh, my Gawd!"

As Urba got up heavily, Wade prodded him in the abdomen with the gun.

"Hold—Brandon," panted Urba, in a horrible earnestness to save his life. "We'll leave cattle—hosses. . . . I'll squeal on Drake. His orders. . . . An' he means to git the gurl—one way or another. I'll tell everythin'. . . . Only give me. . . ."

Wade deliberately cocked his gun and then jabbed it at Urba, who doubled up in mortal terror.

"Don't!——you!" he shrieked. He tripped and fell backwards and as Wade jabbed at him he dragged himself along the gravel road toward the horses.

"No use, Urba. You're done. But pull your gun," called Wade, and he kicked the ruffian over backwards. Urba bellowed with pain and terror and fury, the last of which made him a madman. Like a bent sapling released he sprang up scattering drops of blood, with enough manhood left to draw his gun. Wade shot him in the act.

"Here you fellows," shouted Wade, wheeling to the stunned riders. "Pack these men away from here."

The two broke into action. They led Bill's horse up to the porch and flung him over the saddle. Then they fetched Urba's horse and did the same for Urba. Next they got their own horses and mounted.

"Listen," said Wade, "I know your faces. And if I ever meet you again, guns or no guns, I'll take a shot at you. Savvy? . . . Tell your boss, Band Drake, that Urba squealed on him. Tell him to steer clear of Tex Brandon. Now rustle."

Wade watched the gruesome procession until the pine trees obscured it from sight. Then, released from stress, he slowly walked back toward the house. Pencarrow, who had stood through all this, sat down on a porch chair as if it was relief to get off his legs. White agitated faces appeared inside the far door, and as Wade reached the porch, the girl emerged from the other door just behind her father. Wade had himself in hand; his opportunity had come; and he would not make any mistakes. He thought it best to keep his face averted from the girl, or at least his eyes, for the time being. He had sheathed the gun. He took a step up and addressed the rancher.

"Well, Pencarrow, this Arizona is a wild and hard country for a decent Texas family."

"My God, it is—an' bloody," replied the Texan. "An' I chose the wildest range in the whole damned territory."

At that juncture a manly lad of fourteen came thumping up in his bare feet. He was fair, like his father, showing little resemblance to Jacqueline.

"Mister, I heahed it all," he burst out, "and I saw you shoot the darned skunks."

"Did you? Where were you?" replied Wade, instantly warming to this frank-eyed boy.

"I was in the sitting room with Ma and Rosemary and the kids."

"Why didn't you come out to back me up?" Wade said in fun, but the boy took him seriously.

"I wanted to. But Ma held on to me. And besides, Pa won't let me have guns."

"We'll have to talk your Dad out of that," said Wade, seriously. "You've got to learn to handle guns in Arizona."

"Jackie," interposed the rancher. "Will you tell Mother that everythin' is all right out heah now. Take Hal with you."

"Aw, I want to stay," remonstrated the boy, as his sister led him away. "I like that man. And I'm sick of being. . . ."

Wade heard no more. Then he spoke: "Pencarrow, you're a Texan. It's odd that you keep guns from your boy. Doesn't seem like Texas to me."

"His mother's fault. The boy's uncle was a gunman. Glenn Pencarrow. Killed by rangers. She has always hated guns since. That's one reason why I've failed heah."

"Does your daughter share that feeling?"

"You heahed her, stranger. An' I'll bet she'd have shot thet bastard if you hadn't."

That thrilled Wade back to a remembrance of the girl's denunciation of the black-browed Urba. He was about to address the rancher again when Jacqueline returned, light of step and singularly impelling of presence.

"Dad, I've calmed them somewhat and sent them out of the sitting room," she said. "Hal will look after Mr. Brandon's horse. . . . Let us go indoors."

Wade followed them into a large and well-lighted room, with windows looking out upon both sides. It was richly and colorfully furnished. A huge open fireplace, with Navajo designs on the stones, took Wade's eye. He felt composed and sure of himself though deep down there was tumult.

"Heah, take this chair, stranger," said Pencarrow, hospitably. "Brandon? Was that what you called yourself?"

"Yes. Brandon."

"Where you from?"

"All over the West. But I was born in Missouri. They call me Tex."

"Ahuh. . . . Daughter, would you mind leavin' us alone?"

"I certainly would. What's more I won't do it," replied the

girl, with spirit. "Heahafter, I'm going to sit in on all the deals. . . . Forgive me, Dad, for disobeying. But you have made such a mess of it. . . . This terrible thing that's just happened—it seems the time to change."

"Well! Well!" ejaculated the rancher, surprised, and perhaps secretly pleased. "You're as much of a rebel as Hal.—Brandon, this is my eldest—Jacqueline—just turned twenty-one."

"How do you do, Miss Pencarrow," rejoined Wade, with a bow.

"Brandon, your Arizona has ruined all of us," went on the rancher.

"I couldn't think that," replied Wade with strong feeling. He meant to revive the courage and hope of this Texan. "You're far from old. You still have plenty of fight left. And Miss Jacqueline here—well she didn't strike me as being ruined. The lad Hal has fire and spunk. If I judge the rest of your family by you three I'd be willing to gamble on it that you'll find success here."

"Who are you?" queried Pencarrow, responding to that challenge. His fine piercing eyes narrowed in scrutiny of his visitor.

"Just a wandering rider," replied Wade, with his disarming smile.

"Excuse my curiosity," the rancher hastened to add. "You're not like the riders who pass heah. . . . I don't need to ask if you're a gunman. I'm a Texan. My brother Glenn was swift on the draw. But you had it on him. . . . Who told you about me?"

"I happened to ride into Lawsford's camp, asked for a job. I reckon he liked to talk. Mentioned the few cattlemen of this Cedar Range, among them Aulsbrook. Then he spoke of you and your family. How ashamed he was of the rough deal Arizona has given you. Told about Drake, and in short, how you'd been robbed by all the outfits in this country."

"Ahuh. An' thet is why you rode over heah to ask me for a job?"

"Pencarrow, it struck me that I might be the kind of man you needed."

"Ha! thet struck me, too, most damned hard. . . . But air you shore it wasn't talk about Jacqueline thet fetched you?"

"Oh, Dad," interrupted the young woman, blushing furiously. "Such a question to ask!"

"Wal, why is it?" demanded her father, testily. "Haven't riders too many to count rode up heah—every last one of them to pester an' hound you, an' worry me sick? Or turn out to be scoundrels! Why shouldn't I ask Brandon?"

"I'm not offended, Pencarrow," returned Wade. "Lawsford's cowboys did gossip about Miss Jacqueline—most flatteringly. But I had made up my mind to come before I heard them."

"An' you run plumb into some of Band Drake's outfit! . . . Wal, Brandon, I didn't take kindly to yore comin'. But I'm thankin' God you stayed in spite of my insults."

"Dad, evidently Mr. Brandon had determined to get that job," interposed Jacqueline.

"Brandon, I'm ashamed to admit thet I cain't pay my bills in town let alone wages," said the rancher.

"Never mind wages," rejoined Wade, hastily. "I've saved a little money. I had good luck at Tombstone. Struck a rich gold pocket and dug up a few thousand. Then I was forced off my claim. I gambled a little—and won. I'll lend that money to you."

"See heah, Brandon. The boot is on the other foot now. You don't know me," said Pencarrow, red in the face, and visibly agitated.

"Mr. Brandon!" exclaimed Jacqueline. "How could we accept anything like that!"

"You must be the judge of that. But give me a little chance—a little time. Shooting those two hombres was no particular recommendation for me."

"Brandon, you just came heah—a wanderin' rider, eh?" queried the rancher. "You have no home, no kin—nothin' to hold you. An' it went against yore grain to heah of a decent Texan bein' bamboozled an' robbed—an' a family of nice women an' kids sufferin' because of thet. An' you ride over heah to catch some of these dirty skunks in the act. . . . An' by God you shot them!"

Wade, at a loss how to reply, did not answer.

"I've heahed of thet sort of thing," went on Pencarrow. "I could have done the same when I was young. But I never even hoped it'd happen to me. . . . See heah, now. You look over my ranch. See what's left. Figure if I have any chance on earth to retrieve. An' if you think I have, I'll accept the loan of yore money an' give you the job I see you're fitted for an' which is what I need more than money or stock or riders."

"Thanks, Pencarrow. I'll do my best."

"Heah's my hand."

Wade felt in his powerful grip a sincerity and liking that boded well for the future.

CHAPTER TEN

PENCARROW paced the floor like a man coming out of a daze. "Brandon, I'd lost my faith in my fellow men," he said, "an' God, too, I reckon."

"I've had a hard life," replied Wade, "and I've felt that way often. But in every dark hour something saved me."

"Dark hour? . . . I may be a bloody old Texan, hampered by a squeamish wife, and bound by lovin' ties to beat down my real nature, but when you killed those men it was as if lightnin' struck through the blackness of my despair. I never felt such joy."

"Oh—Dad," cried Jacqueline, tremulously. "We mustn't grow savage."

"We cain't live in Arizona an' turn our other cheeks to every blow. . . . Jackie, I'll go tell Mother thet the first blood spilled on our ranch has turned the tide. . . . You talk to Brandon."

Wade, left alone with the girl, found himself staring at the floor, conscious of a sweeping tide of emotion. She was silent. He felt her eyes upon him. He fought to convince himself that he was no guilty wretch before his judge—that he had never been driven by as exalted a motive—that even if she did recognize him she would not betray him to her father. So much reasoned out. But that did not give him strength.

"Mr. Brandon, did you lie to Dad?" Jacqueline asked, her voice low.

"No," he answered, abruptly, shocked out of the inhibited spell, and for the first time he met her gaze fully. Her great dark eyes searched his with all a woman's gifts of penetration.

"Then you—you did not come heah—because of me?"

"Yes. And your father—all of you. . . . I have no ties. Your plight appealed to me."

"You explained it that way. But I—I doubted you. I have been deceived so often. . . . Tell me frankly—wasn't it because of *me*? . . . Because of the vile range gossip—the name these wild riders have given me—that I'm a—a—heah for the taking?"

Wade burned with the shame and the earnestness of her question. She did not blush. Her face was pearl white. Only a very strong incentive could have overcome her antipathy to interrogation of such a nature.

"Wait," she began again, hurriedly, when he would have spoken. "Whatever your motive, you have saved Dad from God only knows what. . . . You have given him hope again. And for that I am deeply indebted. But I want to *know*. . . . I could not blame you for what you heahed. Only I want to put you right . . . then if you stayed to—to help us—it'd be almost too good to be true."

"Miss Pencarrow, please—" burst out Wade as soon as he could find his tongue—"you don't need to tell me—"

"You deny it?" she interrupted, with a magnificent blaze in her eyes.

"Absolutely. I made up my mind to come before Lawsford's cowboys mentioned you. Then, to be fair to them, they did not speak insultingly . . . they talked only of your charms, as cowboys do round the camp fire."

"Thank you. That makes all the difference in the world," she returned, fervently, and then a scarlet wave did blot out the creaminess of her throat and face. She hid it a moment in her hands, like a young girl, and then again looked up bravely. "You'll understand—I'm sure, when I tell you that I've had a hideous ordeal heah in Arizona. I was sixteen when we took up this ranch. I'm twenty-one now. That five years has been a nightmare. Dad's first outfit of riders had to be discharged one after the other for their—their attentions to me. To tell the truth, they were hounds. Band Drake was the worst—he was the cattleman Dad bought our land from—gave me an undeserved name on this range. That, and the fact I have the misfortune to be pretty, drew riders heah like swarms of bees. A few of them were nice cowboys. The rest, like Urba and his riders. . . . I must confess—when you shot him —I was glad, glad—. But Oh! I've been torn apart heah!"

"How in the world did you come to stay?" asked Wade, incredulously.

"That's the strange thing. We all love this Arizona. It wasn't only that all we had was sunk heah. We were very happy at first. The youngsters went wild—and I guess I did too."

"Who is Band Drake?"

"He pretended to be many things he wasn't. Dad fell in with him at Holbrook, where we lived a while. Drake sold us this land which he and his gang had homesteaded, but had never proved up on it. He ran Dad's outfit and ran off most of the cattle in the bargain. He made life miserable for me. Dad had to drive him away. And I haven't taken any horseback rides since, except near the ranch house."

"What does he look like?"

"Tall, fair, rather good-looking. He must be under forty. Claims to come from Texas. But enough about him. . . . Mr. Brandon, haven't I met you before?"

"What!" ejaculated Wade with a start, and for the first time he really looked fully at her.

"You seem strangely familiar—somehow," she went on. "I went to school at Houston. Have you ever been there?"

"No. I've been in southwest Texas, but never in the civilized parts. . . . You must be mistaken. Perhaps I remind you of some one."

"Perhaps. I cain't remember. . . . It struck me a moment ago. You know the vague groping sensations one has trying to remember a name or a face. It's gone now. I guess I'm a little out of my haid."

Wade experienced intense relief. A tumult stilled within him. She did not recognize him. And he was able to look at her, smiling as if at her mistake. She flushed slightly and averted her eyes. How beautiful she seemed! He had no contrasts, no remembrance of beautiful girls with which to compare her. Since he was sixteen he had not seen any girls of her class. So her vivid charm struck him overpoweringly. Her hair was wavy, between brown and chestnut in hue, with glints of gold; her face a lovely oval with wide low level brows, magnificent eyes that looked black, but were deep dark velvet hazel, a straight clear-cut profile and strong sweet lips, curved and red, haunted by mystery and sadness. Her slenderness, perhaps, exaggerated the rounded outlines of her body, as her singularly sensitive and intense vitality drew attention to them. She appeared to Wade a wonderful breath-taking creature, fine, high-spirited, intelligent.

She caught Wade in his absorbed survey of her and it disturbed her to the extent of restlessness. She got up to walk to the door, then hurriedly left it as if the scene outside brought back the tragedy. She had a lithe grace that the cotton gown and apron failed entirely to hide. Her sleeves were rolled above the elbows of round brown arms, and her shapely hands, supple and strong, showed traces of flour.

"I was baking when the four range cavaliers rode up," she said with a smile.

Wade grasped that his study of her had not displeased her, but was being prolonged too far.

"Miss Pencarrow, forgive me for—for staring," he said, hastily. "I forgot my manners. . . . But you are so wonderful looking."

"Thank you. But wait till you see Rona!"

"Your sister?"

"Yes. Hal's twin. She has not a trace of Spanish. My mother was a Castilian. I resemble her somewhat. But Rona favors Dad's side of the family."

"Hal looked about fourteen," said Wade, thoughtfully. "If she is as pretty as you—"

"Pretty!" exclaimed Jacqueline, as Wade hesitated for words. "Rona is the prettiest girl I ever saw. She looks sixteen, too. She has the famous towhaid of the Pencarrows. Which is a Texas characteristic. And such eyes! Like light-colored violets. The strangest shade."

"Then I'm afraid I've tackled the most terrible job any rider ever wished on himself."

"Oh, true—indeed you have!" she replied, eloquently, with a tinge of regret. "But you wouldn't shirk it, would you? Just because these wild Arizonans flock heah?"

"No. I won't shirk it for that or any other reason," he rejoined, soberly. "Nor will you or your sister ever be—be offended by me."

"There! I'm the one that has offended," she rejoined hastily. "Of late I've thought—" she broke off and did not continue her thought. "But, oh Mr. Brandon, the sight of a rider has become hateful to me. Please try to understand."

"I'm not offended," said Wade. "Women have not entered my life since I was a boy. Then it was only my mother and sister."

"You never had a wife?"

"Me! Good heavens, no! Nor a sweetheart—nor anything. I've never had a woman friend."

"Mr. Brandon, can you expect me to believe that?" she asked incredulously. If he had been a liar her eyes would have discovered it. "You are young, handsome. You have the deference for women so seldom met with in this uncouth West."

"No matter what I have or haven't. It's the simple truth."

"Then you've lived a strange lonely life where there weren't any women."

"Yes. For years I've known only the wilderness and rough men. What little time I've spent in towns, I was too busy just staying alive to think of other things."

"You're what Dad calls a gunman?"

"Yes. And that will help in the work I have to do for him."

"My uncle Glenn was a gunman. He was a hero in this family, except with mother. He was driven to fight for his life. . . . That must apply to you?"

"It does. I've been a hunted man."

"Mr. Brandon, that will never stand in the way of your being respected and—and liked in this family. Ever since I was a little girl my sympathy went out to Uncle Glenn, and men like him, who had no home, no loved ones, no comfort, no rest—nothing but a gun and a terrible skill with it."

"That is well for me," returned Wade, with emotion. "But please do not talk about me any more."

"It was necessary. I wanted to know a little about you."

"Some day, maybe, I'll tell you my story. . . . But let us get back to the reasons I am here. . . . It seemed to me that your father and Aulsbrook were not good friends."

"Indeed they are not," she retorted quickly. "And it's not Dad's fault. Out heah, if not in Texas, Dad has seen the necessity of being on good terms with neighbors. But Aulsbrook hated him in Texas and hates him worse heah."

"Why?"

"They both loved the same girl. My mother."

"Oh, I see. What bad luck they should choose the same range! Has Aulsbrook been a square neighbor?"

"Hardly. He is a shrewd man. Dad has not the haid for any business, much less raising cattle. Aulsbrook took advantage of that."

"Was he crooked?" queried Wade, sharply.

"Morally, yes. But not in the way a court would see it."

"I will want to know all about that. . . . How much stock has your father left?"

"We don't know. Not much compared to what we started with. We have left about a hundred haid of horses, some very fine stock. And perhaps a few thousand haid of cattle."

"Have you been living off them?"

"Yes. And off the ranch. We raise everything we eat. We have a wonderful farm down in the canyon. Snow never lies there. So warm and sunny. And water! There never was such water in Texas."

"I rode by the big spring. That must be on Pencarrow's range."

"It is. And has caused us much trouble. Aulsbrook claims it. Has threatened Dad with suit in Phoenix. It's that sort of thing—and debts—pressing debts, which have troubled Dad even more than the rustlers. Sometimes we never know of a cattle steal until long afterward. All our riders are gone."

"I take it you look after your father's books."

"Yes. And I'm ashamed to look in them."

"You must go over them with me presently."

They were then interrupted by the entrance of Pencarrow, leading a dark woman who had once been very handsome and still had distinction. Following her came the boy Hal with a tall girl unmistakedly his sister. She had an abundance of hair so light as to almost be silver, and like Jacqueline she had eyes that would have made any face beautiful, and of a shade of blue that Wade had never seen. When Pencarrow introduced Wade, both the mother and daughter welcomed him, the former shrinkingly as if he were a bloody monster, and the latter gladly as if he were a savior. That was an embarrassing moment for Wade.

"Rona saw the whole show," piped up Hal, "and then she keeled over."

"Mr. Brandon, I never fainted before," said the girl, apologetically. "I listened before you came and I was furious. Then when you rode up, somehow I guessed you'd take Dad's part. I saw it in your eye. And I was tickled to death when you jumped at that Urba. But the bang of your gun and that other fellow's awful face—and the blood—I just got sick and dizzy, and everything went black."

"Don't talk any more about it," ordered Pencarrow. "Your mother is still sick and dizzy—an' she only heahed the fight. . . . Brandon, we'll have some lunch, an' then Hal can ride about with you while the womenfolks fix up one of the cabins for you. . . . Hal, fetch his hawse around."

The Pencarrows had no servants, which lack certainly had not been anticipated when the master built that house, judging by its size and spaciousness. The dining room, like the living room, looked out upon both sides of the house. The furnishings and tableware further attested to Pencarrow's prosperous days. Some one of the family, and Wade suspected it was Jacqueline, was a very capable housekeeper. Wade ate heartily despite the aftermath of the tragedy. But he was glad to get outdoors again. He found that he could hardly keep his eyes off Jacqueline, and Rona watched him as if utterly fascinated.

The ranch buildings had been erected too recently to be run down, but they showed the lack of use. Bunkhouses and cabins were empty, as were the cribs and other sheds. The huge barn was a superb structure with twenty-five stalls on each side of the wide space that ran from end to end. There did not appear to be any hay or grain on the place. The corrals had not been used for a long time.

At a whistle from Hal, a score or more of horses came trooping up the pasture field. They took Wade's eye. He believed himself to be a judge of horseflesh. These were pips, a ragged, fat, long-maned and lazy bunch of thoroughbreds. Pencarrow claimed to know horses better than cattle.

When Wade rode out with the rancher and Hal he felt the same thrill as when he had emerged from the canyon to get his first view of the ranch. No wilder or more beautiful setting could have been found. Its fragrance of sage, its gray and green vastness, its many pine-crowned knolls, its grand mountain wall on the north, and its gateway, like a window opening out upon the painted desert—these were largely responsible for the hold the country had on the Pencarrows. There was something different about Arizona. The wind in the cedars, the waving grass and the purple sage, the zestful tang in the air, the bigness of everything, and the freedom, appeared to belong only to Arizona. Then Wade remembered the canyon not far away, yet invisible from the range above, and he surrendered himself to the spell of the finest country he had seen. As he had told himself already, his wandering rides had ended at Cedar Range.

Wade saw perhaps two thousand head of cattle, and was of the opinion that Pencarrow had more stock left than he supposed. With the cattle business waning in Texas, past its prime in Kansas and Nebraska and Colorado, badly disrupted by the disastrous Lincoln County War in New Mexico, Arizona had a marvelous opportunity. Wade recognized it. He asked about the winter climate, to be satisfied that the cold and snow offered no serious obstacle to successful ranching.

"There's a big open canyon over heah where you could throw more cattle than I ever owned," Pencarrow said.

"How far to the railroad?"

"Five days herd-drivin' an' good grass an' water all the way."

"Any ranchers along that route?"

"Not one. An' a queer thing, too."

"How many cattlemen living off this Cedar Range?"

"Aulsbrook, Driscoll, Mason, Drill, an' a few homesteaders."

"This range is big. But how big?"

"Thunderin' big, you bet. I never knew exactly. It's more than a hundred miles long an' half as wide. Thet's not countin' the canyons, an' they're a whole range in themselves."

"Any idea how much stock?"

"Yes. Aulsbrook claims he's runnin' ten thousand haid. An' the other three ranchers might throw together all their cattle into thet big a herd."

"Only twenty thousand cattle on a range that'd support half a million! With the price bound to climb! . . . Pencarrow, you can make a fortune here in five years."

"I could have. Damn me, suh, I could have," bellowed the rancher, touched on a sore spot. "I saw it. But I've been deceived, outfigured an' robbed."

"If you have two or three thousand head left we can double them in a couple of years. And double that in two more."

"But I haven't got so many left, an' I'd need more cows, new bulls, an' riders."

"Of course. I've worked on ranches at different times, enough to learn something about the cattle business."

From that moment, Wade began to think too deeply to ask more questions or even to attend strictly to Pencarrow's further statements. Upon their return, they unsaddled at the barn. Hal turned the horses loose in the long lane that led to the pasture. Pencarrow told Hal to show Wade to his cabin and then left for the house.

"Mr. Brandon, I'm doggone glad you came to Cedar Ranch," said the boy, heartily. "So is Rona, and I've a hunch Jacque is, too, for all she's so sick of riders."

"Well, Hal, I'm pretty glad myself," replied Wade, warmed by the lad. "Suppose you cut out the mister and call me Tex."

"Tex? For Texas. I like that. We're getting along first-rate, aren't we? Will you take me riding with you?"

"Say, boy, your lessons begin tomorrow."

"Lessons? Gosh!—I have one hour a day with Jacque in summer and three in winter," complained Hal.

"Fine. But I mean lessons in riding, roping, branding, tracking—and handling guns."

"Oh, Mist . . . Tex! You mean it?" ejaculated Hal, rapturously.

"I shore do."

"*Whoopee!*" yelled Hal.

They had reached the little cabin at the edge of the first pine-clad knoll. Jacqueline emerged from the open door to confront them on the porch.

"What are you whooping about?" she asked, severely.

"Tex is gonna make a cowboy out of me."

"Tex?"

"Yes. Mr. Brandon. But he won't let me call him mister."

"Oh, was that it. Well, Tex has taken another hard job on his hands," replied the girl, demurely. "Mr. Brandon, heah are your quarters. Will you step in?"

"I'm gonna run an' tell Rona," said Hal.

"All right lad. While you're at it, ask Rona if she'd like to be a cowgirl."

Hal ran toward the house whooping for his sister. Jacqueline stood in the door of the cabin, bidding Wade enter.

"Cowgirl?" she asked, with a smile.

"Yes. And that goes for you too, Miss Pencarrow."

"How thrilling! . . . Dad built this cabin for his foreman. But it never was occupied by just one man. . . . Mother and I fixed it up in a hurry. It's quite nice, don't you think? Cozy and light. Running water and open fireplace. There's a shed full of cedar and juniper wood through that back door. Table and lamp are still to come."

Wade took one survey of the interior with its pine-wood furniture, its colored blankets and Indian rugs, its big stone fireplace, its several pictures and shelf of books, and then he laughed outright.

"For me, Miss Pencarrow! This wonderful little cabin? . . . It is far too good. If you could see the holes I've lived and slept in!"

"All the more reason why you should have some little comfort heah."

"If you say I must. . . . But I fear I'll not fit it very well, with my dust and rags."

"You are rather ragged and travel-stained," she said, surveying him from mud-caked boots to his dusty sombrero. "But clothes do not make the man in Arizona."

"What does make him? A horse and gun?"

"I admit their importance. . . . You took a shine to Hal at once, didn't you?"

"I sure did."

"I never saw Hal so happy. He's excited, of course, as we all are. Your introduction was upsetting. Dad insulted you and I—well, I took you for another of these loose range Romeos."

"You had reason to take me for worse."

"No! That was fear. I should have *felt* you were the—the man I prayed for—to come—to help Dad."

"Did you pray? Well, now," replied Wade, weakly, as he sought for words to hide a sudden bursting flood of emotion. He tossed his sombrero on the bed and would have made some movement to break the spell. But she held him with a look, grateful and wondering, and an unfathomable darkness of eyes that struck at his heart.

"I did pray. Many and many a time. I never gave up, but I lost hope. . . . I'm ashamed that I didn't recognize the moment—the meeting—the significance of it all. But hard as this Arizona life has been, I had not seen death and blood."

Her speech was low and full of emotion, propelled by the intensity that seemed a part of her every thought and action. These would have been eloquent and persuasive from the plainest of girls. But from Jacqueline Pencarrow, endowed as she was with spirit and beauty, it proved Wade's undoing. That was the peril in her. He recognized it, even at the birth of a first and overmastering love. Most men would have misunderstood her, have been blind to the fact that a wish of hers, a persuasive request was magnified a thousandfold by the beauty of her person and the intensity of her being.

"Oh, I'm *glad* you've come, Tex Brandon," she cried, suddenly glowing scarlet. "And before this day is done—when I recover from this cold sickness—heah—" she pressed a brown spread hand over her heart, "I shall have had my first happy hour in years."

CHAPTER ELEVEN

WADE was alone at Cedar Ranch.

He had seen all the Pencarrows, in wagon and buck board, drive off for Holbrook, a transformed and happy family. He had watched them go with a deep conviction of the good that would come to a man if he had faith and hope enough. At the turn of the road, where it climbed over a gray ridge, one of the girls had waved a scarf the last time. Rona's had been red. This one was yellow, if his keen sight had not been dimmed.

They were to be gone six days or a week. Wade had lent Pencarrow close to seven thousand dollars, money he had earned through mining and won by games of chance. The rancher was to pay his long-due debts and buy food supplies, ranch tools, saddle equipment, rifles and shells, and many things for his needy family. Wade could picture Hal in a store where guns were sold, and the girls shopping for the first time in five years. It was for this that Wade had clung tenaciously to his money.

When they were out of sight, Wade barred his door, and cut open his worn leather vest and coat to get out the ill-gotten fortune that had been a burden all these years. His intention had been to count the rolls and packets of currency. He unstrapped his father's heavy wallet, as he had with a similar intention once before, but the act brought such a storm of poignant memories that he closed it. What must he do with many thousands of dollars stolen from express trains and banks?

First he must hide the money. What a relief to be free of the feel and the awareness of that burden! Temporarily he hid the wallet and rolls and packets in the woodshed. For a permanent hiding place he concluded to make a strong tight box and bury it under the cabin floor.

Wade pondered his peculiar reaction to the sight of this large sum of stolen money. He did not want to face a guilty conscience at this regenerating period. And with the money off his person, securely hidden, he found it easy to forget.

Leaving the cabin, Wade packed a rifle he had borrowed from Pencarrow, the last of a dozen Winchesters the rancher had brought with him. Wade constructed a makeshift sheath for the rifle and tied it on his saddle. He also carried pencil and notebock he had obtained from Jacqueline. Thus equipped he set out to ride the range, vigilant and hawk-eyed, stern with the earnestness of his purpose. If he encountered any queer-acting riders, he meant to shoot first and see about it afterward.

He rode west to West Canyon and along that rim for a mile, clear to where it headed out upon the range; and he sighted a good many cattle, of which he jotted down an estimated count. Then he rode in a circle along the edge of the slope where the purple sage met the green timber. The ride itself would have been all-satisfying without his search for cattle and study of the range. He covered fifty miles that day, and was well pleased with the stock he had seen in the canyon and among the brushy thickets. Rustlers had, no doubt, driven large numbers of cattle off the open range and then made away with herds as occasion demanded.

Wade cooked his own supper that evening, out under the pines, and he failed to remember when campfare had been more appetizing or place as singularly fascinating. The fragrance, the color, the wildness of Arizona were getting into his blood. He sat there and watched the sunset gold steal over the gray sage, and that gorgeous salmon pink peculiar to Arizona emblazoned on the clouds.

Later he sat in the dusk in his cabin door. Pencarrow's ranch house showed dark through the trees. The upper story, an addition built later, just rose to the tops of the pines, some of which brushed against and shadowed the little balcony. Through an opening gleamed a window with a white curtain. This cupola-like story contained two rooms and a porch for Jacqueline and Rona. The rancher had built that addition, he told Wade, after an attack one night by raiders or abductors who had almost succeeded in snatching Jacqueline out of the open window of her bedroom on the ground floor. This happened when she was seventeen years old.

Wade thought darkly about that attempt at kidnapping. Pencarrow should never have brought his family to this isolated range. Jacqueline, and presently Rona too, would work havoc among honest cowboys and other young Arizonans, to say nothing of rousing hot passion and bad blood among the raw and lawless element which rode this section.

Next day Wade turned to the east and covered even more territory, with as gratifying result. He mapped the distinctive landmarks and got the lay of the land, tasks that came as easily to him as if he had been a cowboy all his days.

On the third day he rode the vast gray rolling tableland between Cedar Canyon and the desert. He gained an eminence from which he could see all over the range, down into the canyon, and out upon the desert, a remarkable lookout point on the summit of a pine knoll. With a good field glass he could cover the whole range. Here was a place three hours' hard ride from the ranch house from which he could command all the west side of Cedar Range. It was also an all-satisfying stand from which to see the unfolding panorama of this strange and beautiful Arizona.

On the return, Wade rode around one of the many knolls to encounter at some distance three horsemen whose appearance tallied with riders of Urba's ilk, and whose actions upon being discovered proved that their business at the range looked doubtful. At sight of Wade they sheered off toward the canyon.

Wade dismounted, and jerking his rifle out he began to shoot. The range was too far for good marksmanship, but he could see where his bullets cut up the dust in open patches in front of the horses. From a lope these riders broke into a dead run and were soon out of range. They halted at the slope of a knoll and watched Wade.

He reloaded the Winchester and then, leading his horse, he walked to the spot where the riders had so quickly halted at sight of him. He knelt and measured the tracks of their horses and studied each minutely.

"Watch, you hombres!" he said aloud, as he saw how the three riders had studied his movements as earnestly as had he their tracks. "Now, where in hell can they be? . . . I've just got to go slow and learn to know the men of this range."

He backtracked the riders for several miles, until he was satisfied that they must have come up out of the big canyon. Then Wade made for the ranch house, arriving there after dark.

Next day he set off early, meaning first to call on Pencarrow's nearest neighbor, a homesteader named Elwood Lightfoot, who had located in a big brake of Cedar Canyon on the west side and adjoining the land claimed by Aulsbrook. Wade was particularly interested in this homesteader because Hal and Rona claimed he was their one friend, and because Pencarrow said Aulsbrook had been unable to drive or buy him off. Secondly, this plot of one hundred and sixty acres made a productive little ranch watered from a sister spring to that in Cedar Canyon.

Once Wade found the trail he came out upon the brake in short order. It was a shallow valley walled by red rock, level and green, bisected by a shining brook, and jumping off into the green void below. Wade exclaimed aloud in sheer delight. Arizona hid little Gardens of Eden in its wide gray timber-belted and stone-walled range. What a farm for alfalfa! It seemed to Wade that this ranch should be kept out of Aulsbrook's hands.

Wade rode down. The homesteader's log cabin stood in the open, at the north end, no doubt built there to get the southern exposure and shelter from the northern winds in winter. The cabin was small, crude in structure, with a yellow chimney built outside and a roof of earth from which weeds and sunflowers grew. There was an open-sided sun shelter, with workbench and couch, and a store of traps and tools and rusty farm implements, also a red earthen oven, and many more things Wade had no time to look at.

Rabbits, quail, chickens, deer and burros appeared to have the run of the ranch at that end. The barking of chained hounds announced Wade's arrival. Then a man, no doubt the homesteader, emerged from the cabin. He appeared to be a lean gray old fellow whose eyes were light blue and keen as a whip.

"Howdy. Are you the fellar Hal was tellin' me about the other day?"

"Howdy yourself. Yes, I'm Tex Brandon. And you're Elwood Lightfoot."

"Pile off. I'm achin' to shake yore hand. . . . By Gawd, I shore am glad to meet you. An' that Pencarrow's got a man at Cedar Ranch at last."

"Let's get in the shade and talk. . . . I'm sure as glad to meet you. The Pencarrows have gone to Holbrook for a much-needed trip."

"So Hal told me they was goin'. But he jest rushed hyar an' left in the same breath. . . . What'd they go for?"

"Pencarrow had debts to pay and supplies to buy. And it was a chance for his family."

"Doggone! I'm shore glad. An' turrible curious. Where'd the money come from?"

"I lent some to Pencarrow. I made a lucky gold strike at Tombstone and doubled it by gambling. In any event I'd have lent that money to Pencarrow. But I reckon it is good business. That's the finest ranch I ever saw. He still has some stock left, mostly out in the brush and canyon. I've taken count of nearly four thousand head, which is twice as many as he thinks he has left. There's big money to be made on this range. And I'm going to help him."

"Wal, if you don't mind me sayin' it, your killin' Urba an' his pard was a helluva good start," remarked the homesteader, his penetrating gaze hard on Wade. "I heahed about it thet same day. It's gone over the range like fire in grass, an' it's seepin' down into the brakes to the dens of rustlers an' hawse thieves an' bad eggs."

"Good news," replied Wade, waving that aside. "Hal and Rona swear by you. Their only friend! Are you Pencarrow's friend?"

"I shore am, more'n he reckons. I've had hell keepin' their homestead, which I'd sold long ago but for his two kids."

"That's straight from the shoulder. Pencarrow has two friends now. And two working together are far stronger than one. . . . Will you take me on Pencarrow's recommendation?"

"Brandon, I'd taken you on Hal's an' Rona's. Hal said Rona was so glad you came thet she cried. You could never fool thet sharp-eyed lass. She's been brought up to see only trouble in men."

"Good. We're for Pencarrow and his youngsters, then?"

"I'll go as far as you can," retorted the homesteader. "I've been on the point of borin' one of these hombres for a long time."

"Band Drake, I'll bet."

"You bet. But I've never had a chance thet couldn't be laid at my door. I've got it in for Drake on more'n one score. Most though I hate him because I used to see Miss Jacque often. She'd ride down to visit me. She's afeared to come any more."

"Ahuh. We'll get around to Drake later. Tell me, Lightfoot. Do you own this homestead?"

"I shore do."

"You have the patent?"

"Yes. I proved up on the land three years ago. But didn't get any patent until last fall."

"Looks like a productive ranch?"

"Say, Brandon, things grow heah as if by magic. I cain't get rid of the peaches an' grapes an' melons an' corn an' vegetables. Tons of them rot on the ground. I used to get good pay from Pencarrow, an' I still furnish them all they eat except beef."

"What was your original idea when you homesteaded this land?"

"I saw the value of the water. Then I wanted to farm the land, 'specially alfalfa, an' run cattle up on the range. Been heah nine years, an' am poorer now than when I started. The rustlers got my stock, so I quit raisin' alfalfa."

"How much alfalfa could you raise here?"

"A hundred tons a summer, an' never hurt my garden or orchard."

"Whew! . . . No wonder Aulsbrook has been trying to get your place."

"He's set on thet, by fair means or foul."

"Aulsbrook better be careful. Tell him next time he approaches you. . . . Now, Lightfoot, here's a most particular question. Do you know cattle?"

"Do I? Wal! From A to Z. Thar's not a cattleman in Arizona thet could hold a candle to me. I've worked cattle for forty years an' have lost half a million. But thet wasn't because I didn't know how to breed, raise, drive an' sell cattle."

Wade got up from his comfortable seat on the couch, and scarcely able to contain himself he stalked to and fro under the shelter.

"Wal, you 'pear mighty tickled about my brag, an' my bad luck," added the homesteader, plainly nonplused.

"Lightfoot, you've just told me Pencarrow's fortune is made, and you and I are trailing along behind."

"Man alive! No wonder Hal raved about you. Thet quick? the lad said. But Brandon, how'n hell do you figger thet?"

"Pencarrow has the range. You have the experience."

"Shore. I figgered thet out myself long ago. But it'll take money. Not a hell of a lot. All the same—money! Wal, thet's the third need. An' all three needs don't sum up what the fourth will take. Thet's the guts an' the power to kill or drive off these rustlers an' thieves hidin' down in the brakes."

"My job, Lightfoot!"

"Hell, man! You alone agin a dozen outfits, some of them bad It cain't be done."

"It can be done!"

The homesteader stared mutely at Wade, powerfully impressed

by the fire and force of Wade's assertion, perhaps more so by his presence.

"Are you with me?" queried Wade, sharply.

"Wal, if you want to know, I haven't felt so happy in years. Reckon I'm loco about them twins. An' I shore like Pencarrow. I don't savvy the old lady. An' Jacque—she jest sweeps me off my feet. Queer about how she effects men! Have you felt it, Brandon?"

"She's very beautiful and alive."

"Shore. But thet ain't sayin' nothin'. She jest sets these Arizona rangemen crazy. An' she'd do it the same if she wore a Mormon hood. . . . Wal, what's yore idea about runnin' Cedar Ranch?"

"My word! Now you've stuck me. I made up my mind to do it without thinking how."

"Thet's the way to do. To hell with obstacles an' difficulties! The harder the job, the madder we'll get."

"You'll take me as a pard then on sight?"

"I shore will. I've felt somethin' big in me tryin' to bust ever since Hal was heah."

"Elwood, I mean you will never regret this. . . . Now that's settled. Let's get our heads together."

"Wait a minnit. I've got a condition, Brandon. An' it's thet you let me be the dark horse in this race—the silent pardner in this deal."

"Why? I don't like that idea."

"Wal, as a matter of fact, all I can do is to be a kind of scout for you an' advise you on matters that pertain to cattle raisin'. The brunt of this turrible job will fall on you. All I want is to keep this homestead an' make it pay a little for my old age."

"Elwood, we can make it pay more than that. Alfalfa alone will yield you a good income. You must have help."

"I know a Mexican and his son. Sheepherders. They've been done out of work by these thievin' riders who hate sheep. I can get them for their keep until we begin to produce. Thet'd give me time to scout for you."

"Scout? You mean ride the range and the brakes to get tab on these parasites?"

"Yes, more than thet. To find out where the stolen cattle goes—the stock they don't drive to the railroad. I've always stood in with some of these outfits. Not Drake's nor Harrobin's. They're the kingpins of this range an' they're rivals. We could make 'em enemies. My idee of bein' a dark horse is to keep on apparently as I've always done—never takin' sides."

"Seen from that angle it's a fine idea," replied Wade, thoughtfully. "I accept. You're my silent partner."

"We gotta go slow. No quick improvements heah. An' to throw in new stock up on Cedar Ranch would be fatal until you get these hombres scared or on the run. For the present it's a big enough job to round up all Pencarrow's stock an' get it back in the open. A thorough search of brakes an' timber might fetch surprisin' results."

"I've already proved that in only four days."

"You might run across some of the stolen cattle. Reckon I can guarantee thet. But you'll need cowboys. There's the rub heah. Riders thet won't steal you out of hide an' hair! Riders thet'll ride fer their keep until we get on our feet! Brandon, I reckon it's impossible."

"Not to me. I can run any bunch of cowboys that ever forked horses," retorted Wade, grim-lipped.

"You can? Did you every try it?"

"No. But I can."

"Would you mind tellin' me how in the hell you can do what no cattleman heah ever could?"

"Give me a few *young* riders. I don't care how lazy, onery, tough, crooked, they are. I believe I could build up an outfit. I've got to, Elwood! . . . I'd make big promises, I'd prove that rustling never paid in the long run. I'd work on each one individually. I'd make them like me. I'd make them see the guts Pencarrow has, to stick it out here. I'd excite sympathy and respect for his game family. . . . Elwood, I've lived among bad men, outlaws, outcasts. Every last one of them had some good in him. I'd work on that principle. All the same I'd be a hard driver. I'd shirk no job myself. Lastly I'd tell them I'd shoot whoever made a false move—and I'd do it!"

During the last of Wade's passionate exposition, Lightfoot rose slowly to his feet, his eyes like glints of pale blue sky, his gray worn face lighting with inspired fire.

"Brandon, I know yore cowboy an' his bunch air the outfit you want," he declared, forcibly, and he cracked his big hands together. "Doggone! It's shore queer how things work out—when the right man shows up."

"Elwood, you're saying a lot without telling me anything. Come on. Explain," returned Wade, in eager impatience.

Lightfoot resumed his seat. "Son, I'm not used to bein' het up. Listen an' you'll see I shore had cause. . . . A year or more ago a cowboy rode down heah, bad shot up. I took him in without askin' questions. An' I pulled him through. He was about the likeablest cuss I ever met. We got to be good friends. Wal, his name was Hogue Kinsey an' he come from a good western family down below Ashfork somewhere. His father had a couple of bad years with drouth thet most cleaned out his cattle. They got pretty pore. Hogue had a sister he must have been plumb fond of. She fell sick an' to get her into a less high an' cold climate, Hogue stole a bunch of cattle an' sold them. Thet must have been several years ago. Anyway he got found out an' had to leave home. Hogue had a meek an' easy-goin' disposition, but he was quick tempered an' thet coupled with a handy knack with a gun put him on the road to the bad. If I'd had any money to hire thet boy, I could have saved him from livin' off this range. As it was I kept him heah a while an' then he drifted over Pine Mound way, where he hangs out with half a dozen boys slated for hell. Hogue hasn't been heah lately. He used to come often. Guess I cussed him an' argued with him too much. Shore they're stealin' cattle but in a two-bit way thet's not botherin' the ranchers yet. I reckon his outfit have stole a few haid from Pencarrow. But I'll add this in Hogue's favor. He's the only cowboy I know who never rode up to Pencarrow's door an' asked for a job."

"How do you account for that?" queried Wade, intensely interested.

"Wal, I reckon Hogue hasn't become hardened yet. He wouldn't ride for a cattleman an' steal behind his back. He remembers his sister an' mother too wal to be a cheat to the Pencarrow girls. Thet's how I figger him, Brandon. An' it's jest the time to get Hogue. Between us we can do it."

"Where is Pine Mound?"

"About thirty miles across country by trail. Much further by road. It's a sleepy little cattle town in winter. But shore hums in summer. All the outlaw outfits buy their supplies there, loaf an' drink an' gamble there. Fights an' killin's common. Pine Mound is on the stage road thet runs into Mariposa an' New Mexico."

"Locate the trail for me and I'll ride over there tomorrow," said Wade.

"Hadn't you better let me get hold of Hogue first?" asked the homesteader.

"I just want to take heap look round, as the Indian says. I'll not force my acquaintance upon Hogue or anyone. Still time and opportunity must not be slighted. . . . Can you get your Mexican friends here today?"

"I can call them from the rim. They live in a log shack not far from heah."

"Well, call them. Tomorrow you come to the ranch and stay until I get back."

"I was thinkin' of thet. . . . It takes a good rider five hours to make Pine Mound from heah. Ride east from the ranch till you pick up Dry Canyon. Go along the rim till you can get down. You'll find a trail. Foller it an' make yore time while it's not so rough. It haids out of Dry Canyon an' through the timber an' rock country down to Pine Mound. You cain't miss it."

"All right, Elwood. I'll rustle back now. I don't mind telling you that Hal and Rona did me a good turn when they talked about you."

"Bless them twins! An' what do you reckon it means to me? . . .

Wal! Wal! Brandon, you're a stranger, but you strike me deep. May these good things be!"

"Put on your thinking cap, old-timer," replied Wade, as he halted with his toe in the stirrup and gazed straight in Lightfoot's troubled blue eyes. "These good things are going to be!"

The dawn broke gray and soft, with a redness streaking over the sage. Bird and beast of the wild were out in force, scarcely moving to evade the approach of the fast-trotting horse. By the hour the sun rose Wade had descended into Dry Canyon and had found the trail.

Though water evidently ran there only in the rainy season the canyon was verdant and rich, full of pines and sycamores, and patches of scrub oak and thickets of manzanita. Fresh bear tracks on the dusty trail showed fresh deer tracks in their rounded depressions. Mockingbirds and jays and squirrels made music and clamor. Small bunches of cattle, wilder than deer, crashed into the thickets at Wade's approach.

The head of Dry Canyon closed almost abruptly with a jumble of splintered and weathered cliffs, through which the trail climbed in zigzags and loops. Once out on top Wade faced a slow descent through timber and sage. Arizona taught Wade its infinite variety of scenes, yet all characterized with that singular red and gray and purple, with a dry fragrance that was as exhilarating as wine, with a brooding solitude, a wilderness of space.

Wade could not have exercised more hawk-eyed vigilance had he once more been in familiar flight from pursuers. He saw the flash of the wings of birds far ahead, the movement of brush, the gray rump of a deer entering a thicket. Whenever he came to an open flat or a long line of trail ahead or the descent of a slope, he slowed his horse and took distrustful measure of rock and bush and tree.

Yet all the while, despite his habit of vigilance and the magnifying of his alert faculties to fit this new phase of his life, despite the grim hard deadliness to survive and to win, which he had deliberately heightened and intensified, he rode as one who had at last come upon the glory and dreams of fulfillment, of atonement, of salvation. The sacred promise to his father, which had so often spurred him on to heroic efforts, gained in the glamour of an adventure that called to all a man could feel. Fight and romance and love! It would take a terrible clash with the evil forces of that range to retrieve Pencarrow's losses and to make his range prosperous, his person safe, his family happy. It was romance because of its setting, its drama against the purple background of that wild sage country, its inevitable fierce and bloody action, its relation of one man to a persecuted girl. Wade confessed his love, breathed it out to the open and the solitude, revelled in all its dawning and exalting transformation, blessed the god of his wandering rides—the unerring fate that had given him the chance and power to pay his debt to the girl who had saved him. He asked no more than to save her if it cost his life.

A few squatters' cabins, and then a long-unused sawmill, and at last a ranch in a green valley, told Wade that he was approaching Pine Mound. At last he saw down its long wide street, with its irrigation ditches on the outskirts and lines of cottonwood trees, leading to the center of the town. Sleepy was the word to describe Pine Mound. Wade rode half the length of the street before he saw horses at the hitching rails, a couple of muddy-wheeled wagons, and several rough-clad men who stared curiously as he passed by.

A few more pretentious structures, old and weather-stained, and some sign of bustle and life, persuaded Wade that he had reached the center of Pine Mound. Dismounting he tied his horse and clanked stiffly into a high signboard-fronted merchandise store. Letters on the signboard had long been obliterated. The size of the store inside and the jumbled mass of its wares attested to the fact that it did business with a relatively large number of customers. Wade saw one woman and several men being waited upon. Then he was accosted by a sloe-eyed individual whose bland smile could not hide his curious interest.

"Mawnin', sir. What can I do for you?"

"I'm Brandon, from Cedar Ranch. Pencarrow's new foreman. Called to make acquaintance."

"Brandon! You're the—— Aw, yes. Pencarrow. We used to do business with him. Fact is, he still owes us a little bill.

"Yes. He sent me to pay it. I'd be obliged if you'll make it out."

"Glad to. New foreman, eh? Pencarrow on his feet again?"

"Solid. But he's not asking for more credit. From now on he'll pay cash. . . . I'll drop in again after I get a bite and a drink."

Wade strode out, aware that his presence had been noted and commented upon by the other occupants of that store. He had worn a cool brazen aloofness, not inviting either curiosity or civility. He strode down the gravel sidewalk, which was on a level with the street, and he did not miss anything there was to be seen. The old buildings were constructed of stone and adobe, and the newer ones of clapboards, some with the bark still on. There appeared to be only one other large store, which Wade entered. It contained a stock of merchandise similar to that of the first, only the amount was small by comparison. A proprietor or clerk sat by the door, tipped back in a chair, smoking a pipe. He looked friendly where the other merchant had been negative. Wade accosted him without preface:

"Do you know Pencarrow?"

"No. I never had no dealin's with him. You see I set up here after he quit buyin' in Pine Mound."

"Pencarrow will be buying again. I'm his new foreman, Brandon."

"Hod do. My name is Hicks. I seen you come out of the Mormon store."

"Mormon, eh? Who runs it?"

"Jed an' Seth Bozeman."

"I take you for a Gentile."

"You're takin' correct. An' here's where you should deal."

"Agree with you. But how will the Bozemans like that?"

"Wal, they've got aplenty of trade without newcomers to this range. An' they'd just as lief you didn't drop in."

"Oho, you don't say?"

"I do say, Brandon, but I'd be obliged to you not to let thet go further."

"I savvy. . . . Kind of a warm place for a Gentile, this Pine Mound, isn't it?"

"Pretty warm, yes. An' what's left of us will be movin' some day."

"Same old story. . . . By the way, Hicks, have you heard what happened out at Pencarrow's?"

"Nope. Ain't heared a thing for a coon's age. What'd you do?"

"I shot Urba and one of his gang."

"Urba! Hell you say? . . . Brandon, you won't be popular here."

"I'd rather be unpopular. . . . Does Band Drake hang out here?"

"About half the time, I reckon. Most all winter, anyway."

"And Harrobin?"

"Wal, he's here most of the time when Drake isn't."

"They don't get along together?"

"Huh. Not so you'd notice it."

"Hicks, I want you to be a friend of Pencarrow's and mine. Savvy?"

"Thet isn't hard to do. But you 'pear a pretty sharp-eyed gent. Not thet I'm not used to such! Only you're different. Brandon, you're not keepin' out of sight. You're lookin' for somebody."

"You're a bright fellow, Hicks. . . . I'll drop in again."

Wade found a little restaurant, conducted by a jolly fat Mormon where good cooking, no doubt, accounted for a motley group of drivers. Wade looked them over while he ate, and he concluded that a couple of cowboys and a backwoodsman out of the round dozen occupants might be given the benefit of a doubt.

"Ridin' through, stranger?" inquired the proprietress, as Wade paid for his meal.

"No. Just scraping acquaintance," replied Wade, in a voice that carried. "I'm Brandon, Pencarrow's new foreman."

"Glad to meet you. Come again," she concluded, heartily.

"Sure will. You're an awful good cook, lady."

Wade went out assurred of the fact that the name Brandon had struck hard on the ears of most of those men. His introduction to Cedar Range and Pine Mound had been one to incite hostility and caution in men whose vocations were doubtful. The success of his championship of Pencarrow depended on the fear he could instill and his ruthless reaction to every circumstance that arose. During his long rides he had thought out his best mode of procedure in every conceivable situation that might arise. In the past he had avoided gunplay until it was forced upon him; here on this range he must invite it. His strength lay in that alone. There could hardly be his match with a gun on this range. He had nothing to fear in an even break with Drake or Harrobin, or any of their crews. But that was only a small side to the risks he would encounter. Many a gunman had faced too many enemies at one time, or had been shot in the back or ambushed along the trails. Wade knew he had the training for this perilous job. And he had begun to feel mounting in him a passion of incentive that would become superhuman.

Pine Mound boasted more drinking dens than stores. The largest had a crudely painted white mule on the high board front.

Wade entered as if looking for someone. The saloon was like hundreds of others he had seen in the west, only there was a vague difference that did not come from the odor of rum and tobacco, or from the half score of noisy men lined up at the bar, nor from the rude drawings and letterings on the whitewashed adobe wall, nor from the card tables and gamblers at the back.

No one paid particular attention to Wade, from which he deduced that his arrival in town had not yet been noised about. But not improbably a loud argument among the gamesters kept attention from the entrance of a stranger.

At the moment two cowboys, young and lithe, with guns swinging and spurs jingling, their lean faces hot and hard, came striding forward, evidently in a hurry to get out.

"Rustle, you two-bit brand blotters!" called a harsh voice. "An' from today you stay out of Pine Mound!"

"Come on Hogue," called one of the cowboys, over his shoulder.

"I'm damned if I will," came the reply, ringing shrilly.

Wade's thought was as swift as his leaping pulse. As the group at the bar, silenced by this row, moved back, curiously, Wade intercepted the two cowboys to whisper coolly in their faces: "Don't show yellow!" And he spun them around to pass ahead of them. His startling action had halted them. "Jerry, who'n hell?—"

Wade was among the foremost of the curious onlookers that crowded back to the gaming tables. Some had been vacated by players, at others the gamblers stood up, their heads craned toward a group at the rear table. Wade saw a handsome flaming-faced youth confronting five men, three of whom were standing.

"Harrobin, you can't drive me off this range," he declared hotly.

"Look here, Kinsey," retorted a dark-bearded man who sat at the table, his hands covering a stack of cards and chips. "I've warned you before. You and your outfit will rustle or take the consequences."

"Bah! You can't bluff me, Harrobin."

"It's no bluff."

"But what have I done? Sure, you owe Jerry an' me money. An' we don't happen to be Mormons—"

"Cut that kind of talk," interrupted Harrobin. "If you'd done no more, you talk too much. Men get shot for that on this range."

"I daresay they do—in the back—or when they're not packin' a gun, as I'm not," flashed Kinsey, scornfully.

"Once more I warn you."

"Aw Hell! I'm not afraid of you, Harrobin. If I had my gun I'd call you right here an' now."

"Cowboys like you are always armed as far as I'm concerned," said Harrobin with cold voice and lowering scowl.

"If I gotta get off this range an' be murdered I've a right to know why," rejoined Kinsey, passionately.

"You talk too much."

"Talk?—Hell, you talk, everybody talks. When I told Band Drake—"

"Shut up!" hissed Harrobin, moving as if to sit back a little from the table.

Wade was swift to seize the opportunity made for him. He leaped out to draw his gun.

"*Hold!*" he yelled, like the clap of a bell. Then cold, measured, menacing he continued: "Don't move, men!—Careful, Harrobin!"

From a violent start the Mormon froze stiff. He had drawn his gun or had a hand on it under the table. Wade's posture, his colorless voice, his bladelike eyes left no room for conjecture.

"Don't shut up, Kinsey," went on Wade, curtly. "Your talk was damn interesting to another Gentile, one Tex Brandon. . . . Go on!"

The cowboy's lean frame strung like a whipcord. "Thanks, stranger," he rejoined quietly, his young face paling. "You bet your life I'll go on. . . . Harrobin, take this in your teeth. . . . You're sore—you're tryin' to hound me off this range—because I told Band Drake about the herd of C. R. Bar cattle you got penned in Green Canyon."

Harrobin turned livid under his dark scant beard. No power but the unknown quality of Wade could have stayed his hand. But his intuition, his wisdom, his experience were not so great as his fury.

"Much obliged, Hogue," rang out Wade. "C. R. Bar cattle. That's Pencarrow's brand. And I happen to be Pencarrow's new foreman. . . . Go on!"

"Aw! . . . Reckon thet'll be about all," drawled the cowboy, who, game as he was, turned white at the situation he had precipitated.

"Harrobin, I want that bunch of C. R. Bar cattle," demanded Wade.

"Kinsey's a liar," hissed the Mormon, malignantly. "No one will believe the sneaking lout. He and his two-bit outfit have run off Pencarrow stock themselves. I know. I've bought it."

"That so, Hogue?" queried Wade, never relaxing a fraction of his quivering readiness.

"Sure it's so. Who hasn't run off Pencarrow cattle? The fool rancher kept no riders to brand his stock. I never drove off a hoof thet wasn't a maverick. An' in Arizona a maverick belongs to the man who brands it."

"Harrobin, you stand corrected. I reckon you're the liar," snapped Wade.

"Brandon?—That your name? Pencarrow's new foreman, eh? . . . Ha! Ha! You'll last long on Cedar Range."

"Drop that gun on the floor," ordered Wade.

"What gun?"

"The gun you have in your hand."

"You're mistaken. I've no gun."

"Do you think any man with a gun in his hand could fool *me*? . . . If I hadn't interfered you'd have shot this cowboy in cold blood."

"I'll shoot him later," retorted Harrobin, who seemed wholly governed by passion.

"Like hell you will!" shouted Kinsey. "I can beat you to a gun any day, you black-faced Mormon!"

"*Drop it!*" thundered Wade.

Harrobin was not yet intimidated to the point of complying. His gaze betrayed a calculation of chances as opposed to releasing his gun. The instant Wade read that conflict of thoughts he took swift aim at the Mormon's right arm and pulled the trigger. The heavy colt filled the room with booming crash. A trenchant silence ensued. It was broken by the metallic thud of a gun striking the floor.

Wade stepped forward to shove the smoking gun almost in the faces of the five men. Harrobin sat rigid, ghastly, his eyes windows of hell. His four comrades were under a spell that gave evidence of a nervous break. Wade placed his foot against the table and gave it a tremendous shove. Table, cards and chips, chairs and men went down in a thumping heap.

"Kinsey, get outside," ordered Wade, beginning to back away, keeping the group covered. "Harrobin, I proved you a liar about your gun. . . . Well, throw it pronto if we ever meet again! Because I'll know then what I suspect now—that you're a cattle thief!"

CHAPTER TWELVE

"SAY, who are you?" drawled Hogue Kinsey, as Wade, leading his horse, halted under a wide-spreading cottonwood on the outskirts of Pine Mound. "I shore want to shake your hand—an' thank you heaps—but I'm not stuck on steppin' under this tree."

"Big shady tree. What's the matter with it?" replied Wade, finding a seat and removing his sombrero.

"Nothin' 'cept there's been a couple of hombres hanged heah."

"Hanged!" ejaculated Wade, his head coming up erect.

"Shore. Makes a fellow feel creepy. I don't mind bein' shot. Been winged a few times. But chokin' to death—kickin' at the end of a rope—in the air! I wouldn't like thet."

"Neither would I, Hogue," laughed Wade, remembering the years when he swore he would never dangle at the end of a rope. "All you Arizonans shy of a noose, eh?"

"Shy isn't the word, mister. Let's dodge the idee. I want to thank—"

"Dodge the thanks. But you've given me an idea, by heaven!" ejaculated Wade, with a swift snatch at the air.

"What'd you say your name was?"

"Brandon. Tex Brandon."

"An' you're Pencarrow's new foreman?"

"Yes. An' damn glad to meet you, Hogue."

"Wal, I'm glad too. I kinda like you, Tex. The way you laid it on to Harrobin! Thet was great. But out here, after it's over, wal, I don't feel so good."

"Why not? We're going to be friends."

"Thet so? You heard me tell Harrobin about Pencarrow's mavericks?"

"Forget it. That's past. We've all done some bad things we're ashamed of. I have. . . . Hogue, you're through training to be a rustler."

"Hell you say!" retorted Kinsey, his face flaming. But at Wade's keen steady look his eyes lost their hot, shamed resentment.

"Yes. . . . You were on the way. But I'm checking you up. . . . You're going to be my right-hand rider. You're going to persuade your outfit to throw in with me. I'll whip them into the hardest-riding, hardest-shooting outfit in Arizona. You weren't cut out for a cattle thief. You just got a wrong start, I'll bet. And you're sore. You've just drifted. Well, I don't need to tell you where you were drifting. But one thing you didn't know—any more than Harrobin or Drake—and that is you were due to run up against a new deal—a chance to square yourself—to turn honest and stay honest—to be able presently to help your Dad—and your sister—and to have them proud of you—proud of the name that'll come to you, just as sure as we sit here. . . . We'll retrieve Pencarrow's losses. We'll make his fortune. We'll clean out these pack-rat nests of rustlers. . . . *We'll* hang Harrobin and Drake!"

"My—Gawd!" gasped the cowboy, as if carried off his feet.

"How do you like the prospect?" flashed Wade. All his bitter youth came back at sight of Kinsey's face. If he had been given a chance like this!

"Like—it!—Say, man, you're loco—or you're bigger caliber—than ever rode to this range."

"Hogue, are you with me?"

"It takes my breath, Brandon. . . . It's a cowboy dream. My head whirls. . . . But the way you walked out to call Harrobin! . . . I got to believe my own eyes. Lord, if I only could. . . . But Pencarrow. I stole from him."

"Boy, Pencarrow's a Texan. Salt of the earth. You'll love him.

You'll start right by telling him straight. Then that'll be the end of your two-bit rustling."

"I've heard of the Pencarrow girls. Never seen them. But I'd shore be afraid—"

"Listen, cowboy. Wipe off your mind whatever rotten range gossip you've heard. Think of this. You'll be riding, fighting for two of the truest finest girls who ever came out here to make the West a better place."

"— —— it! Brandon, you're makin' *me* a better fellow than I am!" fired the cowboy, caught in the throes of mingled uplift and degradation.

"Nope. I just know what's in you, Hogue. Shake hands."

Kinsey had a calloused hand and a grip like steel. He was won. A blaze burned out the tears in his eyes. Something hard, like a shadow of viciousness, passed out of his young face.

"Brandon—I hope—you're not too late," he replied, brokenly.

"Never too late. I can tell you that. . . . Now, Hogue, what about this outfit of yours?"

"Wal, somebody has given you a wrong hunch. It's not exactly an outfit. Bunch of us been livin' together in an old cabin over here. Pretty sick of livin' on beef. An' just about ready for anythin', I'd say. Four of us you can gamble on. An' I reckon Kid Marshall could be worked up. But Rain Carter—I'm not guaranteein' him. I wouldn't trust thet hombre. He's an older fellow. Used to ride for Harrobin."

"When can I talk to this outfit?"

"Right away. Jerry an' Bill are waitin' for me. I'll call them, an' we'll ride out to the cabin."

Before the hour was gone Wade had presented his offer to Kinsey's comrades. The nature of it, the way Wade put it, had the same effect upon four of them that it had had upon Kinsey. Carter, a silent man, thin-lipped and shifty-eyed, manifested a slow amaze, a pondering thoughtfulness, but no eager excitement. His youth lay behind him. The others were all boys under twenty, and Wade had caught them at a critical time. He could as well have persuaded them to a crooked deal that would have made them outlaws. One by one they shook hands with Wade, awed by his force, yet ready to burst into whoops.

"Carter, you're an older man," said Wade, curtly. "I see you've got more to wipe out than these boys. But my offer holds for you. Only think well what you're doing."

"I been thinkin', Brandon," returned the other; and the fact that his glance was enigmatical and his face a mask settled in Wade's mind an unfavorable conviction. "I'll be ridin' my hoss over somebody's toes. But let 'er rip!"

"One last word, fellows, and get me straight," said Wade, uncompromisingly. "I'm giving you a chance to be honest. . . . To escape the noose! For that's what'll come to Arizona rustlers pretty pronto. I'm guaranteeing you work, board, horses and outfits, guns. And if you stick you'll be paid for your services. . . . But if any one of you ever double-crosses me he'll get the same I'm going to hand out to these rustlers."

"Pards," spoke up Kinsey, "Put thet in your pipes an' smoke it. I'm grabbin' this chance like a fellar who's bogged down in quicksand, when you throw him a rope. . . . An' I say to one an' all of you—an' you 'specially, Carter, if you're not shore—good an' straight shore—duck this deal right here an' now."

Carter sat with his head bowed, silenced if not visibly pale and tense like his comrades. After a moment's trenchant pause, Kinsey turned to Wade.

"Boss, it's a deal. May you never regret it!" he announced, coolly. "An' here's an idee thet just popped into my head. . . . Let's rustle down to Meadow Canyon an' drive thet herd of Pencarrow's back to his ranch. Harrobin will be nursin' thet sore arm an' his grouch for a few days. Some of his outfit are away. At what I can't guess. But they're away. An' Stranathon, who sat next to him, an' those other three hombres I don't know—they couldn't stop us if they did find out."

Wade was on his feet in excitement.

"Hogue, by heaven, what a great start!" he yelled. "I guess

maybe I didn't have you figured. . . . Boys, we're off. Tie on your belongings. You'll never come back to this scurvy shack."

Four days later before sunset, a long stream of tired dusty cattle filed into the lower end of Pencarrow's fenced pasture. And seven tattered grimy riders on lame horses wended their weary way toward the ranch house and the cabins.

Two heavy-laden wagons, one of them new, and a buckboard, had come along the road parallel with the lane, accommodating their movements to the slow walk of the riders. This was the Pencarrow caravan returning from Holbrook.

A wild whoop from the driver of that new wagon greeted Wade's ears and wakened him from utter exhaustion to a tremendous throbbing glow of delight. That yell emanated from Hal Pencarrow's lusty throat and heralded the singularly opportune hour of Wade's arrival.

"Boys, we're a scarecrow outfit," said Wade with a laugh. "But we needn't be ashamed to meet the Pencarrows."

But Hogue Kinsey was the only one to follow Wade across the green square to the ranch house. Surely that was the strangest and most all-satisfying ride of Wade's long career as a horseman. How deeply he felt the joy he would give Pencarrow! And when Wade saw Jacqueline stand up in the buckboard to let the reins fall and stare with great dark wide eyes, he felt no less the glory of a victor returning from the war. He did not look up again until he reached the wagon, when he stiffly dismounted and hobbled to the porch where Pencarrow stood, his white hair erect like the mane of a lion. Wade heard Kinsey's slow clinking step behind him.

"*Brandon!*" tolled out the rancher, sonorously. "Is thet you or a niggah?"

"Yes sir, it's me," replied Wade. "We must be pretty black and crumby. No wash, no bed, no grub—nothing but dust and meat these last five days. . . . I have to report, sir—"

"You shore look it. Never saw such ragamuffins! . . . Brandon, I reckon I can see, but I cain't believe my own eyes."

"I have a report to make, sir," went on Wade. "I just drove in four thousand head of cattle. Rough estimate. Most of them are yours. Harrobin rustled them from time to time. He kept this herd in Meadow Canyon. I lost a few on the way."

"Four thousand—haid!" gasped Pencarrow, hoarsely. "Harrobin! . . . Thet Mariposa rancher?"

"Harrobin may be a rancher over there. But here he is a rustler."

"My Gawd! . . . An' what's all the stock I saw as we come up the valley?"

"I drove the brush and canyons. Accounted for about thirty-five hundred head."

"My cattle?"

"Yes, sir. You can count on around eight thousand head."

"Man!—How'd you do this?"

"I made the acquaintance of this cowboy, Hogue Kinsey. He and his outfit of five riders threw in with me."

Kinsey clinked up beside Wade and removed his sombrero to disclose a dust-caked visage and narrow eyes of blue lightning. He might have served as a model from which to sculpture the hard rider of the West.

"Mr. Pencarrow, I reckon I want to come clean right here," he said. "Your man Brandon got me out of a bad scrap over at Pine Mound. He had to shoot Harrobin to do it, but not fatally, I'm sorry to say. I an' my pards have throwed in to ride for Brandon. We're the new C.R.B. outfit. We're gonna make cattle history on this range. Brandon will write it—an' shore in blood. . . . He got me an' my pards to see the error of our ways. . . . I've appropriated a lot of your mavericks in the past. I want thet understood."

"Appropriated?—What do you mean, cowboy?" queried Pencarrow, puzzled.

"Wal, I just branded your mavericks whenever I run across them. An' sold them."

"Brandon, what's he aimin' at?"

"Kinsey did not need to tell you," returned Wade. "But I'm glad he did. . . . You know the law of the Texas range, where the maverick had its origin. If you and I run cattle in the same range, and if I find an unbranded calf I can burn my brand on it. Kinsey's reliance on that law is farfetched, of course, because he did not own any cattle on this range. But that appears to be the free and easy way here in Arizona. What counts with me is that Kinsey has turned his back on such loose work and will ride for me."

"Wal, it counts more with—me thet he told me," replied Pencarrow, huskily. "Brandon, I'll heah all these particulars later. . . . I confess I'm—saggin'. . . . My laigs air weak as my haid."

Rona Pencarrow came running to her father.

"Oh Dad! I think he is wonder—ful!" she cried, hugging Pencarrow's arm.

At that instant Kinsey turned and saw Rona, certainly for the first time. Their glances locked. Wade trembled before that glance. Rona and Hogue became oblivious to the others, to time and place. Wade divined the mysterious and merciless youth and life which struck them blind and mute.

Jacqueline must have seen it, too, for as she came forward her glance followed Rona's.

"Rona, come with Dad," she said, her rich voice unsteady. "Mother has hysterics. . . . Brandon, wait please."

They went down the porch toward the living rooms. Wade turned to the stricken cowboy, and if he had ever felt grim humor and compassion and a feeling of brotherliness it was then.

"Hogue, come out of your trance," he said, "and go fall in the watering trough."

Hogue jerked up without a word and hobbling to his horse he took up the bridle and went plodding toward the bank. Wade sat down on the porch as if his legs had given way under him. What had he done? Then Hal Pencarrow plumped down beside him to save him from chaotic thoughts.

"Tex, what you think? I drove that new team and wagon Dad bought all the way from Holbrook," announced the youth, proudly.

"Hello, Hal. . . . You did? Well, by golly! I'll want to hear all about that drive."

"It shore was hell. Took us four days. I'll tell you—and I shore want to heah about your cattle drive. When you get rested, Tex. Dad thought you was a niggah. Wasn't that funny? But no wonder. . . . Did you see Jacque's face when she stood up in the buckboard?"

"Not distinctly, Hal. Reckon I couldn't see very well. . . . Why?"

"She knew you, and don't you forget it, Tex. I never saw Jacque look so much like that. We're all kinda dumb Texans—Dad all over again. But not Jacque. She's part Spanish. And if you do something that pleases her—something hard to do—Oh! what you get!"

"Hal, did you have—a good time in town?" asked Wade, catching his breath. He was not in any physical condition to face what Hal intimated.

"Did we? My—gosh!" ejaculated the lad. "I heahed Jacque say Dad didn't owe near so much money as he thought. He was so happy he just beamed. Rona said he was like our old Dad, when we was kids. Rona and me—we just went loco. We got sick from eating stuff, but that made no difference. I coaxed Dad out of a cowboy outfit. Guess? You bet. A 44 Winchester and a Colt 45. Dad was tickled when I told him I'd have to ride with you. But when Ma saw the guns she went into a conniption fit. But right then I cut my apron string. Mebbe Jacque helped. Oh, she was just grand. We'd have gone hawg-wild but for her. At that we stayed ten days in town, bought out all the stores, made lots of friends—Gosh! the way these western fellows tumbled before my sister!—and we came away leaving two thousand odd dollars in the bank. I heahed Jacque tell Dad. She handled the money. And I'm darned if saving that didn't please her more than all the clothes she got. . . . Tex, we owe this trip and all to you. . . . If I cain't tell you how we feel, by gosh! Jacque can."

Light quick steps behind Wade and the sense of a dynamic presence sent his blood surging.

"Hal, drive the buckboard down to the bar," said his sister, matter-of-factly. "Then hurry back to unpack the new wagon. Rona and I will help. After that long slow ride we shore need exercise. The old wagon can wait till mawnin'."

"I'll be back pronto," chirped Hal, leaping up to run to the buckboard.

"Miss Pencarrow, let me help," said Wade, rising as if his legs were no longer dead.

"Brandon, in the future we will dispense with the miss," replied Jacqueline, and she came close to him to look up with soft glad eyes, impossible to meet, and to try to shake the dust off his scarf which she found caked stiff. "I didn't dream cowboy work could be so hard. But of course you magnify it. . . . Your beard is all matted. You must be daid on your feet."

"I reck—I was," replied Wade, unsteadily. Her proximity bereft him of all save a masklike exterior.

"You must go to your cabin and clean up. I'll send some supper over to you. We fetched back a cook and a maid. Fancy that, Texas Brandon!—A nice fat Mexican woman and her daughter. Oh, we are on the road back to the proud Pencarrows. It worries me."

"That is just fine, Miss Pen—"

"Jacqueline," she interrupted.

"Oh, yes . . . Jac—que—line. . . . It's not so easy to say. . . . Please don't send me any supper. I'm too tired to eat."

"Some hot soup. You must have some nourishment. Dad will want you to drink mint juleps with him. But I'd rather you didn't."

"I am through with drink."

"That adds to my gladness. But heah I selfishly keep you. Go now. I'll fetch the hot soup myself. . . . You'll have plenty of time to remove all this grime and dust. . . . Do you remember the woman of the Scriptures who used her hair for that purpose? I feel I could do that for you."

"Don't—don't talk so—so wildly," returned Wade, hastily, stung to poignant speech. "You overrate my—my service. It was my duty—my work. Westerners are that way. What else have I done?"

"What *have* you done?" she flashed, and taking hold of the dusty lapels of his coat she gave him a little pull that was a shake as well, while she leaned to gaze up at him. Her breast just touched his, but enough for him to feel the quick swell of hers. It was not a mad weak moment for Wade. Nothing could have made him forget himself. Nevertheless it was terrible in that he shook like a leaf in the wind, that he had no quick barrier against this girl's gratitude, no sudden strength to hide the spell of her loveliness.

"Yes, what have you done?" she went on, after a long pause, during which she gave him a royal benefit of eyes that would have wrought havoc in him if they had not already done so. But they were close now, out in the open light, surrendering with all a woman's heart of simplicity and truth, gloriously dark hazel mirrors of a strong, sweet passionate soul.

"Dad is in there crying like a baby—unmanned as I never saw his misfortunes unman him. 'Eight thousand haid of cattle,' he repeats, 'an' cattle sellin' at thirty dollars, an' goin' to forty. An' I reckoned I was ruined.' . . . Mother is crying with him—happy for him and for us children. We kids had so joyous a time in town that I wept for them. . . . You saw Rona look at that cowboy. Oh, what have you done? She invested *him* with all the glamour of this day. . . . You saw Hal. That sensitive lad, melancholy, burdened by his troubles, transformed in a few days to a wild dauntless, gay youth, ready to fight for us. . . . And as for *me*—upon whom this splendid thing you've begun falls heaviest—because *I* feel that you have saved my loved ones. . . . Oh, Tex Brandon, what haven't you done!"

CHAPTER THIRTEEN

WADE crossed the green to the cabin in the afterglow of sunset. He lingered on his porch, wondering if that golden light was not unreal, if the strange buoyant elation that had dispelled his fatigue was not another illusion. But he was wide awake; the cattle were lowing in the distant pasture; the pines above his cabin swished in the cold night breeze; and the dark clear sky to the east proved that he was in Arizona.

Jacqueline Pencarrow, even more than her father, was generous and impulsive. She was still only a girl, and the visit to town, so long after isolation, with its rapture for the children, had stirred her deeply. Then to return home—find thousands of the Pencarrow cattle back on the range, to see her father break down, —these were enough to make any girl forget herself. She was doomed to radiate infinitely more than she intended. A smile, a word of rich feeling, a glance from her devastating eyes—these Wade felt must not be taken as intimate, as something peculiarly intended for him, because he had made her happy. Then he tried to dismiss the rebellious ecstatic sensations she had aroused in him.

For the rest he was happier than he had ever been in all his life. He marveled that he could stand there, watching the golden light fade, and feel so wonderfully warm—deep down in his heart. It was God, it was blessed; and he clasped the proof of it, and the stern ruthless past that had made it possible, to his soul.

A rustling step arrested his thought. "*Agua caliente, señor,*" came in soft accents, and a Mexican maid set a pail upon the step. Wade went in to take a hot bath, a luxury he had not indulged in for so long. His mind seemed gradually to lose its whirling activity and to slow toward oblivion. He was asleep almost before he got under his blanket.

When Wade awakened, the afternoon sun shone through the door he had forgotten to close. On the table stood a tray with dishes. This puzzled him until he recalled that Jacqueline had told him she would bring something for him to eat. She had come. She had entered his cabin to place the tray there, and she had found him in a dead slumber. The deduction had an unaccountable effect upon Wade. In a moment that uneasy rapturous trouble stirred within him.

"Boss, are you gonna wake up?" called Kinsey's slow voice. "You've slept seventeen hours."

"Devil I have! . . . Come in, Hogue, I sure was dead to the world."

The cowboy entered, his lean young face smooth and glistening.

"We all slept late. But thet was comin' to us," he said. "Cattle was pretty tired. They're still layin' down. Pencarrow was out tryin' to count them."

"Hogue, hand me that tray," said Wade, sitting up. "I'll eat my last night's supper for breakfast. . . . What's on your mind, cowboy?"

"Boss, I shore hate to be a quitter," replied Hogue with difficulty. "But I'm askin' you to let me go."

"Hell no, Hogue! Couldn't think of it. You're my right-hand man, the best of the hardest riding bunch I ever saw. . . . But what's the matter?"

"I'm ashamed to tell you," rejoined Kinsey.

"Never be ashamed to tell me anything. I'll understand. And I'll help you."

"Who was thet towhaided girl with the big eyes?"

"Last night, you mean. . . . Hogue, that was Rona Pencarrow."

"Did you see her look at me? . . . Did you hear what she said to her dad?"

"Yes. She's only a kid for all her height. Hogue, she was grateful, half beside herself. She said she thought you were wonderful. Well, so do I. It was a big thing to do, springing that on Pencarrow. I'm sure glad. All's clear ahead of you, Hogue."

"Will you let me go?"

"No!—Hogue, for heavens' sake, what's eating you? To flunk on a job like this! You're loco."

"Shore I'm loco. Thet's why I'm askin'. . . . But boss, don't—don't think me unfeelin'. My Gawd, I'd love to stay on here—to ride an' fight for thet—for them. Only I oughn't do it."

"Hogue!—I savvy. You hadn't met Rona when you came clean to Pencarrow—admitted you had been a thief?—Then, seeing that swell kid, hearing her defend you—it kind of shamed you?"

"I reckon thet's it—boss," replied the cowboy. "I'd turned my back on girls. . . . Thet last night—kinda jarred me."

"Small wonder. But you could not have done a finer thing. You can stand up now, and look any man in the eye—or any girl, even as fine a one as Rona Pencarrow. For in that act you got back all you had lost."

"Brandon, you make me see things clear," replied the cowboy, ponderingly. "An' I'm beholdin' to you. I'll deserve what you think of me or die tryin'. . . . But don't forget I asked you to let me go."

"I will forget it," rejoined Wade, earnestly. "Rustle back to the barn and round up the boys. I'll be there pronto."

"Boss, I forgot to tell you thet Lightfoot has been lookin' over the herd we drove in. Where does he come in?"

"Good chap, and sure a friend of ours. Cotton to him, Hogue."

After the cowboy stalked out with his clinking step, Wade sat gazing through the open door. "Doggone," he soliloquized. "That boy is a straight shooter. . . . It must be just as I feared last night. Rona is a powder magazine and Hogue is a flint, ready to spark. What will come of that? Jacqueline said, 'What haven't you done?'. . . . I don't know. All I know is that I've troubles of my own. Troubles I wouldn't miss for all the world."

Later Elwood Lightfoot met Wade to tell him bluntly: "Good

job. We'll loosen hell on this range. Those rustlers have it so easy an' are so rich they can afford to hold cattle for fattenin'. I never heard the like of thet in all my ranchin'. . . . Brandon, act pronto now. Cut out all the steers in thet herd—upward of two thousand an' all out on the range, an' drive them to Holbrook an' sell. Thirty dollars a head is worth more than two birds in the bush."

"Gee! that's an idea," ejaculated Wade. "Steers don't build up a herd. They're just fodder for rustlers. Old-timer, thanks for your second hunch. I'll pull that trick this very week."

"Pencarrow 'pears like he used to be. An' the twins! My Gawd, how they've bloomed over night! . . . Brandon, you ought to feel good."

"I do. I feel clean loco. I'm stuck on my job."

"Wal, it's one hell of a job, son. But you've started wonderful. You've struck fire from these boys. Didn't I tell you Hogue Kinsey was some hombre in the makin'? Thet cowboy will be great. His outfit will tear this crooked range wide open. But you will be a target for all the sneakin' riders Drake an' Harrobin have. Never forget thet. Keep in the open. The timber an' canyon trails mean death to you. If they can't kill you pronto, they'll sic a gunman on you."

"Have they any of those in their outfits?"

"Hard-shootin' riders, yes. But Band Drake is thick with the only real gunman in eastern Arizona. His name is Kent. He's a bad man. Hangs out at Holbrook. Brandon, you must be a hawk an' a wolf in one. Thet is to see an' smell danger. Your doin's are already sweepin' the range. But no one knows who or what you are. We haven't the time to let events build you a reputation. We've got to give you a terrible one an' set tongues to waggin'. I'll do thet. I can ride in on every outfit an' talk. An' I'll claim to have known you back in Kansas when times would make riding this range a picnic. All to throw the fear of death into these rustlin' hombres."

"Go as far as you like. Don't forget I shot my way out of Tombstone before I got here. But shooting would be too good for men like Harrobin. He's a thief here and pretends to be an honest cattleman at Mariposa, and no doubt other places. . . . Lightfoot, I'm going to hang Harrobin."

"Wal, by thunder! Thet's an idee. The old Wyomin' an' Nebraska law with cattle an' hoss thieves. I'll swear it'd do more to scare rustlers on this range than all the shootin' your outfit can do."

"Kinsey picked the tree for me," said Wade, significantly.

"Thet big cottonwood outside of Pine Mound?" ejaculated the homesteader.

"Yep. Sure a beautiful tree. Pity to desecrate it with a hangman's rope!"

"Right in their stronghold! . . . Wal, more power to you, Tex Brandon. I'll be ridin' home now.—See you soon, mebbe tomorrow. I want to give you a long talk about the open range. Kinsey swears you're shore at home in the woods."

"What about buying more cattle—that new stock to build up our herd. . . . But never mind now. Think it over. So long, Elwood."

Wade went out to take up the work at hand—so many tasks beside the great one, care of the herd. Pencarrow ordered the cowboys to report at the kitchen for their meals. He asked Wade to eat with the family, saying the invitation came at Jacqueline's suggestion.

"Thanks, indeed. But I had better eat with my outfit," replied Wade, soberly.

Early and late he drove the cowboys, and the harder he drove them, the better they liked it. The drama of this new range situation had seized upon their adventure-loving imaginations. They sensed events, stirring and dire enough for the wildest riders, out of which they would emerge heroes. They took avidly to Wade's plan to develop a notorious outfit.

The morning arrived when they were to start the big drive to Holbrook. Wade designated Jerry and Rain Carter to remain on the ranch and to keep the cattle out of the brush. Hal Pencarrow had been given his first job for Wade—to drive the wagon. With a gun at his belt and a rifle on the wagonseat the lad was in a transport. But he affected a studied pose of *sang-froid*.

Wade had seen the girls every day, though seldom to speak to. This morning before mounting his horse he approached Jacqueline, whose intent eyes kept him restlessly aware of her presence. She stood at the living room door with Rona, who had begged to go with Hal and looked brokenhearted at being laughed at by her father.

"Some day I'll take you, Rona," said Wade. "Wait till I learn the ropes. . . . Promise me you will not ride while we are away or stray far from the house."

"Yes, I promise. But why?"

"There will be risk from now on."

"Of what?"

"Bad riders hanging around the ranch."

Rona did not seem impressed. Her dreamy gaze had fixed on the lithe riders down the lane. It did not occur to her that she ran some risk from one of them, but that thought was in Wade's mind. He turned to Jacqueline, and as always when he looked at her squarely, he was shot through and through with the magnetic charm of her.

"Jacqueline, you will not ride while I am gone—and stay close to the house," he said.

"Is that an order or a request?" she queried with a tilt of her chin.

"I am—just telling you," replied Wade, frozen by her cool query. He divined the only possible way he could have offended, and that was to refuse the invitation to eat with the family.

"Are you my master?" she asked, with somber, unfathomable gaze upon him—a woman's look, to the wonder and peril of which he had never been subjected till then. He felt a quick strange shock.

"Jacqueline, it would not be safe," he replied hurriedly.

"Why not? I hate to be cooped in. I love to ride."

"Because I have enraged these rustlers who lived off this range.

Lightfoot told me they will hang around in the woods. They might kidnap you or Rona. Think how awful that would be! I told your father, but he left it to me."

"Indeed. How sweet of Dad! . . . And what are you going to do about it?" she challenged.

"I can only appeal to your intelligence, your good sense, your loyalty. Pencarrow has a new lease on life. A misfortune like that—a tragedy, for these louts are raw evil men, and they would make away with you—indeed, it would ruin Pencarrow, and it certainly would wreck the plans I've made for him."

"Oh, I see. You think a great deal of Dad, don't you?"

"Yes, and of all of you."

"Brandon, I would do anything you asked me to," she replied without flippancy.

"Oh! . . . Thank you—that relieves me," returned Wade, composed and staggered. "Good-by." And he turned to Pencarrow, who came out of the house with a packet of letters.

"How long will you be gone?" added Jacqueline.

"I don't know. We'll hurry. Believe me."

"If you meet John McComb give him my regards. He was very nice to Rona and me."

"I shall not forget," replied Wade, vaguely disquieted. Then Pencarrow claimed his attention.

"Letters to mail," said the rancher. "Here's three lists. Mine, mother's and the girls'. I shore wouldn't be in your boots. . . . Sell for the best price you can get. Buy complete outfits for yourself an' your riders, not forgettin' the Winchesters an' shells you mentioned. Heah's my bankbook. Deposit to my account. . . . An' rustle back, Brandon."

"Yes, sir. I want to buy a good field glass and to order a telescope. This is a wide long range. We need to see what's going on."

"Buy anythin' you need. Only keep track of it. You must account to Jackie for expenses. . . . Have an eye for Hal."

Wade made the drive to Holbrook in five days, a quick uneventful trip, without loss of steer or any appreciable weight of beef.

He found that his fame had preceded him. And he further stirred gossip and conjecture by stalking into saloons and gambling halls silently, but apparently bent on meeting some particular man. That night in the office of the little hotel he had some pertinent things to say about Band Drake and Harrobin. These rustler barons manifestly had other friends besides Kent in that community. Wade left bitter seed to germinate.

The herd of cattle brought nine thousand six hundred dollars. Wade kept out six hundred and banked the rest, a little business dealing that further set Holbrook by the ears.

"Boys," he said to the eager brown-faced quartet of riders, "here's some hard-earned coin, your first wages. But as you see, hardly enough to go on a toot. Remember now, Tex Brandon's outfit is on trial. Be on deck early in the morning to help me buy rifles, shells, saddles, bridles, spurs, boots, sombreros, clothes, bed-rolls, and whatever else we need."

"Brand new outfit—whoopee!" yelled the cowboys, and arm in arm, their spurs jangling and their high heels thumping, they paraded down the street.

Wade kept Hal with him, to the lad's obvious pride. Before that second day was gone Wade had met John McComb, a young merchant of the town, a dark, good-looking likable westerner. Wade had not found anything harder than delivery of the message to this Arizonan.

"Miss Jacqueline sent her regards to you," he managed to get out.

"She did! . . . That was kind of her," ejaculated McComb and he blushed like a girl.

Wade readily saw how the wind lay in that quarter and it gave him a queer sickening qualm. It was not surprise at evidence of another victim to Miss Pencarrow's charms. It must have been that she chose to remember this fine young fellow. Wade stored away in his mind something to face and fight out at a quieter lovelier time.

Late in the afternoon Wade and his riders started back on the return trip. He let Hal ride a horse and he drove the wagon. They were a merry party. They camped at a spring near the road and feasted on a broiled wild turkey Kinsey had shot from his saddle.

Next day, with the loaded wagon, the cavalcade could make only about twenty miles. On the following morning they started at dawn, intending to reach the ranch by night. Soon they were well down out of the heavy timber, within occasional sight of the purple range and the sentinel knolls and the red rim rocks.

With the riders ahead of the wagon and Kinsey in the lead, under strict orders to keep sharp lookout, Wade drove ten hours at a stretch, and then, where a rocky brook crossed the road, they halted to rest and eat. Starting again in an hour they ran out of the solid timber into the patches of oak and pine that dotted the gray range. The ranch was already in sight and the party was passing a thicket when two whiplike rifle reports, one close after the other, cracked out. Wade saw the puffs of white smoke. Hal's horse was shot from under him and a bullet knocked Wade off the wagon seat.

He lay on the load of supplies, not unconscious but stunned. Still he heard shrill yells from the cowboys and a volley of gunshots, then the crack of ironshod hoofs over rocks. Hal's pale face appeared.

"Oh, Tex! . . . You're alive!—I thought . . . they shot my horse. I got pitched hard. Are you bad hurt? . . . There were two that we saw. They hid behind the bushes—shot from their horses. Kinsey and Marshall chased them, burnin' powder. . . . Oh, you're so white!"

Bilt Wood joined Hal, standing on a wheel to look down at Wade.

"Boss, where'd they hit you?" queried Wood, sharply, his eyes fearful.

"Creased my head. . . . It burns—I'm dizzy. Call Hogue back," replied Wade, with sight waning. Then all went dark for him.

When Wade regained consciousness, it was dusk and he was being carried from the wagon. Excited whispers, a girl's low cry,

Pencarrow's deep voice told him where he had been taken. The cowboys laid him upon a couch. Some one lighted a lamp. Blood dripping down over Wade's forehead kept him from opening his eyes, and an impulse, of which he was perfectly conscious yet did not understand, kept him from speaking.

Pencarrow put a heavy hand on Wade's breast.

"He's alive. Heart all right," he said, in gruff relief. "What a bloody mess! Fetch water an' a towel, somebody."

"Dad, they shot my horse from under me," spoke up Hal, importantly. "I was in the air when I heard the second bullet hit Tex. The tumble dazed me, but I got up on the wagon wheel. Bilt did too. Tex lay back on the canvas. His eyes were wide open. He spoke. . . . Oh, Dad, it couldn't—have been. . . ."

"Hal's right, Mr. Pencarrow," said Wood, as the lad faltered. "Thet hombre bounced lead off Tex's head, sure, but it wasn't no brain shot."

"Hal," called Jacqueline, from the head of the stairs, "have the cowboys come back from town?" Then when the lad failed to answer her, quick footsteps sounded descending to the hall, entering the living room. "Dad! . . . What has happened?—Who—"

"It's Tex. He's been shot. We're not shore how bad."

She reached the couch. Wade felt her before she touched him. "Oh, my God!" she whispered low. Her hands fluttered on his head. "Where?—Show me where it—" She parted his wet hair. Her finger touched the wound and burned like a red hot iron. "It's—here," she went on, with agitation. "No hole, Dad! . . . A long furrow. . . . I feel the bone—smooth all the way."

"Wall now—thet's fine," exploded Pencarrow, thickly.

"Aw!" breathed Hal, as if unbearable oppression had been removed. And then excitedly, "Come in, Rona. I'll tell you all about it. Had my horse shot from under me. And Tex got hit."

Wade decided it was time to relieve these good people further: "Jacqueline, will you make sure my brains are intact?" he asked, clearly. "I can't dispense with any and hold down this job."

"Oh!" cried Jacqueline, startled.

"We thought you were unconscious. . . . Brandon, you just escaped. . . . It's only a scalp wound."

"I'm rather used to gunshots," replied Wade, wildly. "Will you please wash the blood out of my eyes?"

Presently Wade was able to see and the first face happened to be Rona's. It was pale and compassionate. She smiled gladly.

"Tex, you weren't so careful as you made me promise to be," she said.

"Rona, I sure wasn't."

Jacqueline asked Wade to raise his head. "Iodine. It'll hurt."

"I don't believe coats of fire would hurt at this moment," replied Wade, lightly. But his boast and his indifference were only a blind to hide the guilty tumult roused by Jacqueline's soft hands upon his head and face, her close fragrant proximity, her eyes that still caused the havoc of their first shock.

"Indeed you are not badly hurt," she said.

"Boss, you had a narrow squeak," interposed Bilt Wood. "I'll mosey along now with the horses."

"Where's Kinsey?" queried Wade, suddenly remembering.

"Last I seen of him an' Kid Marshall they was shore pullin' leather after them two hombres."

"Bilt, did you ever see them before?" asked Wade.

"I've an idea I've seen one of the horses. But, Boss, we'll know for sure pronto. Hogue an' Kid cain't be beat ridin' on the range."

The cowboy clanked out. Jacqueline finished bandaging Wade's head.

"Thanks. I'll go to my cabin now. Hal, will you lend me a hand?"

"Brandon, you will stay right here where I can look after you," said Jacqueline. "Hal, pull off his boots. Ronn, fetch a blanket and pillow."

Wade gave in gratefully. The truth was he did not feel too well. He had become conscious of a throbbing pain in his head.

"Here's your bankbook and receipt for expenses," he said to

Pencarrow, handing out a packet. "I sold for thirty dollars a head."

"Splendid—all out of a clear sky!" ejaculated the rancher, in glad amaze. "Brandon, it's almost too good to be true."

"Well, it's true—as true as this rustler brand on my head. . . . Pencarrow, the opportunity for you grows. Cattle on the hoof, beef, hides, ought to bring better prices all the time. The market grows. That Lincoln County War has deflected half a million head from the Kansas City and Chicago markets already this year."

"Brandon, you should say *our* opportunity grows," corrected the rancher, pointedly.

"Our! . . . Oh, I savvy. Sure. It's my chance, too. I think I've got an outfit of cowboys. Hogue Kinsey is a wonderful chap. I wonder about that Carter—"

"You must stop talking," interrupted Jacqueline, her cool hand going to Wade's hot face. "Dad—all of you get out of heah."

They left precipitously. She turned the lamp down and shaded the light from Wade's eyes. Then she drew a rocking chair close to the couch.

"You may be Tex Brandon, who has been shot full of holes, and scoffs at them, but all the same you are feverish," she said, softly. "You must go to sleep."

"I couldn't."

"Are you in great pain?"

"It hurts all right. But I'm used to that. I might sleep, if you left me."

"No. I'll stay heah, and be very quiet."

"Jacqueline, the man does not live who could fall asleep with you sitting beside him."

"Indeed, and why?"

"Do you need to ask?"

"Surely. Am I so—so disturbing?"

"Disturbing?" laughed Wade, a little wildly. "You are storm, wind, wildfire in prairie grass, chain lightning!"

"Well! A compliment—a doubtful one—from Tex Brandon at last. Thank you, even if it took a gunshot to get it out of you."

"Don't be sarcastic—or humorous at my expense," said Wade, realizing he was on the verge of a precipice. "It is not *my* place to pay compliments to Jacqueline Pencarrow."

"I do not see why, if they are sincere. I'd like to hear them."

"You—would?" he whispered, unsteadily.

"Yes, but not now. You're getting flighty. And if you *ever* pay me compliments I want you to be very clearhaided indeed. . . . Try to sleep now. . . . I will go. . . . But how can I if you hold my hand?"

"I'm afraid I don't—want you to—go," returned Wade, irrationally, and his eyes fell shut irresistibly. He felt himself drifting. His last sensation was that she ceased to try to withdraw her hand.

When he awoke the room was in deep shadow, the lamp turned very low. He was alone. Coyotes were wailing out on the range. Strange vague thoughts attended him until he drifted off once more. He roused again at dawn, sensing a presence, but fell asleep again. Next time he opened his eyes the sunlight was streaming through the window. His pain was less acute. The house was astir. He heard Mrs. Pencarrow berating Hal. "But you fool boy, why do you wear the horrid thing indoors, to bump into everybody? It gives me the shivers."

"Wal, Ma, you can't never tell when you're gonna need a gun," replied Hal, vaguely. Then the lad appeared at the living room door, bright-eyed and handsome.

"Howdy Tex, old-timer," he said, advancing with the cowboy gait he had assumed. "Jacque says you slept well. She stayed up all night with you, Tex. I'll tell you, cowboy, it's somethin' to have that girl for a nurse."

"No!—Hal, where'd she stay?" asked Wade, incredulously.

"Right heah in Dad's arm chair. She's gone to bed now to get a little sleep. Do you know, Tex, I believe Jacque likes you. I've seen a heap of men come and go heah. She couldn't see them with a telescope. Rona *was* crazy about you, too. But girls are funny. Last night she was more worried about Hogue Kinsey than you."

"Hand me my boots," said Wade, surcharged with energy. "I'll rustle for my cabin before the crowd comes in. . . . All right, Hal, if you want to help me over. Carry my coat and gun belt."

Wade made the distance to his cabin easily enough, but he was glad to fall on his bed.

"I've been out to the barn," Hal was saying. "Bilt was up early looking for Kinsey and Kid Marshall. Hicks rode out at daylight, so they said. Jerry troubled, restless—black as a thundercloud. Rain Carter gone."

"Gone where?" asked Wade.

"They don't know. And they're plumb curious."

"Run along, Hal. I'll want to know pronto when the boys get back."

"I'll send somebody with your breakfast, boss," replied Hal, and rushed off.

Midafternoon came with Wade unable to sleep longer, restless and suffering, worried about the missing cowboys. Jacqueline visited him a little while, to bathe his hot face with cold water, to soothe his pain and strangely ease his unrest. She had little to say and avoided his eyes. When she left him, prey to greater trouble of spirit, and insupportable longing for her presence, her touch remained to torture him.

Then Pencarrow and Lightfoot came in.

"Kinsey an' Marshall been sighted down the range," announced the rancher. "Reckon they're about heah by now. . . . How air you, Brandon?"

The tall homesteader stood over Wade and gazed down at him with narrowed eyes and grim smile.

"So you been an' gone an' done it," he said. "After all my hunch about your seein' them hombres before they seen you."

"Elwood, I didn't expect to be ambushed on our own range in sight of the house," protested Wade.

"Listen. This is Arizona. More desert-bred hombres will shoot you in yore doorway. Anywhere—any time—except when you meet them face to face!"

"I never will be surprised again," promised Wade, quietly.

"Some of them will hide along the trails, watchin' and waitin' while their pards run off a few more cattle."

"But they can't rustle cattle after dark. I tried it. Not in this country of canyon, rocks and thickets. In the daylight we'll see them. We've got the cattle in the open. I'll split my men in couples. We'll ride out before dawn or camp at the edge of the pines. Elwood, these thieves are going to ride square into rifle fire."

"Now you're talkin'. Play them at their own game."

"Heah comes the cowboys," interposed Pencarrow, from the open door. "Hal is with them. An' the girls runnin' from the house."

Wade expected just what he saw when Hogue Kinsey entered the cabin—a dusty weary cowboy, with hard, worn visage from the somber shade of which glittered eyes of fire. At sight of Wade they softened. Kinsey sat down beside Wade to take hold of him.

"Howdy, boss. Them boys told me just now. I never expected to see you alive after thet bullet knocked you off the wagon seat. I seen who shot you an' I went after him."

"Reckon I'm just as glad to see you, Hogue."

Jacqueline entered with Jerry, whose haggard face showed signs of softening. Evidently Jacqueline had heard something to make her tense and white.

Kinsey got up to look from Wade to Pencarrow. "I've a tough report. Shall I make it before Miss Jacqueline?"

"No," rejoined Wade, sharply, as he sat up. Turning to Jacqueline he said: "Please go."

"I asked Kinsey to tell me what had happened. He refused. I regard myself as a part of this Pencarrow outfit and I insist upon staying. I appeal to you, Brandon."

"It was only for your sake," explained Wade.

"Stay, Jackie. I like your spunk. An' it's time you were havin' a say in all my affairs," said Pencarrow.

"All right," went on Kinsey, swallowing hard. "Miss Jacqueline, I wanted to spare you some harrowin' details. . . . Jerry, suppose you tell your story first."

"Thet I will, an' short an' sweet," replied Jerry with fire in his eye. "Boss, after you rode off on your way to town Carter left us. I didn't see him till sundown. An' then he was shore queer. Next day he rode off alone. I waited, made a circle, took up his trail—an' caught him meetin' some riders in the woods. They had a long confab. I left before they got through. I didn't get very close, so couldn't recognize any of them riders, even if I'd known them. Thet night Carter talked queerer than ever, kind of pumpin' me. I got leery an' guessed he was up to somethin' slick. Like wantin' me to say I was tired ridin' for you an' lookin' for a bonanza. If he'd had an openin' he'd made me a proposition—I never knew what. Wal, next day he rode off an' didn't come back."

After a pregnant silence, Kinsey spoke out abruptly:

"Boss, it was Carter who shot you. The other man, Neale, one of Harrobin's riders, as we found out, he shot first an' shot at Hal. I seen them just a second before they pulled trigger. You bet they knew who they wanted to shoot at! . . . I spurred after them an' Kid followed me. They had about five hundred yards start. Kid an' I had the best horses, as I seen pronto. It was fifteen miles across thet sage flat. I reckoned we'd be in range before we got there. But we wasn't. They run in on the Pine Mound trail an' stuck to it. Rocks loomed on each side. We began to gain. The timber was open. If they'd split at Dry Canyon an' gone into the brush we'd lost them. But they appeared hell-bent to get somewhere. They began to shoot back at us, usin' their rifles. Kid an' I kept our fire. We had our new Winchesters full of shells, an' it shore looked bad for Carter an' his pard."

Kinsey wiped the sweat from his face, coughed, drew a deep breath and resumed his story.

"We gained, an' their bullets began to spang off the rocks under our horses' hoofs. So I told Kid, who's the best rifle shot, to open up. He missed half a dozen shots. Then I couldn't stand it any longer. My second shot piled Neal up an' his hoss ran off the trail. We kept on. Carter used up all his shells, threw away his rifle, an' pulled his gun. We knew we had him then an' we let him shoot. Meanwhile we drew close to Pine Mound. I tried to keep Kid from shootin'. I had an idee of my own. But finally Kid broke a laig of Carter's horse. The fall stunned Carter. We got off, took his gun an' what he had on him before he came to. We mounted an' I told Kid to loose his lasso. I did mine. Carter seen thet, an' yellin' like a madman he plunged for the brush. I roped him. . . ."

Here Kinsey broke off, with an expulsion of breath his pallid face working. "Boss, I don't like—to tell the rest—before Miss Jacqueline."

"Go on Kinsey," spoke up the girl for herself, with spirit. "I want to hear every word. These men tried to kill my brother. They almost killed Brandon."

The cowboy, evidently strengthened from a weak and sickening spell, went on in short jerky exclamations.

"I roped him. . . . Rode down the trail. . . . Didn't look back. . . . I came to—that big cottonwood—outside Pine Mound. . . . I jumped off. . . . Kid was right behind. . . . He piled off. . . . Carter was floppin'—like a chicken with it's head cut off. . . . We hanged him—tied the lasso. . . . Carter kicked somethin' terrible. . . . When he quit—I wrote some words on a piece of paper—an' fastened it to his vest button."

Jacqueline turned away to the window. Pencarrow expelled his breath loudly.

"Kinsey," he said, hoarsely, "it was an extreme action. . . . But I must uphold you. . . . Brutal—just!"

"Wal, I say good!" ejaculated Elwood Lightfoot, harshly.

"Kinsey heard my plan," flashed Wade. "I'm responsible. He obeyed orders. . . . Hogue, what did you write on that paper?"

"Warnin' to rustlers. Harrobin an' Drake beware!" replied the cowboy. "But thet wasn't all Kid an' I did. By thet time we was shore mad. We hid our hosses an' went on in to Pine Mound. I'm not sure what was in our heads—maybe unloadin' our guns if we had half a chance—but it darn soon got knocked out."

Jerry said: "Don't forget what we found on Carter."

Then Kinsey produced a large roll of dirty greenbacks which he handed to Wade. "Boss, Carter took this to double-cross you."

"Keep thet," replied Wade, sharply, moving it aside. "Divide it among the boys."

The cowboy let out a nervous laugh, devoid of mirth, hard, metallic, and again he breathed like a man with a weight on his chest.

"Yep, we had any hifalutin' idees knocked plumb galley-west. . . . Boss, we run smack into Harrobin an' Band Drake, with a bunch of men, in front of Bozeman's store. Harrobin spotted us. Half an eye could have seen we'd been ridin' hard."

" 'Hullo there Kinsey,' sang out Harrobin, most damn curious an' mean. He would have drawed his gun then—an' got bored for his pains 'cause I'd have beat him to it—but for Drake, who called him an' stepped between. I'd sold Drake cattle, an' I used to take letters to a girl for him. Drake always liked me.

" 'Let me do the talkin', he said. 'Hogue, what's the idee, bustin' in here, lookin' as if you'd played up the range?'

" 'Kid an' I been trailin' some cattle,' I said, offhand-like. 'Lost their tracks out here close. An' we come in for a drink an' some grub. Mr. Drake, did you happen to see thet bunch of steers?'

"You should have heard them haw! haw! All except Harrobin. They was in a good humor. Been tippin' at a bottle. But Harrobin was sore. He had his arm in a sling, an' I reckon sight of me recalled how he got thet injury. But I've half an idee he doesn't know yet thet we rustled the cattle he stole.

" 'Cowboy, you get thet drink an' mosey without the grub," said Drake. 'Onhealthy for you here.'

" 'All right,' I said. 'We'll mosey, an' much obliged.' . . . Then

Harrobin stepped out, black as the ace of spades. 'Kinsey, is it true you're ridin' for Pencarrow?' he asked me. I told him yes, that we'd got a good offer, an' bein' tired of starvin' we took it up. . . . 'Thet's all right, if you want to risk it,' he went on. 'But keep out of Pine Mound. I'll let you off this time to take a message to your boss, Tex Brandon.'

"'All right, sir. I'll take it,' I chirped, glad to get off so easy. . . . 'Tell Brandon,' lit out Harrobin, 'thet Blue has throwed in with me an' thet Holbrook Kent has come with him!'"

"Blue!" echoed Wade, curiously, a bolt shooting back on a door of memory.

"Shore, Blue," interposed Pencarrow. "Drake's real name is Rand Blue. I forgot to tell you. He hails from the Panhandle of Texas. Bad man. Ran a rustler gang in Colorado. Came to Arizona under the name of Drake. He lived at Windsor for a while, posed as a respectable cattleman. Cut quite a swath. Sold me this ranch an' cheated my eyes out—an' at the same time had the gall to try to win Jacqueline."

"Dad Pencarrow!" burst out Jacqueline, heatedly. "So that was it! You never told me."

"Wal daughter, I didn't know so much then as I learned later. Aulsbrook was mixed up in it. I know now he put Drake or Blue on to me to do me dirt. I wiped it off my mind. . . . But Band Drake is really Rand Blue."

"Wal, the throwin' together of those two rustler outfits is turrible bad news for this range," put in Elwood Lightfoot, gravely concerned.

"Boss," interposed Kinsey. "I knew Drake was or had been Blue. But names mean so little out here. I never thought to tell you."

"*Rand Blue!*" whispered Wade, overwrought beyond his strength. The faces before him strangely faded. He seemed left alone, forced back into the past.

CHAPTER FOURTEEN

IN HIS own mind Wade corroborated Elwood Lightfoot's fears. Rand Blue and Harrobin, with picked riders and the choice of all the rest of the riffraff of the canyoned range, would be too much for any cowboy outfit under any leader. That was the logical way to figure it out.

"No!" muttered Wade. "I'll make figures and facts lie!" His incentive and motive were too great to allow failure to stay an instant before his consciousness. And he began to think as if he had never before exercised that faculty.

He was out of doors and around next day, but did not feel fit for the saddle. In truth he would have stayed in bed but for the fear—the yearning hunger which was worse than fear—that Jacqueline would come to him, a ministering angel, a generous-hearted girl who placed too high a value upon him.

The cowboys had orders to ride out before dawn and return after dark. Wade climbed the nearest knoll and watched the range with his glass. He could not cover the important flats and swales. He saw no riders and but few cattle. The day dragged. When he could stay out no longer he returned to his cabin to find wild flowers on his table. Jacqueline had been there. The golden columbines, that must have come from the green depths of the canyon, seemed to speak to him. Later Lightfoot called and told him that he had fetched the columbines to Jacqueline. She must have picked the bluebells herself.

The homesteader was gloomy. He advised an immediate sale of all Pencarrow's cattle. Wade agreed that would save a good deal of money, but it would make the rustlers master of the situation.

"I'm not cattle wise, Elwood," said Wade, "but I can't see that. . . . If Pencarrow sold out how would that effect this range? It's free, you know."

"It'd be bad. Aulsbrook an' Driscoll would throw their herds up here. An' they'd be hard to dislodge."

"Wouldn't Harrobin and Drake . . . I mean Blue—wouldn't they clean out other cattlemen the same as Pencarrow?"

"They never have."

"Hell you say! That's strange."

"Wal, it always struck me queer. Aulsbrook never lost cattle enough to appreciate. He was friendly with Drake when Drake was lordin' it around Winslow. Driscoll, though, has been hard hit at times, but never cleaned out."

"This cattle game is sure queer—and as crooked as a rail fence," muttered Wade.

"Shore it is. An' I reckon for Pencarrow to sell out would be equivalent to quittin'."

"A Texan quit!—You couldn't make him. And Jacqueline and the twins are as game as he is. That's not the way, Elwood."

"Wal, there *is* only one way as I can see. More cattle an' more riders. An' fight these rustlers tooth an' nail!"

"*Ah!*" It was a sound like a gasp.

"What's the matter, son? Did you hurt your head, jerkin' up thet way?"

"Yes," lied Wade, confronted by an appalling temptation. The old cattleman had solved the problem of the Pencarrows. More cattle—more riders—and fight! Wade remembered the fortune in tainted money he had hidden under the floor of his cabin. He could buy fifty thousand head of cattle—more if he wanted to—at a price far cheaper than the future would ever offer. He could quadruple Hogue Kinsey's hard-riding outfit and rid the range of these parasites. He could save the Pencarrows—make their fortune. But at the price of dishonor. He had been a robber. He still held a robber's ill-gotten, bloodstained wealth. And on the moment Jacqueline's magnificent eyes seemed to shine intent upon him, wondering at him, marveling in her faith, betraying more than gratitude. No! Never that way! She would loathe him if she ever found out. And the old specter of recapture stalked out with the memory of Rand Blue. That traitor had put the ranger hounds upon the trail of his father. They had tracked him to his death. That called for revenge. Of all men, Wade knew Blue would be the one to recognize him—to have a pack of rangers yapping at his heels.

The homesteader left Wade to his strange gloom, no doubt accounting for it by the head wound. Presently it was broken by Jacqueline's quick soft tread on the porch, her pale face in the doorway.

"Brandon! How—are you?" she panted. "Elwood said you looked and talked strange—that your head hurt."

"I reckon I'm—all right," replied Wade, which was a half lie. And he closed his eyes because he had not the courage to look at her. Then he lay there silent, quivering under her soft cool hands as she bathed his hot face and re-dressed his wound. And he strained in a torture of happiness. If he had not been an outlaw, beyond the pale—if he had not owed her more than his life—if fate had not placed him in such an insupportable situation, great if he were great enough to fulfill it—he would not have been at the mercy of a love that made her touch bliss. She left him in the dusk as he feigned sleep.

The cowboys had no report to make which was favorable. The next morning Wade's fever had left him. After breakfast, which the maid brought, he took his glass and went to a farther and higher knoll, from which he could command a view of half the range. It was pleasant and lovely there high up among the pines. He found that he loved this wild, gray, rocky, canyoned, purple Arizona land. The bluebells smiled out of the brown mats of needles, the white grama grass moved in the gentle breeze, the pines sang their soft swishing song, with its eternal note of sadness, the sage stretched away to the black-belted mountain, looming grandly, and to the dim hazy mystic desert with its specters.

Wade sighted strange riders that day. He saw dust clouds over the rolling ridge. At night Kinsey sought him with the news that he and Kid Marshall suspected the rustling of cattle off the far side of the range. Wood and Hicks had been across there, but had not yet ridden in.

"Keep under cover and watch," said Wade. "Shoot if any riders come in range. It's all we can do until I find a better way."

Jerry and Hal, hiding along the cedar belt, had seen no riders. Later Wood and Hicks rode in on lame horses. They had surprised a bunch of rustlers in a brazen raid, driving cattle toward the Holbrook road.

"We emptied three saddles emptyin' our rifles," said Bilt, with dark elation. "Then they bore down on us, six or eight of the bunch, an' tried to head us off from the ranch. Shore we had a ride for ten miles."

Wade was fired anew with that report. His riders began to loom in his sight, cold-nerved, matchless horsemen, imbued with fighting spirit. They were a supreme outfit in the making. As they sat in the starlit night, with cigarettes glowing like sparks, their lean faces clean-cut and cold, Wade talked.

"Boys, the odds seem to be a hundred to one against us. Ranchers on this range wouldn't give two-bits for our cattle or our lives. But I can't see it their way—I can't. Sure I'm burning deep down. All the same I'm thinking hard and clear. *Quien sabe?* Who knows what we can do? *I* know and *you* know. It depends on us—our eyes, our ears, our brains. I tell you, see everything, hear everything and beat these rustlers to it. Outfigure them! Get the jump on their thoughts! They are all slow thinkers. Ride and hide like men who are being hounded to death. And shoot first, as Wood and Hicks did today. . . . For the rest, practice your draw.

"Practice—practice—practice! Use your rifles. Learn their range and accuracy. Shoot at every jack rabbit, coyote, wolf—every sailing hawk you see, when it is safe to shoot. And be deadly about this practice, as if your lives depended on every shot, as indeed they do. Above all *never* be surprised. I repeat, always see the other man first. We've got shells enough for an army—we've got the swiftest horses on this range. . . . I tell you what I can't explain. I feel what I can't prove. . . . We'll kill a lot of these rustlers. We'll hang Blue and Harrobin."

"Boss, how about Holbrook Kent?" queried Hogue Kinsey, slowly.

"He will be my job."

"I've seen Kent. Little man, lame from a bullet still in his hip. Not young. Face full of deep lines. No beard. You won't believe it. He's cockeyed! An' supposed to be lightnin'-swift on the draw. Must be, for he's credited with eight men. While I was in Harrobin's camp one night I heard Blue had a hold of some kind on Kent. If thet's so Kent will be bracin' you right here some day."

"Thanks for the hunch, Hogue. I'd prefer to meet him at Holbrook, or anywhere but here."

"Boss, Kent is a real hombre," spoke up Kid Marshall. "He'll come out in the open, if he's gonna fight you atall. But as for the rest of them fellars, I say fight them Indian fashion."

"Ahuh. Like Hicks and Wood did today?" rejoined Wade.

"We shore did," spoke up Wood with fire. "Boss, mebbe you didn't know Hicks is part Apache. He's the best man with hosses, the best tracker, the slickest in the woods thet I or any of us ever seen."

"Hicks, are you really part Indian?" queried Wade, strongly interested.

"Half-breed, boss," replied Hicks, simply. "Born in Tonto. Crook got me when I was a boy. I ran away from the reservation."

"Well!—Hogue, I'm just getting acquainted with my outfit."

"Boss, we'll shore make this range hum. . . . Cowboys, it's late. Let's turn in."

"Good night. I'll be riding with you in a day or two," returned Wade, and wended a thoughtful way toward his cabin.

After breakfast next morning Wade resumed his seldom neglected practice of the swift drawing of a gun. He had a mirror here to look into which helped considerably. He found that even the few days of neglect had slowed his draw perceptibly. He was stern at this task when a gasp and a little rich laugh at his back made him whirl. Jacqueline and Rona stood framed in the open doorway, contrasting pictures of young and beautiful womanhood. Rona looked awed while Jacqueline wore a fascinated smile.

"Mawnin', Brandon. We saw you just now and wondered if we could slip up on you. . . . Suppose *we* had been rustlers!"

"Good morning, scamps," drawled Wade. "Rustlers wear spurs and boots. They can ride, but not walk—at least not like two slips of girls with pretty little moccasined feet."

"Rona, this man has actually paid me two compliments. . . . Let me hold your gun, Brandon? I saw you move but couldn't see the gun come out. I heard the click."

Wade handed the heavy Colt to her, butt first. She took it, not gingerly yet with dilated eyes.

"Why, the trigger is gone!" she exclaimed.

"Surely. I don't use one."

"But how can you shoot? What makes the hammer fall?"

"I thumb it. Let me show you. . . . See? When I grab the gun my thumb fits over the hammer. The weight of the gun, thrown like this . . . snaps the hammer from under my thumb. So the gun is really fired as it is thrown."

"I couldn't see. How swift you are!—But never mind it again. Sort of chills me. All that magic just to kill some man!"

"Not at all. You have it wrong," replied Wade, his voice a little stiff. "All that is a matter of self-preservation, and perhaps, incidentally, to save some one else now and then."

"Forgive me," said Jacqueline, hastily. "It repelled me—made me remember Uncle Glenn. . . . I'm not quite so stupid when I think."

"Jackie, *I* think he's won—der—ful," piped in Rona, big-eyed and romantic. "Hal is learning to draw. He showed me. Let me try. I dropped the darn thing on my foot."

"If it was loaded I'm surprised at Hal," said Wade, gravely.

"No. It was empty. Hal showed me. He told me you'd given him his first lessons. He said Hogue wasn't so awful swift as you but he was shore swift."

"Hogue?" inquired Jacqueline, a little severely.

"Yes, Hogue," retorted Rona, with a flaming blush. "I cain't go around calling all these cowboys mister. Don't I call Mr. Brandon by his first name, Tex?"

"That is quite different, Rona."

"Sure it's different. So much that *you* never call him Tex," flashed Rona, and ran off in a huff.

A moment's awkward silence followed.

"Rona is growing up," said Jacqueline, thoughtfully. "I'm afraid I cain't manager her any longer."

"She's all right, Jacqueline—a good, lovable, spirited girl."

"Lovable! That's the trouble. Rona is perfectly adorable. I don't mind that. But she's awakening. I've caught her actually making eyes at Hogue Kinsey."

Wade laughed at Jacqueline's tragic intonation.

"What could you expect? What could Pencarrow expect, bringing you pretty—and adorable girls out here to this wild Arizona. Where cowboys are wild, won—der—ful as Rona says, and hungry for love. If I were a girl like Rona I'd fall in love with Hogue."

"Oh! . . . Dad would rage. And Mother—she'd have a fit. And I—"

"Jacqueline, they should have left pride of blood back in southern Texas. . . . I see your point. These wild cowboys are all right to drive your cattle, risk their lives—and lose them sometimes—fighting rustlers. But they are not fit to make friends of—or sweethearts, or husbands."

"Brandon! How bitter you are!" she exclaimed in amaze, and a ruddy color swept up under the golden tan of her skin. "You never spoke that way before."

"Indeed, I forgot myself. But I do think Hogue is a wonderful fellow. His wildness won't make him any less attractive to a young girl like Rona. I advise you to keep her where she can't see him."

"I'll try," she returned, not composedly. "I'm sorry if I offended. It's fine the way you speak up for Hogue. If Rona were my age I—I wouldn't feel such dread. But she's not yet sixteen. . . . To fall in love at that age—with one of these wild-eyed devils—why it'd be terrible. You must help me to prevent it."

"*I!* What on earth can I do?"

"Oh dear! What can anyone do?" wailed Jacqueline. "That cowboy looked at me one day—Oh! I—I could almost love him myself. And Rona! She's got Spanish blood in her, too, and not a very strong haid."

"I can discharge Hogue if you say," rejoined Wade, coldly.

"Certainly not. Brandon, I don't understand you today," she said, in perplexity, and not far from being nettled. "But indeed you have been strange and aloof lately. I forget your injury. I'm not reasonable or kind. Let that annoying subject go for the present."

It was almost beyond Wade's powers to resist her sweet amends—her earnest eloquence—and he never would have succeeded had he looked at her. Doubt ceased right there. She liked him, respected him, wanted him to be her friend, and she had no idea of her devastating charm.

"What I really ran down here to see you for was to ask you to come to dinner tonight."

"That's—very kind of you," he returned haltingly.

"I baked an apple pie. I'm very proud of my southern cooking. Do you like apple pie?"

"Do I. . . . My mother used to make it," he replied.

"Then you will come? Indeed you must, for I've told them all I'm having you."

"Thank you. I'm sorry. . . . I must refuse."

"What!" She appeared utterly astonished.

"I can't come. It's kind of you. . . . I'm only one of your cowboys."

"Absurd!—That can't be your reason. . . . You won't come?"

"No."

"I shall never ask you again."

"That will be well."

"Brandon!" She was bitterly hurt. Her eyes blazed clear dark fire. "That range gossip about me! . . . Could *you*. . . . Oh, you'd insult me."

"Not meaningly. I never heard that gossip until you told me. Then I despised it. . . . But all the same, there's one range rider who is not going to add to your list of miserable victims."

"And that's you?" she flashed, with incredulous scorn and passion.

"That's me," he said, cold and weary with deceit and shame. But he met her eyes, strong in his abnegation, upheld by his secret.

"Oh!—to—to think I—" she cried, brokenly, in distress. Then she drew herself up fighting to regain her pride. "Because you did not hound me like Band Drake or those other—miserable victims—I wanted you to be my very dear friend—my *only* friend in this dark wild land. . . . I am indebted to you for showing me my mistake."

She turned and with head erect and rapid pace she left Wade standing there, sick in his soul, a miserable victim indeed, yet sustained by the consciousness that only then, in that moment when he attained mastery over himself and love and temptation, had he become worthy of the regard she had felt and that he had destroyed.

Like a violent storm that ordeal passed over Wade, leaving him free of the glamour, the weakness, the shame of his position at Cedar Ranch. All the strength engendered in him, the bitter laurel of victory over temptation, the great love that had come, found a sustaining anchor in a single ruthless purpose which went even beyond the saving of Pencarrow and his family.

Before he had recovered sufficiently he went back to riding with his cowboys, to suffer and reel in his saddle, to pant wet and hot in the shade of cedars, to refuse their entreaties of their assistance. Early they rode out and late they returned. Wade had given Hal the job of scout, watching every day with a field glass from the highest knoll on the range. Before sunrise each morning the riders would leave Hal to climb alone to his post, and after dark they would pick him up.

Wade changed the plan of splitting up his riders into couples. Now they all rode together, no longer drivers of cattle but hunters of men. Day by day, here and there on the range, rustlers made swift raids of a few cattle, always driving into the woods or down into the canyons. Hal reported most of these movements and distinguished one group of rustlers from another by their horses. Blue and Harrobin had not yet graduated to the dark-garbed riders and the dark horses adopted by the king rustlers of the eastern ranges. Stealing had been too easy for them in Arizona. No doubt there were several outfits of cattle thieves who were operating in a small way in their own interest.

Before that month was out Wade and his riders, guided by the half-breed's watchless tracking, surprised one of these outfits in the very act. One of them lived long enough to confess his gang had no connection with Drake or Harrobin.

Before midsummer was over, Wade's riders had chased other outfits off the open grazing land. In these instances Wade satisfied himself with seeing a few crippled riders escape, and a riderless horse now and then go galloping off with bridle and mane flying.

But still the herd diminished perceptibly in number.

Late in August the homesteader brought news that made Pencarrow whoop and Wade nod his head as if he had been looking for it. Driscoll had been cleaned out of cattle and Aulsbrook had been reduced to a few thousand head of cows, yearlings and calves.

"I shore knew Rand Blue would rob Aulsbrook some day," roared Pencarrow.

"Thet was the new combine operatin'," said Lightfoot.

"Boss, it means Harrobin's new outfit are stockin' up for the winter," added Hogue Kinsey. "No rustlin' after the snow flies. An' thet'll be pronto. They'll hole up down in the brakes, an' loaf an' gamble an' eat and drink the winter away. I spent one winter with his old outfit. They like hot fires an' plenty of beef."

"Where can they sell?" queried Wade, with exasperation. "Thousands of branded steers!"

"Easy as pie," snorted Lightfoot. "Those hombres have more buyers than they need. Like as not they won't ship a hoof."

"Suppose Aulsbrook and Driscoll were to throw their outfits with mine and we'd trail those stolen cattle?"

"Wal, if they would, it'd be most damn interestin'. An' it might lead to ranchers who never ask questions an' government beef buyers who don't care where they get cattle so long as the price is low."

"What a business!" ejaculated Wade. "What easy living for cattle thieves! And easy profit for crooked ranchers! . . . But it won't last forever on this range."

"Brandon, we'll need to send to town for winter supplies," said Pencarrow. "We'll not be snowed in till November. But there's no tellin'!"

"Make it as late as you can risk," replied Wade.

"Winter will come early an' be a hard one," interposed Lightfoot.

"Bitter up on the divides," added Pencarrow. "But we're low down heah. Snow doesn't lay long. It's an ideal winter range. Only hard on the womenfolk. So lonely."

"Then presently we can count on being shut off from rustlers for a while?" queried Wade.

"Pretty soon now. An' for six months. I reckon Blue an' Harrobin are through right now for this season."

"I can't gamble on that," returned Wade. "Besides there are other outfits of rustlers."

"Have we lost much stock lately?" asked the rancher, gruffly.

"Not that would count, if we had a big herd," said Wade evasively.

"An' what have you an' yore riders been doin'?"

"Riding early and late. Hiding out. Trailing tracks. Chasing rustlers."

"Wal?" rasped the Texan, sitting up to glare at his foreman.

"I've withheld reports because they are insignificant. But—" rejoined Wade, and briefly told facts.

"Ha!—By gad, an' you call thet insignificant!"

"Whew!" whistled Elwood Lightfoot. "Brandon, you're more than makin' good my brag. Thet'll spread over the range an' through Arizona."

"Pencarrow, we can take care of a big herd as easily as a little one," said Wade, spreading his hands. "I've a bunch of Indians in these cowboys."

"We'll buy in the spring. To hell with Blue and Harrobin!"

"They'll lay off Cedar Range till you do get thet big herd," said Lightfoot, warningly.

"If they raid us clean they'll have to travel slow. Through miles of timber in any direction! We'll trail them, hang at their heels, pick them out of their saddles, shoot them in their sleep. If they turn on us we can outrun them. Thanks to your thoroughbreds, Pencarrow."

"For heaven's sake don't tell the girls you're ridin' their hosses."

"Brandon, it's new tactics in these parts," said Lightfoot. "If you can dodge a pitched battle where you're greatly outnumbered you'll go a long way."

September passed. The sage grew more purple in contrast with the sun bleached grass. Frost colored the aspens on the mountains, the oaks on the ridges, the cottonwoods and maples in the lowlands. Cedar Range was approaching a time of unparalleled beauty. Indian summer hovered in the air, with its haze, its melancholy notes of birds, its drowsy dreamy silence in the woods, its goldenrod and purple asters along the trails.

One Sunday the cowboys took one of their few days off.

That morning Hogue Kinsey visited Wade early, stamping into the cabin while Wade was shaving.

"Boss, have you seen who'n the hell is here?" he demanded, in supreme disgust.

"No, Hogue. Who is here?"

"Visitors from Holbrook. Two spruced-up dandies come sparkin' Rona an' Jacqueline."

Wade cut himself with the razor. His chin stung and began to bleed. A strange, hitherto unexperienced sensation stirred in his breast.

"Who are they?"

"John McComb an' a cocky youngster, son of the banker at Holbrook. Hal didn't remember his name."

"Well, what of it, Hogue?" asked Wade, slowly. His hand quivered as he applied the blade again. "It's none of your business—or mine."

"Hell no!" agreed Hogue.

Wade turned in surprise. The cowboy sat on the bed, his lean handsome face fiercely sad, his eyes like green fire.

"Boss, I told you. I begged you to let me go."

"I remember, Hogue. But I couldn't do without you. And I knew you'd put selfish interest—or let us say, cowboy romance—aside for this tremendous job."

"Aw, I know, an' I did. But I gotta tell you—get this off my chest or bust."

"Hogue, I'm your pard or your brother—anyone you need. Go ahead. Spill it."

"Tex, I've made a turrible fool of myself. But I couldn't help it. . . . Thet day Rona looked at me—you remember— an' told her Dad I was won—der—ful. . . . Wal, I fell awful in love with her an' it's grown wuss ever since."

"Is that all, Hogue?"

"All! . . . It was bad enough, but it'll kill me now. . . . I seen Rona with him. She was laughin' an' cuttin' up—the little flirt!"

"Hogue, she's an innocent kid."

"Shore. Innocent of anythin' bad, thank Gawd!—But not of makin' fellows fall in love with her."

"Yes, of that too. Rona is gay, bright, full of fun. She'd get a lot out of some nice boy calling on her. It'll do her good. Poor lonely child! You ought to be glad."

"Tex, you don't know what love is," complained Hogue, in a passion of misery. "I oughtn't hold thet against you. But I do—somehow. An' I oughtn't talk to you this way. But I can't help it.

. . . You're a gunman. You don't care a damn—really—for these Pencarrows. You're just het up over the tough job they give up. You're gonna die fightin' for them—an' I'm gamblin' my life with you thet you'll do for Blue an' Harrobin, an' their rowdies. I like you for thet. It's made a man of me. . . . But for you to expect me to be glad—*glad* some cocky rich youngster has come to make up to Rona—why Boss, you ain't human!"

"Hogue, can I trust you?" asked Wade.

"Trust me! . . . Why, shore you can," replied Hogue, warped out of his despair to gaze wonderingly at Wade.

"You've got me wrong, when you say I'm not human—that I don't know what love is," returned Wade, in a low voice. "I'm in love with Jacqueline. Terribly, hopelessly. I never dreamed of her as attainable. Not for me! But I've been a sick, desperate wretch ever since. This gunman passion to kill you've accused me of—it's true. But I never had it until I came here and saw what Jacqueline Pencarrow was up against. . . . I know all your woes, all your longings. Just now when you told me McComb had come to spark Jacqueline I nearly cut my throat. I wish I had. . . . That was my first stab of jealousy. I dare say I'll learn that hideous and hateful thing. I sympathize with you. We are brothers in misery. . . . But I'll go on, Hogue, just the same—with never a hope to have Jacqueline, though I'd sell my soul to do it—and I'll die trying to save her father, and therefore her."

Kinsey sprang up like a bent sapling released. His fine young face went from red to white.

"My Gawd! . . . Tex, forgive me," he cried, hoarsely, and stalked out of the cabin.

Wade was indeed doomed to intimacy with the green-eyed monster jealousy. Wherever he went that Sunday, and Pencarrow called him to the house, walked with him here and there, he had the misfortune to encounter Jacqueline with her admirer. She wore a becoming gown and she was radiant. He might have been a servant for the little notice she took of him. Yet that did not keep him from seeing her in all her perfection of beauty and overpowering appeal. She might have been as innocent of coquetry as he had sworn to Hogue that Rona was, but he could not absolve her of a woman's wile—that strange inconsistent ghastly need of feeding her vanity by parading her conquest of one man before the eyes of another.

It turned out that Wade, after suffering almost beyond endurance, had yet the worst to face. Returning from the corrals Wade encountered all the Pencarrows and their guests, who were evidently about to make an early start on the long drive to town. Wade assuredly had eyes for the spirited team of blacks hitched to the light buckboard.

Hogue Kinsey stood holding the team, a job that he cordially detested judging from his cold set face and flashing eyes. He shot Wade a warning glance, which quite altered Wade's judgment, and prepared him for anything.

Jacqueline accosted Wade peremptorily: "Brandon, do you instruct your cowboys to keep their mouths shut when questioned?"

"That depends upon who questions them," replied Wade, curtly, feeling the blood go to his face.

"Somebody has been riding my horses. They are thin, scratched and ragged. Pen has a cut on his shoulder and he's lame."

The girl was undoubtedly angry and grieved. Wade made allowance for her sharp tongue. He knew her love for her thoroughbreds and he would not have minded but for her interested and curious admirer. His chief feeling seemed to be dismay at being confronted again at close range by her accusing eyes.

"Kinsey heah is evidently deaf and dumb," she went on. "Will you oblige me by telling me who rode Pen?"

"I did."

"With whose permission?"

"No one's. I just took him."

"How dare you? I don't allow anyone to ride my hawses, especially Pen."

"I'm sorry, Miss Pencarrow," returned Wade, coldly. "I really did not think to ask you. We had ridden out all the other fast horses. They needed a rest. And your fat bunch needed work. They certainly got it. . . . Pen is not lame. He picked up a stone and limps a little."

"Dad, I'm perfectly furious," cried Jacqueline. But to Wade she did not appear as furious as excited. "If I were boss heah I'd—I'd—"

"Wal, I'm glad you're not boss," interrupted Pencarrow, bluntly. "But since you tax Brandon so unkindly, to say the least, why not heah just how Pen came to be lame."

Suddenly Jacqueline descended from her lofty unreasoning anger, proving that she seldom if ever was addressed by her father in that way.

"There is no occasion to tell her," said Wade, hastily. "It was only an incident of every day for us riders."

"Tell her, Hal," cried Rona, resentfully. She had a red spot in each pale cheek.

"Bet your life I'll tell her," retorted Hal. "I'd told her long ago but for Dad."

"What are you keeping from me?" queried Jacqueline, and she paled perceptibly.

"Hal, are you breaking my rule?" interposed Wade.

"Boss, I am, this once. I don't care a damn. Jacque has one of her queer spells today. But she shan't take it out on you."

"Never mind my spell," returned the girl, stiffly, once more prey to a vivid blush. "Tell me what's happened!"

"Nothin' much to us riders, Jacque," answered the lad, nonchalantly. "If we hadn't ridden your horses lately we'd been worse off. You know my job is scoutin' with a glass from the high knoll. Hogue named it Rona's Topknot, cause it's got a bright grassy top. . . . Well, I was watchin' for the boys to show along the edge of the cedars. Sunset right in my eyes the other way. That's how it came I got held up by two geezers. They sneaked up an' got the drop on me. One of them wanted to bust my head open right there. But the other thought they could get money from Dad by kidnappin' me. So they tied my hands, made me get on my horse. We went down the hill. I seen the cowboys off in the cedars an' I yelled bloody murder. My kidnappers wheeled for the open range keeping hold of my bridle an' did they ride! . . . At first we were too far apart for shootin'. But Hogue an' the bunch burned a lot of powder anyway. Brandon was up on Pen. They'd had a hard ride before that. All the horses but Pen were spent. Pen got out ahead an' the others fell back. He began to catch up with us. I never rode so fast in all my life. Then those two geezers began to shoot back at Brandon. They shot all their ammunition away. But he kept comin' an' gainin'. I began to figure I'd soon hear a bullet whistle. But I didn't. I heard Brandon shoot an' I heard his bullet hit the man who had my bridle square in the back. He yelled somethin' awful, let go my bridle an' his own. The other fellow grabbed him an' kept him from fallin' off. He was shot for keeps, that geezer. I got my bridle up an' pulled my horse. Brandon went by like the wind, workin' that Winchester. They went out of sight. I heard more shots. Then Brandon came trotting over the ridge. He says, 'How are you, Hal?' An' I answered, 'Fine outside feelin' kinda cheap for bein' held up.' . . . He didn't say a word about the two rustlers—for sure that's what they were—an' I didn't need to ask. Pen was drippin' wet, but not even winded. We rode back to meet the outfit. I guess that's about all."

If Wade had been capable of a thirst for revenge he could have had his fill. But sight of Jacqueline routed his hurt feelings.

"*Hal!*" she whispered, and reached blindly for her brother, who was quick to take her hand.

"Jacque, it wasn't nothin'—honest it wasn't," he protested, earnestly, shocked at the change he had wrought so quickly in her proud passionate bearing. "But Pen—Aw, what a horse! If you had any idea how good he is you wouldn't be so stingy with him. Jacque, you ought to have heard what the cowboys said about that horse."

Jacqueline raised her head to look at Wade, and it was certain she saw him alone.

"I didn't know. . . . I despise myself—for insulting you. I was terribly wrong."

"It's all right, Miss Pencarrow," rejoined Wade, hurriedly. "Naturally you were upset. You love Pen. He's a grand horse. But neither I or any of us shall ride him again."

"If Pen is that grand he might save Dad or Rona—or *you*, Brandon," she said, with the resonant power back in her voice. "You shall ride him!"

"I'd rather—not," replied Wade, hesitatingly, weakening at the onset of what he felt coming. "I'd never feel right. . . . I lamed him, you know. No one could forget that."

"But Pen is yours, I give him to you," she replied, with finality. And she turned to the others with a mien poised and serious, and in decided contrast to the gay fire which had characterized her that day, and the petulant mood with which it had terminated. "Gentlemen," she said to her guests, "it is too bad you did not get away before I fell into one of my tantrums—to insult Mr. Brandon, who has been our friend and savior. You will appreciate how badly off we are heah—how beset by troubles and dangers—how impossible it is to entertain visitors for a single day without subjecting them to embarrassment. I am sorry. It was kind of you to visit us. Good-by."

CHAPTER FIFTEEN

HAL'S story of his abduction almost split the Pencarrow family. The mother, particularly, went into hysterics and entreated and demanded that her son should no longer be permitted to ride with these wild cowboys. Pencarrow sustained a shock, but he realized that Hal was no longer a child, and he stoutly upheld the lad in his determination to stand by Brandon and do his share. Jacqueline maintained silence during the family dispute, plainly divided between love for her brother and this enlarged and terrifying duty. Rona was strong for Hal. Finally Jacqueline ended the argument by appealing to Brandon: "I think Hal should ride with you. But if possible, give the boy your care and protection while he is learning."

Next day Wade kept Kinsey and Hicks with him while he sent Hal and the other cowboys, and also Lightfoot, to Holbrook for two wagonloads of supplies. Wade took the post of scout on the high knoll. Kinsey and Hicks, with light packs, rode away on the west side of the range, where they were to hide in the timber and watch the open. In case of a raid they were to take the trail of the rustlers, creep up on them in camp, shoot and slip away under cover of the night.

No time that he had ever spent on guard seemed to Wade so thought-compelling and significant as this upon the knoll. He could see the ranch house not far away, and sometimes the girls outdoors, and most of the wide gray range to the north and west. The cattle had scattered over five square miles or more, out in the open, and probably numbered close to four thousand head. Wade sat in the shade of a pine and watched every moving object within range of the powerful field glass. At the same time, thought and feeling were active.

As autumn had advanced the surrounding country had taken on a glorious glamour of gold which the spots of scarlet, the belts of black, and the vast rolling sea of gray appeared only to accentuate. The desert appealed to him most, with its stark and mystic strength, its call of silence and loveliness. Would he ever ride away toward that curtain of blue haze, down into the world of rock and sand?

That day the range, at least as much as he could command, showed no telltale clouds of dust or dots of dark riders on the desert. In the dusk he rode down to the cedars and back to the ranch and a late supper in the kitchen. Pencarrow came in to talk, and Jacqueline, with her all-embracing eyes followed to ask questions he could not answer. The one she came solely to satisfy herself upon was the one she did not ask—and it concerned his return, his safety. Just the fact that she came, to look at him with haunted eyes, sent Wade to his cabin shaken with conflicting tides of emotion.

He sat on his porch in the cool starlight, and he saw Jacqueline's dim face at her open window. Then began a strange duel. She watched him and he knew it, and that gave rise to vaster trouble than his longing to watch her. Why did she lean there? When he could bear it no longer he went inside, almost at once to peep from his dark window, to see with tumult that she at once closed hers and lighted her lamp.

Before dawn he rode off on his lonely vigil, keeping to the open range, and watching with eyes that pierced the gray gloom.

That day was like its predecessor. In the succeeding seven days the first dust clouds he sighted came from the wagons and horses of the returning cowboys. Wade rode in before sunset. Jerry reported so uneventful a round trip to Holbrook that its very quietness seemed ominous. It had turned cold up on the plateaus. Cattle were working down into the draws. Hal, as on the former trip, seemed to grow older and keener by leaps and bounds. Elwood Lightfoot kept silence until the girls had taken Hal and his numerous packages away to the sitting room, and the cowboys had left him with Wade and Pencarrow.

"Wal, Brandon, the seed we sowed has growed powerful rank an' strong," he said. "I never heerd so many conflictin' stories. I took a flyin' trip on the train over to Winslow an' Flagstaff before I looked Holbrook over. All Arizona has heerd of Cedar Ranch doin's. An', Pencarrow, if ever a cattleman was lauded for stickin' it out under impossible circumstances, you are thet man. An', Brandon, if ever a gunman was welcomed on a range you are him. Gossip has magnified everythin' thet's happened, an' created a hundred things thet never happened. You're supposed to have an outfit of wild-ridin' half-breeds an' cowboys. The hangin' of thet rustler at Pine Mound threw the light upon Blue an' Harrobin. I'd almost go so far as to say it made them outlaws. They have powerful friends—all cattle buyers thet ask no questions, you can gamble—an' the hue and cry is not all on one side. But the wedge is entered thet'll split this range wide open. Every cowboy you meet will tell you hangin' rustlers has come to Arizona an' before long the big bones will be decoratin' a cottonwood. That's a juicy quid for cowboys. Some gambler blew in from Tombstone to taunt Holbrook Kent's backers with Tex Brandon's record in Tombstone, Douglas, Yuma. If you were Wess Hardin, Buck Duane an' Billy the Kid rolled into one you couldn't be as vicious, as deadly as they've got you figgered. It's bad news for Blue an' Harrobin. I talked with one man who heerd Blue himself rave about this Tex Brandon. 'But *who'n* hell is he? I knew all the old gunmen in Texas. An' some of the young comers. But I never heerd of Tex Brandon. If he's such a hell of a gunman thet's not his real name.' . . . It's shore put Holbrook Kent on the tip of every one's tongue. Kent is a marked man. If he was a fourflusher, which no one could call him, he'd be forced to meet you. . . . An' to sum up, thet'll be hot-stove an' fireplace gossip all winter. Next summer an' fall will tell the tale."

"It'll be told before summer if I can write my page," said Wade.

"Shore. Hit at them first. They won't be expectin' thet," replied Lightfoot.

"Will they raid me again before winter?" asked Pencarrow.

"I've been expecting a raid every day. But nothing has happened. Kinsey and Hicks are out. I gave them a week. If they're not back by tomorrow we'll hunt them up."

"If I had money, I'd buy cattle," rejoined Pencarrow, decisively. "Rustlers in this section have kept the price low."

"I banked nine thousand dollars for you after I sold the herd we got back," said Wade. "Why not save a thousand out of that and buy with the rest."

"I owe you nearly seven thousand."

"What if you do? Let that ride."

"Pencarrow, you could buy nine hundred head an' more," rejoined Lightfoot. "Cattle will never be so cheap again. Now's the time—if we can only dig up some money."

"Could I mortgage the ranch?"

"Shore. With all this stir, you could borrow big on it."

"No mortgages," cut in Wade, shaking his head. "That's bad. Keep the land and property free."

"I can sell out to Aulsbrook for ten thousand," interfered Lightfoot. "He shore wants thet water right of mine."

"If you sell to anyone it'll be Pencarrow," replied Wade. "If next spring is absolutely the right time to buy then we must raise money some other way."

"Wal, it is absolutely, provided you *know* you can break the power of this rustler outfit."

"I know that I can," rejoined Wade, with grim gravity, but he did not add that he could guarantee coming out of the fight alive.

"Heah we air talkin' big," interrupted Pencarrow, impatiently. "An' it's money thet talks. I'll buy another thousand haid an' then be satisfied to build up slow. Thet was our original idea."

"Yes. But what a pity!" ejaculated Wade, regretfully.

"Beggars cain't be chosers, Brandon. I tell you I'm happy now," retorted the rancher, emphatically. "It's you fellows who egg me on. Heah I have some money in the bank, an' a few thousand cattle when a little while ago I was broke—practically ruined. Brandon, I'd be a poor sort of man if I didn't appreciate what you've done for me an' my family. I can wait."

"But this chance will never come again," protested Wade.

"What chance?"

"To make a fortune."

"No, I reckon not. I shore hope not. At least not owin' to a cattle war on one side an' rustler bands on the other."

"Perhaps I should have said to retrieve the fortune you lost," ventured Wade, significantly.

"Wal, thet hurts, an' if anythin' could upset my equilibrium, thet would. But I was practically ruined. An' I refuse to let dreams of a shore chance to make a fortune cheat me of content now."

That ended the discussion. Wade respected the rancher's fine attitude toward the past and present. But it did not prevent his longing for the realization of this unusual opportunity. He had discarded it before, but it had returned dedoubled and unforgettable.

Kinsey and the half-breed did not return the following day or the next. On the third, Wade made a very early start for the place where the two cowboys had planned to camp, and found that they had not been there for a week. Trailing them was too slow a job. Wade with his cowboys circled the west end of the range and soon ran across recent tracks of a small bunch of cattle traveling in a straight line westward. No doubt Kinsey and Hicks had followed. Before the day was out Wade came upon signs of the first camp of the rustlers, which at once took on deeper significance because of two hastily dug and covered graves.

"Doggone!" drawled Jerry, as he rolled a cigarette. "Hogue an' Hicks paid their respects to this outfit, huh?"

They turned back arriving at the ranch late in the night. Kinsey and Hicks lay in their bunks so dead asleep that they did not awaken. On the following morning Wade let all the cowboys have a much-needed rest, while he went down to see Elwood Lightfoot. The homesteader listened and pondered for a while.

"Lull before the storm, mebbe," he said. "I look to see Pencarrow cleaned out this fall. It'll cost you ten thousand head of steer to bust up this new rustler combine."

"That'd be cheap."

"Make Pencarrow buy more cattle pronto. Blue an' Harrobin will concentrate on the Cedar Range next spring. I've an idee all these ranchers would contribute a lot of cattle to the good cause of eggin' on the rustlers to this range. They'd lose the cattle anyhow."

"What do you mean? Have Aulsbrook, Driscoll, Mason, and even little cattlemen like Drill drive some stock over here to be stolen?"

"Thet's what, if they'd do it. Think it over."

"Wouldn't it be better to buy their contribution cheap."

"It shore would—an' they would sell cheap with thet understandin'. But how'n hell can we buy?"

"Elwood, I haven't figured on that. I always make up my mind first."

"Ahuh. . . . Brandon, I reckon all the cattlemen between the desert an' the White Mountains would be a heap interested in thet idee. Altogether we might buy thirty or forty thousand head for what the rustlers get—provided you can convince the cattlemen you'll clean out the rustlers. Aulsbrook, Driscoll,—they know damn wal they stand to lose *all* their cattle. Blue has been around this range for near five years. Harrobin less. It's about time for them to make some top raids, then move on to their next stampin' ground. So it behooves. . . . Say, what ails you?"

Wade had violently responded to an illuminating thought. It burst like sparks into his mind, making him leap up as if galvanized.

"You've given me a hunch!" After that ejaculation Wade abruptly left.

Hogue Kinsey's report seemed characteristic of what this genius of a cowboy had developed into.

"We tracked nine rustlers drivin' a small herd hell-bent for the brakes. Sneaked up on their first camp just about dark. They were eatin' round the fire. They had dogs an' those dogs gave us away. We each got in a shot an' then run for our horses. Tracked them next day. Found their camp. There was seven of them, an' all damn suspicious an' watchful. We waited till late. Even then some of them were awake, because the instant we opened up they was bouncin' lead off the rocks an' trees. We'd planned to sling some lead ourselves an' vamoose before the rest waked up. We slung it an' vamoosed, but the goin' was hot. Next mornin' we found they'd broke camp in the night, leavin' some seventy odd steers in the woods—an' a couple of their outfit layin' with guns an' spurs gone, an' pockets inside out. Then we mosied for home."

The snows did not come in time to save most of Pencarrow's cattle from the raiders. He had bought fifteen hundred head from Drill, and these five, two- and three-year-old steers went with the rest. While Wade and his cowboys trailed and fought one outfit of rustlers, two or three larger ones made successive raids, leaving only a few hundred cows and calves on the range.

When the winter finally did send the rustlers to their burrows in the brakes, Pencarrow was again on the verge of ruin.

A thin skim of snow lay on the range, except on south exposures where the sun struck warm. The few cows and calves, melancholy reminders of Pencarrow's once big herd, concentrated on those grassy spots. The high ridges and plateaus shone glistening white. Cold wind swept down from the heights. Wolves bayed from the hill slopes, threatening what cattle were left. And the November days came, dark with leaden skies and dreary with the moan in the pine trees.

But the big bunkhouse presented a cheerful sight with its blazing cedar fagots in the open fireplace, and the colorful trappings of the cowboys strewn around.

Pencarrow, accompanied by Jacqueline and the twins, had just addressed the outfit, including Elwood Lightfoot, thanking them in a husky voice for their efforts to save him and his family, and advising them to leave Cedar Ranch to be employed by better ranchers who could pay for their wonderful services.

A silence ensued, Wade sat on a box, gazing sphinxlike into the fire, his face thin and worn, his eyes somber. Elwood stood beside the window gazing out upon the bleak landscape. The cowboys had listened respectfully without the least expression of emotion. Hogue Kinsey gazed at Rona with a strange yearning in his eyes. Perhaps none but Wade saw the look Rona bestowed upon the cowboy.

"Brandon, will you leave?" asked Pencarrow, driven by the silence.

"If you need to ask—no!" replied Wade, without glancing up. His voice rang like steel.

The rancher turned from Wade to Kinsey, and repeated the query.

"Mr. Pencarrow, I'll stick," replied the cowboy, quietly.

"Me too," said Jerry.

"Shucks, we ain't begun to fight," added Bilt Wood, laconically.

The half-breed was slower to reply, his black eyes glittering:

"Boss, I'm half Indian an' never quit a trail."

That left Kid Marshall the bowlegged little desperado of the group, always dry, cool, humorous, long-winded.

"You couldn't drive me away, Mr. Pencarrow," he said. "Somehow we jest fit here. An' it ain't all Tex, either. I never seen any folks I liked to work for so much. Then this cabin is shore a cheerful camp for us. We're gonna start huntin' our winter supply of meat. Deer, elk, turkey—all hung up under the pines to freeze! There won't be much work an' plenty of fun. Among us there's more money than we ever seen before. Shore it'll go from one to another, though I reckon thet when spring comes I'll have most of it. . . . But leavin' all else aside the thing thet nails us here is the deal these hombres have given you. We admire you for standin' pat when most any rancher would quit. We think powerful much of Hal an' the girls for their nerve an' loyalty to you. . . . An' short an' sweet, Mr. Pencarrow, we boys have joined hands with Tex an' we know, if you an' everybody else don't, thet we're gonna kill Blue an' Harrobin."

Pencarrow, red and flustered, spread his hands to Brandon.

"So we're goin' on cattle raisin'?" he asked gruffly.

"We are. All this loss and labor and trouble has just been practice. We won't make the same mistakes twice. These rustlers will make the same mistake too many times."

"Wal, I don't know what to say," rejoined Pencarrow, helplessly.

"Dad, there's nothing to say, except that we understand," said Jacqueline, her dark eyes eloquently upon Wade. The girls went out with their father. Rona had a last look at Hogue, to that worthy's confusion. Then Wade followed to close the door of the bunkhouse.

"Pencarrow, it'd have been a pity to break up that outfit," he said, feelingly.

"I'm beat, Brandon. But to be honest I'm shore happy you're all stayin' on. I'll get up an' fight again."

"Good night, Tex," spoke up Rona, archly, "you're a fine hombre."

"Good night, Star Eyes," replied Wade. "I'm afraid you worked havoc among my cowboys."

"Just you wait," laughed Rona.

Wade turned off on the trail through the snow toward his cabin. "I'll walk over with you," said Jacqueline, as casually as if she had been doing that regularly. She slipped her gloved hand inside his arm. If she had not been on his right, Wade believed she could have felt the great bound of his heart. He was many things besides being dazzled. There was no help for it. She meant to make him her friend. He could not insult her again. She walked in silence, her heavy buckskins crunching the half frozen snow. The sun had set pale and cold in the west; a dull wind blew from the north; calves were bawling in the pasture.

"You had them well coached," said Jacqueline.

"Who?"

"Your cowboys. They like us all, no doubt, as Kid Marshall said. But it is *you* who has. . . ."

She broke off, and then presently: "Did you see Hogue's eyes on Rona?"

"Yes."

"And did you catch her looking at him?"

"That would have been hard to miss."

"Oh, dear! . . . My heart is fighting with my reason—my pride."

"Why?"

"I could almost love that handsome devil myself."

Wade laughed, and it seemed to ease the vise-like pressure in his breast.

"It's always different when we make blunders ourselves."

She was silent again for quite a time, then she queried simply: "Will you come to supper tonight?"

"No—thank you," he replied, surprised into confusion.

"Won't you ever come—Tex?"

"I—I think not."

"We are facing a long cold hard winter. . . . I'll be lonely."

"You will indeed. . . . It's a pity town is shut off. You and Rona need friends—some fun—excitement. It'll be a long time before you'll have neighbors on this range."

"I'll be a little old lady with a lace cap and a querulous voice. . . . But I shall not miss town acquaintances. You remember what I told John McComb?"

"Yes, he understands, apparently. I felt sorry for him. You were cruel. He's desperately in love with you."

"Not cruel, but kind."

They reached his porch, and as Wade stepped up Jacqueline's hand slipped from his arm. She remained standing below, looking up. Her lovely face, cold like pearl, was lit by great eyes of dark fire. Wade distrusted the moment; he dreaded the tiger in ambush within him; he had to look at her and he was afraid to.

"If I were frozen—would you ask me in?" she inquired, calmly.

"What a question! Certainly I would."

"Well, I *am* frozen."

"You! With that fleece-lined leather coat—your woolen dress—and heavy boots?" he ejaculated, feeling as silly and inadequate as his words.

"I did not mean frozen by the snow and wind."

Wade felt helplessly unable to reply to this. He had further realization of the danger of being with her.

"Brandon, I was hateful to you for a long time."

"Perhaps that was right—and best."

"I'm sorry. I'm particularly sorry I stooped so low as to flirt with John McComb. It failed of its purpose—and no doubt gave him the encouragement I later had to deny."

Wade looked the intense surprise and curiosity that he refused to voice.

"Didn't you guess why?"

Wade shook his head.

"I wanted to make you jealous."

"Well! . . ." he burst out, and halted, as if strangled. His veins seemed to swell with blood unable to flow freely.

"You're the only man of all that have come here—who—who never *saw* me," she confessed, frankly. "I liked it at first. Now I don't like it so much. It has been good for my vanity. . . . I shall continue to ask you to come to dinner—and to talk to me a little afterward. Won't you? It'd be a kindness if no more."

"I told you—no," he answered, sadly.

"But don't you like me at all?" she flashed, incredulously and wonderingly, stung by his persistence.

"That has nothing to do with it."

"But don't you?"

"Yes. I—I like you, admire you, respect you more than words can tell."

"You do not!" she exclaimed, petulantly.

She was irresistible. Wade divined the imperative need of cutting short this colloquy.

"I must—since I'm going to die in your service presently," he said, brutally.

"*Oh!*" she cried, as if torn. He went on. "You have common sense, if you stop to think. What could you expect? It's a hundred to one that I'll be shot before I clean out these rustlers' nests. Think! Suppose I more than liked you—or infinitely more, suppose *you* more than like me, which is ridiculous. It would soften me, shake my nerve—and I'd be easy game for Kent or some other gunman before I could save your father. . . . Try to see it that way. Good night."

When the hunting was over, Wade's cowboys had little work outside of mending saddles, bridles, harness, and chopping wood, on which last they gambled as they did on everything.

For Wade to be with them was to stay young. But he had a grave problem which gripped him as soon as he faced it, and which left little time for the cowboys.

That problem was whether or not to spend the hidden fortune on cattle to throw upon Cedar Ranch Range.

There had been a time when he repudiated the idea, scorned it, drove it from his consciousness. But one thing or another brought it back. The still small voice of conscience augmented into a thundering denial, yet the temptation kept pace with it. Some perverse devil argued with him, nagged him relentlessly, told him that it did not matter how he saved Pencarrow so long as he saved him. If it were dishonorable to use this ill-gotten wealth to save the rancher, and indirectly his gallant boy and lovely daughters, such dishonor could fall only upon him, should he ever be found out. Since he asked nothing for himself, how could his act be selfish or base?

Wade feared he had lived so long with dishonest men that he did not know right from wrong. Hours he brooded before his fire over this puzzling moral side of his dilemma.

There would come an hour, often in the dead of night, when he believed he had conquered the temptation, and he rejoiced in his decision. Nevertheless the next day or night the old insidious demanding whispers would be back at his ears.

Every day he weakened in all save passion. The cowboys worried in vain about him. Sweet advances from Jacqueline left him cold. His avoidance of her could not have failed to be observed. Perhaps she saw this and was hurt, because she ceased openly to go out of her way to speak to him. But often when he returned to his cabin from a tramp in the snow down to Lightfoot's place, or from a visit to the cowboys' bunkhouse, he would find an apple pie or some like toothsome delicacy on his table. And many times a day he would look out of his window to see Jacqueline at hers, watching for him. This worked upon Wade so disastrously that for the time being he was incapable of clear thought. What an idiot he was to form the idea that she cared for him! Of all his torturing thoughts this one he most passionately dismissed. It was nothing—this pale sweet face of hers at the window—those dark eyes, seen even at that distance like deep gulfs—this watching so often, and especially from sunset to dusk when he returned from his work to his cabin, —all meant nothing except that she was lovely, and she worried about him because he had said he must die in her service.

That trial did not help him in his ordeal, nor did the gradual loss of hope of Pencarrow, nor the wistful pathos of Rona, nor Hal's failure to hide his dread in gaiety. Nor did the talk of the cowboys, thrilling and loyal and caustic as it was. He had inflamed them with his desire, trained their young hard minds to fear nothing, to hate thieves, and to burn with blood lust. They would talk for hours, planning, creating ways to meet every possible situation that might arise with the rustlers. On pleasant sunny days they would have a shooting match upon which stern practice they made wagers. Nor did Wade's own incessant practice at throwing his gun contribute in any way to a heightening of his moral perception. No gunman ever practiced so relentlessly, so strung with passionless intensity, so coldly, swiftly, surely toward a longed-for meeting. Those winter days made Wade matchless in his speed, his physical perception, his genius to slay.

Christmas Eve brought a surprise in shape of a dinner to the cowboys, kept secret until the very day. The boys whooped with joy, then lapsed into awe, and finally grew scared. But Hogue Kinsey swore he would beat into a jelly any one of them who dared flunk on that occasion. Wade felt both wretched and happy because he could not evade this invitation; he had to go when peace on earth and good will to men was the farthest thing from his mind; when at the peak of his temptation, divided between honor and dishonor, he knew he must see Jacqueline as he had never seen her.

But he went, forgetting himself, glad for the pleasure of these hard homeless cowboys, to whom Christmas usually meant nothing but a debauch at some vile wayside inn. The Pencarrows made it merry for their guests. There was a heap of gifts under the Christmas tree, which told of some one's thoughtfulness far in the past. The dinner was such as to make the cowboys eat as if it were to be the last time in their lives. Rona in a long white gown, new to the cowboys, appeared to have been transformed into a lovely radiant young woman. As for Jacqueline, who also wore white—a gown cut low and without sleeves—she seemed to Wade to move and speak from a glamorous haze. Her beauty when he first saw her that night had blinded him. Her shining eyes, dark as midnight, hiding with gladness some secret, gave his love an insupportable impetus. She had smiled at him, had given her hand, had called him Tex; and seemed to mean that she had dressed thus for him alone.

After the dinner Kid Marshall was the only cowboy who could respond to Jacqueline's merry call for a speech. Kid saw the opportunity of his life, one that he knew he would be unable to grasp. But he was valiant.

"Our lovely hostesses, an' our good boss," he said, "We shore thank you for this grand feast, an' more for the kindness of your hearts. It will never be forgotten by one of us. It has fetched into our lives somethin' different. We, who for years have had no home, no mother, no sisters, no thought of Christ, will be the better for this gatherin' at your table, for the human thought of us. Shore, when another Christmas rolls around some of us will be missin'. But to have been present here, to be made to feel worth kindness, to have the privilege of fightin' for this family, will change our very lives. It will make us forget thet we have been drifters of the range, outcasts who had no hope of good, an' we will be happy to die for you if thet must be."

Marshall's pathos added the only sad touch to thet merry evening—a reminder of the stern menace that hung over Brandon and his riders.

At parting Jacqueline pressed Wade's hand, and with a dancing devil in her dark eyes she said: "After all, I succeeded in getting you to come to dinner, didn't I?"

"Indeed you did. Yet I—must thank you for something I feel and cannot speak."

"Was it so terrible?"

Then Wade looked at her, with all the fire and force of his nature roused to passion. "Yes. For me it was terrible," he said. "But I could have endured more for these cowboys—for what Kid Marshall said it meant to them."

"Terrible?" she whispered, pale in the lamplight that flared through the door. His words had shocked her.

"I shall find it harder to be a man," he returned simply, with regret.

After that night his was a losing struggle. He knew it and suffered. All that he had done to keep true to the promise he had made his father seemed to totter in the balance. At the last, when Simm Bell sat dying, propped against that tree with his guns ready, he had seen clearly the bitter way of his life and the only hope for his son, and he had risen to the heights in his entreaty.

That Christmas night Wade sat before the dying embers of his fire, wretched and elated by turns, trying to end this battle one way or the other. And at a late hour when he crawled into his blankets he had not come to a decision.

The days passed, grew longer, and the sun warmer. All the south slopes were bare. March found the range showing a touch of green. Down on Lightfoot's protected farm the mockingbirds had come back to sing.

Wade welcomed the end of the long winter. The last few weeks he had been almost a recluse. He awaited the wearing out of his will or an illumination of mind.

While practicing with his gun one day—a habit that had become almost mechanical—a thought, a query, coming from no source he divined, halted him. If he were killed presently in the meeting with Kent, what would become of all that money he had hidden. It would mold in the ground. It would do no good to make amends for its evil. It would be wasted.

"It should be put to good use before I meet Kent," he soliloquized. And he became lost in profound thought. The bell that called the cowboys to supper did not stir Wade. He sat in the dusk before the red embers of his neglected fire. And all at once he had a slight strange tremor. In his morbid state Wade took it as an omen of his own death. He would be killed this coming summer. And it magnified his hatred of these cattle thieves and his passion to break their strangle hold on that Arizona range. Also it brought out clearly and vividly from the darkness of his mind the thing that he must do. He would restore Pencarrow's lost property, and therewith the happiness of his family. He would save Jacqueline from poverty, from being driven to sacrifice herself in marriage, perhaps even from being dragged from her home to the dens of these conscienceless outlaws.

Wade seemed to come out of a nightmare. His thought quickened, his feeling eased from a cold clamp. What if he had been the son of a robber, and a robber himself? What if he were wrong in saving the Pencarrows with stolen money? Jacqueline would never know. His death would end forever any chance of his being indentified as Wade Holden, the thief and killer whom Mahaffey and his Texas Rangers had sworn to ride down. Rand Blue would recognize Wade, of that he was deadly certain, but it would then be too late for betrayal. Blue's curse of amaze and fear, his yell of recognition, would be strangled in his throat.

It was over—the long ordeal. He had fallen, but was happy in his debasement. His love for Jacqueline, his resolve to pay his debt to her, were stronger than honor, than his promise to his father, than his slow evolution toward an honest life. That was all there was to it. He had found himself at last. And as if by magic he attained the old cool unassailable spirit. He stood up and shook himself as if to rid himself of a shell, and he threw open his door as if to drive out the other side of him—that boy who still dreamed and hoped.

CHAPTER SIXTEEN

WADE had ridden up to the Pencarrow ranch house at different times and with varied emotions, but the whole sum of them could not compare with his state this lovely May morning, when, after watching eighteen thousand head of dusty tired cattle stream by down into the range, he rode slowly toward the porch.

They were all there, almost strange to him after his absence for so many full weeks of hard action, and their dearness to him flooded over him like a tide. Jacqueline stood behind the rest in the doorway, her face white, her dark eyes dilated and intent. She vanished as Hal and Rona rushed out to meet Wade. They almost dragged him off his horse and Rona kissed him. She appeared to have grown or changed in some striking way. What the twins said Wade never gathered. One on each side they propelled him toward the porch.

Hogue Kinsey, whom Wade had left behind on this trip, leaned against a post, lithe and handsome as always, yet somehow unfamiliar to Wade, with his slight smile and the clear brilliance of his eyes.

"Howdy, Tex," he drawled. "I shore am glad to see you-all."

Pencarrow stood on the porch, his leonine head erect, his gray hair ruffled high, as if he had been running a nervous hand through it. At that moment he had all the fire of Texas about him.

"Wal, heah you air," he said, huskily. "Am I drunk or dreamin'?"

"Wide awake, Pencarrow," replied Wade, with a happy ring

in his cool voice, as he reached for the outstretched hand. "Have you seen our new herd?"

"We been watchin' them come all mawnin', an' reckoned you'd never come. Jackie saw you first, way down the road. Called you 'Aladdin'. . . . Wal, Brandon, you'll excuse me bein' knocked off my pins."

Rona evidently saw Jacqueline inside the dark doorway, for she beckoned eloquently while still clinging to Wade's arm. "Tex," she said, looking up at him with her tawny eyes soft and dim. "Jacque kept us up all this long while. Now she's cracked, as Hogue would say. And Ma ran off crying."

"Aw, I'm doin' thet myself," interposed Hal, as much cowboy as if he had been born on the range. "My Gawd, Tex, but we're glad to see you."

Wade felt strung and cool, his elation as deep as the passion that had actuated him. Anticipation of this dramatic return to Cedar Ranch had haunted him thrillingly for weeks, but he had not been prepared for the sweetness of the reunion. He needed all his nerve to hide his feeling.

"Eighteen thousand odd—the finest herd I ever saw," he said. "None under two years, except the calves born on the way up. Steers and bulls galore, and about fifteen thousand cows. We'll double in a year."

"But—but—" stuttered the rancher, his face purple.

"All paid for—and cheap as dirt. Talk about luck."

"Paid for?" echoed Pencarrow.

"Sure. I had some money, you know. And my hunch was to buy this spring when all the cattlemen south of Cedar Range were broke and scared weak by the fear of a great rustler season."

"Brandon, you *paid* for thet herd?"

"I have the receipts. And I'm your new partner."

"Wal! . . . So thet was what you had up your sleeve? . . . Jackie, come out heah. Somebody's got to thank my new pardner."

But Jacqueline did not come.

"Dad, I'll thank him," exclaimed Rona, her laugh rich and

sweet. She reached up to whisper in Wade's ear. "You're a darling! You're my big brother, Tex. . . . Don't mind about Jacque. She's crazy to see you. Oh, I found out. Give her a little time. She feels things, you know."

Kinsey saved Wade at that juncture from a wild incredible impulse to hug Rona.

"Boss, if you don't mind I'd like to shake your hand," drawled the cowboy.

"Gosh, I'm glad to see you, Hogue," replied Wade. "Did we miss you? I should smile we did. Wait till I tell you! You'll never forgive me."

"I'll never forgive you anyhow," returned Kinsey, enigmatically.

"Brandon, come out with it!" thundered the rancher. "How'd you ever do it? Who're all those riders?"

"Perhaps I'd better tell you in private," said Wade, seriously.

"Private, hell! I have no secrets from my family. . . . Jackie, come out heah."

Jacqueline's face showed so dimly back in the interior of the living room that Wade could make out only a pale oval accentuated by the great dark eyes.

"I'm—not presentable," she said, almost inaudibly. "Send Brandon in."

"We'll all go in," boomed the rancher and led the way.

Wade saw Jacqueline far back in the room, advancing with hesitation, evidently having controlled extreme agitation. Wade's consciousness refuted an electrifying thought, and it made him master of himself.

"Howdy, Jacqueline," he said, taking her hands. "We're all back, safe and sound, with more riders and a lot of cattle; I've gone in partnership with your father. . . . And you'll have two bosses now."

"Oh, what have you done?" she cried.

"Strikes me you've asked me that question before," replied Wade, with a laugh, and he squeezed her hands. "Well, I hardly know what I *have* done. Played the game, I guess, Jacqueline, with the cards dealt me. . . . Nothing for you or Pencarrow—for any of you to feel badly about."

"Wal, Tex, we shore don't feel bad," interposed the rancher. "I reckon Jackie was so relieved to see you alive and well—for she thought you'd be killed—thet she just slumped a little, woman-like, when the dread passed."

Jacqueline drew away from Wade with some return of dignity. "I'm not quite myself lately. I've had my troubles with this family. Then, you come roaring back with a million cattle and horses! It was a little too much. . . . Now what *have* you done?"

"I've gone into partnership with your Dad."

"So you said. I don't see the fairness of such a connection for you. But I'm happy about it."

Wade sat down with the blood drumming in his ears. Jacqueline's eyes were the hardest to face, so eloquent, wondering, all-embracing. Nevertheless he met them, and then the other eager worshiping glances.

"Wal, folks, I was just smothered with luck," he began, easily, as he turned his sombrero round and round, and tried to remember the narrative he had constructed. "You know we rode off intendin' to buy a few thousand head of cattle. Rode to Aulsbrook's ranch first day. I had a bone to pick with him about Lightfoot's homestead and water, which Aulsbrook wanted to get hold of. But I never had a chance to mention that. The man was beside himself with rage and grief. Only the day before, rustlers had run off his herd, leaving only scattered bunches and strays. I had an inspiration. I said: 'Aulsbrook, what'll you sell out for—ranch, horses, including the cattle just raided?' He took me up like a flash. 'Give me ten thousand dollars, and I'll shake this range pronto!' And he began to curse Harrobin and Blue. I said: 'Take you up. Come in and sign a bill of sale on the deal.' . . . I paid him and took on his riders, except a couple, and his foreman. That hombre, I'll bet, could tell something about the raid. We trailed that herd for two days before we caught up. Found them in a canyon valley, a wild beautiful place that Hicks called Red Gulch. It's about a hundred miles from here. . . . We hid our horses and scouted. There were a good many more cattle penned up than Aulsbrook had lost. Round eight thousand, we reckoned. We found where the raiders had camped. They were gone. Hicks knew the lay of the land and the few trails. He made sure of the one these rustlers took—there were about ten riders and some extra horses—and then he led us across country to head them off. It worked. But we had to turn back some, as they had camped. We surprised that outfit. Ha, we sure did! Surprised me to see they had no idea of pursuit. Instead of standing their ground to fight they broke and ran—those that could run—at our first fire. I'll bet most of them carried lead bullets away with them. We captured a couple of cripples. Harrobin's outfit. They confessed and swore they'd leave the country. Harrobin was at Quirts, a little town farther south, a rendezvous for these gangs, same as Pine Mound. They told us who the buyer was. . . . Make a guess, Pencarrow."

"Buyer! You mean who Harrobin was sellin' to?" returned the rancher.

"Yes. You'll throw a fit when I tell you."

"All right. Let me throw it right heah!"

"Mason."

"Mason? Not Lem Mason of Mariposa?—Big cattle dealer an' merchant?"

"Yes, Lem Mason, big cattle dealer and merchant. He ran the M Bar ranch below Quirts as a blind. He sold his own brand at Mariposa and drove stolen brands into New Mexico."

"Wal, for God's sake, who *is* honest on this range?—Tex, am I a rustler, or air *you*?"

"Looks like I was! But it happens I'm not. . . . Well, we left the herd right in Red Gulch and rode down to Quirts. . . . Some bad men escape law and justice for a long time. But few ever do so forever. . . . I rounded up Harrobin and Mason in a saloon, drinking to each other's health and long life, I reckon. . . . Well, to be short and sweet about that meeting—I got the money from

Harrobin—money just paid over by Mason. . . . I hung round Quirts until evening, hoping Mason's tough foreman, Stewart, would ride in. But the little town was agog. Somebody must have tipped off Stewart. He never showed up. . . . We camped, and next day rode south again. By this time we knew where to go. Briefly, I bought ten thousand head from four ranchers, most of these from a cattleman named Drone, who it seems had been marked by the rustlers. He was glad to get rid of his cattle, grateful to sell cheap. His wife was ill—and in short it was good for him to sell out. . . . We drove back. I forgot to say I added five more riders to my sixteen. That was a drive. Two weeks or more back to Red Gulch! I doubt if the Red Gulch herd had stirred except to graze during our absence. . . . All the rest of the time—a month, I reckon, we've been driving our eighteen thousand head home."

"Home?" flashed Jacqueline, with a smile fleeting and beautiful.

"Yes, home! . . . And maybe I'm not glad to get here."

"Will you have a drink with me?" queried Pencarrow, his voice thick.

"No, thanks. I filled up on spring water," said Wade, rising. "And that reminds me, I want a tub of hot water."

"Tex, I'll send some over," drawled Hal. "Shore just got on to the fact thet you look like a niggah. . . . But did you tell us all thet happened?"

"Sure I did, son—at least all I could remember. It was a big job. Lots happened."

"Like the old lady who kept a tavern out West, you did," quoth Hal, and stalked jingling by to the door.

"Boss, you're short a h——er, a right smart storyteller," added Hogue Kinsey.

"Guess I'd better run—before the girls get after me," said Wade, beginning a retreat.

"We'll have lunch in about an hour," interposed Jacqueline. "And if you're not heah by then I'll come after you."

"In that case you can expect me," returned Wade, weakly, and left. Pencarrow and Kinsey followed him, caught up, and strode one on each side.

"I seem to be kinda popular," complained Wade, in cowboy vernacular.

"Out with it!" rang Pencarrow.

"Come clean, Tex, you can't fool us with your stories," added Hogue.

"Will you keep it secret from Hal and the girls?"

"I won't make no promises," declared the rancher.

"Tex, you cain't keep a damn thing from Rona or Hal," said Kinsey.

"Well, do your best. Just so Jacqueline doesn't hear," replied Wade, resignedly. "Listen, your curious bloodthirsty cusses! We cleaned out Harrobin's gang. Killed most—crippled the rest."

"Ahuh! . . . How about Harrobin?"

Wade breathed hard at a grotesque and terrible picture that haunted him. "Wait!" They were silent until they reached the cabin. How the familiar dry sweet-smelling log cabin thrilled him! Wade began to remove gun belt, vest, spurs, halting between each act, as if to speak, then he went on to remove his boots.

"Boss, get it off your chest," advised the cowboy. "You'll feel better. An' so will we."

"Mason bawled like one of his bulls," resumed Wade. "The barefaced front he made!—But it was no good. Harrobin calmly betrayed him. Shore that rustler wanted Mason, and Stewart, too, in on any deal he got. . . . Gosh, he was ugly."

"Mason bawled, huh? He shore was a loudmouthed man," replied Pencarrow. "What else did he do?"

Wade bent over to remove his wet and blackened socks.

"He—drew on me."

"Aw now—he did?" ejaculated Kinsey, his breath whistling.

"Mason drew on you?—Haw! Haw!" returned the Texan, harshly. "Wal, then, how about Harrobin?"

"Pencarrow, we hanged that hombre!"

Wade did not analyze what possessed him when for the first time in years he shaved off his beard. He scarcely recognized the pale lean face, with lines too sad and stern for its youth. But he reflected, also without delving into his feelings, that he was better looking as a man than he had been as a boy. Then he hurriedly dressed in new garments, and masking himself with a handkerchief, he presented himself at the living room door. Rona who saw him first was startled. Then Hal and Jacqueline, coming in with steaming dishes, stopped in their tracks.

"Hands up, Pencarrow," he ordered.

Rona gave a squeal of delight and snatched off his mask.

"I knew you. And all the time you've pretended to be an old geezer! . . . Look at him, Jacque. Isn't he just the darlingest cowboy?"

Jacqueline regarded him gravely. "I don't think I'd call him that, Rona, in the wildest flight of my imagination."

Pencarrow, who had almost failed to recognize his partner, growled his amaze. "Brandon, you're shore the damndest fellow I ever met!"

They had dinner, which seemed a kind of dream to Wade. Often he felt Jacqueline's dark eyes on him, in puzzled wonder. But he was certain this was not caused by any association in her mind with their first meeting so many years ago.

After lunch Pencarrow took him off to a point where they could view the range, and the afternoon passed in discussions and planning for the future.

He had supper with the cowboys. Kinsey had filled the chuck wagon with supplies to use on a very necessary trip to Holbrook. There were twenty-two cowboys, counting Hal, and excluding Wade. They were a merry and a hungry lot.

"Wal, of all the hawgs I ever fed, you hombres take the cake," ejaculated Dickerson, who had been elected cook because he was the best in the outfit.

Their camp was at the edge of the nearest group of pines, on the brook that ran down from the range. A nearby corral shut in a drove of kicking snorting horses. Several canvas tents shone in the light of the camp fires.

Pencarrow brought his daughters down or else they came of their own accord. Wade scarcely approved of the visit. The ejaculations of admiration were loud and profound, not wholly unaccompanied by characteristic comment.

"Jerry, you run this outfit in my absence," Wade was saying. "All you got to do is ride out in bunches of five, day and night, and circle that herd. If you run into any riders shoot first and ask questions afterward. . . . Let's see. I'll take the three wagons, leaving the chuck wagon here. And I'll want Kid Marshall, Bilt Wood, Hal and Hogue to go with me."

"All right, boss," replied the cowboy.

"Get me a list of things you all want."

Hogue Kinsey drew Wade aside. His demeanor was in marked contrast to his usual nonchalance. "Boss, let me off on thet trip to town," he begged. "I'm not atall well an' you know I can't drive a team—an' I don't want to go nohow."

"Hogue! What the hell's wrong with you?" demanded Wade, in curt surprise.

"I'm kinda sick."

"Sick? Say, are you trying to bamboozle me?"

"Honest to Gawd, boss, I ain't myself atall," protested Hogue almost writhing.

"I should smile you're not," snapped Wade, not knowing what to make of his favorite's lame excuses. "Like as not I'll run into Blue's outfit. Some rider dropped in on us last camp. He'd come from Winslow. Said Blue and Kent had been there. . . . Do yo want to stay here when that chance faces me?"

"Hell no!" exclaimed Kinsey, as if wrenched. "I was lyin'-shore, but don't ask me why."

"Well!" ejaculated Wade, as Hogue stalked off in the gloom. Then Wade lounged along the brook, pondering Kinsey's queer statement. Ahead of him a little tent, the kind sheepherders used, gleamed pale in the light of a campfire some rods off. Rounding the tent toward the light he almost ran into Jacqueline. Behind her came her father with some cowboys.

"Oh!" cried Jacqueline, breathlessly, her hands going up.

"Sorry to startle you. I didn't see you coming."

Then, as she stood like a statue, he became acutely aware of her intensity. She appeared as if she had come upon a ghost. Her lips were parted, her magnificent eyes burned like black opals.

"You remind—me—" whispered the girl, breaking off with a hand clapped to tremulous telltale lips.

Wade's panic sent a shudder over him. In the night, with the tent pale in the firelight, she had all but recognized the outlaw fugitive she had succored and whose secret she had kept. What if she did recognize him! All his love, his courage surged in a response to spare her and save himself.

"No wonder," he laughed. "With my clean face and all these beardless cowboys about!"

He passed on, trying not to hurry, pretending some business with his riders. But she called:

"Brandon, don't go! I was hunting for you." He turned back and she approached swiftly and eagerly.

"Miss Jacqueline! What is it?" he rejoined as she halted with a hand half outstretched.

"I'm so worried," she whispered, and taking his arm with both hands she led him away from the camp. Wade's mind whirled with many suppositions, while the fact of her dependence upon him and the sense of her clinging person confused him. Jacqueline looked back at the camp as they crossed the little bridge. The night was balmy, with a fresh smell of dank earth and growing things, and full of the plaintive peep of frogs. From the range came a prolonged bawling of calves. Wade heard the bay of wolves, the yelp of coyotes. He had forgotten these enemies of the cattleman. Jacqueline appeared bent on getting somewhere in a hurry and without being seen.

"What's the rush, Jacqueline?" asked Wade, at length.

"We must—get there—first," panted the girl.

By this time Wade had hazarded a guess at her trouble, and the memory of Hogue's queer talk and action confirmed it. She led him in a wide detour around the ranch house to the north end where the pines grew thickest on the slope of the knoll. A half moon had begun to silver the trees and sage. The range toward the desert gloomed weird and gray, silent as its shadow. Above towered the bulk of the mountain, black under the stars, and deceivingly clear in the night. Jacqueline led the way in among the pines to a secluded nook, which Wade remembered the sisters had frequented on hot days the preceding summer. A hammock and a bench showed dimly in the moonlight. Jacqueline led Wade in behind these where they could see the little moonlit glade without being visible themselves She was out of breath from exertion or emotion, no doubt from both.

"Brandon—they meet—here," she whispered, with tragic incoherence.

"Who meet?" asked Wade, though he had guessed well enough.

"Rona and Hogue. Many nights—since you've—been gone. . . . I discovered by accident. I was—sitting at my window—looking out—wondering how you. . . . And suddenly I saw some one in white—gliding along there—and here. Rona! . . . Then Hogue came—the brazen cowboy! Smoking a cigarette. . . . To make sure I went into—Rona's room. She had fixed her bed—put something in it—that even to the feel fooled me. But she was gone!"

"Well!" ejaculated Wade, soberly. "Damn that cowboy!"

"I don't believe we can—blame Hogue so much," went on Jacqueline. "When Rona wants anything—she always gets it. . . . She has developed into a woman—all at once it seems—full of fire and passion. She has grown so strange of late—older, self-contained, dreamy, secretive—and bold as a lioness. I didn't tell her what I'd seen. But I asked her—about Hogue—if he had made love to her--and she lied. . . . Rona lied!—And she's just passed sixteen!"

"Sixteen is old enough for a girl to fall in love—to lie—to do anything," replied Wade, thoughtfully. "But surely this is only a case of boy and girl love? You know."

"Oh, I don't know," wailed Jacqueline. "And I'm terribly afraid."

"Of what?"

"That they've gone so—so far we cain't—"

"Jacqueline, I swear Hogue wouldn't take advantage of that child."

"Oh, you think so," she exclaimed, grasping at hope. "But how could he help it—if she—if she. . . . Rona has burst out like a full-bloom rose. She takes my breath. . . . And Hogue—that rough, wild, lonely cowboy!—It wouldn't be natural or human to resist her. It's just one of those tragedies that cain't be foreseen."

"All true," agreed Wade. "They must be in love—to dare this. I'm sure I wouldn't blame either of them. Rona is sweet. And Hogue is just what she called him—won—der—ful! All natural and human. I can't see any shame in it. . . . I know Hogue. He wouldn't lay a hand on her."

"No he wouldn't!—Just you wait," returned Jacqueline, passionately. "I couldn't believe my eyes. But I saw."

"What did you see?" demanded Wade, fearfully.

"I saw Rona run—*run* into his arms. . . . They stood back up there—right in the open. They stood clasped together. A long time! Then Hogue picked Rona up and packed her down here."

"My God! It's the real thing. . . . But Jacqueline—that doesn't mean the crazy kids have. . . . I tell you I know Hogue wouldn't lose his head that far."

"How do you know?"

"I don't know how I know. I just feel it," said Wade, thoughtfully. "Hogue is no common sort. He had gone to the bad, sure. He told me. It was for a crippled sister. His people were poor. They had a hard time. . . . I found Hogue before he had become actually a criminal. Believe me, he snatched at the chance I gave him to go straight. And he has been just fine. I mustn't forget to tell you that when he saw Rona first he begged me to let him go. I reckon he fell then. But I wouldn't let him go. . . . Later, one day he told me it had happened—he was crazy about her, and wanted to go get himself killed. Well, I talked him out of it. Jacqueline, despite the look of this, I'll gamble on Hogue's honor."

"Oh—I've hated myself—for being so suspicious," whispered Jacqueline, beginning to cry from over-emotion and relief. "But it scared me so. Rona is the apple of Dad's eye. He'd *kill* Hogue if—if. . . . He'd be furious in any event. . . . Oh, I'm glad—you're back. I've been so helpless. . . . Somehow—I rely—on you."

She wept quietly, but unrestrainedly, and one look at her so close, so helpless in her trouble and her trust in him, was enough for Wade. He felt a great current sweeping him on and on toward a maelstrom.

"Don't cry, Jacqueline," he said, a little huskily. "I'll help you. Maybe it's not so bad. . . . But what are we doing here, spying on them. Hogue is a cowboy—a woodsman. He'll catch us."

"Much *you* know about love, Mr. Brandon," replied Jacqueline. "Neither of them could heah—the crack of doom."

"Even so, Hogue will hear you, if you don't stop crying."

"I'll stop. This is the first time—I've broken down," she said, wiping her eyes. "Your being heah with me—sharing it—standing so loyally by Hogue—just—"

"Quiet!" whispered Wade in her ear. "They're coming." And he drew Jacqueline a little farther back in the shadow. He had heard a light step—too light for the boot of a cowboy unused to walking.

Wade saw a gliding shadow. It vanished—again appeared. Jacqueline saw it, too, for she clutched Wade's warning hand. Then a white slender form came out in the moonlight. Rona! Her hair shone silver. She had the poise of a listening deer, but there was no hint of fear in her intensity. She was an alert girl, impatient for her lover. What a picture she made! Wade was moved to his depths. Could any man, much less a lonely unloved cowboy, resist that youth, loveliness, desire?

Suddenly Rona's slender form appeared to leap! She had heard what she expected. Running to the bench she sat down with her back toward the moonlit aisle down which she expected Hogue to come. The posture she assumed was one of indifference. How strange compared to her former lithe intentness, her listening passion.

Wade saw the red fire of a cigarette before he made out the tall cowboy. Hogue came on slowly and stealthily, and when he gained the aisle his cigarette no longer burned. He peered into the shadow. Sight of Rona completely overcame the caution of his slow approach. Then he reached her, spoke in a low tender tone.

"You're late," she replied, petulantly.

"I'm sorry. Just couldn't help it. Thet outfit an' your Dad. Then Tex—"

"If you loved me you'd not let anyone, even Tex, keep you."

"Love you? My Gawd, girl, I'm mad about you. I'm riskin' my life—for Pencarrow would kill me—an' what's more I'm riskin' more. Tex's friendship an' respect."

"But, darling, I haven't been with you for three whole days," protested Rona, passionately.

"Haven't I longed for you? Haven't I watched you from afar? Haven't I looked at the light in your window till it went out, night after night?"

"You like to talk to those cowboys," replied Rona, jealously. "You'd rather play cairds. And now that Tex is back, you forget me."

"Rona, be sensible," said Hogue, patiently. "I didn't forget you. I lied to Tex, tryin' to get out of somethin'. Told him I was sick."

"Get out of what?" queried Rona, her lovely head coming erect.

"Aw, never mind. But it took my nerve."

"Hogue!—What did Tex want?"

"Wal, he's leavin' for town in the mornin'. Takin' Hal, Kid, Bilt an' me. I tried to get out of it. Tex was some surprised. He looked at me—an' did I sink into my boots? Then he said sort of contemptuous thet I'd let him go to Holbrook when there was a shore chance he'd run into a fight. I just couldn't back out—"

"Fight?" cried Rona.

"Shore they'll be a fight. Blue an' his rustlers are up thet way. Been to Winslow. An' it's ten to one we'll run into them at Holbrook. I couldn't fail Tex. He wants *me*. I'd be so damn proud I'd bust if it wasn't for you. I'm so in love with you I can't be half a man. But I'm goin'. I wouldn't miss seein' Brandon fight Holbrook Kent for anythin' in the world."

Wade became aware of more than his reaction to Hogues passion and Rona's sudden awakening. Jacqueline gave a start. She gripped Wade's hand tight. But it was fear for him in her distended eyes that shook his nerve. A convulsed cry from Rona prevented any wild response in Wade to Jacqueline's fear for his life.

Rona had leaped up to throw her arms around Hogue's neck. Murmuring brokenly, incoherently, she pulled him to her, kissing him passionately, clasping him with frantic hands. Hogue manifestly resisted this avalanche of terror and love until it overcame him. Then he lifted her off the ground and lavished on her all the wild caresses of which any cowboy could have been capable. When he put her down she seemed so spent and weak that she could not stand without his support.

"Rona. Some day—you'll make—me less than half—a man," he panted.

"But—I love you. Hogue, I love you. I'm frightened," she sobbed.

"Shore you are. But you gotta be game. Why can't you have nerve like your sister?"

"Jacque—Pooh! You don't know—what I know. . . . Hogue, I try to be brave. I have been and happy, too, since you've been heah. But now—you're going away with that devil, Tex Brandon —to fight. . . . You might be—be—"

"Darlin', the chances are a hundred to one against my bein' hurt. Ain't you gambler enough to take that long chance? Tex has only an even chance. An' he'll get killed or bad shot, shore, before he's done all he's set himself."

"But *if* you were shot. . . . Oh, Hogue, what'd *I* do?"

"I won't be shot. I'll hide, dodge—I'll be bulletproof."

"Listen," she cried, excitedly, leaning back with her hands locked behind his neck. "When you get back this time, will you run off with me? . . . To Winslow! And—and marry me there?"

"Aw, Rona!" gasped Hogue. "I can't do thet. I can't. . . . Tex trusts me. Your Dad trusts me. They're gonna make me foreman now that Tex is a pardner. . . . Your sister would despise me."

"She would not. Jacque loves you, like a sister. Hogue, they couldn't do a single thing. Dad would raise the roof. But let him. Tex would beat you an' he'd look scorn at me with his terrible eyes. But let him. . . . We'd be married. It'd be too late!"

"Rona, for Gawd's sake, listen to *me*. I love you. An' I'll die for you. But I won't dishonor you! I won't put shame on you."

"Hogue, darling, there is no dishonor in eloping. We just cain't wait," replied the temptress.

"You don't know I was an outlaw—a rustler—when Tex got hold of me," said Hogue, hoarsely.

"*What?*"

"I was. Shore if you split hairs on it, as Tex did. I hadn't gone plumb to the bad yet. But *I* know. . . . Wal, I'd have to wipe thet out, an' square the debt of cattle I stole—even if it wasn't for myself, before I ever, *ever* dare to ask Pencarrow for you. Now, unless you're gonna make it wuss for me, you'll change your tune."

"Forgive me, Hogue," she pleaded. "You've been won—der—ful! You told me before I fell in love with you—that you'd been a wild hombre. But I didn't know—didn't guess. . . . Hogue, I don't care what you've been. I love you. I'll be true to you. . . . If only you'll not let that cold-blooded, flint and steel Brandon thrust you into the very teeth of death. Oh, he's so hard, so relentless. Hal just told me how Brandon shot Mason and hanged Harrobin to a post in the main street of Quirts."

"Wal, your brother ought to be kicked for tellin', an' I'll shore do thet little job," replied Hogue, grimly. "An' you're all wrong about Tex. Shore he's got two sides to him. But thet hard one is the gunman, an' thet ain't uppermost one tenth the time."

"I like Tex. He fascinates me. But now I almost hate him. He is unhuman."

"I'm surprised at you, Rona. But I'll make allowance for the way you feel. Only I hate to see you so set in a wrong idee. Tex Brandon is the finest, biggest hearted, most unselfish man I ever knew."

"Hogue, he hasn't got a heart," retorted Rona.

"What makes you say thet when *I* tell you he has?"

"Well, one reason, a woman's reason, if you will—he's the only man who ever saw Jacqueline and was like the very rocks toward her. He has insulted her, snubbed her, avoided her. It wouldn't have mattered if Jacque hadn't taken it amiss. She likes that man, Hogue, and he hurt her."

"Wal, if thet's one of your reasons I don't want to hear the others. An' I'm gonna make you crawl, Rona Pencarrow. . . . When I found out I was turrible in love with you I went to Tex an' I told him. I confessed. An' I begged him to let me go before I made a fool of myself an' brought trouble to you. I told him I couldn't endure it. An' when he refused again I called him much what you just called him. I was leavin' when he made me come back. . . . Then he told me what *he* was endurin'. From the very first sight of Jacqueline he had loved her—the first an' only girl he ever loved. It grew an' grew until it was the very breath of his life. But he had to hide it. He could never dream of her love—of havin' her—of all thet's so dear to a lonely man. . . . Why Tex near died when thet McComb fellow was here, hangin' around Jacqueline. I saw thet an' I was sorry for him. He has all the turrible feelin's of a lover who can't ever tell his love, let alone have the touch of hands and lips—all thet you an' I know are so precious. . . . But Tex would not leave her. He would not ride off thinkin' of himself, of his unrequited love, when your father was harassed to ruin. No, by Gawd! he wouldn't. An' thet settled me. I'd been happy to do the same if *you* hadn't found me out—an' kissed me—an' made me like wax. . . . But I just couldn't let you think ill of Tex. An' I beg you to keep his secret as I've kept it till now."

"Oh, how won—der—ful!" cried Rona. "That makes me see. . . . Oh, I'm sorry for any pighaidedness. . . . I'll love Tex now. I always wanted to. . . . How strange!—What would Jacque say?"

"Lord only knows. Women are queer. Don't you ever tell her unless you want to lose me."

"I swear. I cross my heart. . . . Oh, Hogue, you've lifted the burden there. But, darling, what will we *do*?"

"Wait. Thet's all. I've got the grandest chance thet ever came to a no-good cowboy. Tex will help me. All I gotta do is be with him. He'll clean out these rustlers. An' if he's killed—which I pray he never is—I'll go on with his work. Peace an' prosperity will come to this range. I see it, Rona. An' then with all thet's black against me washed off an' forgotten—then I may dare to ask Pencarrow for the most precious creature Gawd ever put breath into."

"Oh, Hogue, you have made me ashamed—and glad—and happy all at once," said Rona. "What a brainless little wretch I am. . . . But kiss me. I pledge myself. I am yours."

"Bless you, precious," replied Hogue, his arms tightening about her. "Come now. You must go. Don't worry about me. . . ."

Their voices trailed into silence and their forms melted into the shadows. Wade stood motionless, hardly breathing. The world had come to an end for him. Yet somehow he was glad.

Jacqueline slipped her hand from his. For the moment she seemed concerned mostly with her sister's romance.

"They will never know what they have to forgive in me," she said. "Tex Brandon, your faith, your bigness put me to shame. . . . I shall help them. I shall win Dad for them."

"And I will have a care for Hogue, though I'd never dare to make him shirk danger," replied Wade.

"Will you have a care for yourself?" she asked.

"That I cannot promise. There are times when sheer cold-blooded nerve carries a man like me through. But I am not heedless, ever."

She walked out of the shade into the moonlight and stood by the bench where Rona had waited. Wade followed with hesitation. He could not stay here a moment longer.

"It's getting late," he said, huskily.

"Yes. But I want to stay here to think—alone—"

Then I'll go. Good night."

She stood white and still, her profile turned clear and beautiful in the moonlight. She did not look at him or offer her hand. Silently and swiftly he turned away only to be halted by her voice.

"Did you call?" he queried.

"Yes. . . . Good night, friend of the Pencarrows," she said, softly.

CHAPTER SEVENTEEN

ONCE away from the softening influence of the Pencarrows, Wade caught up with his single and relentless purpose. He did not let his incredible luck undermine the imperative need for eternal vigilance. Even the trees and the stones were enemies. Spring brought more than balmy air and green grass to that range. It brought action for dark riders who had been holed up all winter.

How soon Rand Blue would learn of the fight in Red Gulch and the breaking of that large faction of the rustlers was a matter of conjecture for Wade. Rumor did not fly over ruddy roads. Blue had been seen in Winslow. The chances were that he would not learn of the death of Mason and Harrobin until he went back to Pine Mound.

Wade found travel slow and irksome. When he rode horseback he had to confine his pace to that of the wagons. But up on the plateau the road had dried out, and the drivers made up for dragging mud. They reached Holbrook after dark and unhitched at the corrals just outside of town. Wade called his cowboys together.

"We'll split up and slip into town," he said. "Hogue, you go alone. Kid, you and Bilt go together. Hal, you go alone, and be sure no one sees you. Keep in the dark. I'll follow. The idea is to find out if Blue's gang is in town before they find out we are. Caution is the word. We'll come back here and sleep in the wagons."

"Are we to drop in any saloons?" asked Kid Marshall.

"Yes. But one drink will do you. I won't give you any more specific orders. Use your heads."

Kinsey left the group and disappeared in the gloom. Hal stalked off, his head erect, impressive with importance.

"Wal, come on," said Kid to Bilt who hung back.

Doggone it, boss, can't I call on my gurl for a minute?" he got out, with difficulty.

"Just the thing. Make it longer. Get all the town gossip. . . . Kid, have you a girl?"

"I had one, boss—the same Bilt's got. I reckon he double-crossed me," replied Marshall.

"Dig up another. Remember caution. This is stern business. Now go."

They disappeared up the lane where Hal and Kinsey had preceded them. Wade rolled and smoked a cigarette. He was in no hurry. The hour was early, just after supper. Presently, on this Saturday night, the main street of Holbrook would be thronged. Wade had nothing especial to think over. Every possible contingency that might arise had been considered. In the nature of events, as he calculated them, this visit to Holbrook was critical. It might well be conclusive. He sensed something charged, cumulative, inevitable. If he had been a gambler for gold, instead of life, he would not have hesitated on this still balmy spring night to stake all on the turn of a single card.

Wade left his coat, which was of dark hue, in the wagon. On former visits to Holbrook he had worn black. This time he had on a light shirt and an old tan sombrero. These, with the removal of his beard, would make him difficult to recognize at a glance as Tex Brandon.

Presently he sauntered slowly up town. Lamps flared yellow and dim. Pedestrians on one side of the wide street could be distinguished only as their dark forms passed the lights. Wade walked the length of the long block of stores and saloons, crossed to the opposite side and proceeded along that. Business was good. The saloons were crowded, and there were many hilarious cowboys jostling and jingling up and down the sidewalk.

A lanky high-booted cattleman, leaning against a hitching rail, invited Wade's interest. "Howdy," said Wade. "Just rolled in. What's the news about town?"

"Howdy, stranger," replied the other, with a keen glance. "Lots of news. Any special kind you want?"

"Not particular. Town 'pears pretty lively."

"Yes. First trip in for most cowboys an' all the teamsters. Stores all loaded up with new goods. There's a new store, too, Radwell's—an' they're gettin' trade. Are you buyin', stranger?"

"Three wagonloads. I'm foreman for Pencarrow."

"Pencarrow? Reckon I dont know him. But I'm not an old stager around Holbrook."

"How are cattle sellin'?"

"Steady. Thirty dollars on the hoof. The big ranchers here are holdin' tight. Cattle will climb slowly for several years."

"That Lincoln County War over yet?"

"Hell no. It busted out fresh this spring. I reckon thet fight at McSween's beats them all."

"Thet so? Tell me about it."

"All I know is what I heerd. It 'pears Billy the Kid an' his outfit was on McSween's side in this war. An' the other faction surrounded McSween's. There was a hell of a fight for two days. McSween an' some of his men killed. Billy the Kid held the fort till they set fire to it. Would you believe it, thet cold-blooded little rooster held out till the roof was blazin'. Then in the face of rifle fire an' in light bright as day Billy's outfit made a break for it. Some of them were killed, but most of them got away. Billy came out arunnin' with a gun in each hand spoutin' red. They never touched him."

"Well! Nervy fellow, that Billy the Kid," declared Wade.

"Quiet little chap. I seen him once. Only a boy! But he was shore born without fear."

"What you hear about our own rustler factions?"

"I ain't heerd nothin'. It's about time, though, our ranges got to warmin' up. This'll be a hot year for cattle thieves."

"Reckon it will," agreed Wade. "Well, I'll be moseyin' along."

Wade did not accept this cattleman's talk as conclusive, still he did not want to risk recognition by going into places where he was known. He kept a sharp lookout for his own men, and satisfied himself that not one of them passed him. He ventured peeping in the saloons, where he was greeted by smoke and loud talk and the odor of rum. Finally Wade decided he would let well enough alone and he went back to the wagons, where he smoked and waited.

Kinsey was the first to arrive. "Wide open cow town, boss," he said. "Money an' booze thick as hops. I saw one doubtful lookin' outfit, but the cowboys I asked didn't know them. Or said they didn't! You can buy drinks for anybody, but they're not tellin' you anythin'."

"I had a look up town. Talked with one man. He said there was plenty of news, and asked what particular kind I wanted. I was a little leery of him."

"Here comes somebody. . . . It's Kid. . . . Over this way, Kid."

"Doggone! I can't see straight. Thet drink I had musta been aquafortis. . . . Gimme a cigarette. . . . You hombres don't look worried none."

"What'd you get track of, Kid?" queried Wade.

"Not a damn thing to make us set up an' take notice. Town's full of cowpunchers, all heeled with a winter's wages. Some slick little hawk-eyed gurls thet I never seen before. Shore had to duck them. Plenty of cardsharps. An' a sprinklin' of rustlin' gents, if I know thet brand."

"Did you see anything of Bilt?"

"Not after the locoed galoot seen Susie with some longlaiged cowpuncher," responded Marshall, with a deep laugh. "I guess mebbe thet little chunk of taffy ain't a smart one. Had me believin' she never looked at no puncher but me. Had Bilt the same."

"Kid, this is no time for girls," said Wade, seriously.

"Boss, I know thet. An' I gave Bilt a hunch But he's plumb loco. He loves thet lyin' little wench. An' to be fair to her, I reckon she likes him best. Anyway they was engaged."

"Here he comes now," interposed Hogue.

Bilt's shuffling clinking step announced his approach. He darkened out of the gloom, and his heavy breathing could be heard before he got to the wagon.

"Winded, by gosh!" whispered Kid, dramatically. "Bilt wouldn't run from anythin' on laigs."

"Whar'n hell air you—all?" he growled, gropingly.

"All here but Hal. Did you see him?"

"Nope. I didn't—see nothin'," replied Bilt, slumping down on a wagon tongue. His labored breathing appeared to come more from agitation than activity.

"Hell you didn't," snapped Kid. "I just told the boss. An' he's sore."

"Tex, I was knocked off my saddle," explained Bilt. "Run into Susie with a handsome cowboy. He shore was the dandy. I told her pronto thet I wanted to see her alone. She said she was sorry but I'd have to wait. An' if I'd like to know it there wasn't any particular reason why she should see me nohow. . . . My Gawd! Wimmen shore are no good! . . . Wal, her gentleman friend crowed at me. I asked him polite who he was. An' he said Joe Steele, from Mariposa, one of Mason's riders. He was expectin' his boss on the ten o'clock train from Winslow. I said sarcastic, 'Wal, your boss won't come on thet train or any other. *An'* 'Mr. Steele,' I went on, 'he won't buy no more rustler cattle. . . .'" He yelped angry at thet, an' I got the idee he was honest enough. No doubt Mason had a square outfit. But I shut Steele up an' asked him short an' sweet if he was packin' a gun. Susie bleated thet he wasn't an' for me to go where it was hot. Steele tried to get in a word. Finally he told me he wasn't packin' no gun an' thet if he was he wouldn't throw it on a jealous little runt like me. Not before a lady! . . . Haw! Haw! So I swung on him, biff,

biff! right on his handsome mug, an' left him layin' at Susie's feet."

Wade was silent, pondering Bilt's story, while the other boys made dry comments.

"Boss, lemme go back uptown now an' I'll find out somethin'," begged Bilt.

"You did pretty well," rejoined Wade. "I question the wisdom of telling Steele his boss would never buy any more rustled cattle. But let that go. In another day or so it'll be range news. . . . Will Steele be hunting you up tomorrow?"

"If he's got any guts he will. Mebbe he was talkin' lofty before the girl."

A quick sharp footstep, without the jingling accompaniment of spurs, caught Wade's ear. He held up his hand. It always pleased him to be the first of his outfit to hear or see some one. Hal arrived. He was pale with importance and his big eyes gleamed in the starlight.

"Rand Blue—or Drake, as he's known—an' Holbrook Kent are in town," he announced coolly, breathing hard.

No one made any reply at the moment. Presently Kinsey coughed and said: "Ahuh. . . . Good work, Hal. None of us got even a hunch."

"Tex, I went up one side of the street an' then down the other. Run plumb into McComb. He was surprised an' anxious. I told him we were in town with you. He drew me back in the shadow. . . . That mawnin' he'd been in the bank. He's a director now. An' he learned that Drake an' Kent were in town layin' pretty low. Drake went to the bank. He had four men with him. He has a big sum of money. He had expected to meet Mason at Winslow. But Mason didn't come. Thet's what Drake told the cashier. Seemed pretty anxious."

"He expects to meet Mason here, and probably Harrobin too," said Wade, decisively.

"McComb told me that Drake has had many friends in Holbrook," went on Hal. "This visit is his first since last fall. Seems changed, the cashier said. Thet rustler rumor hangs over him."

"All right. My luck holds," returned Wade, incisively. "We know Blue and Kent are in town. But they don't know we are. And they won't know till we meet Blue or Kent—or both. . . . Listen, boys. Tomorrow early hitch up and drive the three wagons up town. Go to Sloan's. They are friends of Pencarrow. Stick close together. Buy and pack this list of supplies pronto, but not to excite curiosity. . . . Hogue, you hang around the front of the store. Keep your eye peeled. If I happen along don't notice me. I'll be taken for a stranger."

"Ahuh. . . . An' what're you gonna do, boss?" inquired Kid Marshall.

"I'll be on the lookout. That's all."

"Wal, if you meet up with Kent an' Blue's outfit together oughtn't some of us be with you?" asked Kinsey.

"Yes. Probably it won't work out that way. You can trust me to use my head. Remember, no one in Holbrook will recognize me, much less Blue or Kent."

"Boss, has it struck you thet Blue is far from his hole an' has only a few of his outfit with him?" queried Hogue Kinsey.

"It has," returned Wade, vehemently. "Boys, we're riding pretty. Crawl into the wagons and get some sleep. I'll walk a little, then turn in."

Wade strolled along the corral fence. The night was still. There were no sounds from the town. Near at hand the horses munched their feet. Wade could not inhibit his sensorial perceptions, but he set his thought solely in one direction and clamped it inexorably there. Conjectures and doubts formed no part of that thought. His control and restraint were so perfect that when he crawled into Hal's wagon and lay down beside the lad, he went to sleep at once.

Wade awoke at daylight, and got up to join Kid Marshall and Kinsey, who were starting a fire and carrying water. They prepared breakfast right there in the corral. Hal was sound asleep and hard to awaken. While they ate, the sun came up over the red desert bluffs in the east. It was a cool wonderful Arizona morning. The sky and the time in May presaged wind, and wind meant blowing dust and sand.

"Boss, when we get the supplies all bought an' packed, what'll we do?" asked Kid Marshall. He probably knew as well as the silent Kinsey, but he had to talk.

"Wait for me," rejoined Wade. "Don't forget a pack of grub to eat on the way home. . . . Reckon I'll shave my dirty face right now. Bilt will you fetch me some hot water?"

Kinsey stood by while Wade removed a three days' growth of beard. It left his face pale and lean again.

"Well, Hogue, what's on your mind?" queried Wade, presently.

"I was just watchin' you use thet razor," drawled Hogue. "Hand as steady as a rock! An' you shore as hell to meet Holbrook Kent today! . . . You're all cold nerve, Tex."

"Hogue, the advantage is all mine," said Wade.

"Tex, I was thinkin' somethin' else. Holbrook Kent won't know me, either. Would you let me meet him instead of you?"

"No, cowboy, I wouldn't."

"Wal, I didn't expect you would. But I'm tellin' you—I'm gonna stick by you every damn minute this heah day."

"Oh, you are? Against orders?"

"I wish you would fire me."

"Well, then, against my wishes?"

"Against anythin', Tex. I thought it out last night. I cain't do it no more than you'd let me. It's somethin' I feel, but cain't explain. Shore I know you don't run a hell of a risk. But it's not thet. There's a chance, you know, an' I ought to be beside you. Kid said the same thing an' thet if I didn't he would."

"Then let Kid go with me."

"Nope. I can beat Kid to a gun an' thet entitles me to come first."

"But Hogue, suppose we'd run into Kent with Blue's outfit and we'd both be killed? Then who'd take my place at Cedar Ranch?"

"Boss, I reckon thet if you an' I run into this whole outfit today—an' do get bored—Wal, it'd be the end of Blue, too. An' thet means anyone could run Pencarrow's ranch from then on."

"Hogue, you figure pretty keen. I hate to give in. But I'm bound to respect your creed. Only see here, old man, there are extenuating circumstances for you. I've put all else out of my mind—especially Rona and Jacqueline. But I *could* recall them, unwise as that would be. Then I could give you a reason why you should let Kid take the risk with me."

"No, you couldn't."

"Pard, I was out under the pines the other night in the moonlight—"

"No matter," interrupted Kinsey, his voice ringing. He was visibly shaken, but wrenched out of the momentary weakness. "Forget thet, an' anythin' else but the job at hand."

"Right!" ejaculated Wade, soberly. He could no longer go against his own teachings. "Let's argue no more. Stick an extra gun in your left hip pocket, as I'll do. And roll them a bit to loosen up your hands."

Wade secured a second gun from his pack and retiring to a secluded shed behind the stable he spent a few moments in deliberate practice. That physical expression of the lightning-swift coordination between mind and eye and muscle liberated the domination of cold passion over his faculties. He became like a set hair trigger.

Upon returning to the wagons he briefly repeated his orders to the cowboys, then strode off toward town. Kinsey caught up with him, and taking a position on his left side a step apart, maintained that place without further ado.

The main street of Holbrook presented early morning activities. Riders were coming in, singly and in groups; loaded wagons moved out toward the range; stores and saloons were open, and the sidewalks showed loungers and pedestrians.

Wade took a good while to travel leisurely down one side of the street. But lounge along as he did, he was all eyes. He crossed to see the three Pencarrow wagons pull up to Sloan's and the cowboys roll off the seats, cigarettes smoking, their sombreros cocked sidewise, their movements leisurely.

One disturbing factor wedged into Wade's mind—the possibility of a long stalk for the men he sought. If it so happened that he had to promenade the street, peering into stores and saloons, his search would soon become obvious. Then it must develop into a bold hunt, with the advantage switching to his foes. This contingency haunted him, though he did not believe it would come to pass. Things had not run that way. His luck would hold.

Wade did not need Kinsey's slight hist to espy a group of men standing at the rail in front of the Range Well, the main saloon in town. Only one of these idlers had he ever seen before. Wade was trying to place him when the saloon door swung.

Several men strolled out joking among themselves. The foremost was a stout ruddy-faced fellow in his shirt sleeves. He wore a star on his vest. This group did not exactly block Wade's way, but he halted some steps back.

Then a little man came out, guardedly, it appeared to Wade. He had bright sharp eyes like gimlets. Instinctively Wade recognized him as Holbrook Kent. His companion, a lanky uncouth rider, Wade had seen before. At sight of Wade he froze. Suddenly the group ahead sensed or saw that the moment was charged with potentialities.

"Hey, who're you?" called the sheriff to Wade, blusteringly. An intense curiosity appeared in Kent's eyes. But he lacked Wade's long-trained instinct in meeting men.

"Howdy, Kent," said Wade, with cool effrontery.

"You got the best of me," returned the gunman, gruffly.

"Sure I have. I had it on Mason and Harrobin, too."

"What!" bit out Kent.

"Yes. And before nightfall your big pard Drake will swing . . . But you'll never see it, Kent."

"Hell you say? . . . An' who're . . ."

"Thet's Pencarrow's foreman," yelled the rider wildly. "Brandon!"

With ring of spur and scrape of boot Kent's comrades spread to right and left, leaving the principals in the middle of the sidewalk.

"Mason won't be here to meet you, Kent. . . . But I am!" called Wade, meaningly.

The little gunman hesitated only an instant—that appreciable fraction of time it took to react from surprise. Then with a hiss he reached for his gun. He had it coming up when Wade's shot destroyed the action. The gun discharged as it fell and the report rang loud and clapped in echo from the opposite wall. The little man fell, lifeless before he flopped to the sidewalk. Visage and glance set in that last grim expression.

Wade wheeled with his smoking gun low. "Friend of Kent's, eh?"

"Not particular," choked out the sheriff, ghastly of face. "An' so you're Mr. Brandon?"

Wade backed against the wall, where Kinsey joined him. The four men guardedly left the wall to move forward, still aghast, fastening eyes of amaze and incredulity upon the dead Kent. Clatter of boots sounded from up and down the saloon, and the adjoining stores. If Wade had desired an audience, here it was. His glance oscillated like a compass needle. He missed no newcomer while he still held the eyes of this sheriff and his companions. He saw Bilt and Kid approaching, and Hal, white-faced with a strained look.

"Boss, he's Sam Hiles, sheriff down Winslow way, an' not so damn much," drawled Hogue, cool as ice.

"Hey, cowboy, I've seen you somewhere," snapped Hiles, reddening.

"Dare say you have. An' you're seein' me *now*," retorted the cowboy.

At that juncture Kid Marshall and Bilt Wood came sidling in between the gathering crowd and the wall. They got inside the circle but did not at once line up with Hogue. Kid's glittering eyes took in Kent on the sidewalk, Wade backed against the wall, his gun still in his hand. Then they swerved to the sheriff and the others.

"Hiles, are you a friend of Kent's?" repeated Wade, sharply.

"I said not particular. I'm sheriff of this county. But I'll say Holbrook had many friends hyar."

"Did they know he was hand in glove with a cow thief?"

"Who? Holbrook Kent. Say, you're drunk or crazy. You can get away with thet now, shore, after killin' him."

"Declare yourself, Hiles," demanded Wade, coldly. "You've no call on the law against me. It was self-defense. And if you don't clear me I'll consider you one of Kent's many friends."

"Wal, you can consider an' be damned. An' if you don't rustle, I'll arrest you."

"Rustle? That should be a familiar word with you—along with the rest of Kent's many friends."

"What you mean?" rasped Hiles, turning green.

"I mean this. There's a crooked ring in Holbrook, and I'll bet you belong to it."

"Crooked ring? Brandon you're talkin' heap brave with Kent daid there an' you with the drop on me."

Wade's keen intuition sensed the interest of that listening crowd and the moment which had seemingly been made for him.

"Crooked ring, I said. You're one who profits from it directly or indirectly. Holbrook Kent was the right-hand man of Band Drake. And Band Drake is Rand Blue. He's here to meet Mason, the cattle buyer from Mariposa. Mason buys rustled cattle. . . . Hiles, you've got a crook right here with you now. That rider!"

Wade pointed his gun at the man who had recognized him. "He was in the outfit when I shot Urba for trying to rob Pencarrow."

"I don't know him," replied the sheriff.

"Maybe you don't. All the same if I run across him again I'll bore him. And you bet we're going to ramsack this town for Drake."

"By Gawd, man, you're a bold one, whoever you are," replied Hiles, hoarsely, and he looked the guilt he had so brazenly denied. "Mason will have you run out of Arizona for thet."

"No, not Mason!" retorted Wade. "Hiles, you and your town crowd, and your range neighbors, take this and swallow it. . . . Mason was a buyer from Harrobin and Drake. He was that vilest of range corruptors because he fostered rustling and escaped its consequence—for a time. Harrobin rustled Aulsbrook's herd. My outfit with Aulsbrook's riders took that trail. We caught those rustlers, killed most of them and got the confession of others. We rounded up Harrobin and Mason. At Red Gulch, south of Cedar Range. Harrobin gave Mason away, betrayed him, told of the money he had just accepted for Aulsbrook's herd. . . . Gentlemen, cattle-buyer Mason will never buy another head of stock—or try to draw his gun on a better man. . . . Harrobin we hanged! And we're going to hang his pardner Band Drake, otherwise Blue. The day of this rustler combine is done."

"*Brandon!*" cried an excited voice from the crowd. "He's thet Texas gunman with his half-breed outfit!"

CHAPTER EIGHTEEN

WADE had little fear that Blue would make a break to escape by daylight. He would hide until after nightfall. Nor would Rand Blue ever come out to fight! Nevertheless, Wade sent Hal to the highest roof in Holbrook, there to watch, while he and his cowboys ranged about like hounds on the scent.

"Show me thet geezer who called us a half-breed outfit," Kid Marshall kept calling out, as he prodded this and that pedestrian with his rifle.

"Where have you got 'em hid?" Hogue Kinsey demanded of all whom he met.

Wade beat locked doors with his rifle butt until they were opened.

"You may be honest," he said, to merchants, clerks, bartenders, even to white-faced women. "Sure, we know most of you *are* honest. But if you won't help you must permit us to find Rand Blue and his rustlers."

The main street of Holbrook became empty of its customary movement. Holbrook Kent lay dead where he had fallen, his hand still clutching his half-drawn handkerchief.

Wade, lean-faced and pale, like a wolf, led his three cowboys on that hunt. They held their rifles ready. They trusted no roof, no window, no alley, no corner. They kept close to the walls. They had eyes in the backs of their heads. They entered every building on that street, searched high and low, in lofts and cellars, in grain bins and storerooms, in stables. When the day was done, only the private houses remained unsearched. Hal had not seen a single horseman ride away from town.

But when night fell Susie came weeping to Bilt Wood, almost falling at his feet. "Bilt—that cowboy Steele—was one of them," she sobbed. "He hid Drake- -an' three other men—in our house—scared Pa an' Ma half to death. . . . When it got dark, they took a sack—of food an' things—an' left. . . . Pa heard our horses kicking—in the corral.—Soon as he dared he went out. . . . They'd gone—with only two saddles."

"Haw! Haw!" shouted Bilt, but whether he was demented with gladness or ferocity Wade could not tell. "It'd served you right if Steele had made off with you—you damned little hussy. . . . Which way'd they go?"

"South, on the Pine Mound road."

"Where'n hell else could they go?" queried Kinsey, scornfully. "Back to their hole-up. . . . Tex, the yellow dawgs would have done better to come out here an' fight. It's sixty miles to Pine Mound an' the road's bad. Not cut off. Rocks an' mud, dark as hell. Four men on farm hosses with two saddles!"

"Boss, you can head them off," added Kid Marshall exultantly.

"Fork your hawse, Tex," chimed in Bilt. "Ride for home, you hangin' son of a gun! We'll foller with the wagons. You can make the ranch before daybreak. Bust in on the boys. Take Miss Jackie's fast hawses. Ride Pen yourself, an' set Hicks to haid off Blue."

"Boys, you all must be mind readers," flashed Wade, grimly.

"Oh, Tex, let me go with you?" begged Hal, wild-eyed.

"Pard, I'd like to go, too, but heah I cain't," drawled Hogue, with his frank smile. "You won't need me."

"Aw!—I won't get to see thet Rand Blue kick on a rope," wailed Kid Marshall.

"Hell! What's thet to miss?" yelped Bilt Wood. "I won't get to haul on the rope thet strangles Mister Steele. I won't get to see his handsome mug. . . . Ha!"

"That'll do, you-all," returned Wade, peremptorily. "Miss

Susie, thanks for your help. It was a tough place for a girl. But you've made up for what you did. Bilt will forgive you."

"Like hell I will," replied Wood, but it was a crow rather than a growl.

"Rustle, boys. I'm off," added Wade, and turned to run down the vacant dark street.

Holbrook had had a day to remember, he thought, one that augured well for the future. The worst feature of rustling cattle was its almost universal practice in the first days of new ranges. The indifference to fear of ranchers, perhaps the knowledge that they transgressed the letter of the law, the connivance of stock buyers and railroads, the profit to a whole community, more or less—these were the things that gave rustlers more power than the cattle barons. Cattle meant money. Merchants, saloons, gamblers, cowboys, rustlers, dance-hall girls, everybody lived off cattle. It took some such revolution as Wade had started to awaken a rich range to its senses, to what was right and what was wrong.

The only man Wade encountered in his hurry down the main street was Holbrook Kent, lying as he had fallen, ghastly and stark in the moonlight. This time Wade stopped to take the gunman's gun. That the citizen of whom the town had boasted with pride should lie dead all day in the street proved the panic which had prevailed.

Wade arrived at the corrals out of breath from running. It took him a little while to find his horse Baldy, a big rangy roan, noted for his endurance. Wade saddled him and remembered to sheath his rifle. His extra gun and Kent's he put in the saddlebags, one on each side. Then he reflected a moment. The wagons were gone. There was nothing left in the corral. By this time the cowboys would be driving south. Then mounting, he urged Baldy to a gallop. What a clatter the big hoofs of the roan made down the quiet street! Lights had begun to show and groups of men in doorways and at the street corners. These men watched him ride by, his lean horse stretching out. At the outskirts of town Wade caught up with the wagons. He passed them without slowing down. Hal Pencarrow greeted him with a wild whoop.

"Ride thet hoss, Tex!" yelled Hogue, in his clear high voice.

"Fork him, cowboy!" added Kid Marshall. And Bilt Wood's unintelligible shout, fierce and vengeful, floated after him.

The level road, pale in the moonlight, stretched ahead across the desert. Wade eased the horse to a lope, a gait Baldy could hold indefinitely over good ground. Far to the south dark buttes loomed above the horizon. To the west the great mountain stood up black and grand, its ragged peaks splitting the blue.

At the river Wade slowed to a trot. Baldy went splashing across the shallow sand bars. The moonlight glistened on the frostlike margins of alkali. Beyond began the only ascent on that road to Cedar Range, a gradual climb for a mile through rocky country. Wade saved the horse. From the ridge he looked back to see the ragged black patch that was the town marked by a few lights.

From that point the road descended gradually. The roan settled to a steady lope. The bleak desert, denuded of trees, flashed by on either side of Wade, gray and shadowy. Jack rabbits streaked away into the sage. The air was cool and as Wade rode on, his eye piercing the melancholy moonlit obscurity, his thoughts were centered on Rand Blue.

The rustler, with his men, would expect pursuit on the Pine Mound road. But their calculations would begin from the next morning at the earliest. They would spare nothing on that night ride. On the morrow they would be within striking distance of their hiding place in the brakes.

Wade's plan was to head Blue off before he left the road. If that failed, however, it would only prolong the pursuit. Hicks would trail the rustlers to their lair.

Absorbed in his ruthless concentration, Wade rode on. He walked the horse through dark stretches of woods, trotted him over the rough going, and loped him in the open. The moon soared high. The hours passed as swiftly as the miles. By midnight the rolling range of cedars and pines dropped away in front of Wade, a vast gray vale, pale and obscure under the moon. Lost somewhere in that basin grazed his herd of cattle. He had the length of that valley to ride, and calculating he was ahead of his schedule, he gave Baldy a good long walk. The moon began to wane and the desert to lose its opaque curtain. Soon he resumed the alternate lope and pace that had covered distance so satisfactorily. The moon slid behind the mountain and a wan twilight intervened. That gave place to the dark hour before dawn.

When this lightened to gray, Wade was riding across the flat toward the ranch. Dawn soon followed, with ruddy streaks on the horizon. He galloped the last mile along the pasture lane, and on to the bunkhouse of the cowboys. Leaping off he uncinched the heaving Baldy, and threw the saddle with a flop.

Hicks appeared in the door with a gun in his hand.

"Mawnin', boss," he said. "I heard thet hawse comin' an' I kinda reckoned it'd be you."

"It's me, all right. . . . Wake the boys."

"Hyar, you Injuns!" yelled Hicks. "Pile out. . . . Boss hyar rarin' to go."

Wade led the steaming heaving roan to the pasture gate and turned him in, adding to his memorable list another great horse he had ridden.

The cowboys, with tousled hair, were getting into their boots.

"Hogue an' the boys all right?" asked Jerry, anxiously.

"Yes. They left Holbrook before me, just after dark."

"Whew!—I had a peep at Baldy. . . . Wal?"

"How many riders out?"

"Five. They'll be in at sunup."

"We won't wait. . . . Listen, all of you. . . . Rand Blue and three of his men left Holbrook at dark last night. Poorly mounted, two riding bareback. They'd hid from us all day. . . . Do any of you know a cowboy named Steele, from Mariposa?"

"Sure. I rode with Steele. Fancy fellar. He's in Mason's outfit," replied one of Aulsbrook's riders.

"Well, he's with Blue. It seems Steele beat Bilt out of his girl, Susie something. Bilt had a fight with Steele night before last. And that's how we came to find out where Blue hid all day. Susie came and told Bilt that Steele had hid Blue and the other men in her house."

"Was they hidin' from you, boss?" queried Jerry, curiously.

"They were. After I killed Kent, we treated the town pretty rough hunting for Blue. He had friends there. But they all went back on him yesterday. Scared, I reckon. We had rifles and we prodded whoever we run into and banged at the door. Kid and Hogue were tough. This fellow Steele who'd double-crossed Bilt forced Susie's folks to hide him and Blue and the other two till after dark. Then they escaped on farm horses, taking the Pine Mound road. . . . It's our job to head them off. How about that, Hicks?"

"Take some ridin'," replied the half-breed.

"Then jump, all of you. Rustle Miss Jacqueline's horses. Saddle Pen for me while I stretch my legs. Make some strong coffee. Pack some meat and biscuits."

"Want any word left?" asked Jerry.

"No."

Before the sun tipped the gray sage with rose, Wade's riders were up on prancing fiery horses.

"Hicks, you lead. It'll be trail riding."

"I reckon. Shorter across country. But rough. We can beat thet time."

"How far?"

"Thirty odd miles."

"Where will Blue be heading for?"

"Somewhere in the brakes. Harrobin's Hole, they call it. Trail heads beyond Pine Mound."

"Blue will stay on the road as far as Pine Mound," asserted Wade, grimly.

"Yes, an' he'll never get thet far," chimed in Jerry. "Blue's no cowboy. He's got a bad ankle. An' I never seen the farm hoss thet could travel from Holbrook to Pine Mound in one night."

"Boss," spoke up Strothers, another of Aulsbrook's men and one that Wade wanted to keep on at Cedar Ranch. "I calkilate Blue hasn't heard what happened to Harrobin's outfit, or he wouldn't be makin' for Pine Mound atall."

"Any old buck will make for his old stampin' ground," vouchsafed another rider.

"We're not concerned with Blue's reasons," returned Wade. "Probably he hadn't heard about Harrobin. But I told that Holbrook sheriff. About Mason, too. With Kent out of the deal and only a couple of men Blue showed yellow."

"Boss, we're wastin' time," interposed the half-breed. "All you need to know is thet if Blue leaves his tracks anywhere I can trail him."

"Right. . . . Cut loose, Hicks."

With clattering rhythmic beat of swift hoofs on the hard ground the spirited horses swept down the lane and out upon the reddening sage.

Of all Wade's wild cowboy riders the half-breed was the wildest. He had all the Indian's matchless horsemanship and all the range rider's daredevil boldness. Wade expected a breakneck pace which even he would be unable to hold, though he had in Pen the swiftest horse on the range. He expected to have to caution the reckless Hicks.

In this calculation Wade was deceived. The half-breed at the very outset displayed a scrutiny of the ground ahead and consideration for a horse. Nevertheless he rode like the wind, with the cowboys strung out behind.

"For once Hicks is riding careful," called Wade to Jerry who rode beside him.

"Shore. He ain't gonna miss gettin' a shot at Steele. He's Bilt's pard, you know."

"Aha! So that's it." Wade had been giving the half-breed credit for thought of the great importance of this ride, of what its successful issue meant to his boss and to Pencarrow and the range. But Hicks' thought was to avenge the betrayal of his friend.

The rising sun shone on the flat sage and grass valley with its thousands of grazing cattle. Wade's grim mood admitted appreciation of the beauty and color of that scene, of its significance to him. But it was only a fleeting thought. There was also something wonderful about riding this swiftest of the Pencarrow thoroughbreds. Pen's running gait, like his pace, was something to incite a range rider's love for a great horse.

Hicks swerved off the flat into the cedars, on the trail Wade had ridden so often. It wound snakelike through the gray trees, giving up a ringing clatter from the iron hoofs. The flash of gray-green, the reaching out of dead snags, like clutching hands, the dry fragrance of cedar mixed with sage, the rhythmic beat, beat, beat, the dark little half-breed's crouch in the saddle as he peered ahead, the long single file of riders behind, silent, formidable—all these encroached upon Wade's hard concentration of mind, and warned him for a flashing thought that he was not only an engine of destruction but a man who would have to face himself soon.

From the cedar forest Hicks led into rocky country where he trotted his horse and walked him down into the canyon. On a sandy trail he spared the horse. Climbing out he rode into the pine belt that reached all the way to Pine Mound. A bad trail for miles slowed down the cavalcade. An hour's tedious vigilant riding put behind the zone of rocks and gullies. Hicks left the trail to head into the main pine forest. For centuries the Apaches had burned the grass and brush in this forest, so that it was open like a park.

White and bronze glades and aisles stretched away under the brown-barked pines; deer fled in troops before the charge of the horses; golden shafts of sunlight shot down through the canopy of green; patches of bluebells smiled up from the grass and yellow columbines went down under the ruthless hoofs. Again Wade's stern mind reacted to the fact that this act he was performing concerned only the fleeting present. When it had been consummated and these vicious rustlers were gone, this lovely and grand forest, with its stately pines and colorful glades, the sage-blue flats where the cattle grazed, the stonewalled canyons and the luring reach of the desert, all this wonderland that constituted Arizona would be left free, peaceful, prolific, to be loved and lived with, and to prosper by. The thought troubled Wade. What had he to do with thoughts like that? And he drove them away for the grim realism of this ride and its end soon to come.

Hicks made up for his caution. He raced his horse through the forest, down the aisles, dodging branches, leaping logs. The best Wade could do was keep him in sight. And at last he lost the half-breed altogether. But presently Wade saw the road, and a moment later Hicks on foot, bending low, searching for tracks. Wade pulled Pen to a halt and leaped off. And in another moment the cowboys came tearing to the road.

Wade took a look himself. Jerry sat his saddle lighting a cigarette.

"What you fellows lookin' for?" he drawled. "There ain't been any hosses along here for days."

"Jerry, you always was a hombre thet kept your horse lean," replied Hicks, which reply Wade interpreted to mean that Jerry preferred to tie up his horse. "But you're right. No tracks either way for days."

"Blue hasn't come along yet?" querried Wade.

"Not on this road."

"Boss, it's too soon, anyhow," added Strothers.

"We're not ten miles from Pine Mound," said Hicks.

"But men running for their lives do strange things," rejoined Wade. "Hicks, ride on ahead and be sure you see them first, if they do come. If not, find where they turned off. Go slow. We'll follow you."

It was significant that the half-breed started off leading his horse. Wade waited until he turned a bend out of sight, then cautioning the cowboys to be slow and quiet he followed. They had proceeded in this way for a couple of miles when the sight of Hicks waiting made Wade's heart leap fiercely. He was no longer Pencarrow's savior, and foreman of a hard outfit that he had inspired, but back in the past. Rand Blue had betrayed him to the rangers. Wade again saw his chief—his father!—sitting grim and haggard with his guns leveled, his back to that elm tree, his brow already clammy with the dampness of death.

"Reckon Hicks ain't shore of somethin'," said Jerry. "An' I ain't myself."

No one else spoke. Wade tried to read the half-breed's mind before he got to him. A brook crossed the road, making a bend round a great wide-armed sycamore. Wet turkey tracks showed on a dry stone.

"Boss, I heerd somethin' like iron on stone," whispered Hicks. "So far I ain't shore. Get off an' we'll hide our hosses back aways."

This required a few moments, for Hicks went slowly and some distance back into the woods. "Fetch some ropes," ordered Wade, grimly. They returned to the road.

"My hoss kept me from hearin'," said Hicks. "Now all of you be still."

He lay down in the middle of the road and spread himself comfortably with his ear to the ground.

The cowboys watched him with assurance in their intent glinting eyes. Cigarettes had been cast aside. In their standing and sitting postures there was a suggestion of strung readiness.

Wade shared their attention. But he felt that for him there was infinitely more in the charged moment.

The brook tinkled very faintly; an almost indistinguishable sough of wind, like a mysterious breath, came from the tips of the pines; so silent was the forest that it seemed to be waiting in suspense; the faraway plaintive note of a thrush accentuated the silence. For Wade, nature did not seem to be deaf to the tragedy of men.

Hicks rose as if on springs. "Somebody comin'," he whispered. "Slow an' not fur off."

With noiseless steps the cowboys surrounded Wade.

"Six of you slip up along the road and hide," he said in a whisper. "Rest of you stay here."

Jerry and Strothers with four others melted into the green border of the road. Wade motioned some of those remaining to hide across the road. With Hicks and three others Wade took a like position on his side. He knelt behind some alder brush and pulling a scarf from his pocket he tied it round his face up to his eyes. Then he jerked his sombrero down and drew his gun.

They waited. The woodland dreamed in its hush. The brook tinkled over stones. Wade strained his ears in vain. Then he whispered to Hicks. The half-breed glided away, along the edge of the road, to the giant sycamore, from behind which he stealthily peeped. He drew back, appeared to think, and then took another and a longer look, after which he retraced his soft steps.

"Four riders," he whispered. "Blue an' a flash cowboy ahead."

After what seemed an interminable period Wade heard voices before a thud of hoofs. They came closer, ceased for a moment; the pound of hoofs sounded just round the bend marked by the sycamore.

"Blue, you had money for Mason," rang out an angry voice, "an' some of thet was for me."

"How do I know that?" came the reply, deep, throaty, with a tone that sent fire along Wade's cold veins.

"I *tell* you. An' I want my share. . . . Blue, I got you out of thet mess in Holbrook. But for me you'd decorated a tree."

"Bah! . . . Steele, you were scared half to death."

"Hell yes! Who wouldn't be with Brandon an' his hounds right there in town? All the same I saved you."

"We're not out of it yet," growled Blue.

Two riders rounded the bend. The left one was a superbly built cowboy, young, his garb and the trappings of his horse signifying the dandy. The horseman on the right presented a marked contrast to the cowboy.

Wade, with a remembered face and form vividly in his mind, did not at first glance recognize in this heavy-paunched, tawny-bearded man, the only traitor Simm Bell had ever harbored in his band.

The horses splashed into the brook, jerking and bobbing their heads to lengthen their bridles. Then thirstily they drank. Steele looked back. Other horses were close.

"Blue, I want my share of that money," he demanded, menacingly.

The rustler chief took off his sombrero to wipe his sweaty brow. His hollow eyes flared at the cowboy.

"You can go to hell, Steele," he rasped out, malignance distorting his somber features.

Wade then recognized the big eyes, the crafty look, the coarse visage that had once been handsome, and particularly the rough cutting voice. Rand Blue! The years that seemed long as a lifetime were wiped away. Wade drew a deep breath, then expelled it in a stentorian command: "*Hands up!*"

The bushes crashed on each side of the road to emit the cowboys, stony-faced and formidable with guns extended. At that moment the other two rustlers rounded the sycamore to pull frantically at their thirsty horses. Thudding footfalls behind them preceded the appearance of Jerry and Strothers.

"What's—up?" demanded Blue, hoarsely, his jaw wobbling.

"Not your hands. . . . *Quick!*" yelled the half-breed, advancing with rifle held forward.

"Brandon's outfit!" shrieked Steele, in desperate amaze and fury. His hand flashed low.

Hicks fired without raising the rifle. The cowboy lost action. His head sank forward so that his huge sombrero hid his face. He fell over the neck of his horse, which, startled more by that than by the shot, plunged to let him fall into the brook.

Blue's hands went shakily aloft.

"No rope for me!" shouted the rustler farthest back, and he wheeled his horse to flee.

"Wait, boys, an' bore him!" called out Jerry.

The outlaw got a start, and his quickening hoofbeats rang down the road. Then gunshots blended in a roar. The rapid clip-clop ceased in a heavy crash, crash of brush.

The fourth rustler spurred his frightened steed into a magnificent leap back of Blue. A second leap took him into the green, followed by hissing bullets just a fraction of a second too late. Swift as a flash Hicks ran into the woods.

"Blue, you ——! Hang!" came back a mocking taunt from the fleeing rustler. The cracking rush of a horse through thicket, a pound of hoofs, gathering speed ended in a single spiteful rifle shot.

"Rustle, boys!" commanded Wade.

Behind Blue a lasso flew out like an uncoiling snake to whip round the rustler and draw tight. A single pull dragged him off his horse into the brook. Other cowboys laid hold of the rope and dragged Blue over Steel's dead body, out into the road. Coughing, strangled by mud and water, the rustler got to his knees when a second noose whipped round him, pinioning his arms to his sides. Then the cowboys let him get up on his feet.

"Bran—don!" he gasped. "Which of you—is Brandon? . . . Let me—off! . . . I've money—more hidden! I'll pay handsome . . . leave the country!"

"Shet up," called one of Aulsbrook's cowboys, a lean youth with eyes of blue flame, and he tossed a noose around the rustler's neck. He gave the rope a pull that nearly toppled Blue. Then he tossed the other end of the long lasso over a wide arm of the sycamore.

"My—Gawd!" choked out the doomed man.

It took hard men at a hard time to gaze unmoved at his awful visage.

Wade leaped out of the brush. Hicks came gliding from the woods, carrying a gun-belt and a pair of silver spurs. These he laid down with his rifle, and sprang to line up with the cowboys at the taut rope.

"Brandon?—I can put a fortune in your way," hoarsely pleaded the rustler.

"Stand ready, boys!" shouted Wade, in cold and ringing command. He advanced, strode up to Blue, peered into the convulsed face.

"Don't you know me, Blue?"

"Who—who? . . . Hellsfire!"

Wade snatched off his mask and whispered: "Remember Simm Bell!"

The exiled Texan betrayed a profound and terrific emotion. He recognized Wade. Stricken to the point of collapse, he stared at an arisen ghost. Then he opened his gray lips once more to betray. But Wade lifted his hand and all Blue got out was a horrible strangled, "ag-gh!—" while he was jerked into the air like a grotesque jumping jack for the merciless cowboys to jibe at.

CHAPTER NINETEEN

WHILE Wade sat on a log, sweating and shuddering from the reaction to that hideous execution, the cowboys searched the dead rustlers and tied Blue on his saddle.

Jerry brought Wade a heavy money belt and a huge roll of greenbacks surprisingly clean and new. "I found these on Drake," he said. "Steele an' thet oldish hombre were also well-heeled, accordin' to Strothers, who searched them."

"Tell Strothers to divide with you all."

"Doggone it, boss, rustlin' appears to be a profitable business in these parts."

"It *was*, Jerry."

They packed Blue to the outskirts of Pine Mound, where they hanged him on the notorious cottonwood tree. They tagged his slack figure with a paper bearing the word: RUSTLER.

Then the sleepy little hamlet of Pine Mound awakened to the end of the Drake-Harrobin regime of cattle stealing.

There were but few men in the old haunts of the rustlers and these were curtly invited to prove why they should not be hanged alongside Rand Blue. Those who could not give satisfactory proof of the status they claimed were taken out to view the dead rustler chief and then given an hour to leave town. The Bozemans and other store and saloon keepers who had grown rich off the rustlers were told in blunt language to harbor no more cattle thieves.

The cowboys began to drink and grow hilarious. At their departure, which Wade had trouble in bringing about, they shot up the town. And when they rode past the swinging Blue—ghastly object for the villagers to flock to see—they riddled his body with bullets.

It was midafternoon when they finally headed their tired horses into the Cedar Range trail. Wade with Jerry in front of him brought up the rear of that singing merry cavalcade. They knew they had made Arizona history, that any cattleman in all the territory would pay high for their services. The sun set gold over the purple land and dusk had come before the cowboys settled quietly down to the long ride home.

But Wade welcomed the distance, the darkness, the lonely ride through the pines and cedars. His back had hardly been turned upon the terrible spectacle of the hanging Blue, when the hard ruthless clamped mood of the man sloughed off like dead scales. He escaped the sickening aftermath of death dealing. When he realized that the work had been accomplished, a dark and splendid exultation visited him fleetingly. But that, like the powerful revulsion from bloodletting, did not last long before the terrific fact that the structure he had built for his conscience had collapsed. The certainty which he had relied upon—that he would be killed or seriously wounded in this rustler war—had been a vain anchor. He was alive, well, unscathed, and riding back to a range he had freed of its blood-suckers—to a range that was home, to a family who would worship him as their savior, to the girl with the dark proud passionate eyes, who would make a hero of him. And he must know every waking moment, and in his dreams as well, that he was a liar, a hypocrite, a robber still, and a greater villain than ever.

Yet despite his burning realization, and the helplessness that surged over him, and the miserable thought that after all his years of strife to keep his pledge to his father, fate had played him a scurvy trick, there would come moments of irresistible exultation. He could not prevent these; he had to yield to them. He found that he had an insatiable thirst for respect. He gloried in what he had done for the Pencarrows.

Long before Wade reached the cedar flat that night, weary with physical and mental exertion, the insidious tempter began to whisper: take what is your due—the past is dead—your secret is safe. But he had strength still to drive that devil out. It was an hallucination to imagine he had been safe or ever could be. Had not Rand Blue recognized him in that final appalling moment? Nothing could be surer than that Mahaffey, that hawk-eyed ranger, would know him on sight.

By keeping that fact before his consciousness, by fighting harder for Jacqueline Pencarrow in his hour of almost insupportable temptation than ever before, Wade vanquished the soft-voiced, persuasive tempter.

That struggle left him spent. What best to do and how to do it had to be left until he recovered. Late that night he came upon the cowboys at the Pencarrow corrals and realized that he was home. Deaf to the solicitous Jerry, Wade flopped off Pen and staggered through the dark to his cabin. He barred the door and pulled off his boots. Then he unbuckled from his waist the heavy money belt taken from Blue. It dropped to the floor with a thud. His pocket bulged with the roll of greenbacks and his last conscious thought was a query.

Wade slept until late the next afternoon, and probably would have slept longer but for Elwood Lightfoot's onslaught upon the door.

Wade let him in.

"They all been tryin' to wake you," said the homesteader. "Jacque sent me. She's worried. It 'pears somebody peeped through the winder an' seen you layin' there an' reckoned you was dead. . . . Wal, by gosh, no wonder! You couldn't look no wuss if you was dead!"

"Elwood, I'm afraid I came through it very much alive," replied Wade, thoughtfully.

"Anyone would reckon you was sorry. . . . Tex, it was the greatest deal I ever seen pulled in all my years on the border. You can't escape the happiness of these good people. I reckon facin' them will be harder than doin' the job. But you must take your medicine."

"Elwood, I—I couldn't see Ja . . . any of them now. I must look like hell. . . . Besides, I feel like a poisoned hound."

"Wal, thet ain't strange. But if you'll take a stiff drink an' clean up you'll begin to feel better. Then come down an' have supper with me."

"That's a good idea," replied Wade, gratefully.

It was almost dusk when Wade walked down the trail to Lightfoot's ranch. The homesteader had supper ready. After eating they sat outside and smoked. It was drowsy and warm down under the rock wall. The mockingbirds sang after dark; the brook murmured on its way to its melodious fall into the canyon; the nighthawks wheeled low with raucous squeaks and the insects kept up an incessant hum. The sweetness and loveliness of the place pierced Wade's mind.

"Lightfoot, what'll I do with all this money?" asked Wade, suddenly finding his tongue without effort.

"What money?"

"I've got a nose bag full of greenbacks and gold," replied Wade, laughing grimly. "Harrobin had the money Mason paid him, and some of his own, I reckon. Those rustlers packed their ill-gotten gains around with them. Then Blue had a big sum on him. I got it all. What the cowboys found on the other rustlers they divided and it must have been plenty."

"Wal, I'll be doggoned," returned the homesteader, gleefully. "Can you beat thet? . . . Send me an' Hogue down country to pay them cattlemen for their losses."

"I'll do that," said Wade, brightening. "Did I tell you? . . . Of course I did—about buying Aulsbrook out just after he'd been rustled clean. I've a ranch of my own. Of all the luck—if it *is* luck!"

"Luck? Humph, you don't know how lucky you are yet. . . . Thet's a rich one on Aulsbrook. But he's glad to get out. An' it's just as well. I'd have had to shoot thet Texan. Now, with your range adjoinin' Pencarrow's, we can run as many cattle as we want. I'd send Strothers back there with his riders, throw a new herd in, an' figure on the rewards of virtue."

"Ha! Ha! . . . That's a joke, Elwood. . . . I spent the last of my money buying Aulsbrook out."

"I'll bet you won't be able to pay back a quarter of thet money you got off the rustlers. If Mason paid Harrobin five dollars a head for thet eight thousand odd rustled with Aulsbrook's, why there's forty thousand in one lump. An' you got the cattle an' the money too, barrin' what you paid Aulsbrook. Haw! Haw! Thet shore beats hell!"

"You think the balance—after I pay those little ranchers down there—is rightfully mine?"

"Wal, I should smile I do. Pencarrow agrees. Harrobin an' Drake had other resources. Don't forget thet Drake, or Blue, sold out to Pencarrow for twenty thousand. He was a tightfisted geezer with some purpose up his sleeve. He never was a real hard-drinkin', hard-gamblin' rustler.

"I haven't counted it yet," rejoined Wade, with a little laugh. "Guess I won't. . . . How many riders will I keep to run Pencarrow's ranch?"

"Tex, you kinda forget you're his pardner, don't you? Of all the queer cusses I ever seen, you're the queerest. . . . Wal, I'd keep your old bunch an' add, say four more to it, an' let Hogue be foreman."

"I like that. Is Hogue back? No, he couldn't be. . . . I'd like to see his face when he hears."

Wade slept that night under the open shelter beside the brook and awoke at sunrise with the dark and somber mood fading like a nightmare. Lightfoot went up early to the ranch leaving Wade to his own devices.

He spent the day along the shady rim where the brook took its amber-white leap into the canyon. In renouncing all that he might selfishly have gained, he discovered an amazing abundance left by which to live. His memory, his dream—and the companionship of nature that this Arizona land had made clear for him. He could never be lonely again. His wants would be few. There could never be too much time on his hands. These eventful years at

Cedar Ranch had seen him insensibly drawn to the purple desert, the gray cedar range, the Redwall canyons, the mellow gold-lit glades where the streams glided, the fragrant dry forests. His life had been bitter. But there would be part of it sweet to remember.

Next day Hogue and Hal invaded Wade's retreat and hailed him with the worship of youths. They respected his reticence and seemed conscious of a change in him. But they talked and speculated and looked ahead with a vision that was spirited in Hal and touching in Hogue. That cowboy had been with Rona since his return from Holbrook. He was soft, dreamy at times, wild at others, and then again strangely studious of Wade.

"Hogue, I mustn't forget to tell you I'm sending you down country to make good the cattle losses of these ranchers," said Wade.

"Not me you ain't sendin'," declared Hogue. "Pencarrow has called for all his neighbors, even to the Tonto, to come with their proof. He's shore not goin' to let anyone impose on you."

"Well! I hadn't thought of proof. . . . How's a cattleman to prove he lost so much stock?"

"I reckon he cain't. But Lightfoot will get the right of it. Smart old geezer, thet homesteader!"

Wade walked to the foot of the trail with his friends.

"Pard, won't you come on up?" asked Hogue.

"No. Maybe tomorrow."

"Rona sent her love," added Hal, anxiously. "An' she said to tell you thet if you didn't come soon she'd mosey down after you. . . . An' Jacque—well, she's never asked about you or sent any message. But Tex, she's pale. She doesn't smile an' her eyes are too big for her face. . . . I reckon my sister . . . well, never mind what. Only, please come up, Tex."

"You're a couple of locoed kids," retorted Wade harshly, furious that the red blood burned his cheek.

"See here, boss," drawled Hogue, keenly, his eyes narrowed. "Now you got me straightened out an' my boys, an' Pencarrow on his feet, an' Rona an' Hal happy—an' Jacque a ghost of her old self—you wouldn't double-cross us all, would you, an' leave us stumped?"

Wade fled before the warm light in the cowboy's eyes and the suspicious and damning content of his query. For that was what Wade had made up his mind to do. He was not sure of his strength if he once saw Jacqueline again. These loving fools would have her ill on his account, worn pale through fear for him. They would take her gratitude, her strong sense of what the Pencarrows owed him, as something deeper, and they would throw the bighearted girl into his arms. For one instant, when Wade admitted thought of the possibility of Jacqueline's loving him, he was wrapped in a blinding flame and whirled away, passion-swept, overcome with rapture that was pain.

He must take heed of this warning. There were forces at work beyond his ken. He drove himself to the realization that he dared not tarry longer at Cedar Ranch. The old conflict began all over again. After dark he went back up to the ranch, only to return, harassed, torn by conflicting emotions.

"What's on yore mind, son?" asked the homesteader.

"I wish to God I could tell you," answered Wade, poignantly.

"I reckon I can guess. But up there they all think you're sick from the killin', ashamed of the hard man thet you had to be. . . . Do you want my advice?"

"No, friend, I'm beyond advice. I know what to do. But I've been a coward."

"Wal! wal! . . . Ain't you thinkin' too much about yourself? After all, these people believe in you."

"That makes the hell."

"But what people believe is true," protested the homesteader.

Wade rushed out into the moonlit night. To stay longer with this kindly man would be to confess the guilt that harrowed his soul. He could have told Lightfoot, but he feared counsel and wisdom that might deflect him from his prescribed course. How easy and sweet and rapturous to surrender to circumstances and stay on at Cedar Ranch, friend and brother to these good Pencarrows, perhaps more in time to Jacqueline? From Lightfoot's hint he conceived the probability that Jacqueline would marry him to pay their debt. And that thought possessed Wade with a frenzy for hours. Was there any man who would not have won this girl by any means? But he was bound. If she had not saved his life, made it possible for him to keep his pledge to his father—truly, except for this last weakness with the money—he would have succumbed to the temptation. To take advantage of her gratitude, of her faith, to win her with a lie—that was not possible for him. No! he would ride away without a word to Jacqueline. She would never know that he had paid his debt to her. It would come to her fully as time passed how greatly he had loved her. She could not suffer through that. She would regret, she would wonder—and then life would impose its future and some fortunate man might. . . . As always Wade flinched and fell before the flame of jealousy. But even so he rallied and raised his head. Who was he to hold a thought inimical to the future happiness of this girl?

Next day he went back to the ranch, his old cool self, as inexorable in the purpose he had set himself as the doom he had meted out to Pencarrow's enemies. The day proved to be a full one. Wade had to meet the cattlemen who had called at Pencarrow's invitation. They paid him the meed of the range, simple, elemental. Wade found himself deeply touched, almost exalted despite himself. Their losses did not aggregate a third of the sum Wade had found upon the rustlers. Again he felt defeated. He could not escape a fortune. But he eluded the burden, the dread of the past in a few words to Pencarrow: "Here, partner, take this for safekeeping."

Then visitors consumed most of the day, and the cowboys the rest. None of them wanted to leave Cedar Ranch. Wade surrendered the problem to Kinsey and Strothers. He was no longer foreman. He laughed at their perplexities. Once Rona waved to him from the porch and when he waved back, she boldly threw him kisses.

At sunset, when he came out of his cabin to mount Pen, he felt impelled to glance up at Jacqueline's window. Sight of her when he had not expected it gave him a considerable wrench. She waved something white—a handkerchief—no, it was an envelope. A letter! He doffed his sombrero gaily and rode toward the cowboys' camp with death in his soul.

With the visiting cattlemen and cowboys, Pencarrow's outfit had a busy merry time of it at supper. That gave Wade opportunity to listen and watch, and take his farewell of Hal and Hogue, of the volatile Kid and the somber half-breed, of all these riders who meant more to him than they had ever dreamed.

In the early dusk he rode back to his cabin. He meant to take Pen with him—the one and only thing he exacted from the Pencarrows. The full moon had just peeped over the black mountain. He must hurry. What was it that he wanted from his cabin? He sat down to think. The moment had come for his departure and his heart seemed about to burst.

All at once he felt something smooth and cool under his hand upon the blanket of his bed. It was an envelope. The feel of it, the meaning of it transfixed him for an instant. This was the note Jacqueline had waved at him from her window. She had put it there.

All that remained of the cool calculating man advised that it be left there unread. But that self multiplied by a thousand could never have denied the love that surged in anguished renunciation.

Wade's hands, in moments of peril steady as rocks, shook like aspen leaves as he lighted the lamp. What had she written? He felt carried along in a swift current. Fumbling at the envelope to tear it open, he found it unsealed. He read with eyes that blurred.

Dear Tex:

You will find me waiting for you at the bench in the pines where Rona used to meet Hogue. They have graduated to the living room, with Dad's consent.

I would not attempt to tell you in a letter how I feel about what you have done for us. If you have imagination enough you may realize something of what awaits you by magnifying all we saw there one night in the moonlight.

But I must hasten to let you know that you take too tragically what you suppose is my attitude—and that of all of us for that matter—toward you after the terrible things you have done. At first it *did* sicken me, frighten me to see you kill, and to think of it afterward. But that wore away.

I know you would have come to me at once if you had not feared this. But you should have come, for I would have helped you, comforted you. Only such a man as you are could have saved Dad, and all of us, not to say the other families on this wild range. I would not have you the least different.

But you have stayed away from me too long. I am dying for love of you.

Jacqueline

Wade tried to read the note a second time. But he could not see. He found himself erect, tense like a man mortally stricken, but glorying in the blade that had pierced his vitals. He was lost. He had tarried too long. All his struggle and fall and rise must go for naught. An incredulous rapture, like a flood, waved over his whirling thoughts. If Jacqueline was dying for love of him no outlawed past, no blundering shame of the present could keep him from her.

He went forth from the cabin like a man pursued by furies. But as he strode on, faster and faster toward the pine-clad slope, these voices of conscience left off pursuit. He seemed to be driven to hear the truth of written words and to take his course from that. Yet he knew he was lost. This had ever been about to happen.

He reached the pines. The moon was not high enough to light up the aisles between the trees. To the last instant he did not expect to find Jacqueline. But a white form arose from the bench, and advanced into the little open glade to meet him. Jacqueline!

Wade rushed to envelop her. "Jacqueline!" he cried, hoarsely. "You are here! . . . That message of yours! . . . What madness is this?" He crushed her to his breast so that if she had any reply for his passionate entreaty she could not have given it. Then he held her away from him, with strong and shaking hands pressing down her black hair, holding her face to the moonlight. It was indeed pale and thin, but lovely with its smile and the great dark eyes, shining with love.

"Why did you—not come to me?" she whispered, her bare arms sliding to clasp his neck.

"No—matter now," he said, thickly. "It's too late—if you love me."

"I have been dying of love for you."

"Jacqueline, you are so bighearted—so—so—" he faltered.

"My heart might have been big, but it's almost consumed with unrequited love," she said, reproachfully.

"Don't jest. This is death—or life for me. I have worshiped you from the first. . . . I have tried to die for you. I bore a charmed life. They couldn't kill me. . . . Jacqueline, be sure. . . ."

"I *am* sure now, thank heaven, that you do love me," she cried, awakening. "And I can be myself. Oh, I always doubted that terrible cowboy."

"He told the truth, child," said Wade, mournfully.

"But *you* never told me."

"I did not dare."

"Do you think *I* care for what your past has been?" she queried, passionately, her arms tightening. "You need say only one more word to make me the happiest girl in all this West."

"You'll be—my wife?" he whispered, brokenly, carried away, terrified at the inevitable, even in that moment realizing he could never tell her his secret.

"I will, my dearest," she whispered, her heavy eyelids falling, her white face tilting to his. She was quivering in his arms. And when Wade yielded to those upturned lips the intense and vital life of her seemed to pass into him, like magic satisfying all the hunger of his lonely years, and fortifying him with shuddering, ecstatic strength against the future.

CHAPTER TWENTY

A YEAR and more rolled by. Summer came again to Cedar Range—a summer marked by abundant rain and grass that greened the knolls and flats from the mountains to the desert.

Cattlemen had their first year of prosperity in that isolated section of Arizona. Pencarrow's cowboys burned the C.R.B. brand on five thousand new calves! And other ranchers on the range multiplied their herds in like proportion.

The remnants of the several rustler bands that had fared like robber barons vanished as if by magic. Pine Mound dwindled to a deserted village and the road that led from it to Holbrook became a trail overgrown with weeds. From Sycamore Canyon to Harrobin's old hiding place in the brakes this fading road was said to be haunted. Cowboys made use of other trails. Around the campfires of the range, and far into other grazing country, stories were told about the hanging of the rustlers, and that Band Drake, or Rand Blue, had never been cut down from the wide-spreading cottonwood on the trail near Pine Mound. They told uncanny tales. There were no rustlers left to cut down this ghastly thing and the honest cowmen who passed that way let it remain there like a scarcecrow in the fields. They told how the buzzards and the crows picked the carcass clean of flesh and left a belted and booted skeleton to sway in the wind and rattle its bones and jingle its spurs.

The day of the rustler on that range was done. Homesteaders and cattlemen, most of them Texans, moved into the vast unsettled country to the south.

As notoriety and greatness had been thrust upon Tex Brandon

so were prosperity and respect, and the regard of an increasing population. Wade had surrendered with outward grace to the inevitable. But on lonely rides and in the dark hours he contended with a sleepless remorse, and an abiding dread. When June came he had been married to Jacqueline for a year, and a baby Jacqueline had just arrived at Cedar Ranch. Pencarrow was a proud grandfather. In the happiness of that time he consented to the engagement of Rona to Hogue Kinsey. Hogue's crippled sister had been sent to Kansas City where a specialist had cured the unfortunate ailment that had sent Hogue off the straight and narrow trail. She was a pretty blue-eyed girl of eighteen and her advent at Cedar Ranch had sadly upset the equilibrium of the cowboys. Hal appeared to be leading in the race for the young lady's favor, with Kid Marshall running a close second.

It would have been impossible for Wade not to have reveled in all this happiness. He had lived to bless the one gift that had developed out of his hard years in Texas. He shared this happiness and no one could have divined his secret haunting fears.

But there was a step on his trail. He had heard it when he was alone, riding in the dusk, and sometimes when he sat beside the open fire on winter nights. It would catch up with him some day. Until that fateful time he accepted the homage of the Pencarrows and their neighbors, and he clung to Jacqueline's love with a reverent awe and a hidden pitiful hope.

Often he thought of the gunmen and outlaws who had abandoned a locality or a gang of comrades to disappear and never be heard of again. That had come to be a favorite thought of Wade's. He had personally known several men like that. What had happened to them? Perhaps they had gone to other places, joined other bands under other names. But it was conceivable that one here and there might have abandoned the old evil life and made a new one that had elements of good. Wade had done this. He wondered if it would be just and right of fate to track him down now, and in punishing him for an erring past wreck the happiness of a wife and mother.

One morning when little Jacqueline was two weeks old Wade returned from a visit to Lightfoot's ranch. He was thinking of the probable hundred tons of alfalfa that would be cut from the homesteader's rich acres this summer. As he turned Pen toward the corrals he happened to see a group of saddled and packed horses resting by the pine knoll. His heart leaped to his throat. The horsemen lounging there, talking to the cowboys, could be no other than Texas Rangers. He had seen rangers too often ever to be deceived. And a blind terrific fury and fear possessed him. These passed over him like a wave. No more flight for Wade Holden! He had never shed a ranger's blood and he never would. If this were the end he would meet it with the courage that had come to him.

In another moment he turned Pen toward the house, his one thought for Jacqueline. What a passion of regret stormed his soul! He might have told her long ago—might have spared her shock, if not heartbreak and shame. But he had never been able to face the thought of telling her the truth—of losing the incredible esteem in which she held him. Too late! It all rushed over him now and but for her he would have welcomed death.

A powerful horse, with saddle, trappings, bags and rifle such as were used by Texas Rangers, stood bridle down before the porch. In a single leap Wade was down, to stride up on the porch, into the living room. A big sombrero and dusty gloves lay on the table. He heard voices, Pencarrow's and then a deeper, harder one—that of a native Texan. Wade stood an instant like stone. He had to steel himself against two terrific forces—the ruthless will to kill and the more insupportable need to be the way Jacqueline believed him. That was the most cruel moment of his whole life. How strange and incomprehensible that Jacqueline broke it with a happy little laugh!

"Baby favors my husband," she said, proudly.

"Wal, lass, I can shore recognize some Pencarrow heah, an' a whole lot of yore Spanish," drawled her father.

"Dad, please have Captain Mahaffey stay to lunch," Jacqueline went on. "Tex will be back then."

Mahaffey! His had been the step upon the trail. Ride the man down! Always Wade had known—and yet had risked his fool's paradise! But even now Wade found comfort in the fact that it had not all been for himself. Never for his own love, his own peace of mind, his own skin! And the truth upheld him. It would be Tex Brandon and not Wade Holden that Mahaffey would meet.

Wade stepped into the bedroom. The gold sunshine flooded through the white-curtained windows. Jacqueline sat propped up on pillows, the pearl tint of her lovely face, the soft dark splendor of her wonderful eyes, never before so beautiful. The baby lay gurgling beside her. Pencarrow stood on the far side of the bed. On the nearer side to Wade, as he entered, sat a square-shouldered man with iron-gray hair, with his back to the door. It struck Wade then how strange it was that a Texas Ranger captain, famous for riding down notorious criminals, should sit with his back toward any door!

"Heah he is now," cried Jacqueline, with a blush that still came for Wade on occasions. "Darling, we have a visitor from Texas. . . . Captain Mahaffey, this is my husband."

The big man stood up and turned around. Mahaffey indeed—the iron-jawed, hawk-eyed ranger—a little grayer and grimmer, his visage seamed and lined with the records of his stern life.

"Howdy, Captain," said Wade, with cool and easy graciousness. "I haven't been away from Texas long enough to have forgotten your name."

"Howdy, Brandon," replied Mahaffey. "I've heahed of you all the way across. Let me shake yore hand."

The lightning leaped to his gray hawk eyes as he extended his hand. Wade met it. What was the ranger's game? Oh! The old Texas chivalry toward a woman! Mahaffey would make his arrest outside.

"Wal, now," he went on. "Seems like I've felt hands like this one before. Soft most as a woman's—velvet over steel! Like my old friends Buck Duane, Wess Hardin, King Fisher, an' all thet outfit, you don't chop wood or otherwise mistreat this right member."

"I never used to," replied Wade, with a laugh. "But my gun days are over. I'll come yet to chopping wood—or perhaps even breaking stone. . . . Mahaffey, did you by any chance shake with Billy the Kid on the way across?"

"No, wuss luck. For a Texas Ranger, I shore had a weakness for Billy. . . . He was killed not long ago by Pat Garritt."

"No!" exclaimed Wade. "Not an even break?"

"Wal, I should smile not. Garritt hadn't the nerve for thet. Billy would have beat him to a gun. . . . It happened at Pete Maxwell's in Lincoln. Garritt, the sheriff an' his deputies were on Billy's track. They missed him. But at night when Garritt sat in the dark talkin' to Maxwell, Billy came in the door. Maxwell had been his friend. Billy asked who the stranger was, instead of shootin' first. Pat recognized his voice an' bored him."

"Well!—Who'd ever have guessed such an end for Billy the Kid," exclaimed Wade, profoundly moved.

"None of us can figure what our ends will be," replied the ranger.

"Heah, you bloodthirsty men of the draw, never mind such talk!" retorted Jacqueline. "Babies are more important than guns. Look at this one!"

"Wal, thank Gawd, they air," replied Mahaffey, heartily, as he bent to let the little Jacqueline take a final squeeze at his finger. When he stood up again, he appeared a softer, stranger Mahaffey, one without that piercing gray fire of eye. "Brandon, Pencarrow heah told me about you an' yore work on this range. I never heahed the beat of it unless thet job of Buck Duane's—when he joined Cheseldine's outfit in the Big Bend, an' cleaned them out, even to the great Paggin. But Buck carries a lot of lead even to this day an' you didn't get even a bullet burn."

"That's the miracle," admitted Wade. "I owe it to Jacqueline."

"Wal, I reckon. Air you shore you appreciate her?"

"God knows I do—as greatly as I don't deserve her," replied Wade, poignantly.

"Brandon, a man can never tell what's in him till a good woman brings it out. Stand by what you jest said all yore life."

Wade could not speak. His mind seemed to receive with startling vividness, but could give out no response.

"Good-by, mother an' baby," went on Mahaffey. "I shore am the happier for meetin' you."

The ranger strode out, with Pencarrow following.

"Cain't you stay for lunch, Captain?" asked the rancher.

"Sorry, Pencarrow. But it's early—an' I'll be on my way. I'm damn glad to meet you, an' tell you I hadn't nothin' to do with killin' yore brother Glenn. I'm tellin' you all us rangers air not . . ."

They passed out of hearing. Wade found sense in his nerves and muscles, and he sat down beside Jacqueline, to peer out at the purple Arizona range. What was it that had happened? He seemed to be shut out of the sepulcher of his mind. Inside that locked chamber—faces of the old years—his father—a dark stern ghost this strange Mahaffey—the strife and agony of his struggle—seemed to try to burst their confines to explain that quick retreating footstep. Jacqueline gazed up at him with dim wet eyes. There was something about to happen. But the unreality possessed him. A ring of ironshod hoofs on the court outside! The ranger was riding away. Mahaffey—he whose clarion voice broke through the wall of mind—*Ride the Man Down!*

"Wade . . . *Wade*," whispered Jacqueline. "He knew you."

"My God! . . . What did—you—call me?" gasped Wade. This was another and an unbearable nightmare. But Jacqueline lay there, white and convulsed of face, her dark eyes eloquent with love and pity.

"I called you—Wade," she went on, brokenly. "My husband. . . . You are Wade Holden. You are the boy whom I saved long ago—that night in the canyon—saved from this very Mahaffey. . . . I always knew you—yet was never sure until that night—when you came back with the new cowboys—and I met you coming around the tent into the firelight. . . . Oh, Wade, darling . . . all the time I've known."

"*Jacqueline!* . . . And you loved me . . . married me?" cried Wade, hoarsely, falling to his knees beside the bed.

"Yes. I loved you—married you," she whispered. "I would never have told you but for that ranger's coming. He knew you, Wade. He was heah to arrest you—take you back to Texas. He never guessed that I knew you were Wade Holden . . . and as he listened to Dad and me—slowly strangely softening. Oh, it was beautiful to see. . . . *He* knew you, Wade. Did you not divine that?"

"Yes. I—saw," choked Wade.

"But you did not betray yourself. . . . He has gone, big with *his* secret. . . . *That* gave me right and reason to tell *my* secret. . . . Whatever you did in the past it is atoned for. Mahaffey—that stern, hard-lipped man of law—he removed the stigma. You are free, Wade.

"Oh, yes—free of him—and that footstep on my trail. But can I be of that haunting horror—the fortune my father gave me—robber's money! . . . the use I put it to—to help your father?"

"You saved that through all the years of your outlawry?" she asked, wonderingly.

"Yes. Saved it like a miser. But it was money I could never have returned. Where it came from God only knows. . . ."

"Wade, I could have forgiven and forgotten that without Captain Mahaffey's help," said Jacqueline, with sad and persuasive eloquence. "But *he* represents the law. *He* forgave it. The good you have done far outweighs the bad. That is the answer . . . he will forget."

"Brandon is my middle name," said Wade, lifting his head. "It was my mother's."

"What's in a name? But Jacqueline Pencarrow Brandon—that *is* pretty. Lift her up to the window, dear, and let's look out over the range."

Wade gazed a long time before the dimness left his eyes. Then this bright land, this indescribably new Arizona land rolled away to infinitude, speaking, beautiful, wild, with its straggling cattle dotting the gray, and the pine-clad knolls leading out to the purple desert. Then he understood his father and he understood Mahaffey, and this loyal loving wife. Until that moment it had not been given him to see them clearly, nor his unabatable struggle nor the opportunity that had grown unceasingly with it. Now the truth permeated his being. This was what had happened to one evildoer when he made his pledge and rode away with the spirit to rise. Something beside a footstep had followed along his wandering trail. It was that which abided in mother and babe. They were his to hold, to keep, to grow by, together with the endless range out there, with its blue flats and green knolls, its yellow-walled canyons, and the dim red shadows in the desert distance.